Remembering Jody

Remembering Jody

a novel

Randy Sue Coburn

Carroll & Graf Publishers, Inc.
New York

First Carroll & Graf edition 1999

Carroll & Graf Publishers, Inc.
19 West 21st Street
New York, NY 10010-6805

Library of Congress Cataloging-in-Publication Data is available.

ISBN: 0-7867-0566-3

Manufactured in the United States of America

For Nick, and his unlimited quantities of spontaneous art

In a rage, Set cut the body of Osiris into fourteen pieces, one for each night of the waning moon, and then scattered them far and wide throughout the land of Egypt. Isis traveled the whole of the country, re-membering Osiris, as she remembered him in her heart, for to re-member is to heal.

from Jonathan Cott, "Isis and Osiris"

Remembering Jody

Book I

Chapter 1

I'VE NEVER understood what people fall in love with—or what they protect after they do—if they don't first fall in love with each other's stories. Most of my own stories hinge on what I like to think of as rhyming events, and if somebody responds to one of them as nothing more than an interesting coincidence, I make up my mind pretty quickly that love isn't going to be much of an issue between us.

For instance: My assigned roommate at the University of Georgia is an aggressively cheerful Campus Crusader for Christ who seems to believe Jesus personally arranged for us to live together so that I could be saved. On the first day of class, I sit down in World Drama behind a husky-voiced girl who turns out to be my once-adored but long-lost summer camp bunkmate. She not only lives in my dormitory, but *her* roommate didn't show up at all, and so I move in with her that very afternoon.

For instance: After buying a Chinese rug at a New York flea market one morning, I leave it behind in a taxicab. I recall the driver's name—Morris Bromberg—from his license and when the rug doesn't turn up at lost and found, I call every single Morris Bromberg in five boroughs, failing to locate the right one. When it's time to catch my evening train, I hail a cab that turns out to be Morris Bromberg's; he was working back-to-back shifts and wanted to pick up one last fare before dropping off my rug, now beside him on the front seat.

For instance: I meet a man from Seattle, then spend weeks brooding over whether or not I should write him. When I finally do, our letters cross in midair and arrive on the same day.

See, those are just a few examples. But they help explain why Paul, that man from Seattle, came to conceive of my life as a series of Venn diagrams with endlessly overlapping sectors. That seemed right to me. I could easily see how my main measure of significance, whether of people or events, might be interpreted as the degree to which overlap occurred. If the degree was low, things tended to blur. But if it was high, well, then I remembered everything.

As I stood at the bay window of Paul's small apartment and inhaled the low-tide tang, I saw a trio of fish-shaped kites in the park below, all flying from a single stake. There was a big salmon-shaped kite swooping above a smaller replica, and off to the side, a spinning tubular fish that was smaller still. Their colors were magenta, yellow, and cyan. Paul had taught me that these were the subtractive primary colors, the colors that printers mix, sometimes with black, to come up with every other color. I picked up a pair of binoculars that were on the windowsill for a closer look. The kite-flyer came into my sights as he ran to the edge of the bay, where he stopped to light a cigarette. Then he did a goofy little sailor's dance. I couldn't see his face but the way he crouched down low and flung his legs out to the side made me think of Groucho Marx, and of how Jody used to imitate him when we were kids.

I was spending the summer in Seattle, a kind of test-run to see if I could bring myself to move here. Could I freelance enough articles from the West Coast to avoid having to get a real job? After two years of Paul and me flying back and forth from one Washington to the other, was I ready to live with him? Those were the questions noodling through my mind that morning. I wasn't looking for Jody or anyone else.

As far as I knew, Jody was still in South Carolina, working as a cashier in the underwear outlet that his parents continued to finance solely because it gave him something to do. My stomach churned at the picture of him ringing up sales and counting out change. I didn't like that feeling. So I drifted back to when we set up a front yard stand to sell our old comic books for a nickel each, then back further still, to when Jody began calling me Mashie instead of Marsha. Nobody had called me Mashie for a very long time. Thinking of this now filled me with a longing for the Jody that used to be, for the sweetness so incompatible with all my secondhand perceptions of his condition I had practically forgotten it had ever been his. Deep inside the longing, I imagined that Jody had gone off his medication and run away, something I knew he once did on a regular basis. And what if he had? The longing dissolved into fear. Would I ever know the right thing to do?

I tried to talk myself out of this story. It was ridiculous, really, even in light of the Venn diagram effect. I hadn't seen Jody for over ten years, not since the first time he was hospitalized and his doctor made it clear that "no visitors" applied most especially to me. Here I was, goose flesh on my arms in the middle of June, not only romantically reprieved from another swampy summer in Washington, D.C., but with a view spread out before me that even the most ordinary Seattle restaurants could use to justify expensive menus—ferry boats crossing paths in the foreground and, off in the distance, where the sun set at this time of year, the phantomlike, snowcapped Olympic

Mountain peaks. And instead of enjoying all this, I was summoning a ghost sticky with the residue of another time entirely. Conjuring Jody. Out of a silly step that was hardly unique to him. Out of thin air, practically.

I dialed my mother in South Carolina, expecting her to verify the extent of my error. She answered in her distinctive way, a tiny hum preceding "hello," as if setting the pitch of her voice.

"Hi," I began, "I'm in Seattle."

She laughed. "I'm not *that* bad a mother, I know where you are."

"Have you heard anything about Jody?"

"Jody?" She said his name with evident consternation. "Are you all right?"

"Don't worry, Joyce, I'm fine."

"Good. I'll call you back when the rates go down, I don't want you spending your money. What's your number there?"

"Never mind!" Then, more casually, "How's he doing, do you know?"

"Well," she said slowly, "he's had his own apartment for a while, did I tell you that?"

"No." I generally avoided talking about Jody, mainly because I found it difficult to hear him discussed as a bundle of symptoms and tics, and equally hard to hide that difficulty from my mother. Whenever I went home to visit, it was always over the same holidays when, without fail, Jody was either in the hospital or gone for some other reason—at his sister Nancy's house in Atlanta, his parents' vacation place in Florida. I never regarded this as a coincidence, although I did sometimes wonder if I was being paranoid. Paranoid, a word that was part of Jody's first official diagnosis, right before schizophrenic.

"He's in one of those townhouses at Riverbend," Joyce

went on. "I saw him a while back at the mall, just staring out into space. The other week he got arrested there for loitering, poor thing. Usually, they just escort him out to his car, but this policeman was new. Still, I don't understand how it happened. It's not as if he *looks* bad. Except, I mean, for the staring."

From what I could tell, whenever my mother saw Jody it was always by chance—eating barbecue at the Little Pigs, maybe, or filling up his car at the gas station. These sounded like very substantial activities to me. How strange could he be if he went out for barbecue and pumped gas? Looking through the binoculars, I watched the person who most likely wasn't Jody reel in his kites.

"So he hasn't run away?"

"Oh, I doubt it. Of course, we don't see the Lurreys much anymore."

She paused for a moment then rushed on, as though hoping to keep me from mentioning that I didn't see them at all anymore. "I'm sure he hasn't done anything like that lately, not for years. Not since he was wearing that beret. Not since, you know, he thought he was Pablo Picasso. The last time was when he ran off to Hawaii and got a job in a pineapple factory. I forget how they found him. I think after he got fired he was arrested for panhandling. Or maybe he used one of his parents' credit cards. One thing I could never figure out was what pineapples had to do with Picasso."

"It probably doesn't work like that," I said.

"Like what?"

"Logically."

"Oh. Anyway, that was when they still had him on Thorazine. He must be on something different now. He isn't bloated anymore, but he still smokes all the time. Have you quit yet?"

"Not yet."

"Eileen put smoke detectors up all over the place, she's so worried Jody will fall asleep with one still going. I put them up here, too. Your father's liable to do the same thing to me."

I noticed that the kite-flyer in Myrtle Edwards Park was now faced in my direction, head thrown back and gazing upward, the focus of his attention uncertain enough at this distance that he seemed to be fixed on the window where I stood. I put down the binoculars. "Could you call the Lurreys and see if he's there?"

"Why?"

The obvious answer was that I didn't want to call them myself. How would I address them? Mr. and Mrs.? Pretty formal for people who used to be Aunt Eileen and Uncle Sol, honorary relatives I knew better than any of my real ones. They'd probably hate me using their first names, which is something I often did with my own parents. My mother enjoyed this as proof of how close we were, but my father, for whom it was a sad day when I stopped calling him Daddy, always objected when he heard Daniel coming out of my mouth. On the phone with Joyce, though, I stuck to the flimsy facts. I told her there was someone in the park who might be Jody, but I wasn't close enough to make a positive identification. I was beginning to sound like a cop.

Just then, I heard my father in the background, asking who was on the line. "It's Marsha," my mother said, covering the receiver. "She thinks Jody might be out there, but she couldn't see his face."

"What?" My father's voice boomed past her hand. "Has she lost her mind now, too? Let me talk to her."

"Not now, Daniel." Her volume rose to match his.

"But what you just told me doesn't make sense!"

"Nothing I say makes sense to you. Nothing *any* woman says makes sense to you."

"Just tell him you'll explain later," I urged my mother. But she was off and running. "If you want to speak with Marsha," she told my father, "try calling her yourself sometime. That's what *I* do. She's calling on her nickel now, so leave us alone."

There came the sound of my father sneezing, blowing his nose, and finally, a long sigh from my mother when he left as directed. "He's home with a cold," she said, "watching baseball games and following me around the house. He's driving me crazy."

"Will you call them, Mom?"

"I'm sure it's nothing."

"You're probably right. But do it anyway, okay?"

After I said goodbye and hung up, it occurred to me that one of Seattle's major selling points was its location—as far away from where I was raised as you could get without leaving the continental United States.

It would have been bad enough if Jody were the only one. But he wasn't.

Even to outsiders, the incidence of crack-ups among my peers back home might be considered fairly noteworthy. At last count, four former Temple Israel Sunday School classmates had been institutionalized, nearly a quarter of the student body. For a while, whenever I sounded the least bit depressed Joyce would inquire whether I'd been in the vicinity of marijuana. She had taken to blaming it for "ruining" Jody, forgetting that she tried the stuff with me once herself with no more alarming result than a terribly specific craving for a hollowed-out banana filled with crunchy peanut butter. I was home from college then and nothing, so far as we knew, was wrong with Jody. It was a pleasant night, kind of like old times, when Joyce took an unabashed, almost regal pride in being different from all the other mothers, in being a painter who was trained at the Chicago Art Institute, in being South Carolina's very own answer to Helen Frankenthaler and Grace Hartigan—although not many people in our town, much less the state, knew or cared who *they* were.

It still seems strange to me that the place where I'm from is now considered a real city. There used to be lots of civic bragging about Sparta being the Textile Capital of the World. For a while the chamber of commerce even promoted Sparta as the Airlift Capital of the World, but that had to stop when the air force base shut down. Really, it was just a burgeoning mill town with the sort of inferiority complex you might expect from a place that, being nestled in the twangy Blue Ridge foothills, had forever suffered by comparison to Charleston's elegant coastal drawl. Growth, when it came, tended toward the generic. But even before the sprawling tentacles of two-lane highways widened to major thoroughfares, even before the names of residential subdivisions began to resemble those of plantations—or worse, English manors—even then, somehow it was always too large a town and too small a shtetl to offer much in the way of comfort to anyone who was noticeably different.

As a rule, we were considered not so much strange as Biblically Significant. With religiously inclined black people, this sometimes amounted to an ancient sense of recognition, almost as if Mr. Abraham down at the Army-Navy store had been transported directly here from the Old Testament, descended from slaves, like them. With the white people it was trickier. It got to be almost interesting to observe the deft manner, a sort of sideways sociability, with which acceptance gave way to exclusion at certain mysterious junctures, leaving you to wonder if it was really because they were dumb enough to think you had something to do with killing Christ.

When fundamentalist street preachers would accost us downtown and demand to know if we had found Jesus, Jody's idea of a joke was to swoon in mock concern and ask if He was lost, then tell the red-faced proselytizer that, yes, come to think of it, he *did* see someone who looked a whole lot like Jesus over on Crescent Avenue, where everyone— even out-of-state students at the local Bible-beating Baptist college—knew the temple was located.

It was too distressing to think of *Jody* as someone who might be given to accosting people on downtown streets. Or in Myrtle Edwards Park. I tried not to as I waited for Joyce to call back, busying myself instead with tidying the bed on which Paul and I had made urgent love before he left for the studio, neither one of us used to the idea that we had weeks together stretching out before us instead of the usual few days. The nights were still cool enough that we slept beneath a billowy down quilt. I fluffed the quilt and then, forgetting that I had, sat on it to entertain another distraction; how would I ever fit all my stuff into such a small space, much less get it up five flights without an elevator? Maybe if I moved out here we'd have to give up the view, a view that just now, I noticed, included a troop of slate-colored clouds marching in from the south.

What was taking Joyce so long?

Maybe she had to cover for the rudeness of the question I'd forced on her with a lot of polite conversation. Maybe she was receiving instructions for me from Eileen. Or maybe she was just sitting there, waiting for enough time to pass before she could call back to say sorry, she couldn't reach anyone, and didn't I have better things to be doing with my time? The phone rang.

"Marsha, he's been gone for five days."

"Who did you talk to?"

"Juanita, the Lurreys are our of town." Juanita was the Lurreys' maid. "His car's gone, Nancy's filed a missing person report. Just let the police take care of it, do you hear?"

"Look, he's never done anything worse than loiter and panhandle. Aren't you overreacting just a little bit?"

"Marsha," she said, "I suspect I know more than you think."

Either that, I wanted to say, or you suspect more than you know. But splitting hairs and arguing were pointless now, so I got off the phone and hurried to finish dressing. While I was tying my sneakers, the phone rang again. Thinking it was Joyce with more warnings, I let the machine answer. "Are you there?" I heard Paul say. "Are you working? Are you naked in the bathtub? I was thinking lunch out on the pier, on those benches by the Happy Hooker. Call me."

His voice sounded so warm and cozy I wanted to curl up inside of it like a squirrel. But if I started talking to him now, I might lose track of my kite-flyer. I grabbed the keys to Paul's pickup, reluctant to waste any more time walking, and ran down the wide wood stairwell. Outside, on the longest side of this triangular-shaped building, was a painted advertisement for a seafood restaurant. The pickup was parked just beneath the restaurant's motto, "Keep Clam."

I pulled out into traffic and glanced at the sky again while I waited for the light to change at the intersection of Broad and Western. If it wasn't Jody in the park, I could still make it to the studio for lunch. But unless the wind changed, it would probably be raining by then.

Chapter 2

THE AFTERNOON my father drives us into South Carolina for the first time, we descend from the mountains through a storm, the rain coming down so hard that we can't open the windows. It's three days now since we left Chicago and I'm in the back seat with my brother Flip, too hot and restless to fall asleep like he has. "Okay, miss," my father says to distract me. "What's your name?"

"Marsha Rose."

"And where do you live?"

"One-eleven Shannon Drive, Sparta, South Carolina."

"And what are your mommy and daddy's names?"

"Joyce and Daniel Rose."

"Very good, Marsha Rose—you win a fried chicken dinner."

I try to hang onto his attention, but I don't know enough about anything else my father considers important to succeed at this for long. Taking hairpin curves with one hand on the wheel, he lights a cigarette. "Crack the window open," snaps my mother, already braced against the dash to show her displeasure with how fast my father's driving. I crouch down behind his seat where they can't see me, positioning myself so the rainwater leaking in trickles onto my neck.

That night, I eat fried chicken sitting in a booster chair at the Southerner restaurant. Next to me, in another booster chair, is a boy named Jody who shakes a cleanly gnawed chicken bone in my face as if it were a rattle.

When I slap his hand away, his mother leans across the table, drawing her heart-shaped face close to mine. I pull back at first, expecting a reprimand from the way her lips are pressed together. But then I notice the snap in her eyes, the dimples pocking her cheeks, and I realize that what she's doing is cultivating a smile. "It's the wishbone, honey," she tells me through a flash of teeth, big and sparkling against her wavy black hair, Carmen-colored lipstick, and dark summer skin. Then, to Jody, "Tell Marsha what to do, son."

"Make a wish and pull," he says.

I look to my own mother beside me for guidance. "Why don't you wish that we'll all be happy here," she suggests. But that's not nearly specific enough for Marsha Rose of one-eleven Shannon Drive, soon to be sleeping in her very own bedroom for the first time ever. I consider for a moment and then reach for the chicken bone.

Jody's upset when it breaks into two perfectly even pieces, but his mother assures us that this means both of our wishes will come true. If she's right, I won't ever mess up and tell someone that my name is Marsha Rosenfeld.

Outside the Southerner restaurant, Jody's mother and father say goodbye to us with their arms looped affectionately around each other's waists, as though posing for a photograph.

In Chicago my father worked for a small company that made textile machinery, dealing with all his southern clients mostly by mail. As far as those clients knew, my father, Daniel Rosenfeld, was Daniel Rose. My father and his bosses had decided this name would go down more easily among people who, they believed, detested Jews almost as much as blacks and only somewhat less than Catholics. It never occurred to anyone that some day Daniel Rosenfeld would have to move South, where unions weren't the issue they were in Chicago, to build a new factory. Once it did, the four of us were stuck with his pen name.

Changing his name doesn't seem to bother my father, who probably would have been horrified if anyone had expected him to go the distance and change his religion as well. He's been coming to South Carolina for months to scout a factory site and find us a home, meeting Sol and Eileen Lurrey in the process. My father is the kind of man who finds life bursting with possibility after acquiring a new name, a new town, and a new job that is significant enough at last to be in sync with his own ideas of himself. He hires a pretty secretary with out-of-date marcelled hair, one who doesn't mind being called honey and is smart enough not only to make a flattering fuss over the eloquence of his business letters, but over how difficult it is to decide whether he looks most like Glenn Ford or Tyrone Power.

My parents don't accord much credibility to my memories of incidents that occurred before we moved here, of my being wrapped in a blanket and passed like a football over a backyard fence between my father and uncle, or of dancing up and down our concrete driveway for endless hours with the ballerina doll I received for my second birthday, her ankles strapped to mine. In my father's all-too-brief accounts of my earliest years, I am always either bossy, taking toys away from my sweeter-tempered brother Philip, whom I call Flip, or tearful, giving my father endless cause to call me Sarah Heartburn, a name that only signifies to me what a pain I am. When it comes to telling the kind of stories I'd like to hear, my mother isn't any better than my father. Through some murky level of awareness, I figure that if I were a more delightful child, if I were less dark and less quick to cry and just generally more like my freckle-faced, rosy-cheeked older brother, things would be different. What's certain is that my parents, far-flung from their own families and heads of a newly named tribe, find plenty of things more interesting than the reminiscences of a girl who's probably making everything up anyway.

We come from the Land of Lincoln, my father reminds us. And now we live in a place where a hotel, highway, high school, and beauty pageant are all named for Wade Hampton, a Confederate general who never managed to win a major battle in the Civil War. This could never happen in the North, I think, which, like my parents, seems so much more clear and conscious about things like winning and losing.

Jody's parents, Sol and Eileen Lurrey, are southerners, born and bred. As president of the Temple Brotherhood, Sol is duty-bound to offer my family a taste of communal hospitality now that we've all arrived. But in the beginning, Sol and Eileen are wary. They think we might be lepers, which is what the natives privately call Yankee congregants whose employers send them here to live.

Lepers, as I will eventually learn, are transferred because superiors figure this is a good way to get rid of them. Prior to moving here, lepers consider the two Carolinas so equally worthless that they can't tell them apart; once arrived, they tend to find fault with everything, from the lackadaisical temple, which has trouble finding rabbis who aren't lepers themselves, to the dearth of social amenities, which means you have to join the Elks Club or the Air Force Base Officer's Club if you like to dance to live music and don't want to brownbag your liquor.

Since lepers are so unpleasant and generally don't last

for more than a year or two, Sol and Eileen are reluctant to waste energy on them. But it doesn't take long for my parents to win the Lurreys over. It helps that my father is very good at singing all the songs that Sol likes to play on the piano, and that, early on, my mother gives Eileen one of her impastoed abstract cityscapes. It doesn't go at all with the rest of what's hanging in the Lurreys' house— floral still lives just about everywhere but the den, where there are pictures of dogs playing poker—but Eileen gives it a place of prominence, over the living room sofa, anyway.

My mother's greatest disappointment after moving to Sparta is discovering that we live in what she calls hard-shell Baptist country. There's nothing at all here of the charm, gaiety, and genial corruption that she remembers from Mississippi, where she went to school and met my father during the war. My mother's first major mission after we're settled is to have the garage walled-in and insulated so she can turn it into her studio. Once she and Eileen decide to be friends, the two of them start making trips to Charleston and Atlanta, real ports of pleasure compared to where we live, places with galleries, museums, interesting stores.

From my mother, Eileen learns something about contemporary artists, about designers like Bonnie Cashin and Norman Norrell, about what to buy when you can afford only one good piece and where to look for decent knockoffs. From Eileen, my mother learns about who's worth cultivating in Sparta, about which slow-talking businessmen routinely take carpetbaggers to the cleaners by pretending to be simple country boys, and about which plants do best with the short winters and humid summers here. This last my mother listens to out of sheer politeness; she has no interest at all in getting her hands dirty with anything but oil paint.

Soon, my mother begins having what she thinks of as a reasonable life, which entails hiring a maid whose name is Parthenia but is called Patina by everyone, including her own family. Patina is the older sister of Juanita, the Lurreys' maid, which intertwines our lives with the Lurreys' that much more. And of course there are the children, their girl the same age as our boy, our girl the same age as their boy, with the same three years between them.

At the Lurreys' insistence, Flip and I call Sol and Eileen aunt and uncle; Nancy and Jody do the same with our parents. Plenty of people in town think we are actually blood relatives, just because of our religion. For the most part, so do I.

If you're going to have two mothers, you could do a lot worse. You wouldn't go to my mother to learn how things worked. My mother thought wasps had stingers on their noses, like in the cartoons, instead of on their butts. Aunt Eileen not only knew where stingers were located, she knew that when you got stung, damp shredded tobacco from one of her Kents took away the pain. Sometimes it's nice having a ghost mother who doesn't stick out quite so much, one who sounds, dresses, behaves, and cooks more like everybody else's mother.

Jody, meanwhile, thinks that my mother's being an artist makes her some kind of magician. Because to him, growing roses or slapping tobacco on a bee sting is everyday, ordinary stuff.

One Saturday during the summer before Jody and I start school, my mother and Aunt Eileen sit in the Lurreys' backyard sunning themselves. My mother is going to play Maisie in a Little Theater production of *The Boyfriend*, which Jody and I both think means she is going to be famous. She already looks famous, her hair dyed red and cut into a flapper's helmet, more glamorous than ever. My mother came to be in the play by accident. Aunt Eileen had signed her up to help with painting sets, but when the director met my mother, she confirmed his guess that she could dance as well as fake a tune, and he put her directly into the cast. It wasn't as if my mother had been longing to perform onstage, but she's ham enough to enjoy it. There aren't many artists for her to hang out with in Sparta—not many, anyway, who paint things besides flowers and barn scenes. The Little Theater crowd is about as close as she can get to having a gang to laugh, drink, joke, and swear with, a gang something like the one she'd had in Chicago.

While Aunt Eileen cues my mother from a script stained orange with Bain de Soleil, Jody and I hang around at their feet to play a game of checkers, enjoying the Judy Holiday–like voice my mother uses when she says her lines. My mother's only solo song is one about how it's never too late to fall in love. She has a record at home with this and all the other songs from the play on it, and we know the words well enough by now that Jody and I sing along when she practices. There are no songs today, though, just spoken words. When Aunt Eileen and my mother are through with the script, Jody goes to toss his big shooter marbles into the pit that's being dug for a swimming pool, sinking them into the moist red dirt.

Aunt Eileen sprays her face with water from an old Windex bottle as she explains to my mother. "He actually enjoys the risk of losing them. It's a boy's game, not a girl's."

Jody and I are taking swimming lessons so that we won't drown in Saluda Lake when the mothers take us there for picnics, or in the Lurreys' pool when it's finished, with blue tile Roman numerals on the bottom representing how many pairs of little girls' panties Uncle Sol had to manufacture and sell in order to pay for it. Our teacher is Bishop Fulmer, the crew-cut son of the contractor who's building the Lurreys' pool. Aunt Eileen says Bishop has been to divinity school, and we wonder what can be so hard about making candy that you have to study it. Although Bishop is a good swimming teacher, Jody's progress is slowed by the fact that he refuses to put his head under water.

My mother wears a black-and-white check paneled suit that emphasizes her small waist and full breasts. Aunt Eileen's suit isn't nearly so stylish, but she likes to dive and hers is designed so that she won't fall out the top if she does a toe-touching pike, her specialty.

"You know," my mother says to Aunt Eileen, "Margo says Harold is a fairy."

Margo is the English actress who came here to choreograph the play—she has taught me to dance a time step on the off-beat so that it rhymes rhythmically with the chant of "Thanks for the buggy ride"—and Harold plays Maisie's boyfriend. I think of the tooth I pulled out a few nights ago at the Carolina Theater during *West Side Story*, triumphantly holding the bloody root in front of my mother's face during a lull between songs, and wonder if Harold was in any way connected to the quarter I received.

"Well," Aunt Eileen says, looking surprised, "I went to high school with Harold, of course. But I guess the world Margo comes from, she should know."

"There are fairies at the bottom of our garden," my mother flutes in an English accent.

"What's that supposed to mean?" Aunt Eileen asks, frowning.

Bea Lillie, I want to tell her. I know about Bea Lillie because my mother sometimes puts on a long string of my pop beads and twirls them around her neck, like Bea Lillie, she would say, while reciting the fairy poem. But my mother doesn't elaborate. "Oh," she says airily, "it's just a poem."

The fathers are off in Pickens today, playing golf at a country club where, unlike the club in Sparta, the only restrictions are racial. If this were Sunday, all of us would go out to dinner at the New China restaurant, the only restaurant in town open on Sundays. But this is Saturday, and our parents are going to the Officer's Club tonight without us.

Jody and I are the only children around now. Last week we drove with the mothers into the mountains of North Carolina to take Flip and Nancy to Camp Maccabee, a camp created largely for the purpose of adjusting children like us to our heritage. It seemed amazing, so many Jewish people all in one place. Flip turned shy and I clung along with him to my mother's side, suddenly afraid she might decide to leave me here too. But Nancy couldn't wait for us to go so she could meet everybody who wasn't lucky enough yet to know her. Nancy has so much energy it's as though her system operates on rocket fuel instead of blood, and she makes up her mind at the same high speed she does everything else. Jody goes more slowly, like me, but he regarded this as some kind of adventure he was being left out of and pestered his mother to let him stay.

"You're only six," Aunt Eileen told Jody. "You have to be at least seven before you can go to camp."

On the way home, Aunt Eileen scooted closer to my mother, who was driving her new powder-blue Thunderbird convertible with the top down. "I spent a lot of time preparing them," Aunt Eileen said, "telling them about the camp and what it's for. Maybe they're just more outgoing by nature than yours." I took this as one of Aunt Eileen's measuring remarks, with Flip and my mother and me coming up short this time. My mother shrugged and drove in silence, her face a mask of imperturbability, but I could tell she was irritated. It didn't seem to matter to her so much that Aunt Eileen's brow wrinkled thoughtfully, as if to show how hard she tried to measure fairly. It was the measuring itself that sometimes got to my mother, who'd just as soon not chart everything so closely.

Aunt Eileen retied her scarf and turned her attention to Jody, who was picking his nose. "Just what do you think you're doing?" Aunt Eileen demanded.

"I'm hiding my finger," he said, shouting into the wind.

My mother burst into laughter, but Aunt Eileen glared.

That's how it is with them a lot of the time, the other mother turning into an ally when yours is annoyed, always for reasons you can never really trust enough to test.

Today in the Lurreys' backyard, though, the mothers are in perfect harmony. "Come here, Little Bit," Aunt Eileen says to me, "and I'll do your hair."

I love the feeling of Aunt Eileen's hands in my hair as much as that of my mother's nails when she scratches my back. While I sit between Aunt Eileen's legs she sprays my head with water from her bottle and starts wrapping strands around her fingers. "Look at this hair," she coos. "It curls whatever way you comb it."

"Nothing like *mine*," my mother says.

Aunt Eileen laughs. "Maybe she gets it from *me*." I'm so used to being mistaken for Aunt Eileen's child by now that I almost consider this to be within the realm of possibility.

"When Marsha's old enough to start using makeup," Aunt Eileen says, still combing my hair, "she's going to be something."

"Maybe," my mother says, "if the Baptists don't have her too scared of looking like a Jezebel by then. You know the nude I have hanging in the bedroom?"

Aunt Eileen giggles. "The true redhead?"

They're talking about the portrait of a Chicago woman who posed for my mother's class at the Art Institute, a recent source of shame for me. "Marsha's little friends made a fuss," my mother continues. "They told her it was bad, and nothing would do but that I take it down. She said, 'Mama, I don't want to go to hell down a sliding board of nails.' Can you imagine? That's what they told her."

Aunt Eileen sounds a low, judicious tone. "Did they tell her she'd go to hell because of the nude or because of Jesus?"

"She didn't mention Jesus."

"Then it could have been worse."

The others have so much more information about hell than me, all of it delivered with great certainty. I look over my shoulder at Aunt Eileen. "Don't we believe in hell?"

"No," she says crisply. "We believe you make your own heaven or hell right here on earth. That's what we say in our house. Now turn around or you'll come out lopsided." Sinking back against Aunt Eileen's breasts, I wish she could be there to argue for me the next time when I don't know what we believe in compared to everybody else.

While Aunt Eileen and Uncle Sol dress for dinner, Juanita arrives in her husband's truck. Her husband works for a glass company, and always fixes the windows that Flip and his friends break playing baseball.

I like being with Patina well enough, but Jody loves Juanita. After the Lurreys leave with my parents, Juanita cooks a regular dinner for us that Jody pushes around on his plate before talking Juanita into making him a fried Spam sandwich on Wonder Bread with lots of mayonnaise instead. We all watch TV together until it's time for Juanita to bathe us—separately now that we're too old to be bathed together. As I lay freshly washed in Nancy's bed, I listen to Jody, still in the bathtub, repeat something from a cartoon we'd seen that morning.

"My oh my," he sputters, "am I ever mortified."

"Don't say that, Joy-boy," Juanita scolds.

"Why not?"

"Because mortified is how you feel when you're *dead.*"

Jody is just practicing for later. After his bath, when Juanita is watching "Saturday Night at the Movies," Jody will scrape his fingers across the heating grate in the wall between Nancy's room and his, signaling me that it's time for us to meet in the adjoining bathroom and tell each other stories. Although Jody always approaches this enterprise with a lot of thought and preparation, I'm content to embroider whatever he comes up with.

Jody makes motorboat noises for a while before trying out another line. "You can't take my power," he says in a commanding voice, "because my power is in my brain." This reminds me of what Jody tells Nancy when they're fighting and she hits him on the head. "*Don't*—my *brains* are in there."

Jody keeps babbling as Juanita pulls him out of the tub. "You know what I think?" he says. "I think the world is in God's stomach."

After all the snaps on his pajama top click together, Juanita says, "There, we're done, baby. And how do you feel now?"

"Soft," Jody tells her.

"That's nice," Juanita says, sounding every bit as serious as him. "That's a real nice way to go off to sleep."

I wait for Jody's fingers on the grate for what seems like a long time. Tonight we do things differently. Jody brings a blanket and a small lamp, its blue shade decorated with cowboys herding cattle, into the bathroom. After we clear out the wide cabinet beneath the sink, Jody plugs in the lamp and sets it up inside. Then, leaving the cabinet doors open, he drapes the blanket over the sink. We crawl into the back corners on either side of the drain pipe and sit for a while hugging our knees, enjoying the campfire effect.

"My oh my," Jody begins. We're primed for hilarity anyway, and laugh all the harder now that there's something forbidden about these words. Then we take turns, Jody starting off with a boy who lives in a cave, me turning him into a girl, until finally it's the two of them together, doing all sorts of dangerous, scary things, risking their lives repeatedly as they hunt for food and fire wood and stuff to furnish their cave with, only nothing bad can ever really happen to them because the world is in God's stomach and it's safe to go to sleep.

Chapter 3

Seattle

THE KITES were on the ground near their owner, who lay sleeping on a grassy hill using a duffel bag for his pillow. Yes, it was Jody, all right—a more mature version of the toothy, olive-skinned boy who used to be mistaken for my twin in grade school. We still looked like kin, with angular cheeks, sharp chins, and narrow noses shooting down from high, widow's-peaked foreheads. Even closed, Jody's eyes had a way of seeming large and expectant. Eyes don't change and behind their lids Jody's were not only hazel, like mine, but similarly flecked with so many watery-colored dots it looked as if they'd given up about halfway through trying to be blue. I noticed the gold signet ring Nancy had bought for Jody in Mexico City the summer she studied Spanish there, a masculine version of the one she bought for me and that I was wearing today. People sometimes ask me if it's a sorority ring, which I think is funny. Me in a sorority.

Is he *really* asleep, I wondered as I sat down on a nearby bench. I decided he was by the distinctive way his hand was positioned, palm open guilelessly by his head. He looked so vulnerable, younger than his thirty-three years. A child could have stolen from him. Much likelier suspects, though, were closer at hand—two other sleeping men, dressed as Jody was in jeans, flannel shirts, and athletic shoes. But while Jody could easily be mistaken for a slightly overripe camper, someone who'd been a little too long on the trail, these guys who were evidently with him looked more like old hands at street life.

What if I woke Jody? He might see me as an obstacle to his flight, Eileen and Sol's hand-picked emissary, someone whose mere presence would be upsetting. Wasn't this the sort of thing paranoid people thought? It crossed my mind that Jody's instinct to run might be a healthy one. Maybe his troubles would fade apart from familiar places and people. Right, Marsha, and while you're at it, why not leave everything to the police?

I checked my watch. Almost lunch time. I recognized the approaching dense clatter of wheels on the path behind me as signaling the passage of a long-legged blonde who wore her hair in a French braid and roller-skated through the park every day while pushing her baby in a stroller. Soon entire firms of attorneys would be jogging by in perfect pecking order. I remembered what I was supposed to be working on today—a story for a woman's magazine that just happened to have a fairly high overlap factor. The premise of this story was that Family Reunions teach Lessons from the Past that Will Strengthen Your Marriage. "Make it heartwarming," advised Carolyn, my editor in New York. "We want it for the Thanksgiving issue, so just picture your copy facing a turkey layout. These are the subheads I see—Character, Community, Continuity. And remember, most of our readers haven't graduated from college." Paul teased me about contributing to the further befuddlement of the American housewife, but I didn't mind that it was a lame story. I bought my ticket to Seattle with the advance, and besides, with a lame story, editors didn't really care if you made things up, not so long as they didn't know for a fact that you did.

Of course, Jody and I weren't married, and I couldn't

quite see how a reunion with him would fit under any of Carolyn's subheads, much less into the summer that I had planned for myself.

The last time I'd seen Jody, he was standing by the side of the road in Athens, Georgia, thumb stuck out to hitch-hike, refusing to get into my car when I stopped alongside him and never looking in my direction as I slowly drove away, checking the rearview mirror for a signal from him that he wanted me to come back.

This time, I wasn't waiting for a signal. I went to Jody's side and shook his arm. "Jody, wake up. It's Marsha."

"Oh, Mashie," he said, blinking eyelashes that had once been indecently thick and were now sort of sparse and singed looking. "What are you doing here?"

I wished he'd gone on to say something else, something like Finally! Or, Am I awake or still dreaming? He didn't, and I detected enough suspicion in his tone that it ignited my anxiety. "Well, I certainly didn't expect to see *you*. I mean, I wasn't, um, *looking* for you or anything, if that's what you're worried about. Are you . . . on vacation?"

Ignoring my question, Jody took a Swiss Army knife out of his pocket and a hunk of sausage from his duffel bag. He offered me a slice and I refused. I wanted to reach out and straighten Jody's dark hair, flecked with a few scattered threads of silver now but fine like a child's, long enough to lift with the slightest breeze. Instead I sank down on my heels and began fiddling with the grass, silenced by how Jody's eyes turned inward and then diffuse, as though making unhappy equations with how he felt and what he saw around him.

"We're going to pick cherries," Jody said at last.

Our conversation had roused the men behind him. One of them leaned toward me and stretched, baring snaggled teeth in a vocal yawn. "Good crops these last few years," he said.

"It's the volcano ash," offered the bearded second man as he peeled an orange with a long, dirty thumbnail. "Must be some kind of organic fertilizer."

"It's important for artists," Jody said gravely, "to work in nature. But an island would be best. No one would steal your dreams."

His companions rolled their eyes at each other, then at me. Did Jody think he was Gauguin now? Or had the delusion settled into something more general, a kind of free-floating artistic identity? Maybe he was once more headed toward Hawaii, working his way back up to pineapples with smaller fruit. At least he wasn't panhandling. And if these men were sponging off him, eating into whatever money he had managed to put together, at least they showed some interest in earning more. Unless, of course, they planned to rob him first.

"Where are you staying?" I asked Jody.

"Here for now," answered the snaggle-toothed man, untangling his black shoulder-length hair with the tines of a plastic fork.

I tried to ignore him. "How do you plan to get to where the picking is?"

Jody shrugged and pointed vaguely to the train tracks behind the park.

"Say," the bearded man said, aping my frown with a fiercer one of his own, "can you spare us a smile?"

Back east in D.C.—the *other* Washington, as they said in Seattle—a woman once followed me out of a Capitol Hill drugstore screaming, "Tell me to have a nice day! Tell me to have a nice day!" Never mind how much more bizarre it actually was for the bulk of the population to be constantly mouthing the same inane phrase to one another. Since then, this woman had become my own personal measure of derangement. I couldn't imagine Jody doing something like that, and these men with him didn't seem so bad either. *They* were the ones who had probably binged on drugs and ran away for good a long time ago. At the food bank near the Public Market, where Jody could very well have gotten his sausage, you saw characters like them all the time, aging freaks lined up with worn-out looking drunks and faded families who seemed as if they might be second- and third-generation Okies.

"When are you leaving?" I asked Jody.

"I'm not sure," Jody said, his expression so earnest now it bordered on pleading. "But it's a secret, Mashie, a secret."

"Right," I said. "A secret."

Jody turned to his kites and soon became so absorbed in separating their snarled strings that he no longer seemed aware of me, or of anything else. I looked out and saw that the sky above the bay was sheathed in several shades of gray.

"Hey, Mashie," Jody said. "Can you tell what direction the wind's blowing?"

I thought of Dylan, of not needing a weatherman to know which way the wind blows, of listening to records while sprawled out on the floor of Jody's bedroom, which was the best place to do this because not only could he afford to buy all the records he wanted, but he had a Girard turntable and real speakers, not a cheap Sears console like me. All I did, though, was shake my head and shrug. "I think it's blowing in from the south," I said. "I think it's about to rain."

Jody lit a Vantage, studied the first few wispy drifts as

if to verify my report and then, satisfied with his reading, began inhaling the rest in greedy gulps.

"She's right," the snaggle-toothed man told Jody, gathering his things. "Want to come to the mission with us?"

"No," Jody said before I could.

The bearded man laughed. "He's got a girlfriend now, he don't need no stinkin' mission."

As the first drops of rain began to fall, Jody bundled his kites beneath his arm to protect them and began heading for the park's exit. "Where are you going?" I called after him.

"To the library."

The library was downtown, a long walk from here even at the rapid pace Jody had struck, striding on lanky legs that could have easily belonged to someone far taller. As I trailed after him, I thought about trying to get Jody to Paul's apartment, which was much closer but so small that I couldn't possibly make a phone call without him being aware of it. Paul's studio was closer still, but I didn't want to throw Paul in Jody's face so soon. Not only was Paul my lover, he was an actual artist; I worried that Jody might see him as some kind of rival, a reproach to his delusion. The library it was: "Want a ride?" I asked Jody.

Jody nodded. "These fish don't like to get wet."

Jody's companions lingered as I wrapped the kites in plastic sheeting that Paul kept in the back of the pickup, then shoved the rest of Jody's gear onto the floor of the cab. As I got inside, the snaggle-toothed man slapped the fender and winked at me. "Hope this thing works better than it looks," he said.

He was referring to the Datsun's paint job, dulled over the years from its original red to a color something like tomato soup diluted with lots of milk. "Runs like a top," I said, which was true. Paul changed the oil religiously. I drove off hoping he could hear what a happy engine this was.

Slowly, through Jody's foggy aversion to fact, a few details emerged. Sol and Eileen were on a cruise of Scandinavia, or "the blond countries," as Jody put it. After they left, he sold his car for two thousand dollars, five hundred and fifty of which was still in his possession.

"Must have been an old car," I said.

"Nope. Brand new."

Which meant his parents had bought it for him and it would be worth at least three times the amount he accepted. If anyone back home needed proof of Jody's insanity, that would have done it. Driving really matters down there. When people from elsewhere get confused about which of the two Carolinas I come from, I often explain one of the ways I've always distinguished between them: The state of South Carolina spends money on highways, and the state of North Carolina spends money on schools. This rule is effective mainly because it fits so nicely into Yankee preconceptions about North signifying something smarter than South.

"If I got more money," Jody shrugged, "there'd be that much more to worry about. Bruce Springsteen says a man with a million dollars gets million-dollar problems."

"Oh, so you like Bruce, huh?"

"He's okay."

"I don't recall him singing about million-dollar problems."

"He talks about them in *Musician* magazine. Do you ever write for *Musician* magazine?"

I looked at him, surprised. "No."

"I might have a band someday, you know. I'd call my

band the Reverb Motherfuckers because I don't want to sell out. But if I wanted to sell out, I could have million-dollar problems. Plenty of them, too, believe you me."

We stopped for a traffic light close by the entrance to a fashionable department store. There were monorail tracks overhead, now serving as shelter from the rain for a small group of street people. A scrawny old woman in a sleeveless bubblegum-pink shift paced back and forth in front of the store, screaming emphatically. "Every problem you got comes down to the same single solitary thing! You wanna know what that thing is? That thing is love. You wanna know about love? Well, I'll tell you about love."

She had laid out a line of raw eggs on the sidewalk and now she punctuated her argument by stomping on the eggs, drawing cheers from her audience beneath the tracks. "It (stomp) isn't (stomp) easy (stomp)!"

I flinched, mainly at how little notice I would have taken without Jody here beside me. But Jody watched without any real interest, as though this had nothing whatsoever to do with him, much less him being here with me.

"What about medicine?" I ventured. "Do you take any?"

"I don't need to now."

"Why not?"

"I only need it to work in the store, and I don't like working there."

"Well, who *would* like working in an underwear outlet?" I said it before I could stop myself.

"You'd have to be nuts," Jody agreed cheerfully.

"Do you ever hear voices or, um, anything like that?"

"They just watch me now. They're not talking because I'm doing what I'm supposed to do. Hey, do you think I can look at paintings of women in the library?"

"Hey, is that what you're supposed to do?"

Jody nodded, a contented expression on his face.

Once when we were kids, Jody and I found a skin magazine out in a field behind the barn where we went to ride horses, a publication printed on thin, cheesy paper and called something like *Gent* or *Stud*. The rain-pocked pages showed poorly lit but enlightening pictures of women wearing only scraps of leather and disturbing expressions. We went up to the hayloft to hide the magazine, claiming it as a treasure to which we could secretly return on days when the weather was bad or we couldn't cadge a ride, my interest at least as high as Jody's.

"Why's she sticking her tongue out?" Jody asked me as we sat close together, holding the magazine on our knees, examining a dazed-looking model sprawled on her back.

"I don't know. Maybe she's trying to touch her nose." But as Jody pointed out, if that was what she were really doing, she'd be cross-eyed from the strain instead of lying down with her hands between her legs and staring up at the ceiling.

Soon there would be adolescent girls with crushes on Jody, girls who were smarter than average and admired his eyes, how light they looked against his smooth dark skin, or how well he danced. But other kinds of girls liked him, too, the wilder ones who would eventually wind up with jocks and drinkers, boys very much like their daddies and not at all like Jody. They liked how he treated them with the same attentive interest as he treated the smarter girls. Maybe he had lost the chance to grow into what was good about himself. Maybe pictures were all he could have now. What a shame, I could hear the congregation back home chorusing, such a nice-looking boy.

As we headed on through downtown traffic, Jody removed a can of Coke from his duffel bag, popped the top, and took a long drink. "Your hair's different," he said.

That was an understatement. I used to go through all kinds of contortions to make my hair hang straight, but now it fanned out wild and zizzy past my shoulders, impossible to comb. "Yeah," I told him, "I don't care if it's curly anymore."

"So now you've got a permanent."

I frowned at him; how could he have forgotten? "No, it's natural."

"That's what makes it permanent." He took another sip of Coke and belched loudly. "Say, do you remember Benjie Yelverton?" And then, without waiting for my answer, "Benjie Yelverton could drink milk and make it come out his nose."

"What?" I was surprised Jody chose Benjie Yelverton's singular talent as a vehicle for bringing up the past, but also pleased. This was an area in which I excelled—the recollection of obscure data made significant largely because someone has bothered to remember it at all.

"Uh-huh," he went on. "And you balled up your bread in little wads and stuffed it into your milk carton when Miss Abercrombie wasn't looking so you wouldn't have to eat it."

"What about you?" I teased. "You went home every day in the second grade and told your mother you couldn't read the blackboard, just because you were in love with Marilyn Hightower and wanted to wear glasses like she did."

It was apparent by his lack of response that Jody had lost interest in mining this particular vein. "I guess burping on purpose is sort of like playing with your food," was all he said.

If someone else were saying these things, someone like Paul, I would be laughing. Instead, I just concentrated on achieving the perfect balance of gas and clutch so we wouldn't lurch up the steep hill on Spring Street.

Jody ran his hands furtively over the dashboard, like a blind person searching for a familiar feature. "Mashie, why doesn't your car have a radio?"

"It's not my truck," I said carefully. "It's my boyfriend's. Too bad he couldn't buy your car, huh?"

"Yeah. It's too bad, it's too sad. It's two-thirty, go see a dentist."

"He's a painter, Jody. My boyfriend's an artist."

Jody just nodded, as if saying I heard you the first time, as if I'd told him nothing more remarkable than that my boyfriend had ten toes.

At the library, Jody walked directly to the art section on the fourth floor and pulled a huge stack of coffee table art books off the shelves with little regard, so far as I could tell, to artist or style. There was nothing, for instance, featuring Picasso.

"Are you happy with these?" I asked Jody.

"Yeah," he said, flipping through a Matisse book until he found an odalisque.

I went downstairs to the public phones and called Nancy in Atlanta, but she wasn't home so I left a long message telling her I'd found Jody in Seattle and how she could get in touch with me. Then, at the end: "He knows who I am. That doesn't seem to be a problem. I mean, in case you were wondering."

I returned to Jody and asked him to stay put while I looked for a book. Then, driven by my confusion over the state of Jody's delusion, I took the elevator two floors down to the psychology section, where I just as indiscriminately gathered material on the subject of schizophrenia, as though Jody were a term paper topic I'd just been assigned.

I started with the oldest books. The year Jody and I were born—a year, I learned, in which mental patients occupied more hospital beds than all other types of patients combined—research was published which plainly stated, no question about it, that a family's emotional conflicts crystallize in the weakest member, the schizophrenic, and, as a result, everyone else gets to feel a whole lot less anxious. While both parents might be immature, one tends to be overadequate and can force the underadequate parent into submission—even, I gathered, if he is an otherwise successful businessman producing millions of pairs of panties each year.

Schizophrenics and their mothers were evidently considered so symbiotic that one of the psychiatrist/authors in my stack hardly bothered to write about them as separate people. Another noted the remarkable progress schizophrenic patients made living in a group home under his gentle guidance, but claimed they all regressed completely after being released to their families. Meanwhile, I found more than one reference to what appeared to be the biggest schizophrenic joke going: A number of presumably sane researchers were voluntarily institutionalized as part of an experiment, and although they did not attempt to simulate schizophrenic behavior, almost all were diagnosed as schizophrenics themselves.

Before long, though, I could see that more recent authorities considered such material pure and total horseshit. They were outraged; they were righteous. And their position was plain: When it comes to schizophrenia, biological factors far outweigh parental insecurities and the inadequacies of psychiatry. The problem wasn't hysterical mothers but out-of-control neurons, whipping wildly around the brain like hyperactive children in a roomful of toys. Clearly, these guys were modern. And because they were talking brain disease, not neurosis, they rated family therapy as a treatment for schizophrenics about on a par with hot baths for cancer. Antipsychotic drugs seemed to be the only answer, the thing that made all those other psychological theories so passe. But even so, a vocal renegade element condemned drugs, swearing instead by massive doses of megavitamins and love.

Thinking of my mother's theory, I searched for a possible link between marijuana and schizophrenia and found only that schizophrenics who hear unpleasant voices might try to drown them out, to obliterate them, with the psychic distortions of street drugs. This turned into such a technical discussion of the chemical similarities between drug-induced hallucinations and schizophrenic ones that I drifted back to the summer Jody taught me how to smoke grass.

Home from our first year of college, we were driving all the way to a repertory movie house in Columbia to see *McCabe and Mrs. Miller*, and Jody, who had seen it before, wanted me to be in the proper frame of mind. We both claimed to be romantically enraptured with other people, and rather than creating distance, this actually seemed to have the effect of making us more exotic and interesting to each other. Jody was driving his red Triumph, and he lit up as we approached the city limits. "Always present the enemy," he said, "with a moving target."

Although Jody couldn't have been more casual, it took a few drags before my uneasiness passed, before I was looking up from my low-slung seat and giggling at the ordinary weirdness of all the other drivers we were passing. My sense of direction was never a strong point and now I couldn't have found my way out of a paper bag, but Jody navigated with ease, confidently snaking through unfamiliar streets and making it to the theater in plenty of time for us to load up on the Cokes and popcorn that suddenly seemed so imperative. While the movie played, Jody had a way of sighing sharply or touching my shoulder during certain scenes. And each time, I understood exactly what he thought was wonderful about what was going on up there.

Coming back to the present, I went upstairs to check on Jody, who was sitting at a table by himself, examining color plates and twirling his hair in what looked to be absorption. Maybe this quiet solitude was doing Jody good, I thought.

Without interrupting him, I returned to the second floor, convinced now that the brain disease boys must be right. They had scientific proof, didn't they? Then I picked up a book of statistical studies. One of these studies showed that the odds of one identical twin succumbing to schizophrenia if the other already had it were fifty percent. Fifty percent? I read the text carefully, looking for a line that would break through the jargon and explain this study's significance. Even I knew that identical twins had one hundred percent identical genes. Obviously, some other factor was involved. But what? I'd already come across a few suggestions—enzyme deficiencies, mutations, maybe even a virus caught in the womb—but this particular study didn't venture a guess. I don't know why I was surprised. After all, its authors were scholars, not hacks who expected to appear on afternoon talk shows. I pictured a team of guests and experts, all with identifying labels superimposed across their chests—Controversial Psychiatrist, Schizophrenic Twin, Normal Twin, etc.—and the host careening through a baffled studio audience, frantic for an incendiary response. "You say what? What?"

The rest of the studies in this book seemed even more detached, like facts that might be released along with the census. For instance, more schizophrenics are born in the winter and spring months than in the fall (Jody's birthday was in May, exactly three months before mine). Another set of numbers showed how differently various communities respond to "deviancy." Irish Americans, for instance, were found to be more tolerant of relatives with thought disorders than they were of relatives with emotional disorders, whom they're far more apt to have hospitalized, while Jewish Americans were just the opposite. No implications were drawn. Still, I wondered if this meant that Jews were supposed to value logic over emotion, which would make them very different from southerners, or if instead it meant that, like southerners, Jews were so accustomed to emotional excess that disorders in that department were difficult to determine.

From what I could tell, everything figured into this disease, even geography. Eileen's family was Alsatian—a fact that lingered in *my* brain because Jody had discovered his beloved Marx Brothers were Alsatian, too—but I didn't know if Uncle Sol's people were from Russia or Poland, where schizophrenia is apparently very big. If you wanted to avoid schizophrenia entirely, the place to be was somewhere in the Third World because the incidence has been shown to increase in direct proportion to the degree of civilization. What's meant by "civilization"? Oh, money, media, increased mobility, new ideas in art and music, breakdown of the extended family. Oh.

I read about a man who hadn't been particularly political before his illness, but thought he was Gandhi when he began treatment; a few days later he was Gandhi's brother, which his doctor took as a good sign. Finally, the man let go the idea entirely. Grandiose identity delusions, from what I could glean, were common. But what would make one schizophrenic fixate on Picasso and another on the anchorman of "News at Five"? Evidently not a fundable research topic. And while everyone seemed to agree that the first signs of schizophrenia show up in the late teens or early twenties, I couldn't catch one of my authorities speculating as to why this was so. I thought of surging hormones and, in Jody's case, the prospect of attending law school.

Jody was typical, one author assured me, in feeling he needed freedom rather than treatment. So much for the thought he might be right? Reading on, I weeded out disturbing warnings. Excessive loneliness aggravates the condition. Without medication, Jody's voices would probably return. Left on his own, he might become completely primitive. He might begin to wear odd objects or develop peculiar mannerisms. He might lose his sensitivity to pain, putting on far too little clothing in cold weather and far too much in the heat of summer.

He might, in short, become very much like the people sitting around me in the library.

At the table beside mine was a whisker-stubbled man who resembled the Walter Brennan character in *To Have and Have Not*, the rummy fishing guide who kept asking everyone, "Was you ever bit by a dead bee?" He wore a stained white T-shirt, a blue snap-ease cap advertising the Puyallup Fair, and baggy khaki pants with fishing lures attached to the belt loops. Spending no more than a second on each page, he flipped his way through a weighty text that looked as if it might be an unabridged dictionary. After some minutes of quietly pursuing this activity, he suddenly slapped himself on the forehead with such force that everyone else looked up from their books and papers. A steady sort of interval developed between these slaps until finally, in the grip of a particularly violent fit, he smacked himself four times in a row, knocking off his cap to reveal a scab-covered scalp. Obviously disgusted, the woman sitting across from him slammed her own book shut and

hauled her enormous bulk off to another table at the far
end of the room, fleshy feet spilling out over the sides of
her bedroom slippers. It seemed that only someone accustomed to such outbursts would have reacted so strongly;
the rest of us normals were busily pretending we hadn't
noticed.

At my own table, directly across from me, sat a skinny
little man with a scraggly mustache who continually zipped
and unzipped his imitation leather jacket. He had a pile of
out-of-town newspapers laid out between us, and it seemed
the zipping helped him settle down because soon it stopped
and he appeared to be intent on a weather map in the *Phoe-
nix Gazette*. Before long, though, while examining the editorial page of the *Sacramento Bee*, he started rattling a
plastic bag that sounded as if it contained a thousand
safety pins. When I glanced up at him, he apologized for
the racket by raising his eyebrows and shushing the bag
noisily, entreating it to behave.

Paul once explained to me how the perception of a color
depends upon what other color is close by. If you took, say,
a rusty patch of color and surrounded it with an intense
green, that rusty patch would appear to be red; surrounded
instead by red, it would look brown. In color parlance, that
rusty patch is called metamer. Here in the library, Jody
was my fickle color, my metamer dimming and flaring according to whatever information I placed alongside him,
from Sol and Eileen to these poor prematurely discharged
crazies.

Just as I found myself feeling guiltily grateful that Jody
and I were not blood relations, which would have meant
that I too carried a gene for schizophrenia, I came across
this passage underlined in red ink: "No one of sound mind
willingly subjects himself to the emotionally volatile and
often destructive acts of the schizophrenic." Then later, un-

derlined in black, came weak reassurance: "Fortunately for the schizophrenic, many therapists are none too healthy themselves." Very funny. Perhaps a disgruntled therapist underlined the first statement and a disgruntled schizophrenic the second.

My head ached and the room suddenly felt overheated. I checked my watch. After all this random plundering, the only thing I felt fairly certain of was that some charlatan could make a name for himself as a synthesizer, blaming overadequate mom for kicking that nasty old recessive gene into action. I got up, leaving all the schizophrenia books scattered on the table, and took the stairs one flight down to the nearest ladies' room, a small one with only two stalls.

As I splashed my face with cold water, a high thin voice complained over the flush of a toilet. "I'll admit it," the woman sniffed, "I'm intellectual. I'm withdrawn. That's partly why I chose this work."

There quickly followed another flush and sounds of sympathetic agreement from the next stall. I looked below. Sling-backed sandals beside heavy-soled oxfords. Since the two women emerged without purses, umbrellas, or raincoats in tow, they had to be librarians.

"I used to love this job," the sandaled intellectual continued, her pale face pinched and angry. Snatching a handful of her long linen skirt, she held it under the sink faucet and moaned. "I'll never get this out," she said as the water turned pink, the result of running through a dribbly blood stain. It was a funny place for a menstrual stain to develop, right around where her knee would be. "Do I look like Nurse Ratched to you?" she asked the oxfords, her lower lip trembling. "I'm not equipped to handle mentals. And they're driving me out of the only work I can imagine myself doing."

"When you get home," her plump colleague advised, "put some meat tenderizer on that stain."

"Oh, honestly, Elaine—"

"No, I mean it! Mix some water in and let it set for half an hour, and that blood'll pop right out, you'll see."

Makes you wonder what it does to your stomach, I wanted to say. When we were kids, Jody and I used to be afraid that our stomachs wouldn't know when to stop, that they would go on some kind of digestive rampage and start dissolving the rest of us. Everybody said don't worry, it'll never happen. But something a little like that seemed to be happening to me now.

The sandaled intellectual started sobbing, softly at first, then more loudly when Elaine came over to put an arm around her shoulders. "Aw Jane," she said, "why don't you take the rest of the day off? A thing like that would shake anybody up."

Jane blew her nose. "He said his arm itched," she snuffled, "can you believe that? He said it itched deep down inside, in the bone, and this voice told him the itch was poison, and he better use his knife to get it out. I don't think he hit a major artery or anything, and I hope to God he's not diseased, but he definitely ruined the Modigliani book."

I had finished drying my face with a paper towel, but kept dragging it across my forehead anyway.

"Well," Elaine said, "thank God the security budget hasn't been cut yet. It's awful when the police have to come in and take them away."

"At least he went quietly. At least he didn't scream and yell at me like most of them."

When I want something from a stranger, I tend to retrieve the full range of my southern accent, and the graciousness it implies. "Excuse me," I'll say melodiously, "I couldn't *help* but overhear." Sometimes though, urgency pushes my accent into the higher registers of desperation, and I hear myself sounding like Elizabeth Taylor in *Cat on a Hot Tin Roof*. There in the ladies' room, I grabbed Jane's arm, spun her around, and screeched, "Went where quietly?" Jane looked at my hand on her arm and breathed a sigh of resignation; not even the toilet was safe.

"Bayview Hospital. Why?"

I dropped her arm and watched the white print of my fingers fade to pink as she rubbed it. I pictured Jody in medieval-looking restraints, being carried off to some mental unit, calling out my name. I pictured myself staring at a phone that rings incessantly, not wanting to answer because I know Eileen's on the other end.

"Tell me what he looked like," I sighed, still holding a sliver of hope that I might hear about fish lures or imitation leather jackets. Jane's expression softened as her eyes finally connected with mine.

"Much nicer looking than most of them," she began, drying her hands and putting on the glasses that hung from a cord around her neck. She tilted her head quizzically as I came into sharper focus. "As a matter of fact," she said, "he looks kind of like you."

There was a short line of people waiting to use the pay telephones in the lobby. Either I was radiating more distress than I imagined or the man at the head of the line believed in old-fashioned chivalry because he motioned me through and took my place as soon as a phone came free.

I described Jody in detail to three different emergency room nurses at Bayview before I got connected to a CDMHP—a County Designated Mental Health Professional—and learned from her that the individual who had been brought by ambulance from the library was on file

there as "Foxtrot Doe." All the many patients either incapable of or resistant to providing personal information were
given the last name of Doe. Then they were given a first
name in much the same way that meteorologists designate
hurricanes, by going through the alphabet; the mental patient prior to Jody must have been Echo Doe, or maybe
Edsel. "I don't care what you call him," I exploded while
all this was being explained to me, "what's his condition?"

"I'm not authorized to release any further details." Still,
she seemed glad to learn this particular Doe's actual identity and that he had insurance coverage, the details of
which I assured her would soon be forthcoming—from me.
Providing, of course, that *I* received some details from *her*.
And who was I?

I lied. I said I was Jody's sister.

It was not an original lie. The first time Jody was hospitalized he said I was his sister, too, which everyone took
as another proof of his illness, another sign that seeing me
was dangerous for him. But this time the lie unlocked the
only information I cared about, that Jody's injury wasn't a
serious one. Since it was a self-inflicted wound obviously
resulting from a mental disorder, though, he was being
transferred to the psychiatric floor and detained for a
three-day evaluation. As a family member, I was advised
to let him "settle-in" before coming to visit.

I walked back to the pickup wanting the comfort of Paul,
the steadiness with which I knew he would treat the situation, a steadiness that seemed completely beyond me
just then.

As I stepped into the warehouse building where Paul's
studio was located, I could hear the Rolling Stones blasting
upstairs on his stereo, Mick Jagger offering to come to
someone's emotional rescue. I envied Paul because he could

listen to bone-rattling music while he worked and I couldn't, one of the more obvious benefits, as far as I was concerned, of being a visual rather than a verbal.

Because of the volume, Paul didn't notice when I came through the door. He stood across the wide cement floor, barefoot in paint-splattered khaki shorts and a white T-shirt imprinted with a contorted visage, the screaming face from Munch's painting. Three of Paul's large canvases were hung on the wall, and he stood staring at them through a pair of homemade 3-D glasses, one lens red and the other green, which had the effect of making him look extremely demented.

Paul liked the glasses because they created different contrasts, turning the colors of his paintings into three-dimensional assaults on the eye. As I saw them now, though, Paul's paintings weren't so much about color as topography. They reminded me of brain scans, with each hue representing a different neurological function.

I muted the stereo and Paul, finally taking me in, slid the glasses down his nose and compressed his lips into a lizardlike grin. Such behavior didn't exactly mesh with Paul's age, which was thirty-eight, much less than with what the world expects from looks like his. If you trimmed Paul's hair down to where it bends into thick waves and forced him to wear an expensive suit, he would resemble some classically handsome, character-rich man of the world. A single frown furrow solemnized his brow, giving away his tendency to brood, and dark shadows lay beneath his darker eyes. Even so, other lines suggested his smile, an extraordinarily generous one. People seem reassured by this particular facial contradiction, especially when it saves a man from prettiness. Maybe that was why everyone tended to take Paul's honesty for granted, but never his goofiness.

"Buster!" He came over to pick me up, something my size apparently compelled him to do from time to time. "What happened to you?"

"I don't know where to start," I told him, and, since this was true, I began by asking, "Do you think someone can steal your dreams?"

"What?"

"Do you think your brain can be boosted somehow?"

He looked at me with the leer of a nine year old about to inflict torment. "Are you afraid you might be impregnated by an alien being? That you might be forced to suckle a maniac monster? Yes," he nodded grimly, "your fears are justified, for indeed, this is your fate." Then he bit down on my earlobe almost hard enough to draw blood, a dangerous habit of his about which I found it necessary to issue repeated warnings. "It's what you get," he hissed, "for reading scummy newspapers."

He was referring to how I had recently found an abandoned copy of the *National Star* in the park, and read enough of it to later tell him the names of a half-dozen actresses who had ribs removed to accentuate their waistlines. "No," I said, my voice distraught enough that he put me down, "this is from real life."

As I started to cry, Paul looked at me with what I thought of as his man-of-the-family expression. "You're the man of the family now," I could hear all the adults telling a five-year-old Paul after his father died. "You have to take care of everyone." Paul couldn't recall anything like that actually ever happening, but he seemed to like me making up this memory for him, particularly in light of how inadequate he always felt when somebody brought him a problem he couldn't solve.

"It's Jody," I began, "he was like my brother when we were little." Then, while Paul made us some coffee on his hot plate, I told him what had happened in the park and at the library.

"How come you've never talked about him before?" Paul asked.

"You just don't remember, I told you about him."

"I don't think so."

"That's not important now. I better call his sister again."

Nancy's machine answered, and I was in the middle of leaving another message when she picked up the phone. She'd just come home and hadn't received the first message, so she had no idea what I was talking about, except that it had to do with Jody. "Calm down, Marsha, breathe, start over," she said, and soothing as the words were, her voice was rough and raw. Still, it was amazing how easily the habit of following Nancy's instructions returned to me. When I finished giving her the hospital report, she said, "His doctor's name?"

"Right, I'll get it for you." I could hear Nancy's children in the background clamoring for attention.

"There's just too much going on in my life for me to come out there."

"I understand."

"No you don't."

"What?"

"You *don't* understand, Marsha," she said impatiently. "This isn't the first time something like this has happened."

"Did he ever hurt himself before?"

"That's not the point, and anyway, he has now. The point is, we gave Jody a choice, and he couldn't handle it."

"A choice?"

Nancy blew out an exasperated sigh. "Daddy's retiring, he and Mother are moving to Florida year-round. So we told Jody he could get a place in Florida near them, or he could move into the carriage house behind our place. And what happens? Instead of deciding he goes to Seattle, for God's sake, and does something violent."

"He didn't hurt anyone else, and his wound's not serious."

"He's out of control, though. I just don't know if we can handle him anymore."

"I thought he was living alone."

"He was, but maybe he shouldn't. Maybe he needs more supervision. Look, I shouldn't even be discussing this with you. Thanks for trying to help."

"Are you talking about putting him in an institution?"

"This is a family matter, Marsha."

I would have been offended or hurt if I weren't gnawing on something much bigger. "It's not his fault," I told Nancy, "I shouldn't have left him alone." But now Nancy was offended or hurt, probably hearing in my words implied criticism for the way Jody had been left alone in Sparta. The only information we exchanged after that was strictly practical—addresses, insurance policy numbers, the name of Jody's doctor in South Carolina.

When I got off the phone, Paul said, "How responsible do you want to be, Marsha?"

Responsible enough, I decided, to go back to the apartment, change out of my sweatshirt and jeans, and make a trip to Bayview.

Outside, the rain had stopped. It was even cooler than before, maybe that's why I was shivering. I found myself longing to escape into a more familiar kind of summer day, into the steamy southern warmth that could give you a peculiar sense of power if you were a kid, just because it slowed all the older people down and seemed to leave you that much more room to be in the world.

Chapter 4

South Carolina

AFTER FLIP sends plaintive postcards from Camp Maccabee begging to be brought home, my mother decides that it's too big, too organized, too demanding a place. The next summer, Flip and his neighborhood friends attend a basketball camp and I go to one operated by the YWCA, where the big event is Christmas in July. For us, these camps feel more like Sparta, where we've gotten good at pretending to prefer a sense of difference over fitting seamlessly into any group that might define us.

But Jody loves Camp Maccabee, and for the next few summers, he teaches me the Hebrew songs and dances that he learns there. Nancy imitates the accents of campers from the North, which sound just as comical and dumb to me as hers must sound to them.

"They drink brown cows," Nancy tells me on a hot Sunday afternoon while we're playing Spite and Malice by the Lurreys' pool, slapping our cards down on the sunbaked cement. "They have egg creams, too."

I don't know what she's talking about, but I make a face anyway. "Ugh. Egg creams."

"Not *aig* creams, Marsha. You sound like a linthead. What do you call this?" She taps my knee. "Your *laig*?"

"When they start dating," Nancy goes on, "they can only date Jewish boys." Nancy is so anxious to be a teenager that she spends a lot of time contemplating how it will change her life. "I'm sure glad *I* don't have to date Jewish boys till college—I'd *never* go out, I swear."

What she means, of course, is that she can't imagine ever having romantic feelings toward any of the boys now spending the afternoon here swimming with their families, something that's become a Sunday ritual. Not Flip, of course, who's still so juvenile he gets a laugh out of barging in on Nancy when she's taking a pee. Not the rest of the boys her age, whose compelling interests are Ed Big Daddy Roth and customized model cars that they can glue their Ed Big Daddy Roth Rat Fink stickers onto. And not even Stevie Segal, who's older and good-looking enough to be an intriguing candidate, but whose imitations of Bob Newhart and Shelley Berman are a lot more entertaining to adults than they are to any of us. Stevie goes to New York regularly with his parents, Aunt Francine and Uncle Lud, another pair of our parents' friends who aren't related to any of us by blood. Nancy thinks it's irritating, the way Stevie likes describing scenes from all the Broadway shows he's seen (shows the rest of us have to imagine on the basis of the cast albums), throwing his sophistication in our faces.

Today, Uncle Lud brought along samples of the house dresses that his company manufactures. With his Viennese charm in high gear, he bestowed them on the aunts, some of whom are already wearing them as bathing suit cover-ups. Uncle Lud and Aunt Francine both have German accents, and we all know the story of how Uncle Lud came to Sparta from Vienna as a teenaged boy to take a job sweeping floors in a shirt factory. He sent for Aunt Francine before it was too late, but the rest of their families could not be persuaded to leave until it was. Aunt Francine was always very demure until she'd had a drink or two, and then you'd hear her tinkling, melodic laugh. Just now, she's rubbing lotion on Uncle Lud's shoulders, tinkling at a story he's telling.

After Nancy beats me at Spite and Malice, she goes upstairs to wash and set her hair, letting me tag along. Now that I'm older, there are certain things to be learned from Nancy. I've read all her pamphlets about menstruation and some of her books about teenaged girls with names like Toby and Trish, girls who get class rings from their boyfriends, roll their hair on strips of cloth, and never seem to menstruate themselves. They must belong to another era, I decide, but since Nancy only cares that these girls are teenagers with boyfriends, she can forgive a lot.

Still, I'd rather be reading books about horses, and I'd rather be with Jody. I would be, too, if he wasn't with Billy Shane and Eric Brown, chopping and channeling model cars.

Jody and I spend most of our time together now at a barn that's situated on the border of our subdivision in a stretch of undeveloped countryside. We barter for rides with kids who have horses of their own and often end up sharing, my knees locked into Jody's as we jounce off bareback into the woods. Our usual circuit includes visiting Polly, a discovery of Jody's who lives in a blistered farmhouse shielded from the new Winn-Dixie supermarket by a stand of pines beyond her pasture. Old and milky-eyed from cataracts, Polly considers Jody and me Biblically Significant enough to give us each a sterling silver cross on a chain for Christmas. She doesn't expect us to have any problem wearing them. No matter what we say, Polly insists there must be such a thing as Christian Jews, because Dr. Lowe, the urologist her daughter works for, belongs to the country club, and they don't let just plain Jews into the country club—not the one in Sparta, anyway.

The crosses are nice enough that the girl who owns a pony called Jasper accepts them in exchange for an entire afternoon of riding. Although this pleasure is difficult to defer, we decide to wait and take Jasper on the day that the new rabbi moves in next-door to my house. The rabbi has a daughter our age, and we hope that offering her a ride will be a good way of making friends with Rachel Neiderman.

The Temple Brotherhood, of which my father is now president, has hopes of its own. After breaking in a string of rabbis new to the business, they expect that Rabbi Neiderman, with his scholarly gray beard and years of experience, will lend some distinction to the congregation.

When we arrive on Jasper, Marie Gilbert and Wiley Putnam are already there watching as the Neidermans move in. "Is that the rabbit's family, Marsha?" Marie giggles.

"Rabbi," Wiley corrects her. "The rabbi's family, Marie."

Jasper gets things off to a rocky start by taking a dump on the Neidermans' driveway, directly in the path of moving men transporting furniture into the house, and then further distressing Mrs. Neiderman by pawing at her two skittering Chihuahuas. Since nobody cares about befriending Mrs. Neiderman, this isn't nearly so disturbing to us as the sight of her daughter Rachel when she comes running out of the house.

Rachel's face is plain and bony, like her body, and she has a thick wedge of black hair that she wears skinned into barrettes just behind her ears, which stick out too far for this to be a flattering style. When she runs, it's in a way that's prissy and strange, with her chest thrust forward and arms held out straight behind her, as though she learned to run from studying nautical figureheads. Jody and I exchange baleful looks with Wiley and Marie. Clearly, this girl is not going to be any fun at all.

Rachel can't ride Jasper, it turns out, because even if her mother would let her ride a horse, which she won't, not without a saddle or proper supervision, she isn't allowed to leave the house today.

In the weeks that follow, Rachel occasionally crosses the borders separating her yard from those of her closest neighbors, but she's never out of earshot of her house. Once an hour, her mother summons Rachel inside to drink a glass of water. "Rachel," Mrs. Neiderman yells from the kitchen window, "come and get your water!"

Once when it begins to rain, Rachel walks solemnly back to her house while the rest of us go home with Marie, whose mother decides to telephone Mrs. Neiderman and issue a formal invitation. "I don't want to intrude," Mrs. Gilbert says, "but is there a way I can make the water right for Rachel—a special glass or something your people do?" I open my mouth to tell her we're Reform, we don't keep kosher, but Jody shushes me because that would embarrass Mrs. Gilbert even more than she's embarrassing us. "Well, if the child's drinking water for her health, I'd be happy to set the kitchen timer and give it to her here . . . No, they're not watching TV—they're making sugar cookies." Mrs. Gilbert hangs up the phone with a sigh and Rachel, who never goes inside anybody else's house, stays home.

Occasionally, though, Jody and I are allowed inside Rachel's house, which is filled with dark, heavy furniture and lacy antimacassars that only add to the impression of Rachel, like the heroines in Nancy's books, belonging to another time. Rachel never complains or gives any indication that she envies our freedom to roam, but Jody feels sorry enough for her having to drink all that water that he decides to enliven the procedure by dropping a grape-flavored Fizzie tablet into Rachel's glass. Horrified, Mrs. Neiderman grabs the glass from Rachel and pours its still bubbling purple contents down the sink. None of us, not even Rachel, can stop laughing.

"I fail to see the humor," Mrs. Neiderman says. And then, to Jody, "Where did you get this stuff? From your chemistry set?"

"No ma'am," Jody says.

"Don't call me ma'am," Mrs. Neiderman tells him. "It sounds so servile."

"They're just Fizzies," I say. "You're *supposed* to put them in water and drink it."

Jody reaches into his jeans to produce a foil Fizzies packet. "Give that to me," Mrs. Neiderman says, then holds the packet out at arm's length to read it. "Poison, absolute poison. Do your parents know you're spending your allowance on this?"

Jody and I look at each other as she makes a threatening gesture toward the phone. "My mama bought them for me," Jody says.

Mrs. Neiderman's eyes widen. "You see," she tells Rachel. "This is what comes from television. This is what comes from cartoons."

After that, Mrs. Neiderman pays closer attention to everything we do. I get chewed out for loaning Rachel my comic books, for introducing her to Millie the Model and Spiderman. When Mrs. Neiderman raises the issue with my mother one Friday night after services, my mother laughs in a forced way. "Oh," she says, "I'm sure Marsha will give them up before she goes to college."

After Mrs. Neiderman learns from Rachel that Jody has made a chipmunk he found into a pet, she can't decide what is worse, the threat of rabies or the torture of a small animal, so she reports him to both the Public Health Department and the ASPCA. When Wiley makes fun of Mrs.

Neiderman for doing this, Jody turns testy. "She just doesn't like germs," he says, "that's all." But privately, Jody and I agree that the rabbi's wife is a pain.

Queenie and Victor, the Neidermans' two shivering Chihuahuas, come to seem perfect emblems for Mrs. Neiderman. The closest Rachel ever gets to misbehaving is when she turns one of the dogs over on her lap and spreads its legs. She has a term for this procedure—"opening the Torah"—that no one but her finds funny.

For most of the day, Mrs. Neiderman keeps the dogs in a pen behind the house. When they bark, she runs outside and soothes them with dog biscuits, which she calls yummies.

Jody figures out a way for us to rig a rope pulley so that we can tease the Chihuahuas by dangling dog biscuits over their pen. He climbs one of the largest, leafiest trees in my yard to anchor one end of the rope over a branch, then boosts me up into a tree alongside the pen so I can loop the other end. When Jody sends the biscuits sailing out over the pen, the dogs yap madly, and Jody retracts the biscuits just as Mrs. Neiderman comes out to tend to them. Although we do this again and again, we don't get into trouble for the same reason that the game grows boring: Mrs. Neiderman never once looks up.

Rita Ballentine, the girl who owns Jasper, tells me about the summer camp in North Carolina where you get to ride horses every day, which sounds to me like a big improvement over the horseless YWCA camp, so I pester my mother until she finds out how to send me there.

The equestrian camp, located in the Blue Ridge Mountains not far from Camp Maccabee, is small and only for girls, most of whom are destined to someday become debutantes, a word I hear there for the first time. "My sister made her debut this year," my bunkmate Gypsy Claverie, who lives in Atlanta, tells me. "As what?" I ask.

Gypsy thinks I'm joking. "As Princess Peachtree Branch Up Her Butt!" she hoots. When I eventually get all the details, I conclude that cotillions are something like country clubs. And that Gypsy's mother probably wouldn't let her be my friend if I lived in Atlanta.

Our counselor, Kate Brawley from Raleigh, is the only riding instructor who doesn't have broad hips or a mannish walk, which is one reason why Gypsy and I idolize her. Apart from Gypsy and Kate, all that matters to me is the horses, which are so well trained that you have just to call out the gait you want and they start trotting or cantering or slowing to a walk, rarely requiring a kick or much of a pull on the bit. Accustomed to riding bareback and Western, I learn to ride English from Kate and borrow Gypsy's hard hat when I start jumping.

One day, a group of the best riders is rewarded with a trip to Sliding Rock, a gently sloping waterfall in the Pisgah Forest down which it is possible to slide into a basin of icy water. We go there sitting on benches in the covered rear end of a flatbed truck, and the girls who've been to Sliding Rock before warn the rest of us about the perils of slipping off course onto the rough-edged rocks that lead to the Devil's Whirlpool, a churning cauldron impossible to escape without a forest ranger throwing down a rope to pull you out.

At the Sliding Rock parking lot, our truck pulls in next to a blue and white Camp Maccabee bus. I run to the waterfall looking for Jody, but when I don't find him among the Maccabee contingent, I figure he must be back at camp learning horas or Hebrew songs. For a moment, my disappointment brings back the homesickness I haven't felt for weeks. But soon, as my friends and I cling to each other in giddy excitement, wrapping legs around waists to form the chains in which we make our screaming descents into the water, I forget all about Jody.

After a while, the Maccabee group leaves amid a flurry of whistles and instructions about where to change into dry clothes. Between slides, I stop to catch my breath and watch them depart, wishing I were bold enough to send a message back to Jody through one of them. Soon, they're all gone except for one last counselor, a beautiful brunette in a Maccabee sweatshirt who suddenly backtracks in my direction. Grabbing my arm, she practically pulls me off my feet.

"What are you doing out here?" she demands in a grating voice that reminds me of Nancy Lurrey's imitations. "Didn't you hear that we're leaving?"

The Maccabee counselor is holding me by the wrist, ready to haul me off, when Kate Brawley comes to ask what the trouble is. "The trouble," the Maccabee counselor says, "is that we're all ready to go and she's not."

"But she's one of ours," Kate tells her.

As the Maccabee counselor finally loosens her grip, Kate Brawley from Raleigh draws my shivering body into a dry towel. "I'm sorry," comes the apology to Kate, not to me. "She *looks* like one of ours."

Chapter 5

Seattle

BACK AT Paul's apartment, I put on pantyhose and a pair of heels for the first time in ages. For some reason I couldn't have explained—the possibility that I might be required to attend a funeral, maybe—I had brought with me to Seattle one of the silk dresses my mother bestows on me from time to time, always saying that the garment in question no longer suits her, that it's too tight across the bust, or too young, or too short for her but just right for me, or some other polite fib to conceal her worry that I might show up for an interview with someone important in my usual get-up of T-shirt and jeans.

"You have such nice legs," Joyce would say, finally convincing me to accept whatever outfit she was pushing. "Why don't you show them?"

This particular dress was a black-and-gold print with ties at the throat meant to be worn in a bow, but I made a knot and let them droop past my waist. Usually these outfits hung unused in the back of my closet for the requisite two years you were supposed to keep things before donating them to the Goodwill, suitable only for places where I didn't really want to be anyway—a category into which Bayview certainly fit.

On my way to the hospital, I ducked into a drugstore to buy a stenographer's notebook, the kind reporters who don't make up their interviews use. I used to be one of those, when I worked for a D.C. newspaper. I was never much good, though, at hard news, real news. I thought that was because it was so impersonal, so dry. But now here I was, diving into muck but pretending that a notebook and a nice dress might somehow keep me clean.

Mustapha Ghee, the doctor in charge of emergency psychiatric admissions at Bayview that afternoon, stared at my legs as I approached him, then looked a little too directly into my eyes while I explained my connection to Foxtrot Doe, lying again about being his sister. He told me Jody was on the fifth floor, "resting."

We stood in a corridor off the emergency room, quiet as any library even though this was where the egg-stomping ragers and arm-stabbing itchers were brought to be becalmed. I used to know a girl whose little sister was retarded, and whenever we played in her room it seemed we could experience something of her condition merely by breathing the same air as she, a dull hypnotic scent made up of vaporized menthol, mildewed curtains, and the grape juice that stained her mouth. Here, amid an odor of disinfectant and coffee, the doctors and nurses moved slowly past, as though treading their way between crises through air thickened with the residue of malevolent fogs, benign mists, apathetic hazes. For me, it took abnormal energy just to ask Dr. Ghee questions. "Did you give him drugs, is that what you mean by resting?"

"Sorry?"

"Medication?"

"Ah, yes. Medication no problem. Sometimes, yes, but this time, no. The consideration being, as it were, how he caused his body to be injured."

"You mean you could medicate him because he hurt himself?"

"Correct. He did not desire, but this we can do. By law. When mentally disordered individual is danger to self or others, such procedure is legalistically correct."

"What about his medical history? Shouldn't you know that? Who's treating him now? Can I talk to his doctor?"

Dr. Ghee began to look as if I were pelting him with pebbles. He motioned for me to follow him over to the nurse's station, where I was given a visitor's pass. I clipped it onto one of my dangling tie tips and followed Dr. Ghee to a staff elevator that took us up to the locked psychiatric floor.

Dr. Ghee left me waiting in a small common room with several rows of metal folding chairs and a TV hung from the ceiling. I took a chair in the last row, behind a woman who wore an aging pink Chanel-style suit and had her thick gray hair done up in an impeccably neat bun. She attempted to communicate with the man beside her, who sat slumped in bathrobe and pajamas. "I know someone who has emphysema," she told him, "but he smokes two packs of cigarettes a day."

The man beside her flinched and grimaced and lit a cigarette of his own, inhaling ferociously.

The woman leaned in closer. "Does that make sense to you, smoking two packs a day when you have emphysema? Do you think that sounds like a man who's in touch with reality? Do you think that sounds like a man who's committed to *life*?"

"Leave me alone," the man told her. "I want to enjoy my show."

He was looking straight ahead at the wall, not at the TV, which was tuned to a low-rent local station that specialized in programs from the fifties and sixties. "Dobie Gillis" was just beginning. I could have sung along with the theme. *Dobie, wants a girl who's dreamy, Dobie, wants a girl who's creamy, Dobie, wants a girl to call his own.* I once owned a pair of Dobie Gillis sneakers that were purchased one afternoon when Eileen took Jody and me shopping downtown. Jody got a pair of white bucks, the kind Pat Boone wore. Like the man in front of me, I was watching a show of my own, one in which Jody sat in the Carolina Theater, crossing his legs ankle to thigh so that he could feel the velvet of his new shoes. The movie we were watching was *Old Yeller*, the story of a dog that got rabies, which meant he had to drool dementedly and still look lovable enough so that it was really hard for Travis, the boy he belonged to, to shoot him. But it was all okay because pretty soon there was a puppy who looked just like Old Yeller. Young Yeller, presumably. A genuine Disney experience, giving even as it taketh.

Exasperated with her silent companion, the Chanel lady got up and sat down next to me. "Do you enjoy feeling hopeless?" she demanded. Then she was on her feet again, repeatedly clicking a blue disposable lighter that wouldn't light, pacing in a tight little circle while she squinted upward to address the acoustic tiles. "Dr. Thrill Kill wants to keep me for evaluation," she said, "but what does *he* know? Finer minds than his have been baffled by my brilliance."

Dr. Ghee reappeared and motioned for me to join him. "Be careful," the woman told me. "You've no idea what you're in for."

Dr. Ghee led me down the hall, through a locked metal door, and dropped me off at the office of another doctor, identified by the plaque on his desk as Richard Thrailkill. He wore wire-rimmed eyeglasses, a salt-and-pepper woodsman's beard, and was talking now in tones of easy reasonability to an elderly woman in a house dress and athletic shoes who stood smoking in front of his desk.

"Your sister will take you home with her for the weekend, Ivy," Dr. Thrailkill was saying, "but you have to promise not to smoke in her house. The deal is you go outside when you want to smoke. Okay?"

After agreeing to abide by this rule, the woman leaned over Dr. Thrailkill's desk as though to confide in him. "I've got me a nigger baby," she said.

"Come on now, Ivy. You're teasing me again."

Ivy gave him a gap-toothed grin. "Uh-huh, I got a nigger baby, all right. My sister got me one at Nordstrom, that makes sixteen babies now."

"You mean dolls, Ivy." His smile looked relieved, but his tone didn't change. "Sixteen dolls, one of them black."

When Ivy left and I was alone with Dr. Thrailkill, I told him everything I knew about Jody's condition and the transitional nature of his circumstances back home. I also explained who I *really* was, the shorthand version, anyway—an old family friend, the Lurreys' contact person out here in Seattle, not Jody's sister at all. Thrailkill surprised me by shrugging, as if rules didn't matter so much to him under circumstances where he might have told the same lie himself. He motioned me into a chair, picked up a folder on his desk, took out a form, and filled in all the pertinent information I'd brought with me. I noticed that affixed to the form was a mug-shot style photograph of Jody, staring at the camera with a dazed, half-lidded expression, looking like a prime candidate for living in an institution full-time.

"What's Ivy's problem?" I asked while Dr. Thrailkill finished with the form.

"Well, the court said it was 'insufficient personality,' but that was years ago, when she was first institutionalized. Would you like some tea?"

Richard Thrailkill's office smelled a lot like fruit although none was in sight. When I remarked on this, he brightened a little, seemingly cheered by the mere fact of my observation. "People with schizophrenia," he said, "sometimes have a body odor similar to that of fruit."

"That's strange." I was thinking of Jody's pineapples and cherries.

Dr. Thrailkill nodded as he went about his tea-making business, nuking mugs of water in a miniature microwave oven. "I noticed this odor for years myself before I read about it in a book of little-known scientific facts. It must have been under 'f' because the only other fact I remember is about fruit flies. Did you know there are two closely re-lated species which have a mating song that, when ampli-fied, bears a striking resemblance to the tune of 'Yes Sir, That's My Baby'?"

I shook my head mutely.

"So," he said, "what else can you tell me about Jody that might help?"

I told Dr. Thrailkill that I had read up a little on this disease, was familiar with the issues, and was hoping I could learn some things from him. Then I pulled out my notebook. "I'm a journalist, and I remember everything bet-ter if I write it down."

"You're not going to write about this," he said, "are you? For publication, I mean. Because if you are, you'll have to be cleared through public relations." The oven timer beeped and he removed the mugs. "Of course, since there's nothing to prevent you from answering no and writing something anyway, why bother?"

Although he must have had other things to do, Dr. Thrailkill didn't once check his watch as we talked. I found myself struck as though for the first time by the transfor-mative powers of a simple notebook, how it can alter what would otherwise be a painful or intrusive situation by giv-ing one party a shield of questions and the other a flatter-ing sense of authority.

If you asked Dr. Thrailkill—and I didn't—it was a waste of a psychiatrist's medical training to interpret dreams or treat pedestrian psychological problems. Psychiatrists were for people with diseased brains; a sophisticated computer could effectively counsel the troubled well. That was what he called them, the Troubled Well, which sounded to me like a hexagram from the I Ching.

I sat back and sipped my tea, brewed from a Lipton's bag and lightened with the sticky sweetness of condensed milk, a drink you might give to a child. "What about Dr. Ghee?" I asked. "If I told him I had a frog in my throat, he might think *my* brain was diseased."

Dr. Thrailkill sighed wearily. "Dr. Ghee works with us because most psychiatrists in this country would rather treat the troubled well. And why not? It pays better. We have a shortage in the medical pool, and certain problems in communication are inevitable. But I don't believe an imperfect command of English would prevent Dr. Ghee from recognizing a floridly psychotic episode when he saw one."

I wrote "floridly psychotic" slowly, in large block letters that filled half a page. So that was what Jody had been— floridly psychotic. I took a kind of comfort from how inevitable this description made everything seem, as though there was nothing I could have done to prevent what happened.

"Someday," Dr. Thrailkill went on, "we might need a court order to medicate people who come in here like Jody, bleeding and hallucinating and refusing treatment. The problem is, a person with a chemically imbalanced, malfunctioning brain can not reasonably be expected to use that brain for the purpose of determining the need for treatment. That's it, I'm sorry, what else can we do? I'd like to be able to chart his condition for you, but there *is* no objective measurement for schizophrenia."

"You mean there's no way to prove somebody has it?"

"That's right."

"Or why?"

"Or why. But I feel I should tell you, what Jody did isn't so unusual. In the big picture, it's not even so bad."

Dr. Thrailkill told me about a patient of his who, while she was wasn't taking her medication, had tried to slice off her nipples with a piece of glass because voices told her this act would qualify her for sainthood. Another had walked into a Montgomery Ward store, purchased a chain saw, then went into the men's room, where he cut off his leg.

"But Jody said he felt an itch down deep," I said, "in the bone. Isn't it possible he could have been talking about some other kind of urge?"

"What other kind of urge?"

"I don't know, maybe he was speaking metaphorically."

"I doubt it. Schizophrenics might unconsciously *use* metaphors on occasion, but most have a marked inability to actually think in terms of symbols. That's why traditional therapy doesn't work—it can't alter the course of the disease. From what you tell me, Jody's condition is responsive to drugs. You ought to know that if he doesn't take them, the prognosis is not a happy one.'"

Dr. Thrailkill reminded me of an editor I once had who would urge the employment of certain words or phrases of his suggestion because they were "happier." What makes a prognosis happy? Tidiness, maybe, like the stuff of happy endings, the kind that almost always appear happier than the evidence warrants.

"I see patients we've had to release from this hospital out on the streets all the time," Dr. Thrailkill said as he jerked his thumb over his shoulder, indicating his barred office window and the world beyond it. "The assumption was that there would be community mental health centers, and if they took their medication they could get along okay. But the centers basically failed, and a lot of these people are in terrible shape. You don't have to hear the voices, I tell them—get over to the clinic. Usually, they don't. They can't. Too many end up dying out there." He looked at me for a long moment. "Forgive me for being pedantic. You did say you're familiar with the issues, didn't you?"

"No one of sound mind," I said, "willingly subjects himself to the emotionally volatile and often destructive acts of the schizophrenic."

"Pardon me?"

"Fortunately for the schizophrenic," I continued, "many therapists are none too healthy themselves." I made quotation marks with my fingers. "One of the public library's books on the subject."

Dr. Thrailkill laughed out of his nose in staccato snorts and shrugged helplessly, as though apologizing for the library. "Look," he said, "you may have doubts about the circumstances under which Jody was living. There may be room for improvement in all areas, including the kind of drug he should take. For instance, if we find that Jody was on daily doses of haloperidol, as I suspect he was, I'd like to try putting him instead on biweekly injections of a new drug we're trying here. It's easier to control the medication that way, and there might possibly be fewer disagreeable side effects. I'm not saying Jody should be excluded from these matters, but leaving it all up to him is not the answer, either. If he died while he was on his own, would it make you feel any better to know he died exercising his rights?"

Nobody said anything about anybody dying, I wanted to say—nobody *ever* said anything about anybody dying. Nobody, to be specific, had ever said anything much about

Stevie Segal dying. But if I mentioned Stevie, it wouldn't be long before I asked Dr. Thrailkill about the odds of four diagnosed cases coming out of a small temple congregation in South Carolina, or even whether onset in females was typically ten years later than in males, questions I didn't really want to investigate.

"So," I said slowly, "you don't think there's any question Jody is schizophrenic?"

"Not much. His kind of voices and history are usually pretty clear signs."

"*Paranoid* schizophrenic?"

"That's harder to say, especially at this point."

"Wouldn't it help for you to know more about how it was for him before—before he got this way?"

"I don't really need to hear the entire story of his life, if that's what you mean."

"Well, that's good," I snapped, "because I don't think he could tell you the entire story of his life."

"You're right." He nodded sort of sadly. "I suppose one measure of sanity is what you're doing now."

"What? Taking notes?"

"More what you'll do with them later. Making connections between one thing and another—with some measure of control, without repeated errors. If you think about it, the inability to tell stories represents a radical human incompetence." He pushed his glasses up onto his forehead and rubbed his eyes. "I'm wandering. Effective treatment is the point here."

"Well," I ventured, "some people seem to think vitamin therapy is effective treatment. Some people think it's significant that people like Jody hate their medications. Some people think drugs are inhumane, that they prevent an authentic recovery."

Dr. Thrailkill rocked back in his chair, clasping thick

fingers across the gentle bulge of his stomach. "Those people," he said, "are not my problem."

Just now, I longed to live on the Disney Channel, where meaning bobbed cheerfully on the surface. Here Yeller, come back Yeller. Instead, I asked another question. "What would you do if you were in my place?"

"Well, my sister is schizophrenic—"

"Your sister?"

"Yes, my sister. And if she ran off somewhere to find an old friend—"

"Wait a minute. He didn't come here to find me."

I hadn't taken handwritten notes for a long time, and when I looked down, I noticed my cheap ballpoint pen was leaking, smearing gobs of ink all over my right middle finger. I reached for some tissue from the box on Dr. Thrailkill's desk and began blotting up the ink.

"Are you sure of that?" he said.

"He didn't even know I was here, I haven't seen him in ten years!"

"Nevertheless, if my sister did something like that, I would want her friend to get medical help for my sister and notify her primary caretakers so that they could be involved in all the necessary decisions."

The ink on my finger was already dry, but I kept pointlessly blotting the callus on the top joint, my writer's bump. I used to think this callus was a sign that I was supposed to write for a living, when probably it just meant I'd never learned to hold a pencil properly. As it occurred to me that Dr. Thrailkill's vocation might also be a defect in disguise, words came pouring out of my mouth.

"I'm sorry about your sister, but maybe you have a vested interest in thinking the past doesn't matter." He frowned so thoughtfully that I felt instant regret, but I couldn't stop myself from adding, "Maybe you just want the easy way out, fix up a shot, drug what you can't deal with. Maybe you need to believe in your own innocence."

"Maybe," Dr. Thrailkill said. "But maybe I believe in kindness, and maybe I have to extend it even to myself."

I stopped blotting and balled my ink-stained tissue up into a tight little wad. Dr. Thrailkill offered a wastebasket and said, "You seem like a kind person to me. Why don't you go through Jody's stuff and come back with a change of clothes. The ones he had on got pretty bloody, and I don't want to keep him in a hospital gown any longer than we have to. Bring anything else you think he might want for the next few days—pajamas, extra underwear, cigarettes. Then we'll see what we'll see."

Aside from his clothes, here is what I found in Jody's bag:

- A fashion magazine story describing the stages of heartbreak at the end of a love affair (based chiefly on my own experiences but attributed to those of many made-up others).
- A story about a famous singer-songwriter, published in a men's magazine.
- A story about how to avoid fighting with your husband in public places, which appeared in the same women's magazine that assigned me the story about how family reunions strengthen marriage.
- A nature magazine story about the life cycle of lampreys.
- A travel magazine essay about Seattle, hinged on the fact that I would be spending the summer there.

Rummaging through Jody's articles, I found my own.

Once when my phone went dead back in the other Washington and I desperately needed to use it for some reason, I went frantically knocking on all my neighbors' doors. The only other person at home that morning was Ambero, a beautiful Somalian woman who lived with her husband in a basement studio apartment. Ambero didn't speak much English, but I made myself understood and she asked me inside, where I looked around for an endless moment. There on the wall was a framed charcoal portrait of Jimbo, my first serious boyfriend, staring in my direction as if to remind me how the past always comes back at you, even when you trash it. My old print shower curtain hung on a rod from the ceiling, dividing the space between bed and dining table. Ambero's telephone rested on the typing table my computer had made useless, and my Metropolitan Museum of Art date book from the previous year was beside the telephone directory on the rickety bookcase I bought when I was in college. I had thrown all these things away in a recent fit of spring cleaning and now they were here, completely severed from any meaning they might have held for me. Asking Ambero why she'd been moved to appropriate all this from the trash room seemed not only rude but pointless.

Opening Jody's bag was sort of like that. It was sort of like that, only worse.

Chapter 6

South Carolina

I'M SWIMMING at Saluda Lake with Jody on a warm Saturday afternoon in May when I get sick and vomit to the point of dry heaves. My mother comes to pick me up and after we get home she calls the pediatrician, who says it sounds as though I have gas. That night I dream that the Communists have invaded. Jody and I run through the streets of Sparta searching for our parents. Unable to find them, we hide in the Lurreys' rec room, barricading the door with Uncle Sol's piano and every piece of available furniture. I awaken soaked with sweat, with my sheets, pillows, blankets, stuffed animals, and books all in a pile at the foot of my bed.

Two weeks later, Aunt Eileen brings Jody to see me in the hospital, where I'm still being treated for the peritonitis that developed after my appendix, which is no longer inside me, leaked poison into my body. I'm on the pediatrics floor and not supposed to receive any visitors who aren't adults, but I've been here long enough to become an exception to the rules. "See?" Aunt Eileen says to Jody. "She's here, just like I promised."

What I can see is that Jody thought maybe I had died, and that his mother didn't want to tell him so. I can also see by the way he licks his lips and jiggles his foot that while being here in the hospital frightens Jody, not being able to see me frightened him more.

"This is from our class," he says, giving me one of the two packages that he's holding. Inside is a Villager blouse with a circle pin affixed to its Peter Pan collar, part of the unofficial uniform worn by all the popular fifth grade girls at Christ Church Episcopal School.

Jody and I are still going to public school on the day last spring when my mother shows up in a capelike khaki coat, her hair cut short and dramatic, high heels clicking impatiently down the cement walkway outside our classroom. Since she's nothing like the other mothers in their penny loafers and shirtwaist dresses, she effortlessly snares everyone's attention. After our teacher gives Jody and me permission to leave with her, we join Nancy and Flip in the Thunderbird and head off to take our admission test for what my mother assures us is the best school in town.

It's a warm day, and Nancy, who doesn't dread the test as much as the rest of us, talks my mother into putting the top down. Jody bites his nails and babbles, worrying about the kinds of questions we might be asked. Nancy snorts disgustedly. "What do you think, that they're going ask us stuff from the New Testament? Quick, Jody, why did Paul cross the road to Damascus? Bzzzzz, time's up. Boy, are you stupid."

"*We're* not the stupid ones," Jody growls.

My mother holds up a warning hand. "No one here is stupid, and the next person to use that word will be fined." She charges nickels, dimes, and quarters for offensive language, and threatens to have allowance withheld if one of us ever says nigger.

Jody blames Nancy and Flip for the fact that we're being tested at Christ Church School today. Neither one of them has been recommended by their principal for accelerated classes next year. This means they won't be taking algebra and will have to study South Carolina history instead of American. Worst of all, according to my mother, who now makes the only junior high within city limits sound more like a holding pen for juvenile delinquents than a school, this means they'll have to endure another year of over-crowded classes with knife-wielding mill family boys who have flunked so many grades they're old enough to shave. At Christ Church School, everyone takes algebra, everyone takes American history, and if anyone's parents work at a mill, they run it. My mother and father discussed it all endlessly when we weren't supposed to be listening.

"But Daniel," my mother told my father, "Nancy's grades are even better than Flip's, and both of them do as well as most of the kids who made it."

"What about tests, the standardized ones? How'd they do on those?"

"I don't know and I don't care."

"If you're not going to be logical, what's the use in talk-ing?"

Since logic was always the trump card my father played, she had to ambush and divert with drama in order to pre-vail. "Did you know that this principal *preaches* to them?"

"Well, that's against the law—separation of church and state. Something *can* be done about that."

"What's the point in complaining about her *now*? Any-way, I didn't tell you the worst thing. The worst thing is that when I went to see her, she made a nasty remark, something to the effect that she knew Jews were *supposed* to be smart—"

"You're kidding."

"I wish I were."

"Okay, so they're stigmatized by a Baptist. Is that a good reason for handing them over to a bunch of Episcopalians?"

"There's a big difference between Baptists and Episcopalians, Daniel. You're so off-the-boat about these things. It's because your parents weren't born in this country. I went to an Episcopalian school, a *high* Episcopalian school—"

"And look at the snob it made of you."

"I am not a snob. A snob is someone who has different sets of manners for different people. *My* manners are always the same."

After several weeks of this, I hear my father on the phone assuring his brother, a doctor in Chicago, that his children will not be required to partake of the body and the blood, quoting my mother without attribution: "Our public schools are at the bottom of the ladder, Nathan, just above Mississippi's."

I can't imagine this kind of debate going on in the Lurreys' house. Once Aunt Eileen decided my mother was right about what had to be done, something she did without much hesitation, that was pretty much that.

After we take the admission test, Aunt Eileen arrives in her station wagon to pick us up, Juanita sitting in the front seat beside her. On the way to Juanita's wood frame house on the outskirts of town, Aunt Eileen's scent drifts back to us, a mixture of wisteria and cigarette smoke. Jody starts to wheeze, something that only seems to happen when he's upset, although Aunt Eileen thinks it's tree pollen that does it. When we get to her house, Juanita goes inside to fetch a hankie soaked in eucalyptus oil for Jody to stick his nose into. Juanita's son Calvin sits on the edge of the porch, but when Jody waves at him, Calvin follows Juanita wordlessly inside without waving back. Calvin wants his mother all to himself, and Juanita's so wonderful that Jody doesn't blame him.

By the time we get to Bybee's, the drive-in where Aunt Eileen takes us for iced teas and onion rings, Jody's feeling better. Bybee's is jammed with teenagers. The boys are crammed into the tiny indoor restaurant area and the girls, some of whom Nancy and I recognize as fellow students of tap and modern jazz at the Patsy Chalmers School of the Dance, are all packed into cars, shoving over to make room whenever a boy comes to sit with them and visit. When the girls visit each other, they run so fast between cars it seems they're afraid someone might shoot them. Flip thinks they run this way because they've drunk so much iced tea and need to pee, which they can't do at Bybee's because the bathroom is inside, on male territory.

A black car hop attaches a tray to Aunt Eileen's window and she pays him before distributing our food.

While Jody picks the crust off an onion ring—he likes the crust, not the onion—he complains about Christ Church. "They don't even have a cafeteria, and the playground sucks."

"You can just watch your mouth, son," Aunt Eileen warns, "do you hear?"

"Yes," Jody says sullenly.

"Yes what?"

"Yes ma'am."

"Thank you. And just for the record, they have a *gymnasium* at Christ Church and you get to bring your own lunch. If you did well enough on that test to get in, you can have peanut butter sandwiches every day if you want."

Jody stares out the window, watching a group of car hops who are having a contest to see which one can spin a tray on his fingertips for the longest amount of time. "I don't understand why we can't just go to regular school," Jody says, still staring. "You and Daddy did."

"When we were growing up," Aunt Eileen says with an air of explaining the matter once and for all, "the only private school was *Catholic*."

"What about high school?" Nancy asks. Christ Church only goes through the ninth grade, and Nancy has been ready for high school ever since she cracked open the purple box of Kotex that had been sitting for years in the back of her closet. She already sets and teases her hair into the same bubble flip all the girls here at Bybee's wear, anxious enough to be mistaken for one of them that she's slightly embarrassed to be seen here with us. "You're not going to send us away to high school, are you?"

"Who's sending anybody away?"

"Uncle Lud and Aunt Francine," Nancy reminds her mother. Mark Segal went off to prep school in New England this year, which means his brother Stevie will surely follow.

When Nancy tries to dip an onion ring into Jody's ketchup, having used up all her own, he slaps her hand away loudly enough to attract Aunt Eileen's attention. "*I* have no intention of sending anybody away," she says, "unless their behavior in this car continues to deteriorate." Nancy grins at her, reassured.

Without ever really saying so, Aunt Eileen has made it clear that we're expected to be on friendly terms with the children of her former classmates, all the while remembering that in the future we will be moving into another world, a world that has little to do with the one swirling all around us here at Bybee's. She seems to think Christ Church might serve that end, maybe even elevate it somehow.

To cheer Jody up, Aunt Eileen asks how he wants to celebrate his birthday next month. "I don't know," he says. "A swimming party, I guess." He drains his iced tea, picks the lemon wedge out of his cup, and bites into it. "What would it be like, I wonder, if I was the kid next door?"

Aunt Eileen frowns at him. "What do you mean, Jody?"

"What if I was just some kid you knew?"

"Okay, you're just some kid I know—God forbid. What's your question?"

"Would you like me?"

"Like you? I love you, you know that."

"Yeah, but that's because I'm your kid."

Aunt Eileen honks to have her tray taken away and starts the car, talking to herself so we'll all be sure to hear. "Our vines," she says with a shake of her head, "have tender grapes."

Most of our Christ Church classmates live near the country club or in stately old neighborhoods far from ours, one reason why we make so few new friends that first year. And now that we're going to private school, our old friends seem to think we've gone snooty and aren't so friendly anymore. I give up tap dancing and start taking ballet, like the other girls at Christ Church, but when the teacher tells me I'm not suited for ballet, that my toes are much too long for me to ever go up on point without breaking them, my mother lets me quit.

At a loss for diversion, Jody and I take up being morbid. Maybe it's the last presidential campaign, with all those ads suggesting that the candidate who swept our state would drop the atomic bomb. Maybe it's the scholastic journals we read in school, with stories written by Vietnamese children forced by the Communists to flee their homes. Maybe it's the Civil Defense program we inadvertently watch one Saturday morning with its cartoon family holed up in their basement bomb shelter, not emerging until the black plate they slip outside each night is bereft of white dots in the morning, the white dots being traces of the radioactive fallout that will cause them to vomit and die. Now that we're too big to fit into the cabinet underneath the bathroom sink and tell each other stories, happy endings aren't so convincing anymore.

But mainly it's that we're too much alone, and torturing each other with doom draws us closer to something bigger than we are.

Jody finds a book in the public library filled with pictures of Hiroshima survivors, which we examine repeatedly. I sneak *In Cold Blood* off my parents' bookshelf and pass it along to Jody when I'm done with it. The murdered Clutter children are teenagers, but still, they fit into the fearful fabric we're weaving. They fit because they have not been allowed to grow up.

By the time I get sick on Saturday afternoon, we've been doing this for months.

On Monday morning, my mother rules out gas as the thing that's wrong with me, wraps me in a blanket, and drives me to Sparta General Hospital, where Aunt Eileen is waiting for us in the emergency room. After my blood is tested and it's clear what trouble I'm in, Aunt Eileen telephones the surgeon who will take my appendix out. I know my mother and Aunt Eileen aren't actually wheeling me into surgery, but they are the only ones I can see, standing on either side of me, holding my hands.

Later, lying in bed on the pediatrics floor, I hear my mother worriedly discussing with a nurse how distended my belly is. After it's determined I have peritonitis, she sleeps on a cot in my room. When the surgeon comes by, my father argues with him out in the hall.

"There's a dramatic difference of opinion between you and my brother Nathan as to whether Marsha should be treated according to her temperature, as you seem to believe, or according to her pulse, which my brother insists is the correct course of action."

"I don't give a good goddamn what your brother insists! He's not a surgeon, and he's not treating her."

"My brother is an eminent internist, and if he has reason to doubt the wisdom of your treatment, I think it behooves you to speak to him, one professional to another. I give you the choice of doing that, or of bringing on another surgeon who will."

"You think you're some son of a bitch, don't you, Mr. Rose?"

"No, but I think you'll find I can be as big a bastard as you, Dr. Armitage."

Their arguing is just another part of what I long to escape, what I do escape with the shots that let my body melt away. I don't notice when the arguments stop, when the shots taper off, when I begin to improve. But I know the reason why without being told; it is because I am not from here.

After it's decided I would benefit from receiving plasma transfusions, people from the temple and people who work at my father's and Uncle Sol's factories donate blood. I don't realize that this is just to replace what I will be using of the hospital's stock; I think it's actually their blood dripping down into my veins. Soon I'm so much better that my mother stops sleeping at the hospital. During the days, she hires a nurse to be with me, Mrs. Phillips, and when I actually do develop a gas problem, Mrs. Phillips comforts me by saying she thinks her own farts smell good. Sometimes on the way back from getting a milkshake in the cafeteria, she wheels me into the hospital chapel, where she encourages me to join her as she prays to Jesus for my continued recovery.

"Do you do this for all your patients?" I ask her.

"Only the special ones."

"But I don't believe in Jesus."

"That doesn't matter, honey," she says. "He believes in you."

Since only adult visitors are allowed on the pediatrics floor, at my mother's suggestion, I make friends with Ethan, the boy in the room next to mine who has something wrong with his bone marrow. Ethan can't get out of bed so I wheel into his room and we visit there, playing with our Etch-a-Sketch sets. I make pictures of people and Ethan, his wan, sallow face a mask of concentration, makes geometrical designs—ever smaller squares within circles that look as though they're being sucked into a vacuum.

After Ethan dies, the floor restrictions no longer seem to apply to me. One night my mother manages to bring in Flip as well as a pizza. Flip pushes me down the corridor in my wheelchair as though we are in a race, providing action commentary and sound effects as we smash into and past the field of imaginary wheelchairs all around us. "Don't make her laugh so hard," my mother cautions Flip. "She'll burst her incision."

It's the next day when Aunt Eileen brings Jody. As soon as we're alone, I tell him about Ethan. I start to tell him my dream, too, the one about the Communists invading, but he won't let me finish.

"Let's not do that anymore," he says. "Okay?"

Then he gives me the other present, the one that's from him. It's a book called *The Secret Garden*. "Did you pick it out?" I ask, and when he nods, "Have you read it?"

"It's a girl's book," Jody says.

"But have you read it?"

"A little, so I could tell if you might like it." He plops down at the foot of my bed and I wince from the pain of being jostled. "Want me to read it to you?" he asks.

"There's nothing wrong with my eyes."

"You almost died, Marsha. I tried to give blood, but they said I wasn't old enough."

I fall back against my pillows Sarah Heartburn–style, trying to look even weaker than I am. "Jody? Read to me."

And he begins, self-consciously and with not a little embarrassment. It's hard to forget we've already read Truman Capote and give ourselves up to a story about another child, even one who's roughly our age.

But this orphaned Mary is so sour, so bad-tempered and lonely, that she captures our attention. In the next day's reading, we meet her invalid cousin Colin, spoiled and imperious, a match for her in every way. It's all I can do not to finish the book on my own and wait for Jody to get to the hospital after school so we can find out together how Mary will gain entry into the locked, abandoned garden on her uncle's estate, how she'll lure Colin outside to enlist him in her campaign of bringing the garden back to life, how she will end up helping herself by helping him.

It takes another week to finish the book and the day after we do, Jody talks a nurse into letting him wheel me down to where my mother's car is waiting to take me home. It's the first time I've been out in the fresh air for almost a month, and as the mechanical hospital doors open for us, I imagine that the picture of Mary wheeling Colin out into the garden must be as prominent in Jody's mind as it is in mine.

Chapter 7

Seattle

I DECIDED on my way back to the hospital not to tell Dr. Thrailkill about the magazine articles I found in Jody's bag. If I did, I might once again be seen as having too much content in Jody's delusionary life and therefore unfit company for him. Still, I waited nervously in Thrailkill's office while he went to make sure Jody wanted to see me. I was less worried about whether Jody was lucid enough to receive a visitor than I was about how upset he might be at feeling abandoned. Again. By me.

After what seemed a long time, Thrailkill returned to lead me down the hall to a room with a male nurse stationed outside the open door, reading a magazine. Thrailkill gave the supplies I brought for Jody, including a carton of Vantages, to the nurse. "Five minutes," the nurse said as I went in alone.

The room smelled of sweat, but didn't remind me of fruit so much as fear. Bars were on the window, but if you craned your neck you could see through them to a slice of the Cascade Mountains in the east. There was no light other than natural, and no furniture that wasn't bolted to the floor.

Jody sat on the edge of the bed, wearing a hospital gown, shoes, and socks, which somehow made him seem more naked than if he had been wearing nothing at all. His left arm was bandaged from elbow to wrist, so securely that I wondered if that was to prevent him from ripping it off and reopening his wound. He kept his back to the wall, rocking against it while he smoked, eyes nearly shut. It was hard for me to tell if he knew I was there.

"What are you looking at?" Jody asked, his speech slow and slurred.

"You. You look tired, how do you feel?"

"Quit looking at me." He flicked his ash, missing a plastic tray.

"Okay." I walked over to the window and stared out for a while. "I'm sorry about what happened. I'm sorry you have to go through this. I brought some clothes and things for you."

After a long moment: "Does anyone know where I am?"

His voice sounded so flat I couldn't really tell if he *wanted* anyone to know. What was the best thing in his medicated mind? "Nancy knows," I finally said.

Jody stubbed out his cigarette and took another one from the pack on the bed. "Light," he said, and I gave him one. Then, after several deep inhalations, he surprised me by asking, "How long can I stay here?"

Our five minutes were evidently up already. Dr. Thrailkill stuck his head in and said, "Let's get you out of that gown, Jody."

Jody began mechanically undressing, as if he didn't care that I was in the room. I went to get his bag from the nurse and started to open it, but Dr. Thrailkill made it clear that he wanted Jody to dress by himself and at his own speed. While he did, I pulled Thrailkill out into the hall.

"Did you hear? He wants to know how long he can stay here. I didn't know what to tell him."

"Well, the standard evaluation period is three days, but since this is Thursday and we don't evaluate over the weekends, we'll have to stretch it out to Monday. Then the

CDMHP will assess Jody's case and decide whether or not to file with the court for an additional two-week period."

"That's not what I meant. Wouldn't you have expected him to ask when can I get out, not how long can I stay? He doesn't want to go back to South Carolina. He doesn't," I looked pointedly at Dr. Thrailkill, "want to be returned to his primary caretakers. You know, the people I'm supposed to be deferring to."

"Ms. Rose, a person with a malfunctioning brain—"

"I know—'can't be expected to use that brain to determine what's best for himself.'" I sighed. "I'm supposed to go away for the weekend, but I don't want to leave him alone."

"It might be better for both of you if you did. Give him some time to even out, give yourself some time to absorb what's happened. He knows you care about him."

I wanted to believe him, but I couldn't be at all sure about that. Watching how long it took Jody to realize that he had better take off his shoes if he expected to be able to step into his jeans, I doubted he would remember that I had been here at all.

Paul had planned for us to spend this weekend at the cabin that had once belonged to his paternal grandparents. It was our first weekend together since my arrival, and Paul wanted it to be special. He seemed to be operating on the entirely reasonable theory that if we behaved as though Jody were not disrupting our lives, maybe he wouldn't. After all, Jody was not what our summer together was supposed to be about. Our summer together was supposed to be about deciding the twin issues of Commitment and Consolidation in a state free of longing and outrageous cross-country telephone bills. Our summer together was supposed to further dazzle me with the beauty of the Pacific Northwest so that all my reservations about moving to Seattle, a continent away from all the magazine editors I wrote for, might be overcome.

On Friday morning I trailed morosely after Paul while he hurriedly shopped for our trip in the Public Market. "Are you sure we ought to leave Jody?" I asked repeatedly. Paul ignored me, darting from stall to stall buying bread, steaks, vegetables, fruit, and Spanish olives for his martinis. Then he rushed us to the ferry dock, where we were the last car to make it on board. The departure horn tooted and we got out of the pickup to watch the city slipping out of sight from the rear deck, where the boat engine's clackety, calypsolike vibrations seemed to juggle my thoughts of Jody into a more manageable sequence.

After docking in Bremerton, we headed west for the wide, riverlike finger of Puget Sound called Hood Canal. "How's the story going?" Paul asked. He was referring to my family reunions piece.

"I've got a start," I said, then dug in my bag for the first and only page. "Want to hear it?"

At his nod I began to read.

Once a year, Karen and Mark Simpson got together with Mark's family in rural Oregon. Karen always felt awkward around the Simpson women. The first time Karen came to visit, Mark's mother and sisters laughed because she wore snakeskin cowgirl boots with two-inch heels for a rainy-day walk on the beach. When at home, Karen's in-laws seemed forever occupied with cultivating organic gardens or knitting sweaters made from wool they had shorn and spun themselves.

"It's the *sheep* they shear," Paul corrected. "Then they spin the wool."

"Right," I said, marking the page, "kill the sheep."

But one day, Mrs. Simpson gave Karen a sheaf of letters written by Mark's father, a literature professor who died when Mark was five years old.

"Actually," Paul said, "he was teaching high school English. But go on. *Karen.*"

Reading these letters, Karen wondered if a sense of humor could be genetic because she could see how similar Mark's puns and jokes were to those of his dimly remembered father.

"I really don't remember him at all."

"I know, but that's so sad that if I put it in, I'd go on forever speculating about why."

In one letter, Mr. Simpson wrote at length about an author who was a favorite of Karen's. In another, he described a trip to London during which he enjoyed a performance of Gustav Holst's *The Planets.* Only a week before, Karen had given Mark a recording of that same symphony by the London Philharmonic for his birthday.

"And here's the kicker," I warned Paul.

At last, Karen had found a link to someone in Mark's family whose nature seemed similar to her own.

"You think everything is a story," Paul said, laughing. "I like it."

"Really?"

"Yeah, but is it right for that magazine?"

"I should probably make your family more normal—let your mother and stepsisters buy wool in a store like everyone else."

"And change Holst to Frank Sinatra, maybe. Of course, Felicity"—Felicity was Paul's full-blooded sister—"lives in the city and hates to knit. And I was the one who showed you my father's letters, right?"

"Right. And I've never been to Oregon."

It was also Paul who mocked my boots as we sloshed through the sand, somewhat sloshed ourselves, during a trip to the Olympic peninsula that came early in our romantic career. When we had managed to get ourselves out of bed and beyond the beach outside the cabin, which wasn't often, we walked to the river and watched Quillayute Indians hauling salmon out of nets and into their canoes, swigging from Budweiser cans and slugging the more rambunctious fish into submission with baseball bats. But none of that would work in the family reunions story.

"What kind of expert are you anyway," Paul teased. "You've never been married. You've never even lived with anyone."

"Yep, I'm still pure."

"What" he said, his voice softening, "do you suppose you're afraid of?"

"What are *you* afraid of? You've hardly ever lived alone."

"That's a good question."

"I know. So's yours."

It wasn't that I was so desperate for material that I felt I had to plunder my life with Paul, but it was the best way

I knew to stay interested in this story. Even if I could have
afforded to be choosy about assignments, which I couldn't,
I don't know what I would have chosen. If I was inventive
enough, I might be able to embroider my life and those of
my friends without having to conduct any interviews at all.

When I started freelancing, I was relatively cheerful
about what I did for a living. But one of the first lessons I
learned was that my notion of interesting didn't often coincide with those of the magazines that paid real money.
The people I wanted to write about were "quirky" instead
of "representative of their generation." It was supposed to
be a good thing, representing your generation, and my failure to comprehend why this should be true meant that I
often had trouble figuring out what to discuss with these
representative people. By now, it wouldn't have mattered
if my topic were nuclear arms reduction or new life for used
pantyhose. Just the idea of picking up a phone and trying
to interview someone made me morose. I was like the cartoon I'd once seen about a traveling salesman who knocks
on doors thinking to himself, "I hope these jerks aren't
home." I tried not to betray the full extent of this attitude
to Paul. If I did, I'd have a much harder time contending
that a move to Seattle might represent a setback in my
career.

We were driving now past a chain of retirement homes
that marked the beginning of the canal, places with cute,
family-based names like Ankers Aweigh, Idle Waters,
Dunn Movin', all of them set close together and hard
against the water's edge.

The scenery stayed pretty much the same until miles
later, when we passed Betty's Bait and Coffee Shop (breakfast and blood worms in one easy stop). There the landscape turned wild again and the paved road gave way to
one of gravel.

A startled pair of deer froze for a second before vanishing into the woods on sprung legs. Already the air had changed, gone from briny to a fernlike rain-forest scent. The road was so curvy Paul creeped along in second gear for a half hour, until we reached a sparsely strung necklace of aging cabins, not one of them visible to another. Paul pulled into the shallow drive of our nameless destination and killed the engine. It was so quiet you could hear bark peeling off madrona trees and rustling onto the ground. A steep winding path led down to the water, which could also be heard, though not seen, through a hillside thick with firs.

Paul had timed our trip to coincide with a minus tide. "If you want clams," he said, "we better hurry."

"I've done enough hurrying for today."

"Okay, suit yourself. But you'll be sorry when I'm sitting out on the deck drinking a cold beer, dipping my steamers in lemon butter, because no matter how hard you beg, I'm not going to share."

He knew how to get me to hurry.

Paul's grandfather, who was an architect, had built this cabin back in the fifties to be a family retreat. When his grandparents died the cabin went to Paul and his sister Felicity, the only children of their adored only son. It did not at all fit my Carolina-bred conceptions of what vacation cabins were supposed to be like—dark, musty places with heavy furniture, chenille bedspreads, chipped dishes, mildewed volumes of *Reader's Digest* condensed novels, and board games always bereft of vital pieces.

Here it felt more Oriental than American, much less southern—uncluttered yet cozy, private despite the windows everywhere. Here there were books on the shelves that you might actually want to read, a complete Scrabble game (the old-fashioned kind with wood letters), and, in the kitchen, an unblemished set of pearlescent Russell Wright plates that belonged to Paul's grandmother. You could always find at least one jar of cocktail sauce in the refrigerator, left by previous visitors. Paul and Felicity regularly loaned the cabin to friends, and since many of them were artists, various depictions of this place and its surroundings decorated the walls, including an uncharacteristically sweet watercolor of rose hips done by Paul.

Several Indian rugs lay over polished hardwood floors, and scattered by the living room fireplace was a cluster of cushions embroidered by some of the Hmong refugees Felicity had once made a film about. A diaphanous canopy of mosquito netting hung above the bed, largely for romantic effect; even in August, mosquitoes weren't much of a problem here. Each of the cabin's three large rooms had sliding glass doors opening onto a cedar deck, the place Paul and I had established on previous visits as the site of afternoon sunbathing and love-making. Catching glimpses of our reflections in the sliding doors, we were amused at how decadent we appeared, fucking with our sunglasses on, but a Tibetan prayer flag flying from the roof beam seemed to cast a spell of approbation over everything, even this. Or, I sometimes suspected, especially this.

Paul had been to Nepal, where he acquired the prayer flag. "You sure would like those Buddhists up there," he told me more than once. Now I felt particularly inclined to agree. Schizophrenia, I knew, was virtually unheard of in Nepal.

We carried buckets, hand rakes, and a split of champagne down to the beach with us. Farther west were oyster beds, and farther still the smooth sandy expanse where clams were most abundant. Once I washed down a small handful of psilocybin mushrooms with my morning orange juice and sat for hours on this beach with Paul. Before long, I was making no distinctions between myself and whatever happened to capture my attention. I didn't hear voices, nobody told jokes, but the world suddenly seemed infused with an incredible sense of humor. Every cloud in the wind-tossed sky had its own identity, more distinct at the time than my own. When an ordinary seagull landed a few feet away I went bug-eyed, momentarily convinced this was some remarkable prehistoric creature I'd never seen before. When a yellow jacket hovered near my face, it took all my concentration just to speak. "Get out of my picture," I said, and it did. When my body exerted itself with a need, like an itch to be scratched or having to pee, I resented its demands. What a bother, having a body.

At the time, I thought I was in ecstasy, but if I had been whooshed away to an urban intersection, I would have thought I was in hell. How to find the correct change for the bus when at the same time you have to pay attention to an irate face behind a honking horn, streams of pollen in the air, the smell of a stranger's perfume? How to balance all this with the remarks of a disembodied voice, which may or may not have your best interests at heart? How to feel the way it was with Jody?

A circus was in progress on the beach today, a bivalval orgy of clams and oysters squirting, slurping, and sucking with whatever water remained available to them.

Paul opened two small oysters with the edge of a clam shell. "Oh good," he said, "they aren't sperming."

He meant spawning. You could tell when they were spawning by the milky-white film coating their flesh. How this bitter-tasting splooey of theirs resulted in progeny I could never remember. All I knew was that oysters here were always somehow quickening. After you opened one and ate it, barnacles and snails were still alive on the shell, which you were supposed to leave on the beach, not take home for an ashtray, in order to preserve the lives of tiny animals and encourage the mysterious workings of oyster breeding.

I slid the oyster into my mouth while Paul watched, waiting for me to let him know how perfectly sweet and salty it tasted, as though my response would increase his own pleasure. Even in this way, oysters were like sex.

I chased the oyster with champagne, then walked down to the clam beach to start digging. I grabbed every clam shell I saw, yelping when I caught one unaware with its neck still hanging out, but I only saved the dainty, steamer-size clams and reburied the more plentiful monsters, which weren't nearly as tender. Tomorrow the tide wouldn't be so low and even the big ones would be hard to find. I dug shallow trenches, the way Paul had taught me, and kept digging long after my arms grew tired.

"Aren't you hot?" Paul asked, taking off his shirt. The sun was almost directly overhead. I stripped down to my bathing suit and bent over to resume digging. Paul positioned himself behind me so that I could see him upside down, through my legs.

"I like looking at you this way," he said.

"Face it," I said, chucking another clam into the bucket, "you like looking at me, period."

"Bet you don't know why just now, though," he said.

"Sure I do. Because my tits are falling out of my suit."

"That's nice, but it's not the reason. Hey, I can't believe you said tits."

"I'm learning."

"The reason I like it is because you're usually so graceful, but now you look so awkward . . ."

"Gee, thanks."

"All knees and elbows, like a kid."

I stopped to count the clams—two dozen, enough to quit. "Yeah, well, when I was a kid for real," I said, "I never did this. I thought clams just came out of those little Doxee cans, and that you only ate them in dips."

"Didn't you ever go to the shore?"

I scooted down to the water's edge and rinsed the clams. "The beach, nobody ever called it the shore. The first time I saw the ocean was in Florida. We went with the Lurreys so the fathers could play golf."

"Why Florida? South Carolina has a coast."

"But my parents never went there. I used to have this idea that beaches in South Carolina were where Christians went."

"You mean the goys." Paul had picked up more Yiddish than I ever knew from another Jewish woman, his ex-wife. One of his favorite phrases translated into "Kick yourself in the ass and cry for help."

"Gentiles," I corrected him. "I only ever heard them called Gentiles. Must be more refined."

"Vacations were the only times my stepfather didn't seem to be annoyed by having kids. I never really understood why he waited until we were gone to leave my mother."

I duck-walked over to Paul and kissed his cheekbones, just beneath his eyes, one of my favorite places for planting kisses on him. His skin smelled rich and yeasty from the sun. "Is every family screwed up?" I asked.

"No," he said. "I don't think so."

The clams still had to be rid of the sand in their stomachs, so Paul waded into the canal a few feet to fill his bucket with chilly water. "Okay, guys," he said, dumping the clams in, "time to spit up."

I set the clams in the shade of a maple tree, alongside

the oysters Paul had picked. Then Paul, in search of a science project, decided to plant sticks on the beach to mark the tide's inward flow.

Paul kept a note to himself on the surface of one of his worktables: "I am not an artist. I am a scientist with no discipline." In the realm of science, he mostly cared about outer space, and belonged to an organization called the L-5 Society, named for a neutral gravity zone somewhere between here and the moon. The L-5 Society sent him newsletters written by some space-age Horace Greeley who exhorted his readers to prepare for departure from this planet, a prospect Paul found particularly appealing because he thought it might be fun to release colored neon gases into the atmosphere.

There were times when I half expected Paul to vaporize, when he didn't seem particularly substantial. But in my experience, love didn't necessarily correspond to concreteness. For example, my first proposal of marriage was one of the most most insubstantial moments of my life.

I received this proposal while sitting on the steps outside my D.C. apartment. Paul waited for me inside, as baffled as I was by the reappearance of Bennett, my former boyfriend, who knew I was involved with someone else.

Bennett and I had met after I sent my clips to the men's magazine he edited in New York and he began assigning me stories. I wrote about men at work, men at play, men eating out in manly restaurants, and got used to Bennett editing out the places where I sounded too much like a girl. We were constantly breaking up, Bennett and I, always at his instigation. We reconciled at mine. I had been like one of those stupid rubber boppo toys, rebounding in direct proportion to how hard I'd been cracked in the teeth.

"Marsha," he told me once, "I don't think I love you enough."

"You're just confused," I said, as though that was an appealing quality.

As I sat there on the steps with Bennett, I could only imagine that he assumed I had been making myself unavailable so as to appear more desirable, with his proposal the planned result. But I was never smart enough about this kind of thing to be strategic. Now that it was my turn to cause pain, all I could do was cry and apologize until Bennett finally left.

Back inside, Paul said, "Why do you suppose you spent three years with someone who only wanted you when he got to be pretty sure he couldn't have you?"

"I know," I said. "I must have been crazy."

"Maybe it suited you."

"Are you kidding? It made me miserable."

"Yeah, but it kept you safe."

"I didn't *feel* safe."

"It's just something to think about."

But I was so stirred up I didn't really want to think, not about that anyway. If I set my mind to it, I could be very good at not thinking, period.

At the canal, for instance, my beach activities weren't nearly so methodical as Paul's. I liked watching barnacles. It sounds like a silly thing to do, but it's a kind of meditation, really—squatting down low to fix your gaze on a cluster of barnacles that are about to be submerged by the incoming tide, then waiting for the moment when enough water leaks in so they release their lashlike feet and wave them around in a jubilant-looking hunt for microbes of food.

I perched at the water's edge for a long time, not looking up until a sea lion surfaced a few yards away. Before long, all the sunbaked rocks would be covered by incoming water, making it warm enough for Paul and me to swim, too.

I always stepped lightly going in, partly to avoid cutting my feet on barnacles and partly because of an awareness that every time my foot came down, it disrupted some other world.

Paul and I stretched out on towels to wait, neither one of us minding waiting for a change. Just as I began to drift away, there were words in the air, pulling me back.

"I was just wondering," Paul said out of the blue. "When can I meet him?"

I made something resembling oysters Rockefeller for dinner, which we ate by candlelight to the accompaniment of a jazz station out of Tacoma. These oysters were big and baked in their shells, so a lot of barnacles had died in the oven to make our meal possible. Before it ended, Paul chewed lightly into a perfectly round little pearl. He placed it on the ledge above the kitchen sink along with the household's other pearls, culled from many such dinners over the years, giving our evening a phantom sense of tradition.

Afterward Paul went out onto the deck with a flashlight and an astronomy book and tried to identify constellations. "When you look at your average star," Paul said, "you see the light it gave off about twenty years ago."

"So that's what they mean by light years."

"Yeah."

"I never knew."

The Boswell Sisters came on the radio singing "Crazy People." This was the kind of thing *I* knew. I went inside to turn the radio up so Paul could hear the Bozzies race through the first verse, working their mouths faster than it seemed humanly possible.

Goofy people, daffy people,
daffy people like me go crazy over things you do.
When we are underneath the moon, the moon above,
You got me acting just like a loony—
It must be love, sweet love . . .

Paul had never heard of the Boswell Sisters, so I told him they made the Andrew Sisters sound like old crows, that they were from New Orleans, that they weren't black, as he had thought, but had learned to sing from their black nanny. I told him how Betty Jo Lowe and her mother sang Boswell Sisters songs as Dr. Lowe, the Jewish urologist, drove us to their beach house on my first trip to the South Carolina coast. Mrs. Lowe was a portly woman, a devout Baptist. She passed us food from the front seat—cucumber slices that had been soaked in sugar and vinegar—while she came forth with real intensity on "Minnie the Moocher," suggesting that she might once have been as much of a tomato as her daughter, whose purse Mrs. Lowe was given to searching for contraband like cigarettes and notes from the sexy bad boys Betty Jo so easily attracted.

The Boswell Sisters were dawdling in the bridge now, dripping honey over every vowel.

'Cause lovebirds of a feather
always flock together.
It's an old, old custom of the heart
That keeps folks from driftin' apart.
And that's the reason maybe
that I call you baby.
We're each other's counterpart.

"You know what I wonder?" I said, my mind fixing on Jody again. "If he came out here because of me, then why didn't he seem more excited when I found him in the park? Practically the first thing he said was that he was leaving."

"Maybe the farther he goes, the less he remembers about why he was going. Maybe those stories were meant to remind him."

"Yeah," I said while the Boswells scatted. "Maybe."

If Jody was the receding tide here, then I was like some kind of shellfish, mindlessly sucking after it. Or maybe he was an element in a constellation of my own design, something that can be seen only as it was then, not as it is now.

Paul had yet to meet a single blood relative of mine, but I was friends with his sister Felicity before I knew him. She was our Cupid. And I had met Paul's mother and step-sisters when they came to Seattle for Paul's last show. Afterward we all went to dinner at a Chinese restaurant, where everyone giggled over the fortune in Paul's cookie: "A young woman will come tonight." For a family occasion, it was a remarkably healthy evening.

One of the ways Paul liked to tease me was by seizing every available opportunity to express his low opinion of people who live in the South. Whenever I rose to the bait, he'd trump any defense I might offer with the fact of my leaving. Although Paul fully expected to find evidence of normal IQs in my family, largely because we had moved from Elsewhere, I knew they would explode all his positive prejudices about Jews, the foremost being that the compassion born of persecution created this uniformly admirable breed of politically progressive people. I tried to explain. My father was a country club Republican (now that the country club was admitting Jews who *weren't* married to Gentiles), my mother drove paintings to her gallery in a Country Squire station wagon, and my brother was the proud alumnus of a state military college that counted ritualized torture and the singing of "Dixie" chief among its venerable traditions.

Paul and I had dabbled last year with the idea of him meeting me in South Carolina for Christmas. My parents didn't celebrate Christmas, but Flip had married into a large Baptist family that pretty much absorbed everyone over the holidays. I abandoned the trip, though, after a controversy arose over our sleeping arrangements, which my mother reported would have to be separate if we stayed in my parents' house, the only place with enough room for us. My mother had also made it clear to me that my father, the one who was adamant about separate beds, would also be offended if we stayed in a motel. So I told my mother to tell my father that we couldn't make it after all.

I was grateful for a reason not to go even if it seemed like a dumb one to Paul, who was willing to give my parents a lot of slack, if for no other reason than that they had produced me. But then, *his* family routinely adjusted to things that would render mine catatonic—one stepsister who was an unmarried mother, another whose lesbian lover ran off with Paul's cousin, a stepfather who ran off with one of his students, a mother who ran off to live in a double-wide yurt with weeds and wildflowers growing out of its roof.

Paul seemed to find it amusing that my father might think of him in the same terms as he would a horny teenager. I thought it best not to mention that at the age of thirty-two, I was still speaking to my father through an interpreter.

I hadn't talked to anyone in my family since I told my mother about Jody stabbing himself, something I mused about as Paul and I sat in bed the next morning with our coffee, strong and thick with cream that Paul had whipped by hand, twirling a wire whisk between his palms. We drank it slowly, watching as a dense layer of fog rose off the water like a theater curtain. I had half-hoped, half-feared, that Jody would act like a magnet, drawing my parents and the Lurreys out West. But if that were going to happen, I would have heard something by now; we had left the number here at the cabin on Paul's answering machine.

"Well, there *is* a time difference," Paul pointed out. "And are you sure the phone's working? Felicity likes to unplug it, remember."

"I checked, I'm sure."

"Don't be too impatient. People usually rise to the occasion when there's a crisis at hand."

"Maybe they don't think it's a crisis. Maybe they're used to things like this happening."

"He never stabbed himself before."

"No, but he's in the hospital now, so everything's okay."

I smoothed Paul's frown furrow with my fingertips. "Look, it doesn't matter. They're not my real parents anyway."

"Oh, right. I forgot."

"No, it's true. My real father subscribed to *Poetry Review*, and my real mother was a disciple of Martha Graham's. They ate spaghetti on Saturday nights with Woody Guthrie."

"Where was this?"

"New York, of course. Unfortunately, I was kidnapped at an early age by a band of gypsies working out of Weehauken. They had connections in Chicago, which is how I came allegedly to be born there."

Paul laughed. "How do we wind up with these people anyway?"

"The mystery of blood, I guess."

"Kidnapping never occurred to me. But I still sometimes

think about how much happier I would have been if my real father hadn't died."

He wasn't competing with me by saying so, just admitting to a common sadness, the kind lovers so often seem to protect in each other. Maybe there's a genetically encoded reason for this, something to do with survival of the species, like preserving like. What married people did with all that tender regard, especially after assuring species survival in a more obvious way, was another mystery to me. The whole thing looked like a gamble, one with terrible odds, that what you started out protecting wouldn't disappear into altogether different instincts, altogether different imperatives.

When the phone finally rang later that morning, it was Carolyn, my editor for the story about family reunions strengthening marriage.

"Okay," Carolyn said, "you're going to love me for this. Here's the story—the husband is going nuts, your basic midlife crisis, only about ten years early. He's not having an affair and he's not drinking. The wife can't figure it out, she doesn't know what to do."

"Maybe," I said, "she should put Thorazine in his tea." I looked through the desk drawer for paper and pencil, finding only an old wooden duck caller. I blew my lips softly through the mouthpiece, making little *fft fft* sounds that Carolyn couldn't hear.

"That's good," Carolyn said. "You can say this woman thought about putting Thorazine in her husband's tea, only make it coffee."

"Why? Is tea drinking confined to college graduates?"

"Trust me, Marsha. Anyway, this woman and her husband go to visit his family in Ohio, where she learns from her mother-in-law that when her father-in-law was her husband's age, I mean *exactly* her husband's age, he went into business for himself."

I exhaled with the duck caller still against my lips, producing a loud quack. "What's that?" Carolyn asked.

"A duck."

"Wow, you really *are* out in the sticks. I wish *I* were. I nearly passed out this morning on the subway."

"From the heat?"

"No, from the smell of this crazy guy who sat down beside me. The train was so crowded there was nothing I could do, but it really wrecked my morning."

"Did he smell like fruit?"

"Fruit?"

"Never mind," I said, "I know what you mean." And I did, I really did, but she was pissing me off anyway.

"So, the thing is," Carolyn went on, "this woman's husband doesn't have his own business yet. He hasn't even made partner, but don't put that in. Make him a contractor or something. All you need to clinch it is a graph saying how much closer the two of them felt when she defused the problem by bringing it to his attention, that he hadn't even realized the real reason for his frustration, that they had great sex for the first time in months, blah, blah, blah."

I had given up on finding a pencil, but for the sake of form, I asked Carolyn for this woman's phone number. "Maybe I ought to talk to her myself."

"You're already talking to her. Use made-up names 'cause it's Rick and me. It's perfect, don't you think?"

"Gee, Carolyn, I don't know."

"Why? What's your problem?"

"It's just that I wonder why women are always the ones who have to go digging around for the answers when men act like jerks."

"The way of the world, my sweet."

"Don't you think it makes them sound retarded?"

"Yeah, sure."

"I mean the men, Carolyn."

"Me, too. I would never insult our readers like that."

"Well, goddamn it, why don't they figure out their own lives?"

"Indeed," Carolyn said. "Why don't they indeed."

"I mean the women."

"You do? Ah, well. That's another story."

That afternoon, Paul and I dragged a dinghy down to the beach. He tossed in a crab trap baited with a partially opened can of cat food, then rowed us out to drop it at a deep spot far from the shore. We went out again the next morning, our last at the cabin, and hauled up the trap to find it filled with half a dozen squirming Dungeness crabs. Two were keepers, males large enough to be legal size. I cooked them for lunch, which we ate outside on the deck. It was a lovely lunch, but we were both preoccupied— Paul with the watercolor he wanted to finish before we left and me with the condition Jody would be in when I got back.

We planned to return to Seattle on one of the late ferry boats I liked to watch from Paul's apartment window as we finished dinner, slipping through the dark with tourists' flashbulbs popping on the deck like fireflies. For me, the day dragged. I tried to work on my story, got nowhere, started reading a novel, gave up on that, and went back down to the beach by myself. When I returned to the cabin we started cleaning—shaking out rugs, mopping floors, scrubbing the tub and sinks with Felicity's ecologically correct household cleanser, baking soda mixed with Dr. Bronner's eucalyptus soap.

We had already packed the pickup, locked the cabin, and

hidden the key when I heard the phone ringing inside. I ran underneath the house to grab the key from its hook behind a drain pipe and scrambled back up the hill. Paul watched mutely, stunned to see me move so fast and wordlessly. Inside, I grabbed the phone on the fifth ring and an operator with a slight accent said she had a person-to-person call for Marsha Rose. It was Eileen, calling from Denmark.

"Marsha?" she said when the operator clicked off. "Eileen Lurrey."

So much, I thought, for worrying about whether to call her "aunt." "Yes," I said. I was having a hard time catching my breath.

"Are you all right, dear?"

That was better. "I just ran in from outside. Are *you* okay?"

"We're fine, all things considered. We've spoken to the doctor in Seattle, and we've decided that since Jody is in good hands, we'll continue our trip." She stopped to clear her throat. "It's so strange, that it happened there. Where you were."

I didn't want to clarify the strangeness for her any more than I did for Dr. Thrailkill, for much the same reasons. I didn't want to say it was a lucky thing, either, because I didn't know if that were true. So I just agreed with her, it was very strange indeed.

"If I could just ask another favor," Eileen went on, her voice now almost sounding the way I remembered it.

"I *want* to help."

"Well then, when Jody stabilizes, if you could arrange to put him on a flight back home, that would be extremely helpful."

"They might keep him for a while."

"Only if there's a court order, and I don't expect there

will be. Let Nancy know Jody's flight numbers so she can have someone meet him, and let the airline know he might require help changing planes in Charlotte or Atlanta, whichever way you route him, although Charlotte is better because the airport is smaller. Tell Nancy what you've spent on the ticket and she'll reimburse you. Then we'll be home, as planned, in three weeks."

So that was to be the end of it. I tried to picture Eileen somewhere in Denmark, and couldn't help but think of Queen Gertrude and the son whom she supposed to be mad. Eileen, of course, had years of evidence. And unlike Hamlet, Jody couldn't just be sent off to England. He could, though, be sent to live in an institution. I asked Eileen if she was considering this as seriously as Nancy seemed to be.

"It's not exactly an institution," Eileen said, her voice quavering. "I think a better term would be 'assisted living situation.' We're at a point in our lives where we need things to be more steady, more predictable. We're just too old to keep dealing with this. And Jody's a grown man, Marsha. A grown man."

After we said goodbye, I locked the cabin up again and asked Paul if I could drive. While he marveled at the play of light over the mountains, I concentrated on the unpaved road's seemingly endless curves.

Chapter 8

South Carolina

JODY BECOMES a man on a muggy May night while standing on top of a Coca-Cola crate that gives him the extra height he needs to rise above chin-level with the Torah.

At least a third of those filling the pews tonight have never been inside a temple before. For them, this event is mainly theatrical. What counts is how great Jody looks, tan and assured in his new spring suit. They don't notice that although Jody appears to be reading aloud a Hebrew passage while following Rabbi Stein's ivory pointer, his eyes are actually cast off to the side and reading from a cheat sheet, a phonetic translation that the rabbi provided. A blush creeps into Jody's cheeks as he finishes, his smile only a little more relieved than the rabbi's. But our Christ Church classmates are so impressed you would have thought Jody had actually stood up there and sprouted a beard. Dr. Lowe's red-haired daughter, who looks to be our age, pats her tiny gloved hands together in a flurry of silent applause.

At the rabbi's cue, Mrs. Owens, the Christian lady who plays the organ for Friday night services, slips off her right shoe so her foot won't slip on the narrow wooden chord slats. For the High Holidays, the temple hires a trio in addition to Mrs. Owens, a choir gleaned from Little Theater choruses that sits in the loft over the pulpit and sings the sacred songs in Hebrew that has been printed out phonetically, like Jody's Torah passage, inside their leather-bound hymnals.

After the final hymn and prayers, everyone goes downstairs to the social hall. Jody and his family stand in a receiving line with the rabbi just inside the door. I kiss my way through the line and go over to the buffet table, where Juanita and her son, Calvin, are filling glasses with champagne. Calvin, grown tall and handsome, is dressed for serving in black slacks and a stiff white jacket with a high collar.

"Hey, Calvin," I say, but he takes a pair of empty champagne bottles back to the kitchen without speaking.

"He doesn't like wearing that outfit," Juanita explains. "So how'd he do?" she asks with a nod toward Jody.

"Pretty good. Lost his place one time, though."

"How'd he look?"

"Kind of nervous."

"Lord, I don't wonder—testifying in front of all those people. And in Hebrew!"

"It's not like that," I snap meanly. "It's not like he had some vision and made it up."

While it's true that in our temple, the girls aren't celebrated like the boys when they hit thirteen, I actually don't mind this. The only reason I have for being irritated with Jody is that he has committed the sin of becoming more popular than me.

Tomorrow night, at the "young people's party" Jody's parents will give for him at the Poinsett Hotel, I will spend most of the evening avoiding Chip Ashley, the fat pig-nosed mill heir who has repeatedly asked me to go steady with him. I will watch Jody slow dancing with Scott Rammage to a live combo's rendition of " 'Til There Was You." Not only is Scott the smartest girl in our class, she's also one of the prettiest, tall with clear, sharp features and startlingly violet eyes. She'll be wearing a long dress with an empire waist that emphasizes the fact that, unlike me, Scott actually *needs* to wear a bra. In order to rest her head on Jody's shoulder, Scott will have to kick off her heels and bend her knees a little so she won't look as if she's stooping. Jody will smoothly move her around the dance floor, his hand resting easily on the small of her back. Nancy has taught Jody all the right things to do when he dances with girls, which is partly why all our other classmates will be so excited when he tears himself away from Scott to partner them.

Since Aunt Eileen will have taught Jody the importance of being a good host, he will eventually get around to asking me out on the floor. It will be a fast number, we won't touch. And even though my rhythm is every bit as good as his, I'll feel flushed and awkward, my mouth going dry when I try to smile, my lips hanging up on my braces.

This is how I usually end up dancing with Jody at the less formal parties given on a regular basis by the socially active half of our class, of which I am a nominal member. Jody rose to some kind of alpha-male status when he started going out into the night on proms with Scott Rammage. None of the boys except Chip Ashley ever asks me to go on proms. Since proms are really just walks, I figure the term must be short for promenades. Afterward, there's slow dancing. And then, to cap off the evening, one of the boys makes one of the girls faint.

The girl hyperventilates, panting for a minute or so before the boy standing behind her grabs her around the chest and hugs her hard enough to lift her off the ground and cut off her wind. None of us are daring enough to actually kiss yet, but an unspoken understanding exists that boy-on-girl fainting has to do with sex. That sex might require girls like us to lose all consciousness isn't what anybody admits to having in mind. Despite Scott's height, Jody had a pretty easy time of it making her faint, and even while she was out cold, she still managed to look tall and smart and beautiful. I was sure that if I did it, I'd drool and say the sort of senseless things I did in my sleep.

Aunt Eileen picked up Jody and me after that particular party last month. The ride home was the highlight of my evening. When we were alone or with our families, Jody didn't mind paying attention to me and I could be more like myself.

As Aunt Eileen pulled into our driveway, Jody noticed that Mr. Gailey was sitting on his porch next-door with a hunting rifle laid across his lap. "What's he doing?" I asked Aunt Eileen.

"Oh," she said lightly, "practicing for Gin-Gin's wedding, I imagine." Gin-Gin was Mr. Gailey's wild teenage daughter.

"That's not it," Jody said. "At least he's not wearing a sheet."

Mr. Gailey might be country, but I couldn't imagine him burning any crosses, and he was on good enough terms with my parents that they kept his bottle of Jack Daniels in their bar, checking it out to him on nights when his hard-shell wife wasn't around. I frowned at Jody. "Do you know what you're talking about, 'cause I don't."

"He's on the lookout in case there's a riot on Shannon Drive tonight. Remember the riots last year?"

It dawned on me much too slowly that Mr. Gailey's rifle had something to do with what had happened in Memphis. "There weren't any riots in Sparta."

"Tell *him*," Jody said, jerking his thumb in Mr. Gailey's direction.

"Bite your tongue," Aunt Eileen hissed at Jody. "There's no need to go borrowing trouble." Still, she went inside to watch the news with my father, just to make sure that Mr. Gailey didn't have some unlikely leg up on current events, that only someone like him might expect the anniversary of Martin Luther King's assassination to cause trouble here.

Preoccupied with the problem of my plummeting status, I bought a home hair-coloring kit and bleached my hair a shade that the box advertised as honey ash blonde. I might not be able to do anything about my braces, my flat chest, or the way even the smallest-sized Villager skirts drooped mockingly off my hips, making me wonder if some organ crucial to my development hadn't been removed along with my appendix. But I *could* become a blonde. After I went swimming just once in the Lurreys' pool, though, the chlorine turned my hair a burnt red color that my mother, still angry at me for bleaching it in the first place, said I'd just have to live with until it grew out. The texture changed too, to that of twine, so that I had to battle frizz as well as curls. Now that the dark roots have begun to show, Jody says pretty soon it'll look like a cow shat on my head.

These days, Jody doesn't like it if I mention to anyone else at school the time we spend studying together. Then there are more obvious things that I know better than to talk about, like the fact that Jody's crotch enlarged very noticeably one night while we were alone watching a smoldering pair of *danseurs apache* on TV. Jody didn't seem the least bit flustered, but I couldn't have been more surprised if I learned that an animal was growing in his pants.

On Jody, the right clothes fit. His proportions are tidy and tapered, his teeth perfect, his eyelashes thicker than any girl's, and even his hair, which hangs straight and silky to his eyebrows, is better than mine. Our territory, which had always seemed so clear, is murky and confusing.

I write about it in my diary, which I keep locked and hidden so no one will suspect me of nursing a crush. *Does he know me too well to like me that way? Is it better to be friends?* When I run out of questions, I copy down lyrics to those songs Gene Pitney sings with a catch in his voice, slow songs that Jody never dances to with me.

On the night of Jody's bar mitzvah, my father threads through the temple social hall with his Super 8 camera, shooting home movies. I watch for a while as he focuses on Stevie Segal, home from prep school up North, then on Billy Shane, who lifts his latest model sports car up to the lens. Debbie Rittenbaum and Maureen Abrams hold hands and curtsy in perfect unison.

I spot Marie Gilbert with her parents and go off to join them. Marie wears braces now too, but with her thick, shiny blonde mane and long-waisted figure, they seem much more incidental than mine. "What did you do to your hair?" Marie asks, but before I can answer, Mrs. Gilbert nervously adjusts her hat and says, "I look just awful in hats—I thought all the ladies would be wearing them, but they're not."

Champagne seems to make Mr. Gilbert, who owns a sporting goods store, even more jovial than usual. He grabs my mother's hand as she passes and pulls her over. "Now let me see if I got this thing right," he says, his face red and hectic-looking. "First you say *mazel tov* and then you kiss." He leans over to kiss my mother, who turns her cheek toward him sharply.

"Well, thank you," she says, smiling artificially. "But I'm afraid the only things *I* can take credit for tonight are the pigs-in-a-blanket."

"Boy, I sure do like all this kissin' around here," Mr. Gilbert goes on. "Now, that's *my* idea of gettin' religion."

"What a nice hat you're wearing," my mother tells Mrs. Gilbert.

"I joined *Entre Nous*," Marie says to me, naming one of the better junior high sororities. "Which one did you pledge?"

I take this as evidence of the estrangement that began when Jody and I started going to Christ Church. Marie knows full well there's only one junior high sorority that allows Jewish members, the one that Debbie and Maureen both joined. The junior high fraternities are different, without any rules about religion. Jody joined the same one Flip had belonged to. Soon he would be running around the woods wearing nothing but a jockstrap that had been soaked in Deep Heat and filled with bark chips, yet another kind of initiation.

Next year, I know, all social life will revolve around sorority and fraternity parties. But in this matter, as in so many others, I have Nancy Lurrey's confident example to follow. "You don't need a sorority," she told me, "especially not that goofy one Maureen and Debbie joined. The only reason for joining is the parties, and invitations are easy to get if you've got friends who belong." Which is basically what I tell Marie.

Nancy and Flip graduated from Christ Church before going back to public school, but I don't want to wait that long. What was an early start at algebra compared to a crack at a whole new identity? I could begin by taking up tap dancing again and winning back Marie.

But as Aunt Eileen flags me over to meet Betty Jo Lowe, it seems I might as well begin with her. "And *your* daddy," Aunt Eileen is telling Betty Jo, "took care of *Marsha's* daddy when he had kidney stones!" Betty Jo and I have never gone to the same school, but I've seen her a few times at Friday night services with Dr. Lowe, a short, bald, bespectacled man with a soft coastal accent.

Betty Jo sidles up to me, a small smile parting her Kewpie-doll lips. "God," she whispers, "I could just die for a cigarette."

Just now, Uncle Lud is kissing the hand of Betty Jo's mother with his usual Viennese-style courtliness. Mrs. Lowe is making a rare appearance at the temple tonight because she's an old classmate of Aunt Eileen's. "I love your model coats," Mrs. Lowe says, referring to the house dresses that Uncle Lud's company manufactures. "I just *live* in them at home."

I can see why. Uncle Lud's model coats are especially flattering on fat women. Betty Jo and her father are so slim and dainty that standing alongside them, Mrs. Lowe looks as though she might be there for ballast. But more than her size it's her hair, which she wears in a flat pageboy curling into tight rolls about the size of my mother's pigs-in-a-blanket, that makes her seem so much more matronly than my various unofficial aunts circulating through the social hall.

I know that Betty Jo, like her mother and much older brothers, is supposed to be Baptist. But even in her demure, lace-collared black velvet dress, Betty Jo plainly doesn't care much about what's expected of her. Who better to enlist as someone to think well of me?

I accompany Betty Jo to the bathroom and lean against the wall, watching as she brushes her sleek cap of for-real red hair. Then she powders her face with a Pond's compact, applies sugared pink Love lipstick, and sprays herself with a tiny ebony flask of Tabu, filling the room with a vampy amber scent and me with a sharp yearning for every one of these products.

Soon we're standing in the honeysuckled darkness along-side the temple, Betty Jo smoking the Pall-Mall I got for her from Coy Collum and laughing at my choked attempts to inhale.

"You could spend the night with me sometime," Betty Jo says, "and then we could go to Sunday school together."

"Where?" I ask, expecting to hear the names of either Oak Street or First Baptist, the *nice* Baptist churches where they don't howl and roll around in the aisles.

But Betty Jo pops a cherry Lifesaver into her mouth and rounds her eyes at me. "Duh now, George," she says. I don't know yet that this is part of her slang repertoire, a re-sponse to be made when someone fails to grasp the obvious.

"You mean here? Wouldn't your mother mind?"

"I hope so," Betty Jo giggles. "But you don't have to worry about that."

I try to distract her from my worrisomeness—a major liability, I know. "We mostly just read stories about Jewish kids. I don't even have a Bible. I think we get one when we're confirmed, and then you don't have to go to Sunday school anymore, which I'm looking forward to myself."

"You seem smart. Or like you would be in school any-way." Like Marie, Betty Jo goes to the same junior high Jody and I were sent to Christ Church to avoid. "I guess you know Jody pretty well. He's kind of cute, don't you think?"

Back inside, Betty Jo drifts away. After a while, I wan-der off into another part of the temple, a deserted hallway where the Sunday school classrooms are located.

Opposite the closed classroom doors are the rabbi's study and a wall filled with framed photographs documenting the congregation's history. I especially like the older photo-graphs, the ones taken back before they even had a rabbi, much less a temple, when everybody met in parlors to dis-

cuss the latest novels and drove off to Columbia together
for High Holiday services. There are ladies in long linen
dresses and men in straw boaters, gathered around picnic
tables set with platters of fried chicken and pitchers of iced
tea. I know Uncle Sol and Aunt Eileen to be among the
squinting children in muscle-man bathing suits, posed
along the shore of Saluda Lake, but I can't remember which
ones they are.

Aunt Eileen and my mother are in a more recent black-
and-white picture that ran in the newspaper, posed as if
caught in the act of building a *sukkah*. This is the Sister-
hood's big job, making a *sukkah* every year, a kind of display model to supplement lessons about how our ancestors
lived while on the run in the desert.

In another photograph—this one in color—Uncle Lud is
giving Jody and me gift-wrapped watercolor kits, our prizes
for being named King and Queen of the Purim festival. My
mother had made us the costumes that won us our titles.
Jody wears a beard of shredded Coets that was dyed red
in mercurochrome and water, and ballooning out from his
hips is a madly patterned pair of pantaloons that were once
my mother's Capri pants. I look like a regal insect in a tall
gold cardboard crown skewered with two crimson chop-
sticks, each pointing outward with glittered Styrofoam
balls stuck onto the ends—my mother's idea of ancient Per-
sian female attire.

As I walk by the photographs, I notice how my new pat-
ent leather heels click and echo off the checkered linoleum
floor. Taken by the sound, I start doing a favorite tap step
I remember, one with a particularly quick rat-a-tat-tat ca-
dence. Patsy Chalmers, who likes ballet terminology so
much that she named her son DeJon (after *rond de jomb*),
calls this step "back bomberchez," which, like her son's
name, is only supposed to *sound* French.

Once I get up to speed, I begin performing the step full-out, complete with window-washing hand movements. Then I do cramp-roll turns, an even more complicated step. Here is something my body could do well—so well that I forget all my other dissatisfactions with it and smile for an invisible audience, imagining myself twirling across the stage in a fringed, sequined costume.

If the night weren't humid enough to swell the wood classroom doors and make them stick, I wouldn't notice one of them being opened. As it is, a high-pitched creak stops me in mid-twirl. My stomach reacts first, with a lurch of embarrassment that reaches my mouth tasting of cherries and cigarettes. I see Betty Jo first, a pleasantly quizzical expression on her face, and then Jody emerging from the dark just behind her, his mouth smeared with Love lipstick.

Chapter 9

WHEN I arrived at Bayview on Monday morning, Jody was in Dr. Thrailkill's office, conferring, I assumed, about his evaluation period coming to an end. From where I sat waiting in the common room, I could see the Chanel-suited lady pacing in circles. After a while, Jody walked in wearing a hospital bathrobe over jeans. There were dark circles under his eyes, his hair still looked mussed from sleep, and he needed a shave. Still, as he spotted me, a faint smile appeared. "I'm staying now because I want to," he said. "Not because I have to."

"That's great," I told him, but I didn't believe it.

Later, after Jody had gone to have a cigarette in private, Dr. Thrailkill came out to explain. "There's no need for a court order. Jody *asked* to stay for an additional two weeks." Then he put up a hand as if to stop me from speculating. "No, no, no—that's a good sign. I was right, Jody *was* on haloperidol, and he's willing to try injections."

"But his mother is expecting me to send him home now."

"That won't be a problem," he said confidently.

"If you don't mind, I'd prefer that it was you instead of me who informs his family about this."

"I've already called Jody's sister. He told her himself."

Jody stood smoking with one arm—the one he had stabbed—wrapped around his waist as if he were cold. Or frightened. As I watched him, I berated myself for worrying about how Eileen and Nancy would react to Jody staying on, especially since there might well be another institution waiting at the other end of whatever ticket I bought for him. Something that wouldn't even be under consideration if he hadn't come to Seattle, if I hadn't lost sight of him in the library. Today's news was good. Sending Jody home the way he was now would hardly strengthen his case.

"He looks terrible," I said to Thrailkill.

"I'm optimistic about his chances for improvement."

"He'll never be normal, though, will he?"

"If you mean will he ever be who he was before he became ill . . ." Thrailkill's voice trailed off as he shook his head. Then, brightening, "In a couple of days it might be a good idea to sign him out for a few hours. It would emphasize that he's here on a voluntary basis. I'd suggest doing something outdoors. Movies are a bad idea."

"What's wrong with movies?"

"Smoking's not allowed and plots are usually too hard to follow." He frowned thoughtfully. "Although Schwarzenegger seems pretty popular around here."

At that moment, the Chanel-suited lady burst into a loud, angry conversation with no one who could be seen. Dr. Thrailkill rose and started off in her direction, but then he doubled back and leaned down toward me. "Her condition doesn't respond to drugs. Jody's does. I know this is hard for you to believe, but he's one of the lucky ones."

Jody was still hearing voices. Sometimes during that visit he looked so intent that I imagined he might be hearing only one voice, a voice so open to interpretation that he could neither dismiss nor completely comprehend its words. But I noticed that whenever anyone who worked at the hospital spoke of voices it was as if they only occurred in multiples, like a chorus, giving the impression that something singular might be easier to subdue.

Before I left, Thrailkill told me that since there was a strong possibility Jody's voices would continue until his new medication took full effect, music might make them less bothersome. Actually, what he said was, "Music sometimes seems to alleviate the discomfort of auditory hallucinations."

I spent that evening in Paul's studio making tapes for Jody. I had lots of tapes with me already, but they were mostly songs with words. If it troubled Jody to hear voices, how could it possibly help for him to hear more? And so the new tapes I made for him were wordless things: Scarlatti guitar sonatas, Satie's "Gymnopedies," even some Pachelbel and Vivaldi that sounded like the music restaurants play for Sunday brunch. But Jody didn't like these tapes, he preferred the ones I'd made for Paul and myself. It seemed that so long as the melody tracked easily and the lyrics were fairly placid, not too sharp or angry, music with words wasn't a problem. I found myself thinking differently about the people I saw on the streets wearing their stereo headsets, blocking out external stimulation by the same means that helped Jody silence internal bombardments. He listened on the Walkman that I wrote off on my income tax return last year as a machine for taping interviews.

At the end of the week, Jody signed out for an excursion and came to meet me in the common room with neatly combed hair and wearing the salmon-colored T-shirt I had packed for him. Maybe it was just a reflective effect from the shirt, but Jody's skin, which had taken on a sallow sort of tone in the hospital, looked rosier today. Then my eyes went to his arm, where his stitches had come out this morning, and a long, skinny purple welt marked the path of his wound.

Jody had the Walkman in his breast pocket, along with

the earplugs I bought for him after he complained that my
headset put too much pressure on his brains. He also said
it made him look silly—the real reason, I thought. "Where
are we going?" Jody asked me. "I forget."

"To the Hiram M. Chittenden Canal Locks," I told him.
"With Paul." He gave me a quizzical look. "My boyfriend."

We found Paul waiting for us in a loading zone outside
the hospital. I suspected one reason Paul wanted to come
with us was to gather fuel for his argument that I shouldn't
be so concerned about Jody, that he shouldn't be eating into
so much of our time together.

Paul jumped out of the pickup and shook hands with
Jody. This nicety out of the way, Jody put in his earplugs,
turned on the Walkman, cranked the sound up as high as
it would go, and climbed into the cab so that he was sitting
between Paul and me. As Paul drove away, we could
plainly hear the first cut on my "American Tunes" tape.
Jody called out in a loud monotone, "He says you can't be
bright and *bon vivant* far away from home, but you know
what? Common household cleansers can't touch the stain."

While Paul and I exchanged worried glances, Jody spoke
again: "What I want to know, Mashie, is does he send his
blue jeans to the dry cleaners?"

Now Paul gave me a look as if to say See, I told you those
stories have something to do with him being here. Jody was
referring to a snippet from one of the articles of mine that
was in his bag, a sentence describing the famous singer-
songwriter to whom Jody was listening crossing a leg encased in neatly creased blue jeans. I must have thought it
was a telling detail, but I had a hard time accepting that
Jody did too. It was so much easier to see what was wrong
with him than to discern what remained intact.

Listening to music evidently soothed Jody enough that

he didn't smoke quite so constantly, a side-effect that I particularly appreciated in the truck's close quarters. Visiting with him had put a huge dent into my own habit. Smoking now made all Jody's other mannerisms feel too close, as though I might inhale an affectless stare and exhale a tumble of non sequiturs.

As an entertainment for Jody, the Hiram M. Chittenden Canal Locks had several compelling features: There was no plot to comprehend, just the same liquid motion, reversing and repeating itself; admission was free, an increasingly important consideration for me now that I seemed to be abandoning my family reunions story without another assignment in sight; and we could eat the lunch I packed in a park alongside the locks.

With Jody in the middle of "Bourgeois Blues," Paul parked the truck. *"Tell all the colored folk to listen to me, don't try to buy no home in Washington, D.C.,'cause it's a bourgeois town."* If Jody were feeling better, maybe we could talk about why I put that song on the tape. I told him anyway, in my head, where I could address a grownup Jody of my own invention: I've lived there a long time, but it's not really home, either. Yeah, my Jody would say, I went there once, I know what you mean. Too much reality for me, too.

I turned to Jody, the real one beside me in Paul's truck, and signaled him to turn down the sound. Then I asked, as I had been coached to by Dr. Thrailkill, if the voices were bothering him today. According to Dr. Thrailkill, I was to inquire about Jody's symptoms as matter-of-factly as possible, as though he were afflicted with migraines or arthritis.

"Not now," Jody said sweetly, handing the Walkman to me. "But put it in your purse, okay?" Jody's accent had thickened on the drug. He spoke even more lazily than usual, as though there were something between his back teeth that kept him from closing his jaw completely.

We reached the canal locks just as water in one of them fell to the level of the sound, lowering several sailboats and one big commercial fishing ship. Paul explained the process to Jody much as he did to me on our first trip. "They do this to keep the freshwater in Lake Union separate from the saltwater in Puget Sound."

Jody nodded judiciously, plainly making an effort at cohesion as he lit a cigarette and took a series of double drags. "They have to take sides," he managed.

"That's right," Paul told him, "they do."

"Yeah, 'cause otherwise all the fish would die of confusion."

Once again I was struck by how easily Paul might have said exactly what Jody had just said—with different intonations, to be sure, Paul's voice deliciously silly instead of dim and disconnected, but still, using the same words.

Bells rang, signaling that the water in the second lock would start rising to lake level. At Jody's insistence, we stayed for a few more level changes and releases. I got the sense that while he enjoyed watching different boats and the people on them bobbling up and down, like toys in a giant bathtub, what he really relished was the chance to drift away, his privacy undisturbed by our efforts to draw him into conversations where he could so easily get lost in all the spaces between words and sentences. Paul didn't mind, he could stay here and watch all day, but I wanted Jody to see the fish.

With Jody shuffling behind us, we walked beyond the locks atop a dam, looking down on schooling salmon as they leapt into the air. After descending a flight of stairs we entered a small cement-block building and I led Jody to an aquariumlike wall of glass. Behind the glass, chinook salmon were scaling a ladder built to facilitate their migration, gradually adjusting to freshwater. A public service announcement came on, causing Jody to snap his head and look searchingly around the room until he spotted the speakers. A woman's voice was explaining that these fish were returning to their rivers of origin to spawn. The same announcement played several times over before Jody turned to Paul. "What are they doing?" he asked.

Paul put his hand on Jody's shoulder and Jody flinched, but he didn't draw away. Neither did Paul. I would have, assuming that Jody, finding it so difficult to express emotion himself, disliked displays directed toward him, even mild, affectionate ones. I made a mental note that it was only *strong* emotions that were to be avoided around Jody.

"See how they're pushing against the current?" Paul asked him. "They're looking for the opening in the ladder that the water is pouring through. It's like the current of a river. They have to swim against it as hard as they can to reach the next step, to get where they have to go."

"They're going back to the rivers where they were born," I added, in almost the same words as the public service announcement. "Then they'll lay eggs and fertilize them."

"Yeah," Jody said. "And die." Jody pressed against the window and stared sleepily for a long while. "I don't see any suck marks," he said. "Do salmon carry hitchhikers, Mashie?"

"What do you mean, Jody?"

"Don't you remember? You said those sucky things were hitchhikers of the sea."

"He means lampreys, Marsha," Paul said. "The story you wrote about lampreys. Remember?"

I remembered. But the only *fact* I remembered from writing about lampreys was that they're thought to be a delicacy in certain parts of Europe. Look, I wanted to tell Jody, I wrote that story the same way we used to reword the World Book when we wrote reports in the third grade. But that would launch him off in too many different directions at once. I would be asking Jody to consider me in ways he couldn't even consider himself. I knew what I was supposed to do when I talked to Jody. Looking him in the eye, I was supposed to be clear, concise, calm, adult, practical—all the things I found it hard to be under the best of circumstances. "I'm not positive," I told Jody, "but I don't believe lampreys breed off the Pacific."

"That's probably right," Paul said. "I've never seen any of those marks on West Coast salmon. Or tuna, either."

Jody didn't say anything for a while. Then he laughed and stuck a finger in the corner of his mouth, pretending it was a fish hook. "Sorry, Charlie," he said, "we take only quality tuna here at Star Fish." Then, in a flat voice, he sang his own lyric to an old disco tune: " 'I believe in mackerels, you tuna fish.' " The real words, as I recalled, were "I believe in miracles, you sexy thing." I also recalled Jody dancing in Athens to a live band's southern funk version of the song, crouched down low with his palms on his thighs, laughing as he rolled his shoulders to the beat.

Before I could respond to Jody here at the locks, though, he reached into my purse and grabbed the Walkman.

While Paul and I ate our sandwiches, Jody wandered up the hillside to feed the better part of his to a small flock of Canada geese. "For somebody who thought he was Picasso," Paul said, "Jody didn't seem very interested when I asked if he wanted to visit the studio. Maybe he would have reacted differently if I gave him a little painting. Or if I left myself out of it completely and just gave him some paper and oil sticks to play with."

"Maybe," I said. "But maybe being interested in art is one of his symptoms."

"I always thought it was one of mine." Paul stretched out and put his head on my lap. "I don't mind being with Jody," he said. "I like him. Especially when he's being funny on purpose. But I'll be glad to see him go. His family's been dealing with this a lot longer than you have."

"What do you mean?"

"Just that he's not really your brother, you don't have to take on so much."

I didn't quite know how to explain the lingering picture inside my head of Jody refusing to get into my car, of him heading home with some stranger to be hospitalized for the first time. So I got irritable instead. "Can't you see? He's not ready to go home yet."

"I don't mean now, I mean next week, when his time's up. Although I do feel sorry for him, having to go back down South."

"Would you feel as sorry for him if he had to go to Ohio?"

"Probably not."

"Well, it's gotten to be a lot like Ohio down there."

I had never been to Ohio, but I wanted to avoid the sort of mindless defense of home that I knew myself to be all too capable of, despite my being essentially the same kind of southerner as my parents were Jews—the culinary ethnic variety. Where they had craved bagels and blintzes, I would want white corn, home-grown tomatoes, and yellow squash pressure-cooked to a buttery pulp, the kind of food that was always more likely to be found in Jody's house than in mine. I would want to drink beer and listen to music in a place where people automatically clapped on the off-beat. I would want a chopped barbecue sandwich served by the same waitress I once overheard telling off a rambunctious customer. "Oh, you," she scoffed at him, "you could get a hard-on standing out in the rain." I would want all that, and then I would want to be Elsewhere.

Jody had his own ideas about food. "Rye bread is not for sandwiches," he informed me after feeding the geese. He sounded lighter now, more like himself.

"Is that why you didn't eat your sandwich?"

"Yeah. You're only supposed to toast rye bread and eat it with breakfast, so you can dip it in the egg. You know, the soft yellow part?"

"The yolk."

"Yolkey-dokey."

Jody refused the orange Paul offered because, he said, it was bad for you to eat a piece of fruit unless you were eating that piece of fruit some place where it might actually be grown, and he didn't think oranges could grow in Seattle. I took this as further evidence of Jody's illness, but Paul said, "I have a stepsister in Oregon who believes that, too. Won't eat any fruit that's not local. Practically lives on cranberries."

I laughed a touch hysterically. "Sounds pretty woo-woo."

"Yeah, it's pretty woo-woo, all right," Jody said, clearly pleased with the sound of this, and maybe even the sense. "Woo-woo but true-woo."

Paul stopped at a market on the way back to the hospital and bought Jody a basket of Washington state cherries and a prepackaged tuna fish sandwich on white bread. "Be sure to wash the cherries before you eat them," I said.

Jody nodded, but he might easily have been using his head to keep time with "The Traveling Riverside Blues."

We were having dinner with Paul's sister—his full-blooded one—and her husband that night. Feeling aimless after we dropped Jody off, I called Felicity and arranged to come over early and assist with the preparations. As I cut the pickup wheels into the curb alongside her house, I caught sight of Felicity at work in her backyard flower garden. So did two women approaching on the sidewalk, both swathed in the crimson robes and headdresses that meant they lived in a nearby mansion that housed some kind of evangelical karma cult. One of these women waved and called out to Felicity in unnaturally dulcet tones: "You're lucky to have such a beautiful garden."

Felicity squinted at the women from beneath the brim of her gardening hat. "Thank you," she said sharply, "but luck's got nothing to do with it."

Sometimes Felicity reminded me of an enchanted Victorian governess, a strict miss with a ramrod spine who keeps a very effective secret of all her spells and potions. It only made Felicity more remarkable in my eyes that she could impart this impression while being six months pregnant.

I closed the gate behind me and helped Felicity remove drowned slugs from saucers filled with beer. Slugs like beer, and this method was supposed to be more merciful than shriveling them with salt. "Friendly neighbors you've got," I said.

"I just think it's so insulting," she said, "when people confuse work with luck. Wouldn't you be offended if someone told you that you were *lucky* to be with Paul?"

"Oh, I don't know. Sometimes it can seem that way to me. If I hadn't met you, for instance, I would have never met Paul."

"But if you hadn't been ready for someone like him," Felicity insisted, "nothing would have happened. And if you want to stay with him, you'll have to do something about that, too." She tossed me a circumspect look. "The thing about luck is you have to make the effort."

"That's the thing about *good* luck, you mean."

I first met Felicity four years ago, when a snowstorm marooned her back East, in the other Washington. She had come to obtain funding for a documentary about snake-worshipping religious sects. Someone we both knew, another documentary filmmaker who had moved from D.C. to Seattle, suggested my place as a likely port when she called him in a panic, having run through all her hotel money and not gotten a grant yet for her film, what with the snow keeping people she needed to see away from their offices.

She showed up on my doorstep stamping snow off her ladylike suede heels, completely unprepared for this freak April weather. I was equally unprepared for Felicity. She wore a no-nonsense wool suit, pearl stud earrings, barely a trace of makeup, and had her jet-black hair gathered into a barrette at the nape of her neck so that it fanned out over her shoulders like a whisk broom. Here was a woman, I thought, who gave every appearance of being well under fifty, yet probably wore a full slip.

What I didn't realize was that she was in costume. When you want to make movies about things like people who kiss snakes, it's easier to get the money to do it with if you resemble a missionary. If you were around Felicity long enough, though, even if she was in disguise, there were bound to be, well, certain indications of her true self. "I can't stand jogging," she might say, "because I always feel as though my *yoni* is going to fall out."

A few hours into Felicity's D.C. stay, I came down with a fierce case of flu. I insisted that I had all the Coke, juice, Lipton's tea, and crackers I needed to see myself through this, but Felicity tugged on a pair of my snow boots and marched out into the night to find a grocery store that was open. She nursed me through the next day with tea that she boiled from ginger root ("gets the blood flowing," she said), chicken broth made from scratch, and dry, seven-grain toast. While Felicity read my books and played my albums, I dozed off between fits of wonder at how the most familiar music sounds different, more special somehow, when someone else makes the selection.

By the time I drove Felicity to the airport, she had funded her film, arranged my spice rack into alphabetical order, and put me on a vitamin regimen designed to compensate for all the ill effects of cigarettes as well as premenstrual tension. She also analyzed my birth chart.

"No wonder," she said, poring over her tattered paperback ephemeris. "My sun is conjunct your moon, and vice versa."

I didn't know much about astrology, but I knew enough from being with Felicity to guess at what that meant. That meant I felt like family. And so when her recently divorced big brother came through D.C. two years later to check out the museums and galleries there, Felicity made sure he looked me up.

Felicity's husband, Lee, was also a painter and had a studio in the same building as Paul. While Felicity chopped the backbone out of a chicken meant to be dinner for the four of us tonight, I stood in her kitchen, looking at all the latest items she'd magnetized to her refrigerator door. Among them was a short newspaper story about a man in Cincinnati who had felt badly about losing his hair in chemotherapy. In the accompanying photograph, he grinned broadly, surrounded by the Little League team he coached, every member of which had shaved his own head in solidarity with him. Above that was a shot of Felicity, Lee, and Valerie, Lee's daughter from a previous marriage, all soaking in an outdoor hot spring. There was also a single paragraph of newsprint quoting one of this year's contenders for the Miss America title: "I would hate to see them get rid of the swimsuit competition. I have grown enormously from swimsuit."

"Miss South Carolina," I said. "Figures."

"I think it's great," Felicity said, laughing. "I kept it to remind me there are many paths to enlightenment."

"Not in South Carolina, there aren't." I turned to look at her. "Why did you say what you did about me making the effort with Paul?"

"I just wouldn't want to see you taking him for granted."

"Like his ex-wife?"

"Oh, you're *nothing* like Bonnie. She alienated everyone in the family—I've told you this before. She was incredibly narcissistic, jealous of anybody or anything that took Paul's attention away from her for a single second."

"But she was the one who had an affair."

"Like I said, a messed up girl. Speaking of family, how's the reunions article coming?"

"Lousy. I've pretty much run out of ideas."

"You're just preoccupied with Jody." Felicity spread out her spineless chicken and began stuffing the space between flesh and skin with a mixture of bread crumbs and pesto. She knew this was one of my favorite dishes; I was being pampered. "*I'm* married," Felicity said. "I'm practically your *only* married friend."

"That's not true!"

"Okay, your only *happily* married friend. Come on, I'll help you. Ask me some questions."

"Oh, all right." I threw myself into the chair across the table from her. "What have you learned about Lee from being with his family that's helped strengthen your marriage?"

"Aren't you going to take notes?"

"Let's see if it's worth it first."

"Okay. What have I learned about Lee from his family that's helped strengthen my marriage." Felicity considered the question for a moment. "Not much, actually."

"See? That's why I have to make things up. Nobody's life is this stupid."

"No, let me explain. Here, slice this lemon—thinly. Okay, the situation is that Lee's mother always figured it was her job to suss out what was going on with him and explain it to his father. She thinks that it's *my* job now, so she pumps me like crazy. Is he happy with his work? Are things okay financially? How does he feel about becoming a father again? I used to play along, but now I've started to say—very nicely, mind you—'Why in hell don't you ask Lee?' I thought maybe we'd rise to this new level of communication, but all that's happened is we have less to talk about." Felicity took the lemon slices from me and slid them in over the stuffing, then looked up brightly. "Well?"

"Well what?"

"Can you use it?"

"What's the point, Felicity? You have to have a point, and you have to tie the point into character, community, or continuity."

"The point. Let's see." Felicity frowned as she coated the chicken with lemon juice and olive oil, pointing the wings outward so that this bird now looked as though it had been flattened trying to escape. "Okay, the point is that in a patriarchal society, it's the women who are put in charge of tending emotions, and most men fail to discover their feelings because our culture—I mean, community—has yet to develop any collective rituals adequate to the task. Is that better?"

"No." I was laughing at her now.

"What's so funny?"

"Felicity, you sound like a cross between Margaret Mead and the Bagwhan's princess."

"Oh, that's good," Felicity said, lunging for a pencil and piece of paper. "If you won't take notes, I will."

I went back to the refrigerator to look for a bottle of wine. This was a grown-up refrigerator, not a little ice box like Paul's. Felicity considered Birkenstocks a New Age form of birth control and had zero interest in shearing sheep, but her mother and stepsisters had nothing on her when it came to nutrition. Live-culture yogurts sat in her refrigerator alongside organic fruit drinks and eggs from free-running hens. There were leftovers from a salmon that must have been caught in Alaska because Felicity considered the water there appreciably cleaner than that in Washington state. Herbal tinctures and vitamins were wedged into a shelf beside a bottle of sulfite-free white wine. I didn't see how anything bad could possibly happen to a baby born to parents who relied on this refrigerator for sustenance.

I must have stood staring into Felicity's refrigerator for a long time, because when she spoke to me again she used her most tolerant tone. "What are you doing?"

"I don't know. Therapy, I guess. I wonder why it is that looking at a full refrigerator always cheers me up."

"That's easy, Felicity said. It's because your ancestors were peddlers."

As the end of Jody's two weeks drew near, he was clearly well enough to leave, even Dr. Thrailkill said so. But his symptoms seemed to worsen whenever I raised the subject of buying a ticket for him to go home. I knew what I was supposed to do—I was supposed to give him no options. But didn't he already have few enough? And from what I could tell, the option he had exercised himself, to stay and work with Thrailkill, had legitimized his illness and given him insight into it at the same time.

Once while I visited with Jody in the common room, he might have been mistaken for a staff member. "I know you *thought* you saw rats," Jody told the Chanel-suited lady when she jumped screaming onto a chair. "But maybe you should let me take a look for you, because you know what I think? I think your brain is playing tricks on you."

After he coaxed her down from her chair, an ebony-skinned nurse passing by stopped to pat his cheek. "Nice job, baby," she said. "Nice job."

I related this incident to Nancy over the telephone, expecting her to marvel along with me at Jody's progress. Instead she said, "I wish I had a nickel for every time Jody's been told that his brain was playing tricks on him."

"The point is he got out of himself to help somebody else."

"That says just two things to me, Marsha—he's stabilized enough to come home, and he's manipulating you."

"I don't think so."

"Really?" She spoke dryly. "Why not?"

"He wasn't that way before."

"He wasn't schizophrenic before, was he Marsha?"

"I don't think it changes people *that* much. Anyway, how can he be manipulating me when half the time he doesn't even seem to know I'm there?"

"Listen, I've got a basic fact of life for you here, Marsha. When you make excuses for people, you end up with people in your life who you have to make excuses for."

Whom, I could have said, out of nothing but spite and hurt feelings. *For whom you have to make excuses*. Instead, I held my tongue and listened to the background noises on Nancy's end—water splashing and children shrieking.

Maybe being a mother had given Nancy wisdom I did not possess. Anyway, who was I, absent all these years, to question her assessments of Jody, or how she might have acquired them? It sounded as if Nancy must be speaking to me from an outdoor phone, and I guessed that she was enough of a traditionalist to have a swimming pool in the backyard of her house, but probably not so much of one to have it inscribed with Roman numerals representing the number of diseased gums her husband treated in order to pay for it.

When I was with Paul now, I started noticing signs.

- I stopped minding how hard he bit my earlobes.
- When he fashioned a pair of ridiculous-looking pasties for me out of two leaden wine bottle collars, I took note of how perfectly he had gauged the size of my nipples and, instead of laughing, cried.
- For three mornings straight, *I* made the coffee.
- I began marveling at the pleasure I took inhaling the scent of freshly shaved cedar around the ear where he always parked his pencil and at the color of his shirts, so many of which incorporated at least one of the subtractive primaries.

This was how I began to know I would be leaving soon. One morning as we took a bath together in Paul's old clawfoot tub, he decided to shave my legs for me, working with my foot against his chest then over his shoulder, cutting tracks through lather with such care and precision that he reached all the places I usually missed without once drawing blood. After Paul got out of the tub to dry himself, I swiveled around to face the nearest wall, which

Paul had painted Pepto-Bismol pink. Stuck onto the wall with push pins was a Rand McNally map of the United States, encased in plastic and nearly as wide as the tub was long. With all the grace that I could manage, I raised one of my legs, made a ballerina's foot, stabbed Seattle with my big toe, then swooped it across and down the country, trailing off into the Atlantic. When you feel yourself falling, might as well dive. Might as well point your toes.

Chapter 10

New York, 1971

INSTEAD OF going to camp this summer, which at fifteen I think I'm too old for anyway, I go to New York so that I can learn a routine to perform in the Miss Teenage Sparta pageant, an event that Patsy Chalmers encourages all her best students to enter. Patsy is staying at the Americana Hotel with her daughter Boo-Boo—which is short for Bouray, another child named for a misspelled French dance step—who got bleeding blisters on the first day of class and refused to come back. They share a room with Cynthia Carter, who wouldn't dream of missing class no matter how many blisters she had. Cynthia won first runner-up in last year's pageant with a tap dance that Ron LaFarge, our teacher on Eighth Avenue, choreographed for her to Lester Lanin's orchestral arrangement of "Cabaret."

Cynthia is such a pro that even in recitals she performs with Vaseline on her teeth so her lips won't get stuck when she smiles. Her mother is so set on Cynthia having a long career in pageantry that she had a mirrored studio built in their basement and hired a seamstress to make a Cynthia-sized duplicate of the evening gown worn in competition by the current Miss America. Although Cynthia Carter's mother didn't come here with her and mine did, I feel pretty sure that this has nothing to do with my mother's aspirations for me as a beauty queen. She mainly wants to spend a week in New York, like Aunt Eileen and Jody.

I awaken every morning to the wheezing sounds of a window air conditioner and Jody's adenoidal breathing. We are staying at the apartment that Uncle Lud and Aunt Francine rent in an old hotel on Central Park West, the place they use when Uncle Lud comes to town on business. My mother and Aunt Eileen are in the bedroom, I have a sofa bed in the living room, and Jody is on a cot in the adjacent dining room.

One of the hotel bellboys is a midget who, according to my mother, used to be famous in the forties for paging Phillip Morris in cigarette commercials. Like the bellboy, most of the people living here have seen better days. The building's not in such great shape, either. The faucets run rusty water, the pipes screech, and even the hallways smell decrepit, which must be why Aunt Francine has seeded the apartment with little bags of cedar and sachet.

I creep out of bed before my travel alarm goes off, dreading the prospect of spending another long day in the steamy little studio on Eighth Avenue, and slip through the bedroom to get into the bathroom. The mothers are sleeping in the same queen-size bed, Aunt Eileen on her back with one arm flung out to the side and a butterfly-shaped piece of pink adhesive between her eyes that is supposed to smooth out frown lines, and my mother curled into a ball, a pillow wrapped around her head. One of my mother's palette-knifed cityscapes hangs on the wall beside the bed, a nighttime scene in shades of blue and white.

"Have fun, Sister," Aunt Eileen murmurs when I emerge from the bathroom wearing a flowered shift over my leotard and black fishnet tights.

Jody joins me for breakfast downstairs at the coffee shop counter and while we eat, he simulates the question-and-answer portion of the pageant. "Tell us, Marsha," he says, using his orange juice glass as a microphone and talking like a redneck, "if you had a choice, who would you rather be—Florence Nightingale or Janis Joplin? Oh, I see by your expression you consider that a stupid question. Judges, take note. We got us a little smart-ass here. Okay, here's Marsha's *real* question, folks. In the unlikely event that you're selected as our very first He-brew Miss Teenage Prisspot—"

"I'm not listening to you," I tell him. I'm eating bacon and eggs this morning, deviating from my usual half-muffin and not caring if Ron LaFarge later draws attention to my bulging stomach with the criticism he uses only on girls like me, who hide from him in the back row: "I can see your breakfast!"

Jody speaks into his orange juice glass even more loudly. "The question is," he says, "in light of your religious background, would you be able to show up in your crown at a Kiwanis barbecue and devour flesh of the pig?"

I pick up a piece of bacon and wave it in his face before biting into it.

"Try to remember, sugar," he says, "that what we're after here is a *verbal* response. Moving right along, then, do you ever, when you're all alone, tap dance in the nude?"

The elderly woman sitting beside Jody stares at him with horrified interest. Touching his arm lightly, she says, "Where do you come from, darling?" Her accent is German, maybe Yiddish, I can't tell. But I suspect her "darling" has to do somehow with the familiarity of Jody's looks, *our* looks.

Jody is so cracked up by himself that he doesn't hear the woman's question. "Ma'am?" he says, turning to face her.

She looks at him uncomprehendingly. "Excuse me?"

"She wants to know where you live," I prompt Jody.

"I'm from South Carolina," he tells her, his drawl normal now. "We both are."

"South Carolina?"

"Sparta, South Carolina, yes ma'am."

"My God," she murmurs, and goes back to her cereal.

While I finish eating, Jody stares out the window, fascinated by the obviously braless breasts of so many passing young women—another item on his growing list of things that are better here than back home.

Jody had spent most of his time on the plane studying a subway map, already anxious to escape our company and strike out on his own. He worked for a month earlier this summer unloading trucks at Uncle Lud's factory, which gave him the means to do as he pleased while I danced and the mothers amused themselves at stores and museums. Almost since the moment we landed, Jody has been accomplishing things here that I don't have the first notion how to accomplish myself—eating at an automat, shopping at secondhand record stores, going to movies I've never heard of in the middle of the day. Yesterday he met up with a friend from camp and went to a concert in New Jersey given by a couple of groups I've never heard of, either.

Before Jody sets off every day carrying the Army surplus knapsack that he keeps his maps and camera in, Aunt Eileen grills him to make sure he knows how to get wherever he's going and what to do if any problems arise. There aren't any problems—at least, none that he tells us about. Jody gives every indication of having a wonderful time, which is something that I might have resented, given my disappointment with this trip, if Jody were happier at home.

Jody's popularity mysteriously flickered and died by the time we left Christ Church a year early for high school. It seemed that as I grew into my body, Jody began jumping out of his, restlessly impatient with what everybody else seemed to think was important—sports, school spirit, sororities, fraternities. For his birthday in May, Jody asked his parents to finance a trip to Washington so he could demonstrate against the war. Nobody but Jody saw any coolness at all in the prospect of being tear-gassed and arrested. Scott Rammage had gone off to boarding school, Betty Jo Lowe had taken up with a group of hard-drinking older boys, and I was now positioned close enough to the center of things that Jody turning all sideways and moody puzzled me as much as anybody else.

It didn't help that Jody played bass with a band made up of other outcasts who like the same kind of music that he does, a band that practices endlessly but has a repertoire so obscure—by Spartan standards, anyway—that they can't even find free gigs. Jody asked Marie Gilbert to sing with them at Confederate Capers, the school talent show, but she hooked up instead with a group that wanted to play one of the top forty soul songs she did so well. At least Jody's band appreciated his humor. They were the only ones laughing at the pep rally when Jody decided to ridicule the event by running out onto the field and through the goal posts while he waved his arms and rebel-yelled like a maniac.

"That is *not* the right spirit," barked the amplified voice of the Wade Hampton Generals Pep Club president, a girl who considered herself an authority on all matters of spirit because her father was musical director for Bishop Fulmer's evangelical crusades. "Let's everybody try and cheer *together.*"

Even my father, who always seemed to find Jody a far more agreeable creature than me, thinks he's irritating. Compared to the Lurreys, my father is a strict disciplinarian with a low boiling point. He's decided that Uncle Sol and Aunt Eileen indulge Jody—with the too-long hair, with the guitar, with letting him smoke at will (Flip and I sneak all our cigarettes), with the car they gave him even though at fifteen he can only drive by law from dawn to dusk. But Jody's worst sin by far in our house is his open bewilderment at my brother Flip's decision to attend the Citadel.

"Are you *making* Flip go there?" Jody asked my father one Sunday night at the New China restaurant, something in his tone suggesting that in my father's case, coercion seemed a perfectly reasonable explanation.

"Don't be ridiculous," my father harrumphed, "this is Flip's decision."

"Yes, I like boys in uniform," Flip said in an effeminate voice. Then, with exaggerated gruffness, "Did you know it was a *cadet* who fired the first shot on Fort Sumter?"

"What about *this* war?" Jody insisted, but Aunt Eileen shushed him just as my mother's eyes began to moisten. Flip gave Jody a smug smile. "Anybody can get a degree from a civilian school."

"That war will be over by the time Flip graduates," Uncle Sol said to deflate the tension. "Do you think that if we sent Jody to the Citadel, he'd learn how to make his bed?"

Flip and Nancy are working for Uncle Sol this summer, Flip rolling out long sheets of cotton for the panty pattern-cutters and Nancy bored out of her mind filing bills of lading in the office. Soon, because Aunt Eileen said so, Nancy would have to stop seeing Mike Upchurch and only go out with the Jewish boys she was expected to meet through the Jewish college sorority she was expected to join. Aunt Eileen said Mike reminded her of a good-looking truck driver, the kind who might toot his horn and wink at you on the highway. Time and distance were supposed to make Nancy forget how well he could kiss and dance, to make her see there were other ways of kissing and dancing.

Flip is seeing Trisha Williams, a Catholic girl who already subscribes to *Bride* magazine. Flip is not expected to meet any Jewish girls in Charleston, but he's not expected to get married any time soon, either. Sometimes Trisha sits on our front porch clocking Flip while he runs around the neighborhood wearing five-pound ankle weights, an exercise that, like Trisha herself, is supposed to help him survive his freshman year. Trisha plans on going to Charleston for all the parades and drunken parties out on Folly Pier, where she says cadets routinely drop to the floor in puddles of spilt liquor to impersonate dying cockroaches.

These days, the reversal of roles between Jody and me is so apparent that Aunt Eileen seems strangely grateful that I spend any time at all with him. During our freshman year in high school, the closest he ever came to a date was when he went to the library with Marie and me to read the Sunday *New York Times*. Our English teacher, Mr. Clayton, required us to write weekly essays based somehow on something in the Arts and Leisure section.

"This is stupid," Jody would grumble, but he had no trouble coming up with topics, easily spinning two-page opinions on everything from onstage nudity—something he, for one, would like to see—to the lack of a progressive FM rock station in Sparta. He called one of his essays "Psychedelic Shag," although it wasn't exactly an essay; it was his own set of lyrics to the tune of "Psychedelic Shack," and he wrote it to make fun of beach music, the slow, even-beated, usually black songs that people around Sparta have been doing the shag to for years.

Mr. Clayton, being from Wisconsin, didn't know about the shag. But he found Jody's lyrics so amusing that he brought in a record player, put on a song by James and Bobby Purify, and had Marie demonstrate the shag with Jody, who had learned how to do it from Nancy. It seemed strange that Jody would ridicule the shag and then dance it so well, piloting Marie around Mr. Clayton's desk with a soft, sexy shuffle. Fraternity boys in alligator belts and Gant shirts danced like this, not boys like Jody, who wore nothing but jeans and Kmart pocket-tees.

Wiley Putnam, the drummer in Jody's band, has a crush on me, but even though I like Wiley, I've been asked out by enough certifiably cool boys to consider a real date with someone like him an exercise in self-sabotage. Marie says Jody and Wiley are immature, which doesn't have so much to do with their actual behavior as the fact that Marie doesn't want them seen visiting us in her mother's Pontiac at Bybee's. They are especially not welcome on weekend afternoons, when we go to Bybee's with our hair in rollers to indicate that we have dates that night whether we do or not.

My decision to enter the Miss Teenage Sparta pageant and tap dance to the accompaniment of a James Bond movie theme falls much more easily in line with what everybody else enjoys than, say, Jody's cockney-accented rendition of "Your Baby Has Gone Down the Plug Hole." Until we came to New York, though, I never thought that Jody might be actively on his way to a bigger world, one in which he would be far more at home than me.

After we finish breakfast, Jody walks me to class, a protective ritual the mothers insist upon. As we pass Lincoln Center and draw closer to the studio, I see other dancers on their way to Ron LaFarge's classes—taut-bodied girls who live here all the time, girls who take ballet and modern dance to be well-rounded and amaze me with how quickly they learn complicated steps. They think pageants are silly, too. They're going to perform in Broadway shows; some, in fact, already have. Looking at them this morning makes me tired. Even worse, it makes me cry.

"Jesus, Marsha," Jody says when he notices. "I thought you *liked* this."

Almost as if to prove how much I don't, I lurch over to a nearby trash can and throw up. Jody goes to a deli across the street and returns with a bottle of Coca-Cola, Aunt Eileen's remedy for any and all stomach upsets. "Graceful barfing, Marsha," Jody says. "Maybe that's what your talent in the pageant ought to be."

"Stop it," I tell him, starting to cry again.

"Hey," he says, "I meant it. You were real ladylike, hardly anybody even noticed. Drink the Coke. Are you okay?"

Since I'm not the least bit woozy, losing breakfast feels like losing something I hadn't really needed. Still, enough of the real dancers witnessed my performance to make the prospect of class with them today more impossible than ever. "It was just the orange juice," I lie to Jody. "Drinking orange juice on a hot day makes me sick sometimes."

"Are you going to be sick again?"

"No, but I'm not going to be dancing, either."

I refuse his offer to walk me back to the hotel—this is something I do on my own every day—and Jody heads off for the subway. "Wait a minute," I call after him. "I'm coming with you."

Jody stops, looking both pleased and distressed. "You'll have to keep up," he warns. "You'll have to keep up with me and not complain. I don't want to be dragging around somebody who's not having any fun."

He waits outside while I run upstairs to the studio dressing room to shed my leotard and mesh tights and stuff them into my bag, then run back down again feeling weightless.

I have no trouble keeping up with Jody that morning because after our subway ride downtown, we do nothing but stand in a long line with other tourists. Acrobats turn flips down the promenade alongside us, but our view of them is blocked so that we catch only occasional glimpses of body parts overhead. To help the time pass, I take off my sandals and strap on my tap shoes to perform the James Bond dance in a space of less than one square foot, flicking my wrists to indicate turns and sweeping arm movements.

"Pretty goofy," Jody says, but I'm not nearly so goofy as the man we saw over by the refreshment stand, the one who simultaneously plays a neckpiece harmonica, an accordion strapped to his chest, and cymbals tied to his knees. Besides, it's a lot more fun doing the dance goofy down here, at the tip of a place so dense I can barely comprehend it as an island, than serious up there, where it was supposed to really matter, with twenty other sweaty girls all striving for stage presence.

We're by the water now, but that only seems to make the air more humid. Jody takes off his T-shirt and mops the back of his neck with it. Then, without warning, the people behind us begin moving forward at the same moment as the people ahead of us, bearing us along till the concrete beneath our feet changes to a wooden gangplank and we're on board the boat that will take us out to the statue. Jody grabs my hand for purely practical reasons, so we won't be separated.

"She looks kind of dingy, doesn't she?" Jody says after we reach Liberty Island and get a closer look at the statue.

"Yeah, that's a shame, they should take better care of her."

We find the poem at the base, the one written by the Jewish woman whom we learned about years ago in Sunday school, and Jody asks another tourist to take a picture of us standing near it. Jody's determined to climb to the top. "You don't have to come," he says, "you can wait for me down here." But I'm determined to share every bit of this with him, and even though the stairway is so crowded that it takes us two hours to reach the crown, I don't even think about complaining. Instead, I think how right it is we can't hurry through this place that used to take people so long to reach.

On the ride back across the harbor, I hold Jody's hand for reasons that aren't practical at all. I do it because we are taking the same trip that relatives we barely remember or never knew once did, and our boat feels full of ghosts instead of tourists. I do it because coming out here had been his idea, something that would never have occurred to the mothers. But most of all, I'm holding his hand because at this moment, he hardly seems separate from me at all.

On Uncle Lud's recommendation, we all go to a Polynesian restaurant that night for dinner. While we wait for our food, the mothers order drinks called Hurricanes, served in big bowled glasses with fruit and paper umbrellas hanging over the sides. After Aunt Eileen has enough of hers not to mind, Jody sips from her glass.

Pretty soon, my mother's accent is as thick as Aunt Eileen's, a change from her usual way of speaking that irritates me. "You only talk like that when you're drinking," I tell her.

"That's why it doesn't matter if I drink," Jody says, taking another swallow. "I talk like that all the time."

"Maybe *I* only talk like that when I'm relaxed," my mother says, narrowing her eyes at me. Then, to Aunt Eileen, "You'd think I was a drunk."

Aunt Eileen reaches over to flip my hair behind my shoulders. "It's such a pleasure to sit across from you in a restaurant and actually be able to see your faces. I remember when we couldn't go out to dinner without you two sticking your noses into books." Then she gets back around to my bad manners. "We're just having fun, Sister. I think you must be cranky from all that dancing."

"You can tell from her eyes," my mother nods. "Circles down to her knees."

"I didn't dance today," I say, hoping to startle them.

My mother looks suspicious, but hardly startled. Too relaxed, I guess. "But you said your feet hurt."

"From walking all the way uptown with Jody after we saw the Statue of Liberty."

As Aunt Eileen frowns between Jody and me, sabotaging the work of her butterfly adhesives, my mother starts laughing. "What do you think I ought to do, Eileen? Spank her?"

Aunt Eileen cracks a lopsided grin. "Cynthia Carter's mother would."

"So would Uncle Daniel," Jody offers.

"I think that when Daniel's mother was pregnant," says Aunt Eileen, who makes a practice of treating my father as a humorous figure, "she must have been frightened by a policeman."

"Or a tax collector," my mother says, amusing herself so much that she swallows a mouthful of Hurricane the wrong way. Once she recovers, she leans in closer to Aunt Eileen and speaks as if Jody and I aren't there. "Last month I took out a loan to buy frames for my show, and do you know what Thad Mosely told me before I left the bank? He said, 'Let's be discreet, Joyce. I'd rather Daniel found out we were having an affair than that I loaned you money.' "

When the mothers stop giggling, mine seems surprised to realize that Jody and I have not only been listening, but are offended.

"It was just a *joke*," my mother tells us. "Don't take everything so seriously."

"Might as well ask the sun not to shine," Aunt Eileen says as she finishes her Hurricane and flags down our waiter to order another round.

"Men are little boys," my mother says, "they have to be handled." Then she gives Jody a tipsy smile. "What *you* have to remember, sweetheart, is that this is a rule to which you have every right to become an exception."

"He already is," Aunt Eileen says with a fond, misty look in her eyes. "So is Sol, thank God."

After dinner we stand beneath the restaurant canopy in a futile effort to dodge a downpour that comes at us from every angle, driven by the wind and repelled by glass and concrete. My mother runs to the curb and gets soaked to the skin trying to hail a taxi. "See what happens," Aunt Eileen calls out to her, "when you drink Hurricanes?"

My mother hollers back, "Is this what they mean by three sheets to the wind?" They'd each had at least that many drinks by now.

My mother leads us back inside the restaurant and speaks to the owner, a dark-complected man who doesn't look the least bit Polynesian. After she tells him that Uncle Lud sent us and enthuses over our dinner, she asks if he might be able to recommend a reliable taxi company to take us uptown. This is New York, I think, squirming. Why would the owner care about Uncle Lud? Besides, there are pay phones in clear view, right outside the restrooms, and how hard is it to look up Yellow Cab?

But my mother doesn't seem to think there's any reason why she shouldn't behave like a woman who might have a limousine waiting outside for her at this very moment had she only known about the storm. She shivers, as if the restaurant owner can't notice she's wet from how her dress clings.

Aunt Eileen looks almost as uncomfortable as I feel. In this department, my mother's powers are clearly superior to hers. Aunt Eileen clutches her own rain-splattered seersucker jacket around her body, as though hoping my mother will emulate her.

The owner, now on a first-name basis with my mother, has us wait in his office. When he returns, he says that his driver can take us to our hotel after he drops off the payroll at the restaurant's East Side branch. Outside, a white Lincoln Continental is waiting—not quite a limousine, but still, it seems that my mother has manifested the car just by pretending her right to it.

My mother gets into the front seat with the uniformed driver while the rest of us pile into the back. I sit directly behind the driver. Looking into the rearview mirror, I see that he has Oriental eyes. As the Lincoln speeds out into traffic, my mother thanks him for going out of his way to drop us off.

"I take money," the driver says, patting the canvas bag on the seat between them as he swerves to pass a car. "*Beaucoups d'argent.*" He drives one-armed, his right hand resting awkwardly on his waist.

"Then you'd best be careful," Aunt Eileen says, her foot braced against the front seat as though applying imaginary brakes. "Sir? The windows are fogged. Can you see? I can't. Maybe you should turn the defroster on."

"I take money," the driver repeats.

"And we'll be very happy to give you more for a nice safe ride," Aunt Eileen says. When the driver slows down, she turns to Jody and me, feeling her Hurricanes again. "That man in the restaurant is Jewish, you know, and he was responding to southern charm. You see, it's just like I always say—we've got the best of both worlds."

Jody rolls his eyes and leans forward to speak to the driver. "Where do you come from?" No answer. Jody asks the question again in bad high school French.

"Vietnam," the driver says. "I come from Vietnam."

"Which one? *Nord ou sud?*"

"South."

"We're from the South ourselves," my mother interjects, clearly nervous. "Although my daughter and I were both born in Chicago."

At the next stoplight, the driver grins at my mother and pats his waist. "I carry gun," he says.

Jody leans over farther. "Hey, can I see it?"

"Never mind that," Aunt Eileen says, pulling Jody back by the shoulder as the driver reaches beneath his jacket to remove a pistol from his waistband. With the nose pointed skyward, he holds it up for inspection.

"Thank God," Aunt Eileen hisses after the driver finally puts the pistol down on his lap. When we come to a stop in front of the East Side restaurant, he jams the pistol back into his pants and sprints through the rain with the money, leaving the engine running. While he's gone, my mother warns us not to make any sudden movements for the rest of the trip.

"I wish his English was better," Jody mumbles. "I wonder how he got out." After that, nobody says anything until we pull up in front of our hotel. When we get upstairs, my mother goes to bed without removing her makeup and Aunt Eileen totters over to the dining room table to write the Polynesian restaurant owner a thank-you note.

The next morning, while the mothers sleep off their Hurricanes, Jody and I go downstairs for breakfast and divide up the *Times* like an old married couple, Jody keeping the front-page section for himself. I can hardly believe it when I find a story with a South Carolina dateline and a headline that says, "Doesn't Anybody Want to Praise Jesus Anymore?" Among those interviewed is Bishop Fulmer, who says it's difficult to get people to go to church when they can get quality entertainment at home on their television screens.

But Jody doesn't want to hear about Bishop, even though this is the same Bishop who taught us how to swim, the one whose televised sermonettes we used to catch on cartoonless Sunday mornings.

Jody has found a more interesting article on the front page, and he won't talk to me until he's read it all the way through and I have, too.

The story is about a fifteen-year-old Australian boy named Richard who managed to fly first-class all the way from Sydney to Paris with only a few pieces of change in his pocket. He got through customs by pretending to be part of a French family. The plane made stops in Singapore, Bangkok, Colombo, and Athens. Richard saw three movies, ate poached salmon, and when he finally got caught in Paris, he had the nerve to say, "They're real dumb, those airport cops. And the airline people are idiots, too."

"You know what the coolest thing about this is?" Jody asks.

"His parents can't afford to buy him a return ticket, so he'll get to stay in Paris for a while?"

"That's not the coolest thing. The coolest thing is that he'd never been to Paris before in his life, but he knew that was where he belonged."

A photograph accompanying the story shows Richard standing on a Parisian street, grinning while he bites the top off a stick of bread. "I'm happy here," the caption says. "It's the place I feel best. Australia is Paris when it was twenty years old."

For the next hour, we take turns making up the story of Richard's life. I give him a French mother who had to flee Paris when the Nazis came because she was Jewish, and spoke to Richard only in her native tongue. Jody has him getting expelled from high school on purpose because he cut classes, hitchhiking to whatever Australian city might be showing the French films that Jody has been seeing here in New York. We decide that one reason he ran away was his father, who wanted Richard to work in a factory until he was old enough to join the army and go to Vietnam, which might have appealed to Richard if the French still ran things there but they didn't. Instead, Richard will finish high school in Paris, where he'll live with some fond forgotten relative, and fall in love with a Vietnamese girl— this is Jody's invention—who grew up speaking French, too. Neither one of us has the heart to send Richard back to Australia, but we agree that whatever happens to him, he'll be all right because he knows where he's happiest.

Jody tears the article about Richard out of the paper and puts it into his wallet. After we get home, he periodically checks the library's *New York Times* index, looking for further news of Richard that he never finds.

Chapter 11

Seattle

ONCE I started talking to a travel agent, it became clear that there were ways of going to South Carolina by which Jody and I could avoid Charlotte and Atlanta entirely. We could, for instance, change planes in the other Washington, a plan that I found preferable because my experience was that changing planes in the South—the *real* South, which doesn't include the Maryland or Virginia airports that service D.C.—was a lot like trying to avoid stepping in dog shit. There were always connections that couldn't be made, bags that didn't arrive, or nights that had to be spent in airport motels, with the airline picking up the tab only if you were willing to make enough of an insistent, un–southern lady-like scene.

When I went downtown to pick up our tickets, I felt a kind of exhilaration from doing things differently than the way Eileen had planned, the way that required nothing more of me than taking Jody to the airport. But then I wondered if I wasn't just bribing Jody, hustling him out of my life while creating the illusion of giving him a piece of it—a small piece, to be sure, certainly smaller than what I felt obliged to give while he was in the hospital, but large enough to coax him on board an airplane.

"Suit yourself," Paul had said. Nancy said the same thing, but she sounded relieved around the edges, not angry like Paul.

My mother responded to the news of my arrival as if Jody didn't have much to do with it. "We're just thrilled that you're coming," Joyce said. "It's been almost two years since we've seen you here!"

Dr. Thrailkill had called South Carolina to set up a course of treatment for Jody with his regular psychiatrist, who would be administering the next shot. "He'd never even heard of the stuff," Thrailkill marveled, shaking his head. Then, as though to atone for disparaging a fellow professional in my presence: "I understand that in the last few years, there's been great progress down there with services for the mentally ill. Around the time when Jody was first diagnosed, South Carolina was at the bottom of the list, just above Mississippi." Almost the exact words my mother used years ago, describing South Carolina's public school system.

As Thrailkill had predicted, Jody felt better than he did on haloperidol. Not only did his South Carolina records indicate this, but he said so himself. Still, he was altered. Now he often seemed like an agreeably self-absorbed, chain-smoking adolescent, only several years beyond the stage where he might have been happy to have the stewardess pin wings onto his shirt.

Jody sat with Paul and me near the gate for our plane, smoking what I kept reminding him would be his last few cigarettes until we were airborne. "Gotta play by their rules on the plane," I said. And, even more stupidly, "Smoke your brains out while you can." I knew I could live without it, but being with Jody, I felt grateful that smoking sections still existed on domestic flights. Jody couldn't possibly endure five consecutive smokeless hours, not without ingesting more drugs than he already had.

At Jody's feet were his sleeping bag, his duffel bag, and his kites, packed into a fat cardboard tube. On his lap sat the Havana cigar box that Paul had fashioned into a min-iature art kit. Inside the box were a dozen sheets of paper, two charcoal pencils, a sharpener for the pencils, a package of oil sticks, and a black-and-white postcard that showed Pablo Picasso at a dining room table, pretending that the baguettes spread out before him were his out-sized fingers. I had doubts about the Picasso postcard, but when Jody saw it, he said only two words: "Optical delusion."

If he were more attuned to subtleties, Jody might have been trying to distract Paul and me from the distress that had erupted last night and still hung thickly between us. The worst thing about Paul's apartment, I had discovered, was that there was nowhere to go to be alone.

"Mashie," Jody said in the airport, tapping my shoulder. "I got to go check out them urinal cakes." He sounded as though he was imitating somebody else, somebody who was black, and I had no idea what he was talking about.

"He has to pee," Paul explained, laughing.

"Yep," Jody said, "got to bleed my lizard," still using this other voice, but not laughing himself.

"Wonder who *that* was," Paul said after Jody left, and I could tell he wondered if Jody was being racist.

Except for a brief trip to Florida, Paul had spent little time in the South and comprehended racism there in mon-olithic terms. Whenever I tried drawing distinctions for him, he'd say, "All you're talking about is manners." He was right, but so was I.

Once when Paul and I were visiting New York, a tall black man inadvertently stepped on Paul's foot in a crowded subway car, then apologized so elaborately that we both looked up to grin at him. "Wouldn't you know it," the man said, "my last night in New York City and I finally meet some friendly white people." He told us about how he hated the way everybody here, black *and* white, looked at him like he was either crazy or about to rob them if he smiled or said hello. Paul asked where he came from, and he said, "I'm from Emporia, Virginia, where people know how to treat each other, and I can't wait to get back." When Paul cut his eyes at me, I gave him a knowing look.

But now that I was going South myself, such distinctions seemed useless. I did not feel as though I were headed into a situation where people treated each other especially well; I could wait a long time to get back. When I admitted as much last night to Paul, he looked exasperated and said, "I've never heard you have such a hard time agreeing with yourself."

My only luggage today was my laptop computer and a carry-on shoulder bag, which was supposed to help us pretend that I wouldn't be gone for long. My father had offered to pay my fare, as he always did when I came to South Carolina, but I refused and bought a short-notice, full-fare ticket with an open-ended return. Even though I had no idea where my next paycheck was coming from, this time my father's offer made my own condition seem too much akin to Jody's for me to consider accepting it.

I remembered my father once telling Flip and me, "The reason I let you two stick around is that your assets outweigh your liabilities." He had been in high spirits at the time, teasing his children. But even so, his humor seemed cautionary. As I watched Jody wander past our gate and then double back, realizing his mistake, it occurred to me that my father must consider Jody roughly equivalent to a tragically lopsided balance sheet.

"I feel awful," Paul said.

"No you don't." I hugged him as though proving my point, but he didn't smile and it was hard to ignore that this was the first of our airport goodbyes without any tear-salted kisses. Still, I couldn't bring myself to make any guarantees. "Look at it this way, buster," I said. "By the time you see me again, you won't be mad anymore."

"Don't be too sure. I don't much like counting on someone who lets me down."

"I'm not your ex-wife. What are you scared of?"

"That you'll get down there and decide as long as you're on the East Coast, you might as well stay to drum up some more work. You'll get all anxious about this reunion story falling through and going into debt to take this trip with Jody, and the summer will end with us exactly where we were to begin with—still dating. I think that's exactly where you want us to stay."

"You know, of course, that this is more about Jody than anybody else."

"Sure, I know. I'm not so sure you do, is the problem. What's he got on you?"

In our traveling back and forth to each other, Paul and I had developed the habit of requesting seats in the first row behind first class—bulkhead aisle. There were other advantages to this location besides the extra leg room. Meal service began at the front of the plane, so you never got stuck with Salisbury steak because they had run out of chicken, and you didn't have to wait as long after landing to get off and breathe real air. If you wanted to smoke, you could slip off to the rear, find an empty seat, and have a cigarette with your wine. There were almost always empty seats in the rear, and you didn't have to spend the whole flight breathing other people's smoke. Today, however, Jody and I would be sitting in the rear, and I already resented the people up front who'd be slipping back for a cigarette.

I had waited to board until the last possible minute, hoping for a real moment of sweetness with Paul that never came, so the aisles were clear by the time Jody and I made our way back to a middle row with five seats. I moved to the center, leaving an empty seat between myself and the woman sitting to my left, and Jody took the remaining aisle seat, leaving another empty seat between us.

The woman to my left looked to be my age, with an angular, strong-jawed face and a haircut that might have been butch if it weren't for how it dipped into a thick wave over one eye. She was thumbing through the airline magazine when she said to no one, "Oh good, I've been wanting to see this movie." She had one of her bags on the seat between us, and I saw from its tag that her name was Janice.

I decided that Janice not only traveled by herself fairly often, but lived alone, too. I could easily imagine her planning a solitary evening, as I often did, around what television show she might be willing to watch with dinner, what book she'd read afterward, and at what point she might take a bath. Since an evening like this seemed impossible for me now, I found myself actively yearning for what I presumed to be the familiarity of Janice's life.

Jody was already plugged into the Walkman. He opened the cigar box and took out a piece of paper, staring at it for a while before choosing a pencil over the oil sticks. When he noticed me watching, he turned in my direction. "I took art lessons at the museum," Jody said, loud enough to hear himself over the music.

I reached into Jody's breast pocket and turned down the music, feeling as though I had flipped a switch in his brain that would modulate his voice. "Did you enjoy the class?"

"We got to draw a naked lady," he said with a nod. "We couldn't draw a man, though. A naked man was against the rules."

"I guess that's not surprising. Especially down there."

"I was supposed to learn how to draw down there, though."

I felt Thrailkill's friendly, amused-but-not-condescending smile come over my face. "I meant that part of the country, Jody."

"Right. That's all I want to say now, so I'm going to turn the music back up."

"Are the voices bothering you?"

"Mostly I just want to be alone."

"Okay, then."

A few people seated in our vicinity were looking at Jody now, none so intently as Janice.

Jody bent over his paper and began drawing in the upper right-hand corner. It took a long time for his hand to move down far enough along the paper's edge for me to see what he was doing, and even then, it didn't appear to be much more than a jagged line, a series of painstakingly delineated niches, hooks, and hollows.

Jody looked particularly nice today—handsome, even. I had taken him to Kimmie, the Japanese woman who cut Paul's hair. She left Jody's long enough to skim his collar in the back, but shaped it into a flattering slant around his face. His eyes were clear, his cheeks patched with color, and he drew with such concentration that it seemed plain he didn't really need me here to keep him calm. I was the one who needed calming.

When the stewardess came by with beverages after take-off, I got two miniature bottles of wine. I fished around in my bag for a yoga magazine—a magazine I could never imagine myself writing for, which was one of the reasons I bought it when I went to the health food store to stock up on vitamins.

Health food stores were almost as good as full refrigerators when it came to imparting a sense of well-being. They all smelled the same, a blend of dried beans, herb teas, and aromatic oils. It didn't diminish their effectiveness for me one bit that I always walked in carrying cigarettes, or that I didn't plan on giving up red meat any time soon. I didn't practice yoga, either. But what if holding your body in a certain pose every day for a certain amount of time could change your life? I didn't want to rule out anything so simple.

Once in a while, I stole a look at Jody. When he reached the bottom right-hand corner of his paper, he turned it sideways and curved his line without making a break in it. He worked at a rate of about one cigarette for every six inches. By the time the stewardess laid down our trays of Salisbury steak, Jody's line went all the way around the paper like an agitated frame.

The vitamins I bought were a month's worth of individually wrapped packets that were supposed to be specifically designed for women under stress. I tore open a packet with my teeth and gulped the vitamins down with wine, which seemed an appropriate way to take them.

After I finished eating, I had a cup of coffee and my first cigarette of the day, hoping the wine and the vitamins might balance out the caffeine and smoke. I knew I should give up one or two of these habits sooner or later. "You don't want to get too pure," Paul once told me. But then he just hated the idea of turning into one of those people who define themselves by everything they *don't* do.

Jody had finally grown tired of my "American Tunes" tape. Working on his drawing again, he played one that I had labeled "Songs That Make Me Cry."

"Sounds like nice music," Janice said, nodding at Jody.

"He likes it loud," I apologized.

"That's okay, I'm a big Rickie Lee Jones fan."

Some of the songs that make me cry were actually sad, but most seemed to have been written to cheer up sad people, filled with search-your-heart, love-will-find-a-way kind of lyrics. The actual words weren't so important, though, as their tone. Even an infant with no language would find this stuff comforting, like being submerged in warm, lapping liquid.

When the stewardess came around with earphones for the in-flight movie, Janice reached over me to pass her money. "I'm fixin' to run out of headsets," the stewardess told her, "but there'll be someone coming down your aisle in just a minute. You girls just flag her down." Everything about the stewardess was pert and flippy as her north Georgia accent.

"How about you, sir?" the stewardess asked Jody, sitting at her elbow. "I'll be happy to take *your* money."

Jody, who couldn't hear her, didn't respond. "He doesn't like movies," I said, and before she moved on, the stewardess, to whom Jody must have seemed perfectly ordinary, gave me one of those "Men, what are you gonna do" looks that women seem to share so often.

"Are you going to watch?" my neighbor asked me.

"Nah," I said. "I'll catch it on video."

I wondered if Jody had a VCR at home, or if he was cut off from the rental movies that were everywhere now. Even Betty's Bait and Coffee Shop out by Hood Canal carried them. I wouldn't want to be confused with Bible-beating fanatics who boycott movies altogether, the kind of people I grew up around and always considered weird mainly for that reason. But in a way I could begin to see their point. This was the kind of bloodless penetration Christians never quite achieved. They were probably jealous.

I flicked on the overhead reading lights for Jody and me as, somewhere over the Rocky Mountains, the movie began.

Then I sat back and opened my second wine bottle. Feeling for the first time that day as though I had some kind of privacy, I drank and read an article about the enormous physical and mental benefits of doing the spinal twist.

Even if I had never heard of the in-flight movie being shown, I could have told from my occasional glances at the overhead screen that it was about a mentally impaired man with certain special abilities—hardly a stunning conclusion, since the mentally impaired man was played by a movie star so famous that he would have never taken the part if the character were someone afflicted with merely ordinary impairments. I checked on this man's progress nearly as often as I did on Jody's, finally watching for a solid soundless ten minutes at the end, when it seemed as though the impaired man was being sent away to a place that represented an end to the development of his special abilities.

From the way Janice sniffled through the credits, I thought she had been very involved with the movie, very caught up in it. But when the lights on the plane came up again, Janice blew her nose into an airline napkin and said to me, "I think it was cheap."

"Really? It kind of looked to me like it was supposed to be inspiring."

"It was, but you see, I'm a therapist and—"

"You're a therapist?"

"That's right," she said, and for a second I wished that Paul was here so I could share this latest example of the Venn effect. "Anyway," Janice went on, "what I resent is the implication that emotional and mental deficiencies are interesting only to the extent that they enrich the lives of everybody else."

This wasn't the first time I'd noticed that even people who love movies in general seem to get pissed off in very particular ways when they step into their areas of special knowledge. Still, it was hard not to think Janice was saying this for my benefit, and that I might as well be wearing a sign. Maybe the pilot would come over the loudspeaker next, announcing the presence on board of women anxious to speak about how family reunions had strengthened their marriages. Maybe there would be a shuttle from Dulles leaving for L-5, a new space colony created especially for those who could not feel at home on this planet in general, and for southern Jewish schizophrenics in particular.

I went to the bathroom and returned to find Jody with his tray folded up, seat tilted back, and eyes closed, leaning on a pillow wedged against the headrest beside him. While vaulting over his legs, I noticed his drawing on the seat beside mine. Now I could see that the frame he had sketched was actually a continuous series of faces in profile; the addition of eyes, ears, forelocks, and mustaches made this clear. These profiles were all very crude, but all easily identifiable as happy or sad, young or old, male or female.

When I was a kid, before I got sick of everybody asking if I wanted to be an artist like my mother, faces were my favorite things to draw. Usually they were ladies' faces— ladies with big eyes, long curls, narrow noses, and solemn expressions because I couldn't get smiles to come out right. Once my mother glanced at the face I was drawing and murmured in an offhand way, "They say you always draw yourself." I didn't know what she was talking about; these women looked nothing like me. But now that I had in fact come to resemble one of my ladies, it seemed she had been right.

I didn't think Jody was drawing himself though—not unless his self was the blank white space on the inside of this frame of faces, and the faces represented how he perceived the world around him, an incomprehensibly endless chain of variable expressions.

"We're coming into Dulles now," I told Jody, patting his arm until he opened his eyes.

This was the airport that Paul called Dullest, a name that matched his perception of the other Washington. After almost a decade of living here, it took Paul to make me notice the blandness of it, how so many of the lawyers, journalists, bureaucrats, and politicians who seemed to be attracted by power were really only drawn to the structure of it, which is a very different thing. Still, as the plane touched down, it seemed odd that I'd pass through without going home to read my mail, check my messages, sleep in my bed.

We arrived on time, around six o'clock. Still groggy from sleep, Jody was confused when we walked off the plane and into the weirdly segmented, caterpillarlike bus that would take us to the terminal. It was called a people-mover, a name that, along with most everything else about Dulles, struck me as retro-modern and coldly inefficient. I usually flew into National Airport, which had a more human scale, but it was too obsolete to accommodate wide-bodied jets like the one we'd been on.

As the bus began moving, I told Jody about my apartment, trying to distract him from another smokeless interval. Of course, if he'd known about me visiting Seattle, he must have known I lived in D.C., too. Some of the articles he had in his possession said so.

But before I could give this much thought, a dense, bone-rattling noise filled the air, the sound of metal striking concrete. Inside the bus a long unnatural silence separated that sound from the next, sirens wailing at close range.

Then, as the bus lurched into reverse, it seemed as though the same words dawned on almost everyone at once—terrorism, bomb, crash—stirring up flurries of meaningless activity to compensate for lack of knowledge and forward motion. All at once, people were reaching for children, jostling each other for views, shouting out for explanations.

I grabbed Jody's hand, as much for my comfort as for his. When his other hand fluttered to his breast pocket for a cigarette, I grabbed that one, too. Janice was sitting across the bus and down the aisle from us, eyes fixed on the bus loudspeakers, looking determined to remain calm until advised to be otherwise.

"Please keep your seats," the driver's amplified voice finally said. "There's an accident on the runway, and we've been instructed to sit tight to avoid the path of oncoming emergency vehicles. We apologize for the delay and will be moving to the terminal shortly."

"It's okay, we'll be all right," a mother near us told her child. As I echoed her words to Jody, other information began to circulate. Nothing of the accident was visible from the rear segment of the bus, where we were seated, but news filtered back from passengers in the forward car, who could make out the distant runway where a 747 sat, its tail end cracked in two. Some thought they could see people sliding out of the plane on chutes. Meanwhile, everyone on the bus waited to hear something else—an explosion that never came. Lightning did, though, and the dull crash of thunder. As the bus headed off for the terminal again, a heavy rain began to slant through what looked to be thick, humid air.

Inside the terminal, we stepped into the midst of frantic relatives and waylaid travelers standing in nonplussed clumps. Already carrying Jody's kites, now I picked up his sleeping bag, hoping to move him along faster through the crowd and to the counter for the airline we were supposed to fly to South Carolina.

"What's happening?" Jody asked.

"Well, there's been an accident. Probably wind shear, maybe engine failure. We'll have to wait to know for sure." In my effort to be reassuring, I succeeded only in sounding like a happy-talk newscaster.

"I know," Jody said. "What are *we* doing?"

"We're supposed to get on another plane, remember?" But my uncertainty must have been so big and obvious that even Jody could tell I didn't know what I was doing. His hands were shaking.

I walked him over to an urn so he could have a cigarette and told him to wait for me there. I wasn't worried about Jody leaving because, as per Thrailkill's instructions, I was holding his wallet—a different wallet than the one he used to keep the story about Richard going to Paris in, but I thought about it anyway.

It didn't take long for an airline representative to present me with our options. We could hang around here and hope that our flight wouldn't be canceled—it most certainly would be delayed, for several hours at the very least. If the next flight out of National weren't already fully booked, we could have left on that. As it was, it seemed the best tack would be leaving from either airport in the morning. Would my companion and I be requiring overnight accommodations?

As I looped back to Jody, I couldn't help feeling small for thinking this was what I got for trying so hard to avoid travel complications. I could hear Nancy in my head, chastising me for not following Eileen's instructions, for putting Jody in the path of trouble again. I wanted to call Nancy and tell her about the delay, but it seemed silly to stand around waiting in one of the long lines extending out from every public telephone, especially when it was action that seemed required.

I found Jody rocking on his heels, plugged into the Walkman once more, staring out over everyone's heads. Loudly and off-key, he sang the chorus of a song he especially liked, a repetitive string of "I love yous."

I signaled Jody to quiet him, but he sang the line three more times anyway, then yelled over the music, "Are we still going home, Mashie?"

I had heard somewhere that if you want to calm someone it's a good idea to speak softly, so I removed Jody's ear plugs and practically whispered that I had something to tell him. He stopped rocking. "Here's the deal," I said, sounding as clear, concise, and adult as I could manage. "We can't get on another flight until tomorrow, so we're taking a cab to my apartment now."

Outside the airport, we took our place at the end of a line for cabs even longer than the lines for phones. Every few minutes, I inched our bags along on the sidewalk with my foot and lightly nudged the toe of Jody's sneaker to bring him forward with me, doing my best not to jangle his nerves any further.

Chapter 12

College

SOMETIMES ON dateless Saturday nights, I collect a stack of quarters and then, crouched beneath the pay phone in a cubicle down the hall from my dormitory room, I call Jody in New York. He seems to suffer none of the queer, inverted yearnings I experience at the Missouri women's college that I chose to attend in a burst of ignorant enthusiasm. Here, I thought, was a place that would not only let me major in dance—a kind of dance sure to be more sophisticated than what Patsy Chalmers teaches—but didn't care about my terrible math scores.

"Are you telling me," Jody says, "that you'd rather be at home?"

"It's just that it's not so different out here as I thought it would be."

"What about dancing?"

"I'm flexible, which is good, but I'm not strong, which is bad. My only C is in choreography, which I hate. We have to interpret things like menstrual cramps."

"Minstrel cramps? Do you get to wear black face?"

Jody has a phone in his room and when I call, there are always voices and music in the background, all of which I take as evidence of his healthier collegiate existence. On the rare occasions that boys are allowed to visit our rooms, we're required to leave the doors open as a safeguard against carnal activity. Elsewhere, I know, school clinics issue birth control pills on demand. Our clinic is more like a camp infirmary, with a nurse who, when you inquire about the pill, sends you to a devout Catholic gynecologist with tufts of white hair growing out of his ears.

"Screw this," my boyfriend Jimbo said, and flew out from South Carolina with three wheels of little pink tablets that he had acquired with the same mysterious ease as his plane ticket. He didn't realize the pills took a while to go into effect, but I was close enough to my period to take the risk, especially after he'd come all this way for me. I hadn't gone out with Jimbo very long before I left for school, not really expecting us to survive the distance. But now, after months with dorky blind dates as my only possibility for a social life, Jimbo looked especially good. The Cherokee blood on his mother's side showed up in a high-bridged nose and lips so sharply defined they seemed drawn onto his face. But his hair was the color of corn silk, and his lazy-lidded eyes a soft, susceptible shade of blue. Once we were alone in the motel room Jimbo got for us, he opened a bottle of George Dickel and poured into plastic cups. Then, tasting of bourbon, there came the flood of emotion I was so hungry for, the thing that sex, even awkward, painful, fearful sex, seemed the best way of reaching. After Jimbo left to go back to school, I was more homesick than ever. Which I took as an indication of being in love.

When I talk to Jody, though, I don't tell him about any of this. Jody doesn't think much of Jimbo, who was in our high school class and fit in everywhere Jody didn't. At least, that's what I assume Jody's problem with Jimbo is. And it's my own fault that I ended up in a college that now seems like more of a finishing school, my own fault for not having as good an idea as Jody of where I am happiest. So I just hang up the phone letting Jody think I'm stupid.

When our vacations coincide, I see Jody at family get-togethers. Usually these entail dinners at Piedmont Valley, the same country club where the parents once wouldn't allow us to swim with our Christ Church classmates because of its restrictive membership policies. Which obviously aren't so restrictive anymore. We start off in the Piedmont Valley bar, walnut-paneled and trimmed with green leather, where the fathers chat up golf buddies over their Manhattans, and the mothers, who have little in common with the tanned Junior League ladies in their jersey wrap dresses and pearls, talk mainly to each other.

These days, it's Aunt Eileen who leads the parade when the mothers go to New York, putting them up at fancy hotels. Since Uncle Sol's company expanded into grown-up ladies' lingerie, Aunt Eileen has made sizable enough donations to get on the boards of both the Little Theater and the new museum. Now she subscribes to more art magazines than my mother, who seems to be less concerned with painting these days than coloring her hair, now a coppery amber shade and tightly skinned back into a sleek chignon. Aunt Eileen's elegance isn't so studied, and she makes no attempt to hide all the silver that's come into her short, dark curls.

After several years of these country club outings, Nancy and Flip are no longer regular participants. Nancy teaches Head Start classes in Boston while her fiancé finishes dental school. "There are actually five year olds out there," she told me with ill-concealed horror, "who don't know their primary colors." Her wedding will be in Boston, where all her friends are, and no one expects Nancy to continue teaching beyond her first baby.

Uncle Sol was right—the war winded down in time for Flip to fulfill his military obligation with stateside duty and go to a civilian graduate school for a business degree. Flip spends all his vacations studying and clerking at the 7-

Eleven store in suburban Atlanta where my mother is forever envisioning him getting shot in a late-night robbery.
Graduate school is anticlimactic for Flip after being a company commander at the Citadel, where an underclassman
valet would help dress him in the sash, scabbard, and
sword that he wore in the parades I was occasionally required to witness. He didn't mind so much when Trisha
Williams finally found someone else to marry, but he does
seem depressed about losing his place in so many realms
all at once. Even Jody and I think of him as carrying a
strange sort of onus, the stigma of a Vietnam vet somehow
aggravated by the fact that he didn't actually go there.

With Nancy inciting such positive attention and Flip
generating so much concern, I find it easy to be unobtru-
sive. Now that I've given up dancing, I go to a state university in Georgia, which is supposed to have a better
journalism school than the one in South Carolina. The parents, who are impressed that I'm bound to graduate with
honors this year, obviously never heard the joke about how
if you drive through Athens with your windows rolled
down, someone will toss you a diploma. To save money for
a trip to Europe this summer with Gypsy Claverie, my old
camp bunkmate and current roommate, I work part-time
in a book store. I still don't have a Jewish boyfriend, but
while this seems to bother Aunt Eileen, my mother takes
the tack of treating Jimbo as if he's a style I will eventually
outgrow. After all, my mother had proposals of marriage
from six different men before she settled on my father, and
only some of them were Jewish.

Unlike me, Jody refuses to be ignored. It's hard to miss
the fact that he's been pining all year for a girl named
Sydney, under whose influence Jody has affected a
peculiar-sounding northern accent, with vowels so flat and
thin they remind me of pancakes. And it almost seems as

though he's taunting the parents with how casually he treats his academic career. He's changed majors from history to sociology to literature and now to American Studies, a kind of hodgepodge of everything else he's been drawn to study at Columbia. When he comes home for spring break, he brings everyone copies of his school literary magazine, which contains a poem he wrote.

"I don't read much poetry," Uncle Sol says, sawing away at a Piedmont Valley prime rib, "but I'm sure it means something to be selected."

"It means he's a pretty good bullshitter," my father says.

When it becomes obvious that Jody's feelings are hurt, Uncle Sol tries to make amends. "I'm proud of you, son. It's just that I don't exactly know what for."

"For what reason," Aunt Eileen quietly corrects him. She adds, almost defensively, "He can always go to law school."

"Why not?" Jody says. "Everybody else does."

"Glad to hear it," my father chimes in heartily. "I hope they all end up pumping gas."

Pretty soon, he and Uncle Sol are deeply embroiled in discussing union efforts to organize the textile industry, which is the main reason *they* consult lawyers.

Since we are here to celebrate my father's birthday, my mother and Aunt Eileen let the men talk business. "At least they're not talking politics," Aunt Eileen says.

"Dad said he wasn't going to pay my tuition if I voted for Carter," I tell her. "It's a good thing we have secret ballots."

Aunt Eileen laughs instructively. "He obviously didn't mean it now, did he? The important thing is that you voted your conscience. That's what we say in our house."

The overhead lights dim and a candle-studded cake comes toward our table, carried by an aging black waiter wearing chevrons sewn to his sleeve to indicate how many years of service he's put in at Piedmont Valley. The cake is for my father, but since he always insists that no fuss be made over him on this occasion—we'd toasted him in the bar; that was supposed to be enough—my mother wonders out loud who ordered the cake.

"I did," Jody says, and my father looks not only surprised but touched. "They give members free cakes on their birthdays. I didn't want you to miss out on anything, Uncle Daniel."

"When you're as old as I am, you can't afford to."

"Bet I'll be younger than you even then."

"Obviously."

"No, I mean when I get to be your age, I won't be all stuffy and narrow-minded."

Unperturbed, my father blows out his fifty-five candles and cuts into the cake. "We'll see," he tells Jody, handing him the first slice. "With age grows reason."

"Not for me."

"All right, now," Uncle Sol says. "Settle down, son."

"I mean it," Jody insists. He separates a pink rose from the frosting and puts it on the tip of his tongue, holding it there for a second before flipping it inside his mouth like a nervous lizard.

One reason why politics has become such a dicey topic is that Uncle Lud, a two-term mayor of Sparta, ran for Congress in the last election. Although everyone agreed going to Washington would help Uncle Lud and Aunt Francine recover from Stevie's suicide, nobody talked much about the suicide itself. Maybe that was because outsiders aren't supposed to know how Stevie lost his job in Philadelphia, went to New York to drive a cab, and killed himself with pills he'd stolen from Aunt Francine's medicine

cabinet in the hotel on Central Park West, the place where
Jody and I had stayed with the mothers. Stevie was buried
up North, his funeral restricted to immediate family.

Like most of the community, swollen now with lepers
who give no indication of leaving, Uncle Sol supported Uncle Lud's run for office. My father didn't. He said the reason
was principle, pure and simple, that he couldn't support a
Democrat who, if elected, would support the Democratic
national agenda. Uncle Sol argued that no one expected
southern Democrats to behave like Democrats from anywhere else in the country, but this didn't sway my father,
who remained unswayed even when Uncle Lud's opponent
sponsored a telephone poll asking state residents if they'd
feel right voting for someone who doesn't believe in Jesus,
then mentioned Stevie's suicide in a way that cast doubt
on Uncle Lud's fitness as a family man. My father seemed
more disturbed by Uncle Lud's campaign, which he thought
exploited tragedy by making too much of how Uncle Lud
fled Hitler and arrived here a penniless teenager. But what
about Stevie, what about the tragedy Uncle Lud's oppo-
nents were exploiting? And how could someone who was
delighted by a book called *Jews in Sports* (the birthday gift
I bought my father largely as a joke), a man who brags
about his son being one of the only Jewish company com-
manders in the history of the Citadel, deny Uncle Lud his
vote? Maybe if Uncle Lud had won, the subject wouldn't
remain such a sore one.

"I'm just an old-fashioned Republican from the Land of
Lincoln," my father says, as though this removes any question of racism from his politics, as though he never wor-
shipped Roosevelt, as though he never voted for Truman
and Stevenson. It's just another sign of how confused
things are that Uncle Sol and Aunt Eileen are trailing left-

ward and becoming culture mavens along the way, taking up space that ought to be occupied by my parents.

After dinner, Jody and I leave in the three-speed yellow Maverick that I inherited when Flip bought an MG. Although I don't read enough poetry to know if Jody's poem is any good, one line sticks in my head—something about taking one step forward, three steps back, and forever falling. As we speed down Country Club Drive, I ask Jody if his poem was inspired by Sydney.

"I don't want to talk about it, that's why I wrote a poem." Then, changing the subject, "How's Wiley?"

Like me, Wiley goes to school in Athens. "In love with Gypsy," I tell Jody. "Well, maybe not in love. But they're sleeping together."

Jody fishes in his pockets for the Piedmont Valley matchbox in which he's hidden a joint. Then he lights up and speaks in a voice that sounds constipated because he's holding his breath. "Everybody's got somebody but me."

"Why you poor thing. Tell me all your troubles and I'll tell you all mine."

Jody exhales loudly as he passes the joint. "You mean you'll make some up so I'll feel better."

"Fine, have it your way. My life is perfect and yours is shit. Are you sure you want to go to Snake's tonight?" Snake's is the beer joint where we're supposed to meet Jimbo. "Maybe you'd rather be home suffering so you can write another poem."

"Wait," Jody yells as I approach an intersection at Powdersville Road. "Turn right!"

I figure Jody is leading me back into town by a way I don't know. But when his route begins to wind back on itself, I realize where we're heading. We're going to where

Juanita lives. Following Jody's instructions, I pull over near the bottom of a gravel drive, killing the lights and engine. Juanita's wood farmhouse has long since been replaced by a brick ranch-style model. While we sit staring up the hill at her living room window, lit by the glow of a television screen, someone gets up to change channels. Our being here probably has something to do with how Jody's parents recently moved into a house they had built on Stone Mountain, a huge place that the architect for the new museum designed so that none of the wall junctures form right angles. Everything inside seems so planned and plotted that I find it hard to relax there. Even on days when Juanita is working, warming the atmosphere for him, Jody must feel a little like a guest himself.

"Do you want to go up and say hey to Juanita?" I ask.

"I don't want to bother her. Don't you ever wish you could just be with someone without them seeing you, without your being there making a difference?"

"I don't know. I think I *like* making a difference."

Jody nods dreamily, still staring at the house. "I'll just go back the way we came," I tell him, and since this is a dark, winding road where people get lost all the time, I don't think twice about using the drive to turn around. I pull in alongside a truck, the vehicle Juanita's husband uses to make deliveries for the glass company that he owns now. Fastened across the truck's flank is a huge mirror that reflects the Maverick's headlights back on us with such intensity that I almost drive straight into it.

Inside Snake's, Jimbo is playing pool with several of his fraternity brothers. The fraternity that Jimbo belongs to at Clemson conducts annual Old South celebrations at a Myrtle Beach hotel. As Old South unfolds, the brothers split into two factions—those who drink beer and re-create the

State's Rights Secession Ceremony on the ballroom floor, and those who, like Jimbo and his friends, smoke dope and giggle on the sidelines as this occurs.

"South Carolina is too small for a Republic and too large for an insane asylum," Jody intones after I describe this ritual. "Somebody important said that, but I forget who."

Jimbo catches sight of us and waves his pool cue in our direction, then leans down to make a shot. I wonder what he has riding on this game. Jimbo is a born hustler—the person to call for tickets to a sold-out campus concert, a prefab term paper, or pills that will keep you up studying all night. But he radiates such fond generosity that everyone he does business with seems to feel as if they owe him favors in return. If Jimbo graduates this year without getting expelled or arrested, he could easily become a politician.

"Come on," I tell Jody as we push past the bar, "let's get a table." Before we can find one, we run into Marie Gilbert and Mack, her husband.

"Well, hey," Marie says. "Y'all home from school?"

I move to hug her, but since she's smoking a cigarette with one hand and holding a beer in the other, we end up exchanging awkward pats that leave my shoulder damp with Pabst Blue Ribbon. Marie pouts and complains that I never call when I'm in town, but we both know that ever since she got pregnant, right after we graduated from high school, it's she who avoids me.

"You should come see LaDonna," Marie says, mentioning the child she named after a recent Miss South Carolina. "She looks just like Mack spit her."

Mack sells real estate now, but Marie met him when he hired her to sing in his band, one of the few white bands to ever have a big beach music hit. Because Snake's is noted for its beachlike atmosphere—the proprietor goes so far as to sprinkle the floor with sand and infuse the air with Coppertone—I figure that's why Mack and Marie are here; their song is sure to be on the jukebox. Marie wrote the lyrics, sung over the sound of crashing waves, which promise that one love will be enough to last a lifetime.

While we were still in high school, I used to go with Marie to fraternity parties and dance clubs around the state, watching her exchange smoldering onstage glances with Mack. Marie and I had spent endless hours formulating high-minded reasons for why we shouldn't have sex, not yet, a muddy mix of the warnings Marie heard at church and from her mother and the lessons I'd gleaned from *Consecrated Unto Me*, my confirmation class textbook about marriage. We invested so much energy into reinforcing each other's resistance that we could never bring ourselves to discuss what it was like after we changed our minds. Still, I wonder if she had the same thoughts I did—"I am fucking," and "What do I have to give up for this?"

For a crazy moment, I think we might actually be able to discuss such things tonight. Then Marie makes an excuse about getting home to the baby-sitter and leaves. So I talk to Jody instead.

"I'll bet she got pregnant the first time they did it," I say as we sit at a table purposely chosen because it's too small to accommodate Jimbo's fraternity brothers.

"And I'll bet," Jody says, "she never does it with anyone else, ever, not in her whole life. On top of getting knocked up, adultery or divorce would probably kill her. And by the time Mack kicks, she won't be interested anymore."

"Jesus, Jody. She's only twenty-two, don't be so dramatic."

"I know Sparta, and I know Marie. That's not drama, that's reality."

"No wonder she resents me. I didn't get caught."

"That's not it. Stay in this town too long and your head gets stuck permanently up your ass."

Jimbo joins us in time to register this last remark. "Well," he says dryly to Jody, "everybody always speaks highly of *you*."

Jody stands to solemnly shake Jimbo's hand. "I come from the North in peace, General," he says, but if Jody really liked Jimbo, he would have insulted him in kind.

It soon becomes clear that Jimbo isn't going to help Jody and me turn the night around, to redeem it from being another disappointing homecoming. "We're leaving for the low country," Jimbo says. "Going to do some dove hunting over the weekend." He gathers my hair in one hand and raises it to kiss my neck, suggesting that he wouldn't be going away if I weren't expected to sleep in my parents' house tonight. Jody's back stiffens and I think he might be feeling sorry for himself again. But I have begun to see Jody's lack of attachment as something desirable, as though my ties to Jimbo make me too uncomfortably close to being like Marie. Even though I'm pretty sure Jimbo has been with other girls over the last four years, he is, as they say, the sum of my experience. It's true that next to Jimbo, Jody seems more brash and boyish than ever. Compared to Jody, though, Jimbo just now seems like someone who, if you broke his heart, would be much more likely to go creep through a salt marsh drinking bourbon and stalking small animals than write a poem about it.

"I'll bring you back a nice perlo," Jimbo says, referring to the rice dish he makes with dove, which actually tastes very good. At this moment, though, perlo is just another indication of Jimbo's shortcomings.

"We're leaving, too," I tell him. "Jody and I are going to Athens."

Jody and Jimbo both look startled by this announcement, but the difference is that Jody seems pleased.

I'm so obviously sober that I don't have any trouble justifying our departure to my mother, who figures I've done my duty showing up for my father's birthday. "You two drive safely," she says, "I'll explain to Daniel." We go to Stone Mountain and Jody leaves a note for his parents, who went on from the country club to another party.

An hour later, Jody and I are drinking coffee at a Stuckey's just beyond the Georgia state line. Jody reaches for a jar that's part of a pyramid display on the counter and reads from the label. " 'Redneck Fixin's! A super special seasoning fer all yer dishes. Powerful good eatin'! Mix with sour cream for a Redneck Dixie Dip!' "

I attribute his too-loud, jittery speech to high traveling spirits and the effects of caffeine. "A redneck dip," he says, "what's that? Another name for a dumb cracker? Say, let's get some for Jimbo, he can put it in his purloin. Geez, who do you suppose buys this stuff anyway?"

The black woman who served us answers from the grill, where she's frying hamburgers. "Folks from up North," she says. "Retired folks on their way to Florida."

"Doesn't it bother you?" Jody asks. "I mean, the Confederate flag and all. You could complain to the owner."

She flips the burgers. "I *am* the owner. Selling shit like that is what keeps this place in business."

Jody buys a jar when he pays for our coffee, as though apologizing for being a smart-ass white college kid.

Back in the car, Jody fishes out his matchbox again. "It's funny," he says. "As long as I'm on my own and moving around, there are ways I like being down here better than being up there. It's not as interesting, but it's not as exhausting, either. When people seem strange, it's easier to talk yourself into thinking you know why."

"Easier to laugh at them, too."

"Yeah. That's the part we really like, isn't it?"

I exit the interstate to take a two-lane highway the rest of the way to Athens. The countryside isn't visible but the stars are, and a sense of season returns through the open windows. This is the same route the parents had taken before the interstate was built, when we went south for weekends in Atlanta. We traveled in the dark then, too, because the fathers insisted on leaving well before sunrise. That way, they could get in a full day of golf at the Standard Club—a whole, entire country club with nothing but Jewish members. "Remember?" I say, and Jody nods, knowing what I mean. There's enough of an unspoken transition, felt by us both, that I understand when Jody shakes his head and says, "Stevie Segal. Still seems weird."

"I know. Almost like it never happened, and we'd see him again if everybody still got together the way we used to."

"It's not so much like that anymore."

"Not so small, you mean."

"Not so family."

"Not so nice."

"Well," Jody says, "it's different, anyway." Then he tells me a story he heard from his mother over breakfast this morning, a story about Betty Jo Lowe. Rumors flew about her last year when Betty Jo dropped her purse at the end of Friday night services, during all the kissing and wishing of good Sabbaths, and out rolled her works—rubber tubing, syringe, spoon, needle. Now Betty Jo's ring finger has to be amputated because of a hopeless infection; having exhausted all the veins in her arms, Betty Jo had taken to shooting heroin into her hands.

"Gross," I say, and tell Jody a story I've just heard from *my* mother, a story about Debbie Rittenbaum and Maureen Abrams. They had gone off to college the way they did everything else—in tandem. But according to my mother, Debbie decided that Maureen was turning everyone in their sorority against her, and despite Maureen's protestations of innocence, Debbie dropped out of Sophie Newcomb and transferred to the University of Tennessee, where another conspiracy against her is evidently afoot. I expect Jody to laugh, but instead he gets edgy. "You know what they say," he snaps. "Just because you're paranoid doesn't mean they're not out to get you."

"Sorry I mentioned it. It's just gossip. Just trash."

"You really think so?"

"Sure. Southern Jewish psycho-trash."

"Now there's an idea!" Animated again, Jody impersonates an announcer's voice. "Live from the Standard Club— Hebrew Hee-Haw!"

Apart from Kinky Friedman and the Texas Jewboys, who aren't technically southern on account of being from Texas, and Randy Newman, who isn't southern at all but sings with an accent, it's hard to think up any acts for this imaginary show of Jody's. Still, he likes the concept so much that he sings one of the Israeli songs he learned at Camp Maccabee with a Hank Williams yodel that gets me laughing so hard I have to pull over to the side of the road.

There are few signs to let us know we're approaching Athens, but lots of religious billboards. "If Jesus Said It, It's Guaranteed," is the one that marks the turn-off I take into town. Late as it is, I decide to go by way of Jackson Street, where most of the clubs are. I have no intention of stopping, but it's reassuring somehow to see people still coming and going, knowing that the insides of these places are pulsing with sounds you couldn't hear at Snake's.

Last fall, Gypsy and I moved out of the dormitory and into Crescent Garden Apartments, a single-level, motel-style complex where we rent a one-bedroom that came furnished with chunky maple pieces. When Jody and I get there, Gypsy and Wiley are still awake. If they weren't such haphazard, circumstantial lovers, they might not be so glad to see us. As it is, we all drink from Wiley's bottle of whiskey and listen to whatever music he feels inspired to play for Jody, his former band-mate.

"Take it up, baby," Wiley says, skittering across the green shag rug with Gypsy. "It'll get all over you, you'll have to *itch* it off." Part of Wiley's charm for Gypsy, whose mother still hasn't forgiven her for refusing to become a debutante, is that Wiley always talks like this, drunk or sober.

So that Gypsy and Wiley can have some privacy, Jody and I drag the mattress off my twin bed and put it on the living room floor for me. Jody takes the couch. The effects of bourbon and lying in the dark with Jody nearby make me turn talkative. I lean toward the wall and rake my fingers over the heating grate, wondering if Jody will remember the signal we'd invented for storytelling when I slept over at his house. I have to do it several times before he responds.

"Okay, okay. But I'm too tired to make up anything."

"Then I'll do the talking." I lie back and close my eyes. "There was a girl who met a boy from India, a beautiful boy with bronze skin, enormous eyes, and a red dot smack in the middle of his forehead. He told her he knew how to read palms, so she asked him to read hers. He stared at her hand for so long without speaking that he made her nervous. She asked if he saw anything bad in her hand, and he shook his head in a kind of figure-eight motion. 'Not bad,' he said. 'Just complicated.'

"He told her she had the kind of lines in her palm that only the most accomplished readers can decipher. Then he showed her the creases in his own palm, which were deep and unbroken, while hers were feathery and chained, like a necklace. She asked what this meant, and he said, for one thing, it meant that she would have many lovers. Which she found disturbing, but exciting, too."

"Let me see your hand," Jody says.

"Be quiet—this is a made-up story."

"Come on, let me see."

I turn on the light for a moment so we can compare palms. Jody has the same chained lines on his that I have on mine. "Okay, okay," I say, "you get to be complicated, too."

"I don't care about that," he says. "Just give me lots of lovers."

In the dark again, I tell Jody good night. "What about your story?" he says. "How does it end?"

"If you could have pretended it was made up, maybe I could have come up with an ending. Now I can't."

"I'll finish it for you. Let's see, now. The boy who told her fortune wasn't from India at all—the red dot on his forehead was a chicken pox scar. But she was so convinced of his identity that she didn't realize he wasn't who he pretended to be until after they were lovers, and he began speaking to her in his regular voice. Actually, she could never be sure what his regular voice was, he used so many different ones. And this is how he became all the lovers in the world to her, and how the fortune he saw in her palm came true. The end."

"Not exactly what I had in mind," I tell him, "but nice. Better than I could have done."

"I know . . . And now it's safe to go to sleep."

I wonder drowsily if being without Jimbo—even more than being with Jody—accounts for how happy I feel just now, but the notion soon wisps off, absorbed by soft, rhythmic moans coming from the bedroom. The couch springs creak as Jody shifts positions, and I think maybe the sounds have made him uncomfortable, but for me they ascend in soothing waves, confidential and comforting as the lullaby of adult voices to a sleepy child.

When I awaken the next afternoon, Jody is in the kitchen with Gypsy and Wiley, preparing a picnic we end up having in a blooming meadow on the outskirts of town. That night, we all go to my favorite club, which has an outdoor dance floor suspended over the Oconee River. We drink pitchers of cold beer and dance until our sunburned faces are damp and gleaming. The band plays throbbing, insistent stuff, turning even the disco song they cover for laughs into something fierce and cutting. There's no name for how we're dancing but it's about as far from a smooth, shaglike shuffle as you can get. We stomp and punch the air and fling ourselves in time to the music, hanging on to each other in wild careening spins, loose-limbed and manic as monkeys until finally we have to stop because the club is closing.

Gypsy and Wiley decide to spend the night in Wiley's trailer. Back at the Crescent Garden Apartments, Jody and I are alone. It soon becomes evident that Jody has drunk a lot more than I have. He throws up, neatly and quietly, in the bathroom. I stand outside the door, waiting with Coke and saltines.

"Whoa," Jody says as he emerges. "Still wobbly." He drops back to the edge of the tub and takes the Coke. "I'm sorry."

I sit down beside him. "It's okay. Happens all the time

with Gypsy, that's why we have a lot of Cokes and crackers around here."

"I'm really sorry, Marsha,"

"Hey, your aim was good."

At that, Jody lunges for the toilet again. When he's done, I wet a washcloth and clamp it on his forehead. "Jesus," he groans, but this time he keeps the Coke and crackers down. I convince Jody that he'll feel better if he takes a shower, then leave to put a fresh set of sheets on Gypsy's bed for him.

Jody showers for so long that I stick my head into the bathroom twice to make sure he's still on his feet. "I'm sorry," he says again as he stumbles into bed wearing his briefs, hair all clumpy and wet. I turn off the lights and go out on the porch for one last cigarette. Before I slide into my own bed across the room, I check Jody's breathing, already deep and steady.

It's morning when I hear the sound of my name, whispered softly at close range, and there's the familiar weekend feeling of another body companionably close to mine. A hand runs beneath the sheet along the length of my thigh, drawing up my leg to rest comfortably along the warmth of another thigh, not nearly so long as the one I'm accustomed to, but the significant thing is that it's nice, nice as the breath on my neck and then the lips brushing my mouth, the sensation there different enough by contrast to make me open my eyes. I close them again just as quickly, the better to blur the image of who I'm with and enhance the possibility of discovering someone new, someone unexpected. But I caught a glimpse of Jody's face, and I could tell he's scared. Like I am.

I assume we're scared for the same reasons. Uncertainty over how we might physically mesh amplified by a stark inability to picture either one of us casually mentioning to our parents that we had, by the way, become lovers, although who knows, they might be pleased. I could imagine, at least, that Aunt Eileen might be, if she knew it was serious. But lovers, I remind myself, are experiences. Just about everyone I know outside of Sparta acts as if they believe this. And so if Jody is in my bed, this is an opportunity for an experience. I don't really like the idea of people as experiences, of tossing them—or being tossed—away like pieces of Kleenex. Still, if Jody and I are going to have complicated lives with lots of lovers, what better, safer place to start than with each other?

I am preparing myself to be as sophisticated about all this as I imagine Jody is. As sophisticated, say, as Sydney, or any other bright northern girl about to get a degree from Columbia who might inspire Jody to write a poem. And so I'm surprised when Jody takes my face in his hands and says, "Oh God, Marsha, I hope you need this as much as me," sounding much too raw and jagged for sophistication.

I put my arms around Jody and say it's all right, don't worry. Rubbing my face against his silky hair, I breathe in the citrus smell of my own shampoo. Even as my heart begins to race, I grow oddly calm with the certainty of knowing what I want to do.

More words might stop us, might shatter the secret that I start to share with Jody in a kiss that begins all experimental and exploratory, tracing the outlines of lips, teeth, and tongue to get these new boundaries straight, then ends so deep and sure that Jody is pressing urgently against me, as if my body holds the answer to an earth-shattering question that his can only ask inside mine. Always before, we lacked the mystery it took to be lovestruck and willful and filled with longing, like everybody was in the songs we used to sit around in Jody's bedroom listening to for hours on end, letting our hearts splinter without ever really causing each other pain. Now, there is mystery. And the very real possibility of pain.

Soon distinctions are impossible to make, between him and me, then and now, right and wrong. Somehow it feels as though I am comforting Jody as much as making love with him, but since the urge to comfort comes from love, I find myself hoping in the end that this will be enough to soothe the aftermath, when our bodies separate and we're faced with untangling everything else from the strangeness of what we've done.

Jody trembles as he falls against me, goose flesh breaking out on his arms and legs as though a cool breeze just grazed his skin. It hasn't. The bedroom is warm, almost hot, and we're layered with sweat. Bright light breaks through the drawn blinds and I hear a splash outside as someone dives into the Crescent Garden Apartments swimming pool. I wish for a moment that Jody and I could just jump up and go swimming ourselves, replacing the aroma of sex in which we're enveloped with the familiar, innocent scent of chlorinated water.

Jody is the first to speak. "That was different. Touching you was almost like touching myself."

I don't know how to take this, as something wonderful or not so thrilling, so I try for a joke. "Oh, do you do that a lot?"

"Sure, don't you?"

"Girls don't so much, I guess. Especially girls with roommates. Or maybe I'm just weird."

"No, I'm the weird one."

"Right, I forgot. And I'm the one who's way too normal."

"This wasn't normal."

"No, it wasn't."

Jody pulls away from me, irritated. "Is that all you have to say?"

"I didn't mean anything bad. What do you want me to say?"

Jody sits up to wrap his arms around his knees and for a second, I think he's going to cry. "I have to know I'm okay, Marsha."

I scoot forward to sit beside him. "I really liked that. You were fine. Honest."

"That's not what I meant."

"Tell me what you meant, then."

"I don't know, exactly. But if you think I'm okay, I'll feel a whole lot better about myself." As Jody raises his head to look at me, the telephone rings.

"It might be the parents."

"It might be Jimbo."

I agonize for a few more rings, clutching the sheet against my chest. "I better answer," I tell Jody, and pick up the phone. Jody was right—it's Jimbo, calling collect from a gas station in Beaufort. "Are you mad at me?" he asks.

"No, Jimbo, I'm not," I say, letting Jody know who's on the line.

Jody gets up, puts on his jeans, and starts pacing back and forth while Jimbo apologizes for abandoning me the other night. This is rare. Jimbo must suspect what happened between me and Jody, and what that might bode for us. I'm not good enough at endings to attempt one over the telephone, especially with Jody here, wearing a track in the shag rug, so I just listen and wait for my chance to hang up. But Jimbo won't let me, not until I've told him that I love him. "You know I do," isn't enough for Jimbo. He has to hear me say it, he has to bring his hustling charm to bear and cajole me into an outright declaration. Finally, I let him.

The words are no sooner out of my mouth, as dopey and

dismissive as I can make them sound, than Jody jerks the telephone receiver out of my hand and hurls it against the wall hard enough to dislodge a huge chunk of plaster. Then we're yelling, each so angry that I'm completely dressed before I realize that Jody's rage is more dangerous than mine. It's more dangerous because it's not directed enough at me. There are plenty of fine, righteous things Jody could say when I demand to know what in the goddamn hell is wrong with him that he had to start destroying property. Plenty of things besides, "That's too easy, Marsha! What's *right* with me, can you tell me that?"

I just look at Jody, crying, expecting that my tears will calm him. But he's too caught up in his own emotion for that and slams out of the apartment instead. I can see where he's headed from the porch—to the two-lane highway that runs across the hill above Crescent Gardens. I go back inside and grab my car keys.

When I reach the highway, I spot Jody standing on the shoulder with one hand jammed in his pocket and the other stuck out to hitchhike. His unbuttoned shirt flaps as cars whoosh by, baring the smooth skin on his chest and belly. I pull up alongside him, but he spins away to put more distance between us and pokes his thumb back into the air. "I'll take you home," I yell through the open passenger window. "Come on, Jody, please get in." When he doesn't respond, I tell him that if he's trying to get to Sparta, he's standing on the wrong side of the highway. He just glares at me and crosses the road. I drive away slowly enough to give him time to change his mind, watching in the rearview mirror all the while, but he doesn't so much as glance in my direction. Fine, I think, let him try to catch a ride looking like he just fell out of bed. He knows where I live, the door's unlocked.

I go alone to a restaurant for breakfast, wanting the com-

fort now of a public place. While I wait for my one-egg special, I work the crossword puzzle in a newspaper someone
has left behind. Using a pencil stub the waitress gave me,
I fill in the five-letter word for repent: *atone*. But how am
I supposed to atone for this sense of rejection, vying with
the guilt? I do not want to answer this question. I do not
want to be this grown up.

When I leave, I pass by the spot where Jody was standing. He's gone. By dusk, I figure he's had plenty of time to
get home. I've certainly had plenty of time to formulate my
apology. And so I call Jody at his parents' house. Aunt Eileen answers, her voice high and strained. "I can't talk to
you now, Marsha, I'm expecting a call from the doctor. We
have to get Jody to the hospital."

"Why, what's wrong with him?"

She responds with an anger I've never heard before.
"How could you be so reckless when it's obvious what a
difficult time he's going through?" Then Aunt Eileen stops
herself with a sob. "Oh God, I don't know *why* this is happening," she says, and hangs up the phone.

I start to dial my mother's number, but then realize she
won't know anything more than I do. I have a sick feeling
that whatever's wrong with Jody can't be addressed by a
white cell count or a surgeon. I doubt Aunt Eileen will want
my mother there by her side. I'm not at all sure she will
want me there, either, but I know I have to go.

It takes me a while to find Aunt Eileen because visitors
aren't allowed on the floor where Jody is and I have to
sneak up on a staff elevator. When I get there, she and
Uncle Sol are talking with a doctor in the waiting room. I
stay out by the elevators, where they can't see me. After
Uncle Sol leaves with the doctor, I go to Aunt Eileen. At
the sight of her red and swollen-looking eyes, I burst into

fresh tears. We stand together for a long time, just holding each other.

"I'm so sorry," I tell her.

"I know you are, Sister, I know."

"I have to tell Jody, maybe it'll help."

Aunt Eileen sighs and sits. "The doctor doesn't want him seeing you, Marsha."

"Not now, you mean."

"This is serious, dear. It could be for a long time."

"Why would he say that? That doesn't make sense."

Aunt Eileen hands me a Kleenex and I blow my nose. "There's been trouble for a while. His grades taking a dip, his having to live alone." She shakes her head to stop me when I protest the normalcy of these things. "There's more you don't know. The point is, it didn't start today. It just got worse. Much worse."

"What happened?"

"Jody was mad at you when he got home, that was plain enough."

"We had a fight."

"I know. After he locked himself in his room, I could hear him arguing with you."

"But he didn't call, I didn't talk to him after he left."

"You don't understand. I didn't either, at first. You were in his head, Marsha, not on the telephone."

I sit down beside Aunt Eileen, silent with wondering just how much she learned from Jody's end of this imaginary conversation, just how much I was obliged to tell her. Would things go better for Jody if she knew what happened? "While we were in Athens," I say, beginning my confession, then I stop, unable to finish.

"So that part's true." It's a statement, not a question.

"Yes."

She takes a moment to absorb this, looking more sad

than surprised, then picks up where she left off. "When Jody came out of his room, he didn't seem angry anymore, but he was wild. He went through so many changes I couldn't keep up. First he was going to Europe with you this summer instead of to school. His father tried to reason with him, but he just got wilder. He told us he was going to marry you. And now, what he seems to be sticking with—what he keeps telling the doctor—is that you are his sister."

"He's just confused, that's what *you* call me."

"He's not calling you that, Marsha. He's saying this is who you are. It's not your fault, what's happening to him, we know and the doctor does, too. But I hope you can see why . . ."

Aunt Eileen takes out another Kleenex, this one for herself, and I feel her pulling back, gathering strength for Jody. She hasn't enough extra to take care of me, and I can tell from her goodbye that she doesn't expect to be seeing me anytime soon, either.

"I won't be talking about . . . Athens," she says, "with your parents, so you don't have to worry about that. Just concentrate on finishing school and enjoying your trip. All right?"

I nod in agreement as the guilt worms deeper into my heart, taking on a parasitic life of its own.

Book II

Chapter 13

As WE drew close to the front of the taxi line outside Dulles, Jody started counting out loud by thousands. After a while, it dawned on me that he was counting the seconds between thunder and lightning, reversing the way you were supposed to determine an approaching storm's nearness in miles. The storm, of course, had already arrived.

"You know what my mother used to tell me thunder was," I said, thinking out loud. "She said it was the sound of fairies bowling. Guess hers must have been blue-collar fairies."

It was cool now, strange weather for July in this part of the country, made all the more peculiar when knuckle-sized pieces of hail began to fall, clattering off the metal roof. "Now they're shooting craps," Jody said.

It made as much sense as anything else to think that maybe God, who wasn't supposed to play dice with the universe, might let the fairies do it for Him. Considering the God we'd been brought up on, it wasn't so surprising that Jody had been one of the only patients on the ward at Bayview who made no claims for transmitting His word. Our God seemed to have said everything He had to say a long time ago—definitely not the type to offer words of wisdom to someone having trouble with their brain, or someone trying to understand why someone else's brain goes haywire. Still, I wouldn't put it past Him to throw a little senseless death our way, just to keep things in perspective.

"Do you live in an apartment complex?" Jody asked.

"Kind of. But it's not much like a complex back home."

"No swimming pool?"

"Nope."

"I've got my sleeping bag"—he kicked it with his foot—"maybe I can sleep outside tonight."

"What if it's still raining? What if it gets hot again?"

"That's not the point," Jody said, jamming his hands into his jeans.

"Okay, what's the point?"

"I don't know, you ask too many questions."

He was right. "I have a couch in my office that opens up into a bed," I told him slowly. "You can close the door and be alone if you like. We won't get in each other's way, don't worry."

"Do you have air conditioning?"

"Yes."

"Okay," he said. "I'll sleep inside."

We advanced to the front of the line and climbed into the back seat of a cab. I was about to give the driver basic directions to my place when I remembered that the storm had probably made rush hour traffic even more impossible than usual. I didn't want to leave Nancy any room to reproach me for not letting her know sooner what had happened to delay us. "Do you think you could find a gas station so I can use a telephone before we hit the beltway?" I asked the driver.

"Sure." He drove several miles before reaching a likely exit.

"Vienna," Jody said, reading an overhead sign.

"Vienna, Virginia," I explained.

"Waltzing Matilda," he said pleasantly.

"Matilda." After a moment's thought, " '*She take me money and run Venezuela. Everybody now.*' "

Looking out the window, Jody said, "You have a car, don't you?"

"Yes."

"I like to drive. Could we could drive home from here?"

Nancy didn't care much for the idea, which I didn't give Jody any credit whatsoever for hatching, of us driving to South Carolina from D.C. "You're safer in the air than on the road," she said, referring to the crash that had caused our delay.

"But that's not it. If I'm starting to feel like a police escort here, Jody must be feeling like he's done something bad and I'm just returning him to the proper authorities."

"He's not upset, is he, Marsha?"

"No, he's fine."

"I hope you haven't said anything to him about, you know, an assisted living situation."

"No, not a word. Look, just a few more days, that's all I'm asking."

To Nancy, I must have seemed just as unreliable as Jody in the throes of a relapse. What reason could there be for Nancy to believe I held her brother's interests above my own? Why should she think I wouldn't be just as careless with Jody as when I spontaneously drove him off to Athens? I wanted to tell her that after all my years of neglect, it didn't feel right getting out of this so fast. But that smacked of Janice's movie review on the plane, and I saw how easily it might appear that I was embracing some Hollywood notion of affliction, looking to elevate myself with Jody's deficiencies only so long as I enjoyed the view.

According to the arrangements Nancy made with me before I left Seattle, my mission would end when Calvin Thomas, Juanita's son, picked Jody up at the airport in South Carolina. Nancy might have laid these plans out for me in a way that didn't invite discussion, but my willingness to accept them without question hadn't exactly suggested an interest beyond the escort mode that I'd described. Nancy deserved convincing, so I promised that we'd be on the first airplane out of here in the morning if that was what Jody wanted.

"I still have my doubts," she said before we hung up. "But I'm hoping you'll prove me wrong."

Over the years, I had fallen into the convenient habit of lumping Nancy's existence in with my brother Flip's, both of them leading ordered lives in interchangeably lush, shaded neighborhoods, places where all the drunks and crazies lived *inside* the houses, not camped out on the curving curbed sidewalks. But it had been a long time since we were all part of the same family. And unlike Flip, Nancy would someday probably feel compelled to start checking her own children for signs of Jody's illness.

After Nancy hung up, I punched the star button to get a dial tone and called Joyce. "I was just making dinner and watching the world weather channel," she said. "Is your plane delayed?"

Afterward, I couldn't decide which was stranger—my mother, a woman who had never crossed the Atlantic, keeping up with atmospheric conditions in Budapest, or the way that my father, who had planned to pick me up at the airport, responded to the news that I would probably be driving down. "You're making a big mistake," he said, "if you don't get vouchers for the unused portion of your airfare."

I hit the star button again and dialed Paul's studio. Usually when we parted, Paul would leave special messages on his answering machine—something along the order of "If this is my girlfriend, I miss you already." This time, the message said only that he was out of town for a couple of days. This was news to me, so surprising I barely managed a coherent message of my own.

Back in the taxi, Jody was listening to the "Songs That Make Me Cry" tape again. A white girl singer was doing her cover of an old Five Stairsteps tune. *"Ooooh child,"* she sang, *"things are gonna be easier."* I was like the schizophrenics I'd read about who interpreted every external occurrence as a message meant especially for them: I wanted to take that song as a promise.

By the time we pulled up in front of my apartment building, it was hot enough again that steam rose from the streets. The building sounded as if it might take off, propelled by the humming motors of window air conditioners. There were three in my second-floor apartment, and the first thing I did after we walked in was turn them all on as cold as they would go.

Compared to Paul's tiny place, mine was luxuriously large. Instead of painted pine floors there were parquet squares of dark oak. The kitchen and bathroom sinks had single faucets, not one for hot water and another for cold. There was room for lots of books and places besides bed in which to read them. Here was all my music, too, a huge block of records and tapes. Each room contained a painting of Paul's, and since the many windows looked out into tree branches or across a courtyard into other windows, his paintings provided the best views in the place, shifting fields and fragments of color so openhearted that I used to think they made up for the lack of horizon. Now I wasn't so sure. For all the extra square footage here, I found myself unable to summon any corresponding sense of spaciousness inside.

I was changing into shorts and a fresh T-shirt when Jody, who was supposed to be taking a nap on the couch in my office, knocked on my bedroom door. In his hand was a postcard-sized piece of cardboard that had been tacked to my office bulletin board, a pen-and-ink diagram of the buckle on Paul's favorite belt, which used to give me trouble in the early days of our romance. The caption said, *To impress your friends and avoid embarrassing delays, you really should . . . know your belt buckle!* Underneath were step-by-step instructions for undoing the labeled parts of a standard issue, friction lock, brass webbed-belt buckle:

1. *Place thumb and index finger on the knob on opposite ends of special locking pin.*
2. *Slide special locking pin to position "u" in the slot.*
3. *Pull the end of belt through buckle.*
4. *See how easy it is? And you don't have to worry about putting it back together.*

"You know what this looks like?" Jody asked, waving Paul's card in the air.

"I'm interested in what you think it looks like," I said evenly, although I was worrying that Jody would be pawing through all my things in there, maybe even trying to add to his collection of my work.

"It looks like an illustration in *Boy's Life*," he said. "You know—for the belt buckle merit badge."

"Maybe you've got a point. Paul made it, and he was an Eagle Scout." Jody examined the card more closely. "It's supposed to be a joke," I offered.

"Oh," he said. "Very funny." Then he slammed the door, and I couldn't tell if he had to because it was swollen with heat, or if he did it because he was annoyed.

* * *

One reason I didn't sublet my apartment for the summer was that I needed an escape route if things didn't work out with Paul. "Plan plans," Paul had scrawled onto one of his worktables in a note to himself, "don't plan outcomes." The only positive effect of my inability to do this, it seemed, was that Jody and I could stay here, in this lonesome home, instead of in a lonesome airport motel room.

I went shopping while Jody slept and poured myself a glass of wine before I started preparing dinner. In something of a daze, I stood staring at my refrigerator door. Not nearly so varied and editorial as Felicity's, it was mostly decorated with snapshots of Paul and my Seattle friends. In fact, if you judged by my refrigerator, I didn't know anyone in D.C. except for the crowd of perfectly good and decent people who posed for me last Thanksgiving around a Cleveland Park fireplace. It wasn't their fault that I didn't want to call any of them up right now.

It was eight o'clock Seattle time when Jody finished napping and we sat down to a dinner of poached tuna, green beans, and salad. But here the eleven o'clock news was on. I rolled my old Motorola into the dining room so we could watch reports of the crash.

According to the newscaster, five people were dead, including two children, and seven were in serious condition. Among those interviewed was a businessman who missed the flight because a tire on his rental car went flat on the way to the airport. He had already been issued his ticket and boarding pass, though, and his seat would have been in the section where everyone who was killed or injured had been sitting.

"I guess you must feel like you're living right," the reporter interviewing him said.

"What's this," I moaned, "a beer commercial?" I turned

the television off and dimmed the lamp by the table. "I watch television when I eat at home," Jody said in a factual, uncomplaining tone.

"Me, too. If there's anything good on."

"I don't care about that," Jody said. "Do you have cable?"

I shook my head, not bothering to add that cable had only recently become available in the District of Columbia—another way in which the city seemed out of sync with the rest of the country.

Jody turned his attention to compiling a careful forkful of beans, tuna, tomato, and lettuce. "Some people," he said, "might think my apartment is nicer than yours, Mashie. But I don't."

Without falling back into cop mode, I tried to steer Jody toward discussing the choice of where to live that his family had given him. "Will you be glad to be back in your own place?"

"I don't know. It hasn't happened yet." Jody kept his eyes on his fork. "It has regular air conditioning, anyway—not boxes in the windows. And cable, too." His voice brightened as he recited what sounded like an advertising litany. "Chicago sports, New York movies, Atlanta news, weather all over the world." Then he tore off a piece of bread, spread on some of the butter that I had thawed on the window sill, and covered it with a thick layer of salt.

After dinner, Jody studied the shelves in the living room where I kept all my children's books. Among them were twelve volumes of My Book House, a series that covered everything from nursery rhymes to sword and sorcery. There was also a My Book House guide for parents called *In Your Hands*, which had an illustration on the cover showing a naked baby sitting in a pair of hands, Mom's wrist encircled by lace and Dad's by pin-striped cuffs.

"Children quickly sense your attitude and actions toward

books as well as other things," the guide said. "As a special treat, let your baby turn a page in his own book and never fail to praise him when he has done it well."

Maybe I'd been moved to smuggle My Book House out of my parents' house because they had actually followed this advice with me. I doubted it, though. My proprietary feelings about books seemed too instinctive to have been taught. I used to think just reading a book made it mine, which might have been why I still had in my possession a hardbound, color-illustrated copy of *The Little Engine That Could* that bore a sticker identifying it as the property of Jody Lurrey.

"Do you want it back?" I teased, showing Jody the book.

"No," he said, "I don't read much anymore." Then he pulled off the shelf a volume called *A Child's History of the World*. "I remember this."

"Me, too. Especially that scary story about the Spartans—the *Greek* Spartans, that was confusing. About how they took boys away from their families when they were just babies and made them sleep outside without blankets and hike without shoes. That way, they'd either have to die or be tough and strong. Remember?"

"Yeah," Jody said vaguely, replacing the book. "Sort of."

I was thinking about how Jody's situation had come to be the reverse of what I'd described—how he was now fully grown, a man being sent back to where he came from so that he *wouldn't* sleep outside without blankets and wander the streets shoeless—when he removed another book, *The Secret Garden*. Sitting down on the couch, Jody slowly flipped through the book's oversized pages and color plates. "I like the pictures," he said.

"But that's not why you gave it to me, is it?"

"I don't remember why, exactly."

Because of fallout and poison pills and the dead Clutter

children, I was tempted to say. Instead, wanting to touch
him—*really* touch him—but not wanting to hurt him this
time, I leaned forward to very carefully lay my hand on his
shoulder. "I treasure that book because it came from you."

"That's okay," he said, edging away. "I didn't pay for it."
He closed the book and lit a Vantage, one sneakered foot
jiggling madly against the leg of the coffee table.

If Jody weren't altered, I would have offered him some
brandy. But since he couldn't drink on the medication that
he was taking, and since the living room was almost chilly
from the air conditioner, I made him some hot chocolate
from a hardened packet of Dutch Girl cocoa powder that I
found in the back of a cupboard.

"I need to talk to you about the rest of our trip," I said,
handing him a mug. "If you really want to, we could take
a couple of days and drive down there in my car."

"I used to drive it in one day," Jody said. "I'd take pills
and drive from New York in one day."

He had to be talking about speed. I remembered the
Black Beauties and Pink Hearts Jimbo used to sell, how
easy they were to come by then, and wondered if Jody had
ever tried to silence the voices that way. But rather than
take another detour, I only said, "Believe me, if we drive,
it'll take a couple of days. I have no intention of spending
nine straight hours on the interstate. So think about it.
Which way would you rather go—road or airplane?"

Jody frowned and bit his lip, almost as though to convince me that he was giving the matter serious thought; I
could tell he had already made up his mind. "Is your *car*
air conditioned?"

"Good question. Yes."

"Does it have a tape deck?" I nodded. "A stick shift?"
"Yes."

"Okay," he chirped, and started to sing. " '*Roll down the*

window and let the wind blow back your hair.' " Then, a line of his own: "*Leave it up if it's hot and we'll have to turn on the frigid air . . .*"

It was late, but neither of us felt sleepy. When Jody said he'd like to play chess, I unearthed an old set made out of corkboard and plastic, something I had unaccountably neglected to throw away in the fit of cleaning that overtook me before I left for Seattle. We both played wildly, without strategy, but by the time I begged off to go to bed, I was down to three pieces and Jody still had five, including his king and queen.

I usually slept naked, but out of deference to Jody's presence in the apartment I wore the closest thing to pajamas that I possessed—gym shorts and a T-shirt. Once in bed, though, I had trouble falling asleep. One thing that kept my mind spinning was the last time Jody and I were alone together in the same apartment, and how poorly I read the real nature of what was occurring. Another was Paul's current inaccessibility, which led me to imagining another woman, who at this very moment might be trying to convince Paul that he deserved someone who could love without the longing of long distance, who could be consistently passionate about a man who lived in the same area code as she. "Just look at her history," this woman would say, wisdom glistening in her eyes as she shook her head sadly. "I'm sure Marsha loves you, in her way. But her way is so . . . limited. Don't you think?"

It seemed that except for the time it took to have a dream, I stayed awake all night. In this dream, I am walking through a mountain meadow. These are the small, gentle mountains of my childhood, not the grand, jagged snowcapped peaks of the Pacific Northwest. At the edge of a grove I find a pair of silky panties. Oh no, I think—someone has been raped. But when I see a price tag still attached, I realize the panties have never been worn. Nearby I find a shopping bag containing more new, unused clothing and an empty suitcase. I pick up all these things and take them with me, wandering into a makeshift shack where a young woman paces in circles, talking to herself. There is a bed nearby and a Degas ballerina print tacked to the wall. "Are these your things I've got?" I ask the young woman. She looks at me, eyes ablaze and defensive. "I finished the chapter and answered all the questions," she says. "What more do you want from me?" I tell her that I'm sorry she's upset. "Is it because you're hearing voices? Is that what's wrong? Because if it is, it's not your fault, and there are things that help make the voices go away. Would you like that?" As she cries and nods I wake up crying too, my T-shirt twisted underneath my arms.

The digital clock by my bed read 4:15 A.M. I got up to get a glass of water. In the living room I tripped over an object on the rug that, after regaining balance, I could see was Jody's arm. He was stretched out in his sleeping bag, with nothing but a hand between his head and the floor. When he didn't stir, I wondered if the drugs were the reason why I hadn't disturbed him. I wondered, too, if they allowed him to dream. Maybe this was another thing lost to Jody, part of the price paid so that he could function less painfully in what was commonly agreed to be the real world. It always seemed sad when Jody was far away and I heard reports of his condition. Now that he had come close, it was even sadder that he was more distant than I had allowed myself to imagine. But this seemed a backward way of perceiving things—like thinking of myself as the sensible, awakened one stumbling across the sleeping runaway, like counting the seconds between lightning and thunder.

Chapter 14

I COULD tell Jody was awake by the television sounds coming from the next room. I slipped unseen into the bathroom and, before emerging, showered and put on a long cotton dress selected because it allowed me to look like an adult without wearing pantyhose. Did I imagine that an otherwise bothersome stranger might take in the sight of Jody and me together and think, "Well, that fellow there is a little peculiar, but the lady with him is wearing a second-hand Cacharel print"? Probably.

"You look special," Jody said when I joined him.

"Well, it's a special day."

He shook his head emphatically, spraying smoke out of his nostrils. "That's not it."

I was already cranky for coffee, and breathing his smoke this early in the morning made me even crankier. "Listen," I said, switching off the TV, "let's not make too much of this, okay? It's just a dress and a little bit of makeup." A *very* little bit of makeup. My leeriness of emitting unintended sexual signals had made my hand with powder and paint even lighter than usual.

"Don't you remember, Mashie?"

"Remember what?"

"How you go into your room and work all by yourself, but you get fixed up to do it anyway."

It took more time than it should have for me to realize

Jody was referring to an article that was *not* among those in his collection, one about makeup that had been published in a fashion magazine last year. In this piece I claimed to make a practice of wearing makeup while working at home because I lived in fear that otherwise I might find myself sprawled on the couch in a faded chenille robe, a cigarette dangling from my mouth, watching "I Love Lucy." It wasn't exactly true, of course. For one thing, I was more susceptible to televangelists and "Family" reruns than "I Love Lucy." But all that seemed beside the point now.

"Jesus, Jody," I said. "You remember the crap I write better than I do."

He sat at the dining room table and didn't speak again until my coffee was ready. "Your air conditioner in there"— he gestured toward the office—"is awfully loud."

"Is that why you slept in the living room?" His sleeping bag was still on the floor, so I didn't have to violate his privacy by mentioning this. I wanted to talk about my articles the same way, without saying I'd seen them in his bag. "Come on, Jody, I'd really like to know why you remember the stories I wrote so well."

"It's not like I read them all the way through. Just the parts that seemed interesting. Then I'd take notes."

"Notes?"

"Yeah. For my research."

"Really? What were you researching?"

Jody avoided my eyes and began fiddling with the fringe on the place mat in front of him. I expected the conversation to go no further. Then he said, "I was researching you."

As my eyes grazed the scar on Jody's arm, I wondered if I still had another existence, separate from the one I experienced, as a voice in Jody's head, one that said, "Read me!" That was a scary enough idea to make me want to change the subject. But if Jody could be brave, so could I.

"How would you find these articles?"

"There's this librarian who smells nice—she said your name's in the green book."

"The green book?"

"Yeah, the one that says who writes what."

He was right; the indexed guide to periodicals came bound in a green cover. I'd used it often enough myself. "So you'd find my name and ask for the magazines?"

"Uh-huh."

"And would you take them home from the library?"

"Sometimes. But that's against the rules."

"Right. They'd rather you Xerox them."

"Yeah, but then you have to have perfect dollars for the change machine and wait in line for the other one that copies."

I put some fruit and cereal on the table and we started to eat. "You shouldn't call them crap, Marsha," Jody said. "But you *are* a pretty good bullshitter."

"Thank you."

Jody drank a glass of orange juice and chopped a banana into his cereal. Unless he thought oranges and bananas could be grown here, his food fixations were waning.

There were no clouds in the sky today, just a thin haze of heat and smog. After locking up the apartment I led Jody down a hilly paved path through shrubbery filled with chorusing crickets to the parking lot where I'd left my car. Since most of my neighbors had already gone to work, my car stood nearly alone in the lot, a green Honda covered with a coat of pollen so thick that even yesterday's rain had failed to wash it away.

Jody helped me wedge the tube containing his kites into the hatchback trunk, a dutiful bit of assistance so bereft of any sense of ownership he seemed to have already forgotten why he bought them. More interesting to him was the plastic monkey head he spotted in a corner of the trunk. He picked it up for a closer look. "It's Dr. Zaeus," I said, answering his uncomprehending expression. "You know, from *Planet of the Apes*? I got it for a nickel at a flea market, don't ask me why."

"I liked that movie. I would have bought it for a nickel, too."

"Then it's yours."

"Thanks."

We got into the car and, with the doors still open, I started up the engine and the air conditioning. "How come you still have South Carolina license plates," Jody asked. "You don't live in South Carolina anymore."

"I know, I know. It's embarrassing, but my father bought this car and it's in his name, not mine."

"My father bought my car, too."

I couldn't help thinking that if Jody had managed to sell his car, Sol must have been generous enough—or foolish enough, my father would probably say, especially now—to put it in Jody's name. But I just said, "Yeah, they like buying cars, those guys."

"Do I have to be embarrassed?"

"Nah," I said, "Neither one of us does."

I drove into Georgetown to pick up some sandwiches at a health food store. Then, at Jody's insistence, we made another stop at the Safeway for barbecued potato chips and Cokes. Since I still held Jody's money, I gave him his wallet so he could run this errand himself.

While he was gone I reached into the glove compartment, removed the car registration, and put it in my purse as a reminder to finally do something about having the car signed over to me. If I lived anyplace else, I might have done this sooner. In D.C., though, there were so many de-racinated people that just about everyone seemed to think that where they came from was more valid, more real somehow, than where they were living. But not having the car in my name was a bother. Since I hadn't been to South Carolina for two years, I had to ask Jimbo, still a friend and still something of a hustler, to illicitly obtain and mail me my inspection stickers. If a local cop discovered I lived here and had out-of-state plates, I'd get a big fine. But at the actual point of purchase, I was happy enough to accept the Honda without question; the Maverick I'd inherited from Flip had given out at about the same time I became an erratically employed freelancer. Besides, this car was the only gift my father had ever personally selected for me, and it seemed then that my only choice was to accept it as offered or not at all.

While I waited for Jody, I noticed he had left his duffel bag unzipped on the floor board. I could see how neatly his clothes were packed. I could also see Paul's handwriting on the back of a postcard. For a second I suspected Jody of stealing mail from my office. But then I saw that it was the Picasso postcard Paul had given Jody, with a message I hadn't read. It said: "God is really only another artist. He invented the giraffe, the elephant, and the cat. He has no real style. He just keeps on trying other things. P. Picasso."

My heart leapt right up into my mouth, as though it were on springs. I had already left three messages for Paul, and now I wanted to leave another.

When Jody returned, I didn't ask for his wallet back. If I was going to have more faith in the bigger things, I might as well start with the smaller ones. "Ready?" I asked, and he nodded, unsnapping a Coke top. But instead of heading straight for the interstate as I had planned, I exited off Rock Creek Park and swung through the heart of official Washington—not because of any sudden impulse to play tour guide, but because it didn't feel right to begin our trip yet.

The White House came up on Jody's side of Pennsylvania Avenue, the homeless and deranged in Lafayette Park on mine. Some of them, I imagined, were no less ill than Jody.

"Looks like a stamp," Jody said.

He meant the White House, of course, but for a severed second I imagined my view rendered stately in an inch-square commemorative scene, with some appropriate thought printed underneath. The one that came to me would never fit on a stamp: "Let those in quest of God be careful lest appearances deceive them in these people who are peculiar and hard to place." I couldn't remember who wrote that—probably someone who got burned at the stake a long time ago—but these words were undoubtedly filed in my brain right alongside a dozen different situation comedy theme song lyrics, and it was only what Dr. Thrailkill would call a relative measure of sanity that kept me from spewing it all out in a jumble to the world.

I passed the Mall and headed down Constitution Avenue toward the Capitol, then made a U-turn when I saw a "space available" sign in front of a public parking lot near the Hirschorn Gallery. What the hell, I thought, at least admission is free.

I led us in and out of the building's doughnut-shaped corridor, weaving through the permanent collection. We stayed for less than an hour. Nothing remarkable occurred. Even the nudes, which Jody seemed to like, didn't hold his interest for very long, and his reaction to the work by the painter whose identity he had once fixed on only elicited: "I used to have a thing about him. It was really something."

In a way this was a relief, a sign that he was not in pain. But in another way it seemed sad, if only because I'd come to consider Jody's Picasso delusion his clearest response to his condition, the antidote he must have concocted for himself. If not God, then maybe being a genius could unravel the knots inside his brain. Or, failing that, at least make them understandable to others.

There were certainly plenty of people in the museum who appeared far odder than Jody, some meditating upon a chosen image, some looking aimlessly stupefied, as though they'd only wandered in because this place was on their way to the Air and Space Museum. Jody finally exhausted his attention in a room filled with conceptual pieces. After that, nothing seemed to interest him except the hot dog stand he had spied out by the sculpture garden. "Have a nice day," the Vietnamese vendor told Jody, handing him his hot dog and change.

"Thank you," Jody replied. "That's a very American thing to say."

Jody cracked the window when he smoked, letting in blasts of interstate noise and baked air smelling of rubber. For the better part of five hours, we spent our time in separate musical worlds, him listening to the Walkman and me playing tapes on the car deck. He emerged only once from the earphones to announce a full-blown craving for a sandwich—fried Spam on white bread with lots of mayonnaise. I laughed, thinking he was kidding, but he wasn't.

"That stuff's not so good for you," I said. "Especially after a hot dog. Why don't you try one of those hummus pitas I bought?"

He ate only half, with no noticeable pleasure. "It's just not what I was hungry for," he said, and I figured he must not have been very hungry, period.

Just as Paul had predicted, money worries got me thinking of ways to generate more income. Apart from flogging
the family reunions piece, the easiest option was to get in
touch with the editor who had called before I went to Seattle to say I'd be "just right" for a survey piece he had in
mind, something about newlyweds around the country and
the sorts of places where they had met. Of course, I could
always suggest ideas of my own. But in my experience, that
meant writing lengthy proposals that were usually re-
jected.

Once when I was stuck for work, my ex-boyfriend Bennett, who loved to give me advice, suggested that I capi-
talize on my experience writing women's magazine pieces
by translating them into pieces for the men's magazine he
edited. "The trick," he said, "is to play upon all the same
insecurities about love, sex, appearance, and disease. Only
think flip, think upscale." His example, as I recall, involved
substituting "The Appeal of Older Men" for "How Can You
Tell If He's Having an Affair?" He made it sound so easy
that I actually sat down to try it, but I didn't get very far
before all the implications made my brain hurt.

By now, the choice seemed to be either earning a living
by writing stories that didn't matter at all, or scraping by
writing stories that might matter at least to me. Maybe
this was just an excuse, though, a rationalization for allow-
ing myself to settle for what everybody already knew they
wanted, which was never so intriguing as what nobody
knew they needed yet.

Thinking about my precarious career made me even
more tired than I was to begin with. The dreamy music
playing now on the car deck—instrumentals inspired by
filmed footage of the *Apollo* moon landings, a gift from
Paul—didn't do much to help keep me awake. I turned off
the machine and drove along in silence, entertaining my-

self with headlined verse inspired by the spirit of freeze-dried airwaves that seemed to be hovering above the Honda just then.

We meet mates at bars and beaches!
We work while we play!
We like combination pizzas!
We, like sheep, have gone astray!

This seemed worth saving, so I took a pen and notebook out of my purse—the same notebook I'd used while questioning Dr. Thrailkill—and jotted it down without looking, something I learned how to do when I had to interview people during restaurant lunches. With no room among the plates and silverware to take notes on the tabletop, I'd write on my lap, eyes fixed solicitously on my interview subject. During one of these interviews, my subject said he found the motion of my arm movements beneath the tablecloth exciting, a comment I recorded but didn't understand until later, when I typed up my notes.

As I drove, though, scribbling this way didn't remind me of masturbation so much as make me wonder if I just might find something to write about in the course of this trip. That way, I could at least earn money and deduct my expenses. But given the circumstances, I couldn't come up with a topic that didn't feel cheap or diversionary.

Just then, a passing car pulled into my lane bearing a bumper sticker that I took as a personal response from the muse of highway headlines. "Pinocchio," the bumper sticker said, "was a liar and a runaway."

Our connecting single rooms at the Greensboro Holiday Inn that I checked us into were on the balcony level, overlooking a courtyard with a swimming pool in the center. I had asked for second-story rooms out of habit, conditioned by years of my mother insisting upon them because she believed there wouldn't be so many insects as on the first level, as though bugs were subject to vertigo. It seemed appropriate, then, when Jody turned on the television and settled on a show about insects, becoming so absorbed in spider mating rituals that he didn't want to have dinner with me in the motel restaurant. "I'd rather eat here," he said, eyes still glued to the screen. Before leaving, I ordered Jody fried chicken from room service and called Nancy to tell her where we were.

When she asked for Jody I listened, curious to hear him speaking for the first time since his reappearance in my life to someone more firmly anchored in his. I heard none of the irritation I recalled from their childhood exchanges, which now seemed to color mine with Nancy. Instead, Jody spoke with a puppyish eagerness as he gave her to understand that he was enjoying himself.

"This is much nicer than buses," he said, which I supposed was how he got himself to Seattle. "And airplanes are sort of like buses now, too." Before hanging up, he thanked Nancy for calling in a routine way that suggested they never spoke on the phone unless she called him.

"Do you miss her?" I asked.

He looked at me blankly. "She's my sister," he said, as though he'd never run away and this explained everything.

The Holiday Inn restaurant hostess not only spared me the question about whether I'd be just one for dinner tonight, she made a show of generosity out of leading me to a table for four in the center of the half-filled dining room. "I'll bet you've been in an itty-bitty car all day long," she said, her accent fixing my location in this particular part of the world more effectively than any map could. "The last thing you probably want is an itty-bitty table!"

The pin she wore on her chest said her name was Carol Gosnell. She looked like a big-hipped Mary Kay Place with a bad haircut, a little too severe on the sides for how long it was in the back. I sat down and Carol Gosnell winked before leaving me alone with a menu. "If anything good-looking comes along," she said, "I'll send him your way." What a romantic, I thought, trying to assume the best.

Judging by the accents in the air, more locals than transients seemed to be eating here tonight. Probably they were drawn by what the photocopied menu insert referred to as "Calabash Seafood Night!" Which meant frozen stuff that had been thickly breaded and fried, like almost every other entree on the menu. But the good thing about having nostalgic associations with greasy, pressure-cooked food was that I really didn't mind. Even here, in a restaurant physically identical to hundreds of others in various parts of the country, I could find some drama and comfort in just the facts of it being in the South and me being solitary and unknown. This was as much a treat for me as I assumed room service was for Jody.

It seemed silly now that I'd been worried about how Jody and I might be perceived traveling together. If Jody were with me, Carol Gosnell would probably flirt with him in the same way she seemed to flirt with all her customers, male and female. She did this with such energy that she probably wouldn't have enough left over to notice Jody's differences, so long as he didn't smell bad or turn his food onto the floor.

While I finished my beer and ordered another, the flow of customers into the restaurant slowed enough for Carol Gosnell to think it a good idea to come back by my table.

Since I only wanted to observe things here tonight, I bent down toward the Greensboro paper I'd brought with me, hoping to discourage her. It didn't work. "Anything interesting going on in the world today?" she asked.

"Well, somebody firebombed a Mecklenberg County abortion clinic. What do you think of that?" I was hoping that the topic I'd broached—about as objectionable, by local standards, as talk of existential philosophy or oral sex— might send her off in search of a more upbeat customer. But Carol Gosnell stayed on, clucking "land sakes," a phrase I hadn't heard in so long that it startled me, though not so much as the next words out of her mouth. "Sometimes," she said as she settled into the seat across from me, "I'm amazed there's only been one civil war."

I put down the paper. As we talked on, Carol still too diplomatic to let me know exactly where her sympathies lay, I noticed my own accent thickening into a closer approximation of hers. This used to annoy me when Joyce did it, but now I realized that she wasn't being pretentious, as I had suspected, so much as searching for common ground.

"Sometimes I write for women's magazines," I said, although Carol hadn't asked what I did for a living. Then I told her about the family reunions story, briefly and in as neutral terms as possible. I couldn't really determine if she was the right age to be an appropriate interview subject; her skin appeared so plump and smooth in the dim restaurant light that she could have been anywhere between thirty-five, the upper limits of my audience, and forty-five. But I didn't want to interview Carol. I wanted to see if someone as smart as her, someone who most likely fit the magazine's typical reader profile in terms of marital status, motherhood, education, and income, could get a handle on what this was supposed to be about without me leading her through all the captioned contortions.

"Well," Carol said, "I'm not married anymore. I just wear this ring so men customers don't get the wrong idea about me being friendly. But I don't care how many of his family reunions I would have gone to, and I went to plenty, I'd still be sitting before you today a divorced woman and happier for it. Not better off, mind you, but happier. So I'm probably the wrong one to be talking to, hon. If you ask me—and you did, remember—I'd a whole lot rather train a man than adjust to him. I have a boyfriend now who's twenty-three." Her voice went up at the end in that southern way that didn't signify a question so much as a request for special attention, a little noise of complicity like the one I instinctively made. "I started seeing him when he was twenty," she went on, "before anybody else had a chance to mess him up."

I had drunk enough beer on an empty stomach for this information to seem much more fascinating than family reunions. "What about your ex-husband—is he still single?"

"Lord, no. He couldn't survive alone. He's got two little girls with his new wife, and she controls everything, absolutely everything. My sons are working for him this summer, and I just tell them, 'Keep your fingers in that till, boys.' I mean, if mine don't say, 'Daddy, I love you' every minute of the day they won't get squat."

The Boston Pops-ish version of "American Pie" playing on the restaurant sound system became eclipsed by "Happy Birthday" being sung at a nearby table. "That's Lucy Gillespie having the birthday," Carol said, nodding toward the older woman who was blowing out candles while several others cheered her on. "I just love her to death. She's still married. They all are, as a matter of fact. Would you like to talk to them?"

A waiter arrived with my Calabashed shrimp. "No, thanks. I'd rather just eat and eavesdrop."

"Me and thee," Carol chirped as she left. "As a matter of fact, that's exactly why I took this job. Food and talk, hon—can't beat it."

Watching Carol join the ladies for a piece of cake, I thought it doubtful that she even read the magazine I was supposed to be writing for. She probably considered herself more of a *Cosmo* girl.

After dinner, I stopped by the pool and watched a couple of small children, one a toddler, swimming with their mother. In daylight it would be an ordinary enough sight, but in the growing dark with the pool lights not yet on, you had to strain to see the floats velcroed around the baby's wrists. It appeared as if she were being borne away from her mother by unseen currents rather than by fast-kicking legs so tiny they didn't break the water.

"Bye-bye," the baby said.

"Bye-bye," her mother answered. "Don't forget to write."

Jody's picked-clean dinner tray sat outside his door, and his light was still on. After I went into my room, I saw that Jody had closed the door on his side, which was fine with me. I got out my laptop, turned it on, and pressed a button to delete the family reunions article. "Are you sure you want to delete this file?" the computer asked. I pressed *y* for yes.

For the fifth time that day, I called Paul. I had already begun my message, telling him where I was in North Carolina, when he picked up the phone. "Are you screening your calls?" I asked suspiciously.

"I was just unloading the truck," he said.

"What were you doing out of town?"

"I told you last week—I had an appointment with a woman at a gallery in Portland."

"You did? Well, how did it go?"

"Lousy. I guess she couldn't think of any couches my paintings might fit over."

"Well, fuck her," I said, relieved that he evidently hadn't.

But the other woman I imagined the night before returned to taunt me anyway with the inadequacy of my love. "Marsha's so . . . *defended*," I heard her say, "don't you think?" I wanted to prove her wrong, but I didn't quite know where to start.

"I got your messages," Paul said. "And I can't pretend I'm not disappointed. Driving will only make everything take longer."

"Well, I guess it's too bad *I* wasn't on the plane that crashed."

"That was a dumb thing to say."

"I know. I just wish you'd try to believe it's all for the best."

"That you didn't get killed?"

"That I'm doing this."

I stared at my empty screen for a minute before turning off the computer and shutting its lid. "There's something I need to tell you," I said, and then the words came out in a jumbled rush. "Jody was with me in Athens once, he came to visit right before we graduated—or before I did, anyway; he never made it back to school. And he was kind of jumpy and out there, I guess, but I didn't see that then. We drank and sang and danced and told stories and it was more fun than I'd had in a long time, a lot more fun than being with Jimbo. So when we were alone and Jody got into my bed, it didn't seem like such a horrible thing to make love with him. But that's when he got sick, really sick, and had this delusion that I was his sister—that happened before Picasso—so I guess it was."

There was a long silence on Paul's end. "Why did it take

you so long to let me know something so important?" he asked.

"I didn't think it would be so important to *you*."

"You do too much goddamn thinking *for* me sometimes. I hate the idea that you keep me informed on a need-to-know basis. How's that supposed to help me trust you?"

"I didn't think you'd understand. And it seems as though I was right."

"Look, it was a long time ago—"

I made an effort to keep the tears out of my voice. "But you're thinking it was like doing it with my brother, and I already had a boyfriend, and why the fuck haven't I got a better grip on it all by now anyway?"

"Hey, hey," he said gently. "That's what *you're* thinking." And then, after a few moments, "Maybe I was thinking some of those things. But I'm not proud of it. I'm sorry." I heard him swallow and guessed it was gin. "Look," he sighed. "This is too much to handle over the phone. Let's plan to take it up when we see each other."

"Plan plans," I said, "don't plan outcomes," and he laughed. "Do you still love me?"

"I don't know, I may have to reevaluate if you go to work for Uncle Walt."

"Huh?"

"Disney wants you."

"What are you talking about, Paul?"

"The message you got while I was gone. Wait a sec—I'll rewind the tape and play it for you."

There came a whirring sound and then, a formal, preppy, once-familiar telephone voice. "This is Bennett Avery with a message for Marsha Rose. As you may or may not know, Marsha, I am now married and living in California, working with writers at Disney. One of our producers is shepherding an animated feature, and he's looking for someone to punch up the dialogue for a character who's a cat. A fluffy feature writer, as it happens. Think Ruth Hussey in *The Philadelphia Story*. Think pay the equivalent of several magazine pieces. But of course, you'll have to earn it. Call and I'll walk you through the details."

"Oh my God," I said when Paul came back on the line. "Do you think he's still trying to punish me?"

"With a cartoon? He said he worked at Disney, not Mousechwitz."

"Very funny. You've never felt the sting of his blue pencil. Do you know what this is?"

"No, what?"

"This," I sputtered, "is a perfect example of my life!"

I heard a snort and then coughing sounds on Paul's end. "Hold on," he said, hacking some more. "You made me swallow the wrong way."

The person who slept in my motel room the night before had evidently gotten up at 5:00 A.M., which was when I awoke to the sound of a coastal weather report coming from the clock radio by the bed. It took me a while to figure out how to silence the thing, discovering in the process that it was one of those arrangements where if you didn't release the alarm button, the radio would turn on at the same time the next day.

While dealing with that, I noticed the smell of more cigarettes than the one I had smoked in bed last night while watching the original, black-and-white version of *Invasion of the Body Snatchers*. I also noticed that both doors separating my room from Jody's were wide open, and my purse, which I had left on the dresser, was now on the floor.

I jumped out of bed and pawed through the purse looking for my car keys, which weren't there, then dashed into Jody's room, banging my knee on the dresser as I passed.

He had stripped the bed, just as he had my couch yesterday morning, leaving the sheets and bedspread in a folded pile on the center of the mattress. I crumpled against the wall, assuming he had taken flight again. Now I thought I understood what Nancy had meant by manipulation. Maybe she wasn't suggesting that Jody would maliciously use me, as I had suspected, but that it would be remarkably easy for him to conceal his intentions in the fog of my own. Not only had I failed to ration his cigarettes, I'd even been stupid enough to return his wallet, still fairly fat with cash, and make my purse easy prey.

I stepped out onto the balcony, not caring that I still wore only my T-shirt and panties, and ran down the length of it to verify my car's absence, already imagining how strange my report to the police might sound: "My car, which is really my father's, was stolen by a mentally impaired man who was my adjoining roommate last night here at the Holiday Inn . . ."

But before the parking lot came in view, I saw someone who could only be Jody in the swimming pool. Although my eyes registered him floating on his back, lazily sculling his hands, my panic was such that I had to consciously remind myself that drowned people floated facedown. I was already running downstairs when I remembered to go back for a pair of shorts. On my way out again, I checked Jody's room until I found his open duffel bag wedged behind the bathroom door with two cartons of cheap North Carolina cigarettes that he'd bought yesterday sticking out of the top.

Jody apparently didn't envision any Holiday Inn dips when he packed to run away. He swam in his underwear instead of trunks. But since this was a pair of striped briefs—most likely manufactured by Sol's company after its expansion into men's things—they looked appropriate enough that only Jody's aimless enjoyment of the water might startle anyone happening by in pursuit of coffee or the morning paper. Any normal adult in a swimming pool at this hour would be wearing goggles and swimming dogged laps.

I sat on Jody's sleeping bag, rolled up by the pool with his clothes and my car keys on top of it, trying to calm down my heart.

"Hi," Jody said, as if expecting me.

"What's going on?"

Seeing how annoyed I was, Jody ducked his head and went under with legs forked out behind him, surfacing beneath the diving board. With his hair splattered down across his forehead, he looked more like a teenager in need of a shave than someone old enough to be guiding his own toddler around the pool. "I really enjoy how the water smells," he said, grabbing the board with both hands. "What's that stuff called?"

"Chlorine. Listen, Jody, don't take off like that again without telling me."

"You were sleeping."

"You could have left a note."

"That was my job, putting chlorine in the pool. I think I used to have a turtle, and I felt sorry for him because he lived in such a little tub. I put him in the swimming pool so he'd have more room, but he died. The chlorine killed him."

"I'm serious, now, okay?"

"Okay," he said, chinning himself distractedly a few times on the board. I watched him for a minute, remembering our swimming lessons with Bishop Fulmer. "Bishop baptized you, Marsha," Jody would taunt me later, when Bishop started showing up in televised sermons. "He did!

When you were doing the breaststroke one time, I heard him. I'm the only one who never put my head underwater. I'm the only one who heard everything."

I stuck my foot into the water, which seemed even warmer than the morning air, and stepped onto the diving board, tucking my shirt into my shorts and stamping at Jody's hands until he let go laughing, then sprang off into the only fancy dive I ever mastered, a toe-touching pike that Eileen had taught me. The chlorine stung my eyes so that I was soon swimming with them closed, the noise of escalating traffic from the nearby interstate providing a surflike sound convincing as an ear-cupped seashell.

Later, as salesmen began emerging from their rooms, we splatted barefoot back to ours, Jody shirtless in his jeans and clutching his sleeping bag, me running with my arms crossed over my chest to hide the wet-cottoned contour of my breasts.

It didn't seem to matter so much today that I look any more mature than I felt, but I hadn't entirely abandoned faith in fashion statements. The purple T-shirt I decided to wear was one onto which Paul had silkscreened a design meant to illustrate "Get your ducks in a row," a phrase I used that, for some reason, most likely love, had struck Paul as amusingly ridiculous. A few ducks sat primly in a line across the chest, waiting to be joined by several ghost ducks tumbling down into the dotted outlines indicating their proper places.

Jody had left his razor in Washington, so I paid too much money to buy a pack of disposable razors from a vending machine in the motel lobby.

While Jody shaved in the bathroom with the door open, I sat down on the edge of his stripped bed. The television was on, a morning cartoon show. I clicked the remote control to the news and a report about the president playing

golf in Kennebunkport. When I leaned a hand back on the
bed, I noticed that the mattress felt damp. Inhaling
sharply, I also noticed a faint, alleylike odor.

Muting the television volume, I called out to Jody in the
bathroom, an act that felt oddly marital considering that I
now suspected him of wetting the bed. "So what made you
go and get your sleeping bag?"

"I needed it to travel." The words came out funny, as
though through lips twisted to facilitate shaving a cheek.

"I meant this morning. Why did you get it this morning?"

"I had a bad dream."

"Really?" Jody must have taken the excitement in my
voice as a sign of interest in this particular dream rather
than in just the mere fact of him dreaming and remembering at all. He hurriedly finished up in the bathroom and
came out to tell me more.

"It was really kind of a good dream. I mean, it wasn't a
nightmare. But something bad happened."

"Something scary?"

"Not really. I was at this beautiful place, on a lake. People were singing on the other side. It was Jesus music, but
not like on the gospel shows. This was good Jesus music,
black people singing it. I wanted to go there so I got into a
boat. I didn't have to row or anything. The water just
started to carry me to the other side. And that's when the
bad thing happened."

He turned away, actually blushing, so I got up and went
into the other room. "I can still hear you," I said.

I was cruising my room, making sure I'd left nothing
behind, when I heard Jody speak again. "I was out on the
lake, just sort of enjoying the ride?"

"Uh-huh."

"Then I saw this tin can float by, a piece of trash, and I
knew it was my job to get rid of it. Only I couldn't quite

reach the can with my hand, and there wasn't a paddle or anything for me to use to bring it closer. So I decided the only thing I could do was piss on the can as hard as I could and try to sink it. So I did. Only then . . ." His voice trailed off again.

"Only then you woke up."

"Yeah." I looked up to see Jody standing in the doorway, his face either blank or deadpan. "Do we have to be embarrassed *now*?"

"No," I said confidently, as though I made it my business to interpret dreams every day. "Water is a good sign."

Chapter 15

IF WE made a beeline for Sparta, we'd get there before noon. That was too soon for me. When I suggested an indirect route through the mountains, Jody quickly agreed. Once we started climbing, Jody and I changed places in the Honda. He got behind the wheel like someone determined to leave nothing to chance, painstakingly adjusting the seat and rearview mirrors, then familiarizing himself with the gear box, the feel of the clutch, and how the windshield wipers worked. Although it wasn't raining, he had the foresight to expect that we would be killing a lot of bugs.

After Jody had proved how disinclined he was to pass slower drivers and I stopped being afraid he might accidentally throw the car into reverse instead of fifth gear, I decided all I had to do was be a vigilant passenger, reading out loud every sign about speed, curves, and steep inclines. "You don't have to do that," Jody told me.

I lit a cigarette and tried to unclench my jaw. "Am I getting on your nerves?"

"Yeah, a little." With the watched caution of someone taking a driving test, he signaled and slowed down to pull over. I expected that I'd spoiled it for him, that he would now come around to my side of the car and change places just to shut me up. But all he did was mumble something about bleeding his lizard and head for the drift of bushes that lay down an embankment off the side of the road. He was gone long enough for me to notice the last of the cool air evaporating from the car, the mounting pressure of my own bladder, and then, after I got out of the car for a better look, no signs of life from behind the bushes.

I scrambled down the embankment and was wondering which way to go when I heard a twig snap behind me. Jody stood there looking like some errant knight, with a trashed McDonald's cup in one hand and a cluster of wildflowers in the other. "There's a creek down there," he said, wiggling the cup. When we got back to the car, he dribbled water from the cup into a tiny bud vase that Paul had glued onto my dashboard. Then he put the flowers into the vase stem by stem, as though threading an impossibly small needle. "Hope the water's not polluted," he said.

It was still early enough for the café in what passed for downtown Roaring Gap to be serving breakfast. While we sat waiting for ours, I decided it was a good time to work on Jody's relapse list. This was the series of symptoms that Dr. Thrailkill wanted posted on Jody's bathroom mirror when he got home, something to remind him what was going on if he should find himself slipping and unable to realize why. Then he would know he needed to see his doctor and have his medication adjusted.

Jody watched while I flipped my notebook open, then took it from me to examine the scrawls I'd made the day before. "Your handwriting's terrible. What's this say?"

" 'We, like sheep, have gone astray.' It's a line from that Christmas song—Handel's *Messiah*. We used to think it was peculiar, everybody singing about how much they liked sheep. Remember?"

"Not really."

"They'd sing that one phrase, 'We like sheep,' over and over before they ever got to the part about going astray."

"Oh," Jody said, rubbing his chin. "I get it."

I took the notebook back from him and turned to a blank page. "Okay, Dr. Thrailkill said we should make a list for you. Here's what we need to do—you tell me what happens when you start feeling bad, and I'll write it down."

Jody slumped over his coffee cup, frowning. "You want to know what happens when I feel bad in a good way, or good in a bad way? There's a difference."

"What's feeling bad in a good way?"

"That's when I'm supposed to be better because I don't hear voices so much, but I feel like I'm walking around in somebody else's body because I can't make it do what I want when I want or how I want."

"Have you felt that way lately?"

"Yeah."

"Do you feel that way now?"

"No, I'm just hungry now."

"What's feeling good in a bad way?"

"That's when I stop taking medicine."

"Okay, I think it's good in a bad way we're after here. What's the first thing you notice when that happens?"

"Well, everything seems great—real bright and sharp and clear. And I feel lucky because all I had to do was *stop* taking stuff to get better."

I lifted my eyes to his, but he was still looking into his cup like an old-fashioned gypsy reading the grounds, letting a long ash grow on the end of his cigarette. "Do you think you're cured?"

"It's more like nothing was ever wrong with me to begin with."

This seemed too true and cruel a thing to write down and make him look at every day: *1. You know you're in trouble when you think there's nothing wrong with you.*

But these were just notes, I reminded myself—I'd try for

a more positive tone when I typed the list up later. "What else happens?"

"My voice starts to echo, like I'm in the shower all the time. Which is kind of fun at first, but then I get to where I don't want to talk to anybody because what they're saying doesn't fit into the space between the echoes. I'd rather not be around anybody anyway because when I am, I think they're talking about me. Or laughing at me in their brains."

As our waitress brought our food, Jody rattled on, oblivious, as though just discussing this manic state brought it back to him a little. "Terrible things start to happen, so I try to get on top of it all. I get real food instead of frozen—maybe a steak and a potato to bake and some broccoli because it's supposed to be good for you, but I can never remember how to cook it so it always turns out too hard or too squishy. I do the laundry, I clean up real good, I watch TV and listen to the radio so I'll know what to be on the lookout for." The waitress, a generously built young woman who seemed to know everybody there but us, gave Jody a sympathetic little smile before moving on, as though she had plenty of days like that herself.

Jody stubbed out his cigarette and flooded his thin slices of French toast in so much butter and syrup that the goop reached the rim of his plate. "Is that enough?" he asked.

"Looks like it to me."

"Have I *told* you enough?"

"Do you think you can remember more?" I put my notebook on my lap and used my left hand to eat my oatmeal—I could tell it was the instant kind when I bit into an insufficiently moistened dried blueberry—leaving my right hand free to write. "What else happens?"

"I start thinking crazy." As I wrote this down Jody leaned over the table and jabbed my arm with the dull end of his fork. "Don't do that where I can't see," he said. "It looks sneaky. If you're going to interview me, Marsha, you can't be sneaky. Plus, try to remember that when I say 'off-the-record,' that means no comment."

"I'm sorry, did you say off-the-record?"

"Not out loud, maybe."

I shoved the bowl to one side and made room on the table for my notebook. "Okay, what do you want me to write down?"

"Just say that after I argue with myself for a while I decide it's not my fault I'm thinking crazy. It's *their* fault. I wonder why they want to make me crazy, and I figure the reason is I must be in the wrong place, with the wrong kind of people, and I have to do something about it."

"So you leave?"

"If I can."

"What's it like then?"

"I don't think about what I'm doing anymore. I'm just doing, and it all seems to go according to some kind of plan that's bigger than me. Everything that happens, whatever it is, it all seems like part of the plan. There's no good or bad anymore. It's all okay because I'm protected."

The waitress, back for coffee refills now, caught the last of what Jody was saying. "That's just how it is," she said, "when you're right with the Lord."

"No, it's not," Jody said without looking at her, his voice flat and impassive, as if *her* voice had come to him from inside his head. "That's just how it is when I'm sick."

The waitress cocked a hip and bit her lip, seeming to ponder this information in light of her own religious experience.

"Are you done?" I asked Jody.

"I guess."

I reached over to spear some French toast off his plate,

which he then guarded with crossed arms to keep me from taking more. "That's not," he said, "what I'm done with."

I closed my notebook, took my vitamins for women under stress, and asked the waitress to put in my own order of French toast.

If Jody had in fact been giving an interview, I thought while I waited, this would be the story: The Brain Has a Life of Its Own. It makes sense, it makes its own movies, it makes war on itself. It makes you homesick for something that was never really yours to begin with, then defies you to find it with only a lot of vague, powerful longings for guides. I remembered Dr. Thrailkill explaining how a sick brain can't be expected to understand its deficiencies on account of its disease. But even a presumably healthy one, like mine, could only understand another to the limited extent that it understood itself—a situation bound to account for a high run of tragic results. It didn't really seem to matter anymore if what was wrong with Jody had to do with how he was raised or a virus he caught while still in the womb. It only seemed to matter that he enjoy what he could without being further damaged.

Since no editor would be laying out this story, I could picture the copy any way I pleased. The way I saw it just then was facing a fried Spam and Wonder Bread layout, the text an uninterrupted block of print assuming the reader's interest and attention, with no subheads at all.

Leaving Roaring Gap, I had to bite my tongue to keep from announcing detour signs. Jody followed them on his own, driving us through a pass along which modest wooden houses, most of them in dire need of paint, were dug into a shady wooded hillside. It was not exactly an uplifting landscape.

"This reminds me of that old cartoon they used to run

all the time on the Cowboy Bob show," I said, "the one with the happy elves and the sad elves. The happy elves lived in a sunny meadow where they ran a dairy, and the sad elves didn't do anything except live in a dark valley like this and go around saying—"

Jody chimed in with me on the sad elves' line: "I don't want to be happy, I want to be sad."

"Then the happy elves bombed through the sad elf valley throwing milk bottles, and when the bottles broke on the sad elves' heads, there was sunlight everywhere and they got happy in spite of themselves. You know, if that was supposed to be the milk of human kindness, why couldn't they just give it to the sad elves and let them drink it?"

"Cowboy Bob's not on anymore," Jody informed me. "They've got Muppet Babies now instead."

"Really? What are they like?"

"They're happy *all* the time."

"How boring."

"Yeah, we hate them."

It was then, almost as if on cue, that the head of a Tiny Tears doll appeared to me through the roadside shrubbery. As we drew closer, I could see that the doll was lashed onto a fence, riding a portable vacuum cleaner canister and wearing a halo that appeared to be made from an oven heating element. "Pull over," I said, and we got out to examine the doll more closely. The heating element had bits of colored glass stuck on to it, and a string of little flame-shaped lights hung around the doll's shoulders, reflecting off the halo and enhancing the angelic impression. Close by was a line of low-kicking, green-skinned Barbie doll chorus girls, gathered on a circuit board stage and dressed in everything from beach wear to wedding gowns.

Jody roamed the fence with such interest that I went back to the car and got the little point-and-shoot camera that I hadn't really expected to use on this trip. I snapped a shot of Jody examining what looked to be an electronic fertility goddess—an hourglass-shaped lamp with a portable television picture tube head, and, hung around what would be its hips, a cable girdle laced with little naked dime-store baby dolls. "This is better than Tweetsie Railroad," Jody said. Tweetsie Railroad was the Blue Ridge Mountains train ride for kids that Sol and Eileen had once taken us on as a result of Jody's incessant badgering, a sort of low-rent but satisfying surrogate for our enraptured ideas of Disneyland.

The fence itself was a handmade thing with wood posts and horizontal boards. Lengths of wire radiated out from objects like spiderwebs, holding them in place. From somewhere nearby there came an underground hum from the generator that fed the fence power. A lot of the dolls on display were in bits and pieces—torsos and appendages—mixed up with all kinds of other stuff that humans had once found useful. The fence ran around both sides of what was obviously a residence, although one arm was sparsely populated, a work in progress.

A bearded old man emerged from behind the house, pushing a wheelbarrow toward the unfinished section of fence. He put down the wheelbarrow, pushed back the brim of his straw hat, and waved shyly. "Got me a load of stuff in town," he shouted. "Y'all want to come see?"

And so we went to marvel at his new collection of glass insulators, the bell-shaped wire protectors that were once used on telephone poles. "These'll look real good with arms poking out of 'em," he said, nodding sagely.

I found myself wishing that Paul could be here.

Despite the name he had given himself, it turned out that Nevada Messenger had never once been outside the state of North Carolina. His wife told me this as we sat in her leveled-out backyard, which was cleared of trees and sunny as the front of the house was dark. We sipped iced tea and looked through her family scrapbook, filled mostly with stories that had been written about her husband. Nevada had survived the Depression by peddling handmade twig furniture, and had always intended to head west someday. "It's probably just as well he never made it to Nevada," Mrs. Messenger said. "Nothing could have lived up to Nevada in his mind."

Mrs. Messenger made things herself, crocheted Christmas ornaments that a business-minded niece sold to shops in the tourist towns. "She tells me country is popular these days," Mrs. Messenger said. "I don't know what that means. Do you?"

"Maybe. Maybe everybody's homesick."

"For *country?*" She said the word with all the disbelief of a woman whose "facility," as she called it, was a wooden outhouse.

"That's right. In fact, there are some people who'd say that what you have here is an alternative lifestyle, Mrs. Messenger."

"They would?" She thought about this for a moment. "Hah!"

I envied Nevada Messenger on behalf of Jody, for whom envy now seemed a blessedly out-of-reach emotion. He was a character who would never be forced, for his own good, to deal with doctors or drugs; he could fool around with dolls and be thought colorful—legendary, even, judging from the ink he'd garnered. What would the scientists find if they could chemically analyze the contents of Nevada Messenger's brain? Probably, I thought, that he was lucky. I once read about a woman who'd fallen on her head as a child and later became convinced that in another life she had been the lover of an Egyptian pharaoh, a belief that no one held against her because her delusion, if that's what it was, led her to become a world-renowned Egyptologist. She was lucky, too.

Before we left, I took a picture of Jody with the Messengers. As I wrote down their address, Jody went off to the car and returned with the plastic head that was in my trunk. "It's Dr. Zaeus," Jody said. "From *Planet of the Apes*." Mr. Messenger accepted the head with a puzzled look. "It's a movie," Jody explained. "Charlton Heston and a bunch of actors dressed like monkeys, and the monkeys are all better than the people."

"Is that right?" Mr. Messenger said. Then, "You know what? This would look real good with a lightbulb stuck in its mouth."

Somewhere near Black Mountain, Jody began to find mountain driving monotonous. This was mainly because we'd been stuck for miles behind a Winnebago determined to distinguish itself from other Winnebagos by never once stopping at an overlook to partake of the view—which would have been all right if the driver didn't slow down anyway, not wanting to miss anything.

I took over behind the wheel, heading us into the heart of summer camp country. The landscape was so familiar now that as far as I was concerned, we were practically in the suburbs of home.

We stopped for ice cream in a shop filled with camp kids, a dozen little well-bred southern girls having hysterical fits of excitement merely because they'd been taken somewhere in a motorized vehicle to eat something sweet. After they'd all been served, one of their counselors clapped her hands to silence them. "All right, y'all," she said, "let's go to work on your song."

The few other adults in the place positioned themselves as far away as possible from these children, none of whom was older than eight or nine. I purposely chose a nearby table so I could track their musical progress. After agreeing upon "Swanee" as the tune for their song, the campers huddled to confer on lyrics, finally emerging with a first line they were so happy with that they couldn't wait to sing it. Or, rather, scream it. *"Snakes, bugs, butterflies and salamanders—all part of nature!"*

Jody gathered up the plastic dishes that held our half-eaten lumps of ice cream and tossed them into a garbage can. "Come on," he said, heading for the door, a cigarette already in his mouth. "They're nuts. They're *completely* out of control."

When we stopped for gas, I asked directions to the Grove Park Inn, a sign for which I'd seen a few miles back. I was still hungry and liked the idea of treating us to a late lunch in a quiet, elegant place.

If the parents had ever taken us to the Grove Park Inn, it would have been on one of those rainy Sundays when we all fled our movieless South Carolina county for a matinee in Asheville, where cinematic entertainment on the Sabbath wasn't considered a sin. But I doubted they did because I had no recollection of the sweeping vistas, the manicured grounds at the Grove Park Inn.

As we walked through the lobby with its massive stone fireplace, I picked up a hotel brochure that reminded me of what I actually did once know about this place and now couldn't believe I had ever forgotten. F. Scott Fitzgerald used to stay here. He stayed here when he came to visit Zelda, who was being treated in a nearby private hospital for—what else?—schizophrenia. I mean, what else given the way things were going. Had we landed here on account of Jody contacting Zelda in some occluded corner of *my* brain? I remembered my dream of the other night, with the screaming girl in the mountains, by the grove, and her Degas print. Zelda had tried to be a ballet dancer in Paris, hadn't she?

I was never attracted to the story of Zelda's life because of her illness; it was her wildness I cared about. Still, I could recall that while she was here in these mountains, she was treated with a strict diet, exercise regimens, and insulin injections, none of which seemed to do much good. I remembered something else, too. After many relapses (had someone made a list for her?) and repeated hospitalizations, Zelda died at this place in a fire, which most people who knew her thought was a blessing.

If those were the bad old days, what, then, were these?

It startled me when Jody said later, as we were being handed menus in the Blue Ridge Dining Room, that his parents used to stay at this hotel when they came to visit him. Thinking that he, too, had once been institutionalized in Asheville, I asked, "Where were you when they came to visit?"

"At camp," he said. "Camp Whatchamacallit. You know—the Jewish one."

Chapter 16

DOWNTOWN SPARTA was supposed to be revitalized, which meant it had been trimmed back and reduced to a brick-inlaid pedestrian thoroughfare rimmed by new office buildings, restaurants, and a Marriott Hotel that was a scaled-down version of the one in Atlanta. Then there were the crown jewels of Uncle Lud's mayorship—the library that looked like a shoe box with too large a lid; the performing arts center that booked traveling symphonies and Broadway road shows, leaving the old Memorial Auditorium a haven for heavy metal concerts and Friday night wrestling; and, of course, the museum, a triangular-shaped building staffed by docents who were refugees from garden clubs and bridge tables. All the old movie theaters, department stores, and luncheonettes were gone, defunct or moved to the malls. The Poinsett Hotel, where the Lurreys held Jody's bar mitzvah party, was distant enough from the hub of renewal that it had been turned into welfare housing for senior citizens. And the *Sparta News Herald* building, with its chiming clock tower, was untouched except for a fancy new sign.

In a way, it struck me as a bad dream of a downtown, the kind of place you'd find yourself running through, frantic and probably naked, attracting barely a glance from suspendered stockbrokers and women looking like sedated Alices in Wonderland in their white stockings and Laura

Ashley dresses. At the same time, though, the place seemed only a flawed and familiar extension of itself, almost admirable for holding on to at least this much old ground while making way for the new.

Downtown was our first stop because Calvin Thomas had the keys to Jody's apartment, which Jody had locked inside when he left. "What's Calvin like now?" I asked Jody as I looked for a parking place.

"He's all right," Jody said. "Only he's got his foot in his mouth."

"You mean he's sort of a bumbler?"

"I mean it's sort of a joke. He's always saying how you got to walk it like you talk it, so I'm always saying he's got his foot in his mouth."

I would soon consider this an unlikely description of Calvin, but then nothing had prepared me for the elegance of him standing slim, erect, and European-tailored in his men's wear shop. Since I couldn't imagine any of the boys from high school purchasing anything to wear here, I wanted to ask Calvin what he was doing with a store like this in a town like this. But then, the town had obviously changed enough into a city for there to be customers such as the man Calvin was helping when we arrived—a man who, considering how Sparta's lack of unions had extended its appeal well beyond the textile industry, could easily be an executive with the French tire company that had recently opened a factory.

Once Calvin's customer left with a new tie, I babbled to Calvin about what a wonderful place he had here, great location, nice displays, and every other inane thing that popped into my head.

"Thanks," Calvin said. Eyeing the T-shirt Paul had made for me, he strained for a compliment to offer in return. "You look good in ducks." Turning to Jody, he clapped a hand on his shoulder. "So, you've been traveling!"

The Lurreys were due back in town at the end of the week. In the meantime, it was Calvin's job to get Jody settled and see to any needs that Jody, now being carless, couldn't see to himself. Calvin seemed to be doing a lot for someone who only happened to be related to the Lurreys' maid, so I wasn't really surprised when he gave me to understand that the Lurreys were involved in his store. "Let's put it this way," he said coolly. "I own it. But if something bad happens, they get a piece of the trouble." Maybe, I thought, Calvin's business was part of how the Lurreys took care of Jody, something they wouldn't have done if their son had been healthy.

When Jody went across the street to get a Coke, Calvin responded to the evaluations he evidently suspected me of making. "Look, I'm not hanging around with him just because it's some kind of family tradition," he said. "Is that so hard to understand?"

"No." I tried to swallow past the lump in my throat. "Not so hard at all."

"Good. Just wanted to get that out of the way. And something else. We're so behind the times around here that my people won't be pissed off at your people for, oh, at least another ten years."

I didn't know whether to be offended until Calvin snapped his fingers and spun around on his heels, punctuating his joke with the physical equivalent of a drummer's "ba da boom." "You're good," I told him.

"Uh-huh."

"But it doesn't look like you'll be hanging around with Jody much longer."

"Well, how can I, if he moves out to be with his sister or parents?"

"Or into an institution."

"What? Did they say that's what they're doing?"

"They're seriously considering it."

As Jody returned, Calvin distracted him from our emotion with a dazzling, Juanita-like smile. "You up for some poker tonight?"

"Sure," Jody said. He reached for his wallet and fanned his stash out at Calvin. "I didn't get around to spending as much as I expected while I was gone."

"Don't go giving her the wrong idea," Calvin said. "We generally come out about even," he told me, then thumped Jody's shoulder again. "Of course, things just might change. I don't know what they did for you, man, but you're looking sharp, looking like a sharpster."

I brightened at this, glad that Calvin, with his broader frame of reference, saw improvement. If he could, maybe the Lurreys would, too. "You've got an appointment with the doctor tomorrow," Calvin told Jody. "For your shot."

"I've been thinking about that," I said. "I don't like it that his doctor never heard of the drug Jody's taking." Then, to Jody, "What do you think of this guy?"

"He's not," Jody shrugged, "much like Dr. Thrailkill."

"I'll get on the phone in the morning, see if I can find someone here who is."

"Awful short notice," Calvin said.

"Worth a try, though."

After that, it wasn't difficult talking Calvin into relinquishing his custodial role for the afternoon. He even offered to call Nancy with a five-star report.

With Jody driving, we hit the Winn-Dixie, bought a bunch of groceries (including Spam and Sunbeam bread—they didn't have the Wonder brand), and went to Jody's apartment at Riverbend Village.

In walking distance primarily of itself, Riverbend was a

complex of townhouses done along quasi-antebellum lines, with white wrought-ironed verandahs fighting to sustain the illusion of Charlestonian charm beneath the weight of Kmart garden furniture and barbecue equipment.

Judging from the scent of Pine-Sol in the air, someone—probably Juanita—had recently been in to clean. Still, the smell of smoke clung to everything. I recognized Jody's living room furniture as having once been in his parents' home, overstuffed things that hadn't fit into the Lurreys' right angle–less house. There was little in the way of art on the walls except for a large floral print from the Met and the solemn-eyed, unsmiling portrait of Jody that my mother had painted the summer when we were six and she did a series of the four of us, working mostly from snapshots of Jody and me because, unlike Flip and Nancy, we couldn't be bribed with money into sitting still for long. A cabinet against the wall held a television, a Sony receiver, and a tape deck. Very few tapes were in evidence, and there was no turntable to play all the records Jody had collected before he'd gotten ill, none of which were here anyway. I wondered if they weren't because Jody found them painful reminders of his previous life, disturbing in a way the portrait wasn't, or because he didn't care about them anymore.

The living room's tidiness gave way upstairs in Jody's bedroom, which even a thorough cleaning couldn't completely de-weirdify. This was Jody's lair, the carpet food-stained and divoted from what looked to be cigarette burns, the ceiling covered with iridescent patches of stars and planets arranged into constellations that Jody must have found meaningful, but that bore little resemblance to those in the heavens.

One wall was almost completely taken up by a grocery

store–style pyramid of empty pineapple cans that seemed to have been chosen not only for their state of origin, but for their eyeball-searing labels of red and yellow. Another wall had been made into a kind of bulletin board containing a tacked-on jumble of old TV schedules, wrestling programs, and the biorhythm charts that Jody said a clerk at the outlet store had made for him every month.

There was a Jews for Jesus poster on the closet door that asked the question, "Would you buy just half a bagel?" Above this message one half of a bagel floated through blank space, apparently unable to find its mate without the help of Christ. "Nice poster," I said.

"Got it off TV," Jody answered, and I assumed he was referring to one of those low-rent, fanatic-friendly stations that came to him by cable. "They were giving it to Jewish people for calling in to say if they'd buy half a bagel."

"What did you say?"

"I said yes, if it was half the price."

"Good answer."

"Yeah, but now they've got my phone number, and they call a lot." He squinted as though trying to remember something. "Before I left, I think I thought they were after me."

I wondered how to rephrase this for Jody's relapse list: "Jews for Jesus seem to be among those out to do you harm."

Beside Jody's narrow bed was a hefty stack of *Playboys* and *Penthouses*, which, under other circumstances, I might have found disturbing. Now I just thought, Good, at least that's something he can enjoy. Another television set, a small one, stood in close proximity to the bed. But the sight I lingered on while Jody finished unpacking his duffel bag was one that made me feel as though I was back in my D.C. bed still dreaming: a crude papier mâché female torso (something from art class?) that wore a lacy pair of panties out of which dangled an underwear outlet price tag.

I stood in the doorway delivering the news that I had, not so long ago, anticipated coming as a great relief—to me, not to Jody—but now seemed absolutely alarming, which was that after I finished unloading the groceries and Calvin got here, I would be leaving for my parents' house. Jody lit a cigarette, turned on the television set, and flopped down on his bed with a Coke and a bag of Fritos by his side. He nodded without looking at me as I told him I'd leave my parents' number downstairs and that he should call if he needed anything. It made me uncomfortable, being ignored at a fraught moment like this. Then I thought of certain farewell scenes I'd observed between parents and small children, the kind in which evidently gratifying gushes of unhappy tears are incited by saying such things as, "Don't worry, I won't be gone forever, I'll miss you, too." Wasn't it better to follow Jody's form and act nonchalant?

As if in response, a gruff, husky voice issued an advisory from the TV. "I've got something to say to all you ladies out there—make sure you're ready to go where you're headed when you start your engines."

I couldn't see the set from where I stood. "Who's that?" I asked Jody. "Sergeant Willy Falaw?"

"*Captain* Willy Falaw," Jody corrected. " 'P.M. Magazine Road Safety Tips.' "

"No kidding." When we were kids, Sergeant Willy Falaw's Highway Sermonette came on early every Sunday morning, just after Bishop Fulmer. Once he smashed a hammer down on a rose to illustrate how easily human beings can be crushed by motorized vehicles, cutting short a person's journey down the highway of life.

Now in Jody's bedroom, I grabbed a handful of Fritos and sat down on the floor to watch as Captain Falaw waved a tube of lipstick in the air. "This ordinary cosmetic product might *look* harmless enough," he said, "but in the wrong hands, it's a lethal weapon. Remember, applying makeup behind the wheel is asking for trouble. Don't do it if you want a safe and pleasant journey down the highway of life."

"He's still a jerkhole," Jody said, "isn't he?"

"Only now he's a *fat* jerkhole."

Jody sang a line from an old country song—" *'Roly-poly, Daddy's little fatty'* "—then flipped channels and settled for a while on a Christian exercise program which, according to the promotional commercial that came on in the middle of sit-ups, was locally produced and soon to be nationally syndicated. The sole featured exerciser of this aerobic ministry was Cynthia Carter, former Miss Teenage Piedmont and star pupil at the Patsy Chalmers School of the Dance.

Possibly for different reasons, Jody and I sat transfixed through Cynthia's buttock tucks, the erotic nature of pelvic thrusting completely dispelled by Cynthia's running commentary. "Exhale as you tighten those glutteals," Cynthia was saying into the mike that occasionally dangled into view, "inhale as you release. And just to get you through it, remember—we're not only working to get rid of all that Jell-O on our backsides. We're working to be fit vessels for the Lord's light!"

"All right, Cynthia," I said. "Shape up those vessels."

"Yeah," Jody said. "Better butts for Jesus!"

He flipped channels again, this time to a cartoon program. "See, I told you," he said scornfully. "There they are. The goddamn Muppet Babies."

My parents saw Sol and Eileen only several times a year, and from Joyce's accounts of these get-togethers, I got the sense that the subject of their children had led them into a loaded stalemate. It was easy enough to imagine my parents' mixed feelings about Our Boy's half-Baptist brood interfering with their response to the Lurreys' overamplified pride in Our Girl, raising her family in the dynamic southern Jewish community that Eileen had envisioned all along. The Lurreys, for their part, would be similarly resistant to what I suspected was the golden web my parents wove around Our Girl, flourishing in a larger world that the Lurreys couldn't help remember Our Boy visited only when floridly psychotic. The situation used to remind me of a demented communal divorce, one in which the parents remained on amicable terms while the children no longer spoke.

I let myself into my parents' house through the kitchen door, experiencing once again the distinction between coming home and coming to visit. When I called out my hello, Joyce came running downstairs from her bedroom. As we threw our arms around each other, I inhaled Norrell, her latest signature scent. She gave a start when I moved to kiss her on the lips, having forgotten that in my family, unlike Paul's, nobody lip-kissed.

"Marsha!" my father yelled from the living room.

"Daniel!" I hollered back.

"I'm your father," he cried out in all apparent seriousness. "Show some respect!"

"He probably wants you to run out and hug him," Joyce whispered, giggling.

"He probably wants a dog," I said, but I ran out and hugged him anyway. With his dark tan and a build that still suggested the athlete he'd been in his youth, Daniel looked like a tout for some golden years elixir. Pretty soon, though, an aggrieved expression came over his face, as if he already suspected Joyce and me of excluding him from something in which he had absolutely no interest, but would nevertheless appreciate the opportunity to dismiss as inconsequential.

We then had one of our usual exchanges. "How's the car running?" Daniel asked, hearty and good-humored again.

"Fine."

"Glad to hear it."

"How are the Cubs doing?"

"Lousy!"

"Glad to hear it."

"Traitor!"

"Don't look at me—*I'm* not the one who bets against them."

And so forth.

While Daniel occupied himself with patrolling the network news broadcasts, simultaneously taping the PBS news hour for later viewing, Joyce quizzed me on the nature of my trip. Had Jody "behaved"? Yes. Were there any more "incidents"? No. Then she took me to her studio to show me her latest work, small canvases filled with organic shapes and calligraphic squiggles. As far as I could tell, the paint had long since dried. Little pieces sold best at the gallery where she showed her work, a place that was owned by several art faculty members at the hard-shell Baptist college; at openings, they served white grape juice and Pepperidge Farm Goldfish.

In a basket by her easel was a stash of Amway catalogues. "What's this?" I asked.

"I'm not sure yet—maybe a way to pay off my debt."

The bulk of Joyce's current debt, I knew, came from her tendency to shop whenever she felt blue, a postmenopausal habit of hers that she defended as being healthier than drinking or Valium. Pretty soon, I would be able to gauge how blue she'd been lately by the number of garments she pulled out of her closet and tried to give me. Real generosity could always be detected in her gifts; some clothes and shoes had never been worn and were obviously purchased with me in mind. But her closets were her gardens and basically, this was weeding.

"Randolph," Joyce continued, "says I could be in the clear in anywhere from three to six months."

"Who's Randolph?"

"Someone I met in my hypnosis class. He lives out in Moonville."

"Hypnosis?"

"Didn't I tell you? I'm learning to hypnotize myself out of anxiety attacks."

"What's Randolph in for?"

"He needs a lot of dental work, and he's allergic to Novocain."

"I don't know," I said, shaking my head, "I just can't picture you going door-to-door."

She nodded agreeably. "Me neither, but Randolph says that's what happens at the bottom of the pyramid. I'll be more like at the top. Of course, we can't mention this to your father. And don't tell Flip, either. I asked, and Flip thinks Amway's a redneck hustle. He'd probably think Randolph is a redneck hustle, too, and he wouldn't be entirely wrong. I mean, Randolph's country, no doubt about it, but he's smart and sweet. Anyway, I really don't give a damn. Flip and Daniel are so busy fighting these days that frankly, hypnosis and Randolph are about the only breaks I get . . ."

We went back upstairs and while Joyce changed her clothes—we were going out to dinner—I noticed how trim she was, a testament, since she never exercised, to hormone treatments and her oft-cited observation that short-waisted women keep their figures longer. "I hope Sol and Eileen are reimbursing you for this trip," she said.

"Nope. It was my idea to do it this way."

"Well, maybe your father can help. But don't ask him yourself, let me handle it."

"Forget it, Mom. I'm not doing that stuff anymore."

As Joyce zipped up her skirt, her hurt expression was visible in the full-length mirror. I came closer to touch her hair, a golden chestnut color now, cut into soft layers that reached past her jaw. "This is nice," I said, still looking at her in the mirror, fluffing out the back with my fingertips.

"Do you really think so? We're trying to work in a few different shades so it looks more natural."

She moved into the bathroom to repair her makeup and I followed, watching in some latter-day equivalent of the amazement these rituals used to engender when I was a child. "You think I'm bad," Joyce said, cutting her eyes at me, "because *I* still do that stuff."

"I don't think you're bad. I think you're a gifted con artist." Then I gave her a don't-worry kiss on the cheek and went off to Flip's old bedroom to change into a dress, leaving before Joyce could tell me any more secrets or give me any clothes, activities that now seemed uncomfortably connected.

I was supposed to sleep tonight among the cadet memorabilia in Flip's room. Several years ago, my own old bedroom was appropriated by Daniel and made to look more masculine by Joyce, who ordered a new bedspread and curtains. I knew this wasn't an ordinary arrangement, but it had never seemed so peculiar to me before that my father, who had once snapped Polaroids of me dreaming in this small room, now spent his later evening hours here in a routine reminiscent of Jody's—smoking, watching TV, and

absorbing the effects of drugs, which in his case were designed to bring on sleep.

As I changed clothes, I ordered in my mind the dance
card Joyce had just presented me with, the list of things
that were expected to be soothed, eased, and mediated
somehow during my visit. Apart from the ongoing antago-
nism between my parents, there was, evidently, tension between Daniel and Flip, who had joined the textile
machinery business with the promise from Daniel, now an
owner, that Flip would inherit his share. Then, too, there
was the matter of Joyce distracting herself with what was,
at the very least, a flirtation—a flirtation, appropriately
enough, out in Moonville.

My parents took me to dinner at a new Northern Italian
restaurant. "It's not the little town we moved to anymore,"
Joyce chirped. The restaurant was catty-corner from Calvin's store, and on our way from the parking lot, a panhandler who said he was a Vietnam vet trailed us with his
rap—he'd killed for his country and could use a little help
now himself—until I gave him some change. Once we were
out of earshot, Daniel said grimly, "It's not the little town
we moved to anymore, all right."

After our drinks came and everyone was a little more
relaxed, I passed around snapshots of Paul. "He's a good-
looking guy," Daniel said. "Is he serious?"

"In a ridiculous sort of way."

"She means he has a sense of humor," Joyce clarified.
"That's a *wonderful* quality."

"What *I* meant was—"

"I know what you meant," I told him. And then, "Paul
got along really well with Jody. Better than I did, at first."

It soon become apparent that neither one of my parents,
for all the bulletins that Eileen passed along, actually knew

much more about schizophrenia than I did when Jody showed up in Seattle. I emphasized scientific data for Daniel's benefit and stressed the blamelessness of marijuana for Joyce, who blinked attentively as she listened, almost giddy with interest compared to her somber, silver-haired husband. All the differences that once presumably attracted them to each other now took expression in such wildly divergent manners it appeared there could have been something in having the Lurreys to scratch up against that, for a time, had made Joyce and Daniel seem more probable a couple, had made us seem more probable a family.

"It can be so heartbreaking, having children," Daniel said. "You'll see, Marsha, when you get married and—"

"Dad," I interrupted, "do you remember all those times when you told Flip to never get married?"

"Sure. He obviously wasn't listening."

"*I* was."

"As I was saying, I love your brother, but I can't say right now that I like him."

"You're just like your mother," Joyce said to him, mentioning a relative I could barely remember, "running down one child to another. Anyway, I'm sure you don't have a heart to be broken, it's much too illogical a thing for you to possess. What you have is a . . . bicycle pump!"

"I wish that were true, dear. That way, when your son causes me to burst an artery, it would be easier to repair."

"Arteries don't burst, they clog—with all that junk you go out and have for breakfast every morning."

On earlier visits, I would have taken this as my cue to come up with a more cheerful subject. But tonight I resisted the impulse. "I thought we were talking about Jody," I said, and at that moment, the panhandler from before passed by the window we were sitting near.

Daniel nodded in the panhandler's direction. "I suppose Jody was up to that sort of nonsense in Seattle."

"What sort of nonsense?"

"Begging, acting crazy." He spoke in the same tone he had once employed for faulting Jody's haircut and messy room, as though begging and acting crazy summed up everything wrong with our generation. "I find that behavior offensive."

"And you wonder why," I said, "you should be subjected to it?"

"Exactly."

"In that case, I could think of lots better people than Jody to blame. Like, for instance, these jerkholes you keep voting into office."

"What's a jerkhole?" Joyce asked.

"Look, Marsha," Daniel said patiently, "I'm talking apples and you're talking oranges."

"Well, stop the presses."

Our food appeared and somehow, we got through dinner. Before we left the restaurant, I called Jody's apartment; he and Calvin were playing poker, and yes, it was all right with Jody if I wanted to spend the night there.

"What's the matter, baby?" Calvin said when he opened the door and saw my face. "Someone leave your cake out in the rain?"

Paul was beginning to make dinner at the studio when I called from Jody's bedroom. By the time I finished describing the evening's events, he was eating. "I'm kind of surprised," I told him, "but I don't know what else I expected."

"Maybe a little comfort."

"That's what they had us for, isn't it—comfort in their

old age?" He was chewing and didn't answer. "That's okay, it was a rhetorical question anyway. What's for dinner?"

"A one-dish, single-burner, hot plate special—corkscrew pasta with store-bought cheese sauce. Very tasty. So how did you leave them?"

"When I said I was going to stay at Jody's, Joyce cried and Daniel threw up his hands."

"Too bad you just can't get on a plane and leave, period."

"I can't go like this. Besides, I have to see the Lurreys."

He went on eating and drinking in a way that sounded so thoughtful and familiar that I felt as though I was across the table from him. "Maybe it would be easier," he said, "if you weren't alone."

"How do you mean?"

"Maybe the novelty and wonderfulness of me would balance out all this other crapola."

"I can't ask you to do that."

"I finally figured that out. That's why I offered."

"You'd hate it here."

"I know."

"You might even hate *me* here."

"That's a chance you'd have to take, just like I did. You've done time with my family, and they're not normal."

"They just wear Birkenstocks. Mine are hillbillies."

"They've got too much money to be hillbillies."

"Believe me, you'd prefer the genuine articles."

"You can dish it out, bub, but you can't take it. 'At last,'" he said, his voice going squeaky as he paraphrased my family reunions story, "'Paul found a link with someone in Marsha's family whose nature seemed similar to his own. Unfortunately, it was with someone who'd spent a lot of time in mental institutions.'"

"That's not funny."

"If your link can be dead, why can't mine be mentally ill?"

It didn't occur to me until after we said goodbye that I wouldn't have been in this position at all if it weren't for Paul. It was almost as if having Paul in my life had somehow opened the only door through which Jody could have reentered. Thanking Paul would have been as ridiculous as blaming him. Still, on my way back downstairs, I found myself feeling almost as grateful as I was apprehensive.

"Paul's coming," I said, sitting down to be dealt into the poker game.

"He's her boyfriend," Jody told Calvin, who was shuffling. "He's cute. You'll like him."

"Yeah? Is he a sharp dresser?"

"He wears a standard issue, friction-lock, brass webbed-belt buckle."

"Really," Calvin said, flipping out the cards. "White people are going to put me out of business."

Chapter 17

ONCE, ON a crowded subway car bound for Wall Street, I sat next to an immaculately dressed businessman who scribbled steadily into a leather-bound notebook, frowning as he wrote what I assumed to be information fraught with financial significance. But when I actually caught a glimpse of his notebook, I saw that he was using his Waterman pen to write a single phrase, over and over again: "In it, but not of it." The notion of being in it but not of it seemed pretty implausible to me, sort of like wearing a white silk blouse while you eat a big, two-fisted hamburger with everything on it oozing out the sides.

Calvin, however, had been raised with the New Testament, and his assessment of how I ought to be conducting myself, issued after Jody went to bed, was basically the same. "Don't worry so much about your folks. The more you act like everything's cool, the more they'll have to act like everything's cool."

"What's the good if it's all an act?" He looked at me as though I were being willfully stupid. "And what about the Lurreys? Won't they think I'm meddling?"

"If they do," Calvin said, "I got two more pieces of advice. Hold tight, and leave me out of it."

The next morning, within the space of three phone calls, I had set up an afternoon appointment for Jody to see Dr. Frank Gower, an old hand at administering fluphenazine shots. Then I took Jody with me to have breakfast at the Wade Hampton Pharmacy, located in an aging flat-topped shopping center that, like the town itself, appeared to have grown without any real design. With its rusted sign and jagged roof lines, the shopping center was a definite eyesore. But compared to the malls, it did seem somehow more honest.

I parked in front of the Patsy Chalmers School of the Dance so I could take a look at this year's recital portraits, taped up inside the window. A pronounced age gap existed between the littlest tap dancers and the older students, who looked to be their mothers and could have easily been veterans of the same recitals as me. Patsy's picture was not in the window, but there was a shot of her daughter Boo-Boo, who had apparently inherited the place from Patsy without bothering to change the name. I couldn't decide which would be worse (or better, depending on your point of view); the Bouray or the Boo-Boo Chalmers School of the Dance.

"Everybody looks ugly," Jody said.

He was right. The camera had foreshortened bodies and the lighting didn't do anyone any favors, either. Still, disconcerting as it would have been to imagine myself coming here to click off double pull-backs, I enjoyed knowing these others would be doing so come fall. Compared to the women in the aerobics classes I sometimes took, toned-up specimens who wore fancy leotards and performed dumb cheerleader combinations with all the self-importance of prima ballerinas, Boo-Boo's older students were overweight and paunchy. But at least they were really dancing.

Jody and I walked several doors down to the Wade Hampton Pharmacy, which, as it turned out, had changed far more than the dancing school. For one thing, it was no longer the Wade Hampton Pharmacy. Since my last breakfast here with Daniel, the place had been made over into the Wade Hampton Diner. There was still a horseshoe-shaped counter with swivel stools, but where the racks of hair dye, cold medicines, and magazines had once been there were now booths and tables. The decor, like the waitresses' uniforms, was aggressively fifties. Painted onto the walls were black-and-white, photo-realistic renderings of local scenes—a downtown intersection that no longer existed, a hula hoop contest in Pinkney Park, and the 1960 Ping-Pong Ball Drop, an Easter egglike affair in which Ping-Pong balls were dumped all over the county from a prop-engine airplane.

The clientele, however, was still the same old pharmacy breakfast crowd. And there sat Daniel, at a table in the center of the restaurant, reading the paper while he waited for his food. I watched him for a moment before he caught sight of us. Because Daniel had developed an allergic reaction to newsprint, he now read the paper wearing white cotton gloves. Wearing the gloves in public not only made my father seem vulnerable—a word I had never before associated with him—they also, in combination with his natty business clothes, gave him a vaguely comic, Mad Hatterish sort of air, an impression that held when, after spying Jody and me, he waved us over and began to hold court as though we were visiting emissaries from some strange planet where nobody had any interest in sports or his political views. Which was good practice, I thought, for Daniel meeting Paul.

"This is my daughter Marsha," Daniel told all the waitresses and customers he saw here every morning. "And this is Jody Lurrey, an old friend of the family."

"When they sold magazines here," a chipper insurance agent informed me, "Dan used to show us your articles."

"Oh, God," I groaned, "how embarrassing."

"You don't have to be embarrassed, Marsha," Jody said.

"Attaboy." Daniel clapped Jody on the back as though he had just caught me out at first. "*You* tell her."

"I tell her and she tells me," Jody said. "We made a relapse list together. Plus, Mashie stayed on my couch last night, which sort of makes us even but not really, because I got a headache and ended up sleeping on her floor."

"That's nice," Daniel said, "but I hope you won't mind if Marsha comes back to stay with us. We haven't seen her in so long, and we miss her."

"I don't mind," Jody said, and then to me, "How about you?"

Without waiting for my answer, Daniel smacked the table. "So *that's* settled." He looked around for our waitress. "If Dottie takes your order now, she might be able to get our food out at about the same time."

Dottie was a veteran, noticeably older than the other waitresses who worked here. I guessed that Daniel made a point of sitting at her table because she would put up with him in ways her younger colleagues wouldn't. "I'll do my darnedest, Mr. Rose," Dottie said. "You can be sure of that."

Jody made an effort to sustain the level of conviviality that had been established. "Are y'all proud," he asked Dottie, "of your sausages?"

"They're excellent," Daniel said, following up with a question that routinely accompanied every piece of advice he gave us as children. "Have I ever given you a bum steer?" It was Nancy who had enlightened us when Jody and I took this literally, as some sort of an assurance about degenerate cattle.

Daniel also introduced us to the Chinese-American man behind the cash register—Bobby Lee, the new proprietor. He was about our age, Jody's and mine, maybe a little older. When Daniel told us that Bobby Lee's parents owned the New China restaurant, I guessed that it was him I remembered seeing hunched over a table in the rear of the restaurant doing his homework on Sunday nights, when it always seemed that the temple congregation rented the New China for its exclusive use. That same studiousness was evident now in Bobby Lee, who could easily be one of those wholesomely ethnic models in preppy clothes catalogues.

It figured, I thought, that a boy whose refugee parents probably didn't realize they were naming him for a Confederate general would wind up owning a place named for another, literally making it his business to commemorate the town as he first knew it. Of course, fifties-style diners had become so popular by now that Bobby Lee could have ordered almost everything he needed from a restaurant supplier specializing in the genre. Still, I enjoyed my suspicion that transforming the New China into a place such as this, a restaurant with grits and fries and minced barbecue sandwiches on the menu, had once been Bobby Lee's guilty childhood dream.

After polishing off his breakfast, Jody lit a cigarette and lapsed into a wide-eyed stare. I could feel the truth of Calvin's advice applying now because as I tried to discern if Jody's stare was similar to the ones I remembered from his unstabilized days in Seattle, Daniel grew visibly disturbed by Jody, hurriedly finishing his own food and asking Dottie for the check. Showing some interest in the trouble between my father and Flip was the only way I could think of to act like everything was cool.

"Here we are," Daniel said, instantly warming to the topic, "heading into a recession. And Flip wants to refuse a very handsome offer for the company."

Flip was something of an exception because, unlike most of the other Jewish sons in town, he had stayed and gone into his father's business. Daniel might be ready to retire, but I could see how the notion of selling now would seem like a betrayal to Flip, no matter how golden the parachute he might be offered. "Who wants to buy?"

"A mower manufacturer in Michigan," he said, and mentioned the name of a nationally known company.

"Really? I thought those days were just about over."

"What do you mean?"

"Oh, you know," I said, waving my hand as though the matter were of no consequence to me. "The days of corporate rape and pillage."

Daniel narrowed his eyes. "Have you been talking to Flip?"

"Not lately."

"I've got news for you, Marsha," he said. "This time around, it's the South that's going to save the North's ass."

From the way he sat back and folded his arms, I expected that maybe some of our fellow diners had applauded this sentiment more than once. But before I could respond, Jody spoke. "There's something wrong with this picture," he said.

I wanted to tell him he didn't know how right he was, but Jody made it clear that the picture *he* meant was the one on the wall behind us, which he had evidently been studying all along. "That's the Ottoway Hotel," Jody said. "Right?"

Daniel swiveled around to examine the downtown intersection depicted on the wall, long since razed for a parking lot which in turn was razed for a freeway that made it easier for people to avoid downtown altogether and head straight for the malls. "That's right," Daniel said. "I almost stayed at the Ottoway when I first came to town, when I was looking for a place to build the plant. But their plumbing was so out-of-date they only had bathtubs, no showers."

Since bathrooms were not shown in this painting, Jody must have been referring to something else. "What's wrong with it?" I asked.

"It's on the wrong side of the street."

Daniel looked more closely and motioned Bobby Lee over to the table. "Jody here thinks he's detected a geographical discrepancy in your mural. Is there a chance that the Ottoway Hotel might be on the wrong side of the street?"

Bobby disappeared into the kitchen and came back with a stack of shiny new black-and-white photographs that had obviously been printed from scratched old negatives. They were all street scenes of Sparta. If this were a northern city, the vintage of the cars would make you think the pictures dated from well before World War II. But since most people here were still pretty poor then, they were probably taken later.

"I got these from the newspaper," Bobby said, "for the guy I hired to paint the murals."

Daniel found the photographs at least as entertaining as the crossword puzzle he would be finishing now if we hadn't shown up. We all looked through them together, finding a wide-angled shot in which the Ottoway Hotel appeared just as it did in the mural. It must have been printed from a flopped negative, though, because several other photographs, none quite as all-encompassing as the first, showed the Ottoway Hotel on the opposite corner, where Jody recalled it being.

"Mystery solved," Daniel said, grinning at Jody as though nothing I'd previously said about his condition was significant as this, as though willing Jody to go on from here to solve the mystery of himself.

"I kind of like that it's backward," Jody said.

"It's funny no one else ever noticed," Bobby Lee said. "But I guess most anyone old enough to remember the place is happy to see it here at all."

Since this was roughly my response to the tap dancers' pictures, I thought I understood.

Although Jody wasn't exactly an insider as far as the rest of my family was concerned, he wasn't really an outsider anymore, either. If anything, his reentry into our lives over the next few days made us *all* seem kind of inside-out, seams showing and threads unraveling in ways that were, for a change, fairly obvious.

Daniel came home with a videocassette onto which all his Super 8 home movies had been copied. None of us had seen these movies for years, not since Daniel's old projector broke, so Joyce and I sat down to watch with him. "The Rose Family Memories," a superimposed title said at the beginning of the tape. Then, set to Muzak, came the grainy, jumpy footage of the past. By the time the tape ended, it was clear it should have been called, "The Rose *and* Lurrey Family Memories." There was at least as much footage of Jody as anyone else—shooting baskets with Flip, doing the cha-cha with me, being celebrated at his bar mitzvah, receiving his high school diploma.

"We should show this to Jody," Daniel said afterward.

"Maybe not," Joyce said. "It might be hard for him to watch."

Daniel sank into a long silence from which he emerged to telephone Flip, ostensibly to discuss the finer points of the Cubs' latest loss. "By the way," I heard Daniel say before he hung up, "if we don't sell, I'm not so sure I want to retire."

Without a single warning about who should or should

not know about it, Joyce took me out to Moonville to meet Randolph Shipley, a surprisingly youthful-looking widower. "We're building up your mother's confidence," he said, shaking my hand.

"Just think of us," Joyce told me, "as friends who have helped each other through some tough times."

It was hard to tell whether they were talking about their relationship or the Amway meeting that was about to begin in Randolph's living room, where one of Joyce's paintings had been hung; it looked odd against the floral wallpaper. But it did seem significant that Joyce used the past tense.

I saw it as a measure of Jody's continuing progress when he wanted to join Flip's children and me for a movie. It was a science fiction movie that the twins, Jamie and Missy, were dying to see. I expected that Jody might not be able to sit through the whole thing, but there couldn't possibly have been a live-action movie more cartoonlike than this. I was the one, as it turned out, who couldn't take it.

I left Jody alone with the twins, who sat raptly cross-legged eating popcorn, and two-year-old Jason, who, at the first sound of scary music, had climbed out of his seat and into the nearest adult lap, which happened to be Jody's. There he promptly fell asleep, just as Cathy, his mother, had promised he would. I bought a magazine and spent the duration in the lobby. When the movie ended, Jody came out carrying Jason, who, for some reason, he insisted upon calling Baby Eugene.

"Baby Eugene peed his pants," Jody informed me, his lip curling slightly, but still, he seemed to enjoy the clinging warmth of Jason's body. Jody was ready to be alone then and declined to join us all for dinner, but with such polite appreciation for the invitation that I began practicing my speech for the Lurreys, the one about all the positive ramifications of Jody's running away.

Flip also started referring to Jason as Baby Eugene. "Somehow it suits him," Flip said at dinner that night, scraping corn off the cob for Jason. "Maybe because he's still bald."

"Must be something he gets from his mother's side of the family," said Daniel, who was inordinately proud of his full head of hair.

"Must be," said Cathy, "if it's something bad. Although I fail to see what my being Baptist might have to do with Baby Eugene's—I mean Jason's—still having a little duck down on his head."

A big-boned, open-faced Alabama girl, Cathy usually bore Daniel's comments with humoring smiles. But tonight, after the twins went outside to catch fireflies, she continued to challenge him. "There's something I've been meaning to ask you," Cathy said, cheerful as ever. "Do you think I'm stupid?" Joyce and I toasted her with the dregs of our iced teas. "Y'all stop," Cathy told us, "you're making me self-conscious. It's just that I've been wondering for a long time, and I'd honestly like to know."

"Perhaps I can be of some assistance here," Flip said in exaggeratedly judicious tones. "Considering that you, Catherine, are a woman, and that he, Daniel, is my father, I'd say the chances are excellent that he does, in fact, think you're stupid."

"So," I said to Cathy later, after we finished loading the dishwasher. "Would you say you learned a valuable lesson here tonight that strengthened your marriage?"

She popped open a can of Diet Coke and lit one of the three Marlboros she allowed herself each day. "They're really getting to you," she said, "aren't they?"

"Well, well, jump back and kiss yourself," Wiley Putnam said when I answered the telephone at my parents' house.

" 'Jump back and kiss yourself,' " I repeated. "Where'd you get that?"

"James Brown," said Patina, who was ironing Daniel's shirts on the other side of the kitchen, working to the easy listening station my parents always kept the radio dial on.

Wiley was calling from Nashville, where he was in the music publishing business. His job, he once told me, consisted mostly of "plugging tunes in the pitching room," whatever that meant.

"What's up?" I asked him.

"Well, I'm a very busy boy. Punk and rap have got to be the best things that ever happened to country music."

"How'd you know I was here?"

"Got your boyfriend's number off your answering machine, and I talked to him last night. Listen, I wasn't planning on coming down there myself, but since you're going to subject that man to all those fools we went to high school with, sounds like Uncle Wiley better ease on down the mountain and see if this fellow's up to snuff."

"I don't know what you're talking about, Wiley."

"Our reunion, Marsha—our fifteenth reunion. Don't you read your mail?"

"Not lately."

"Then what the hell are you doing down there? Did somebody die?"

"I found Jody in Seattle."

Wiley whistled low into the telephone. "How is he?"

"Evened-out is the short answer, which is about all I have time for because I've got to be at the airport soon to pick up Paul. There's a doctor in Seattle who says it's the lucky ones who even out after thirty. They might not get much better, but as long as they're on medication, they probably won't get any worse."

"You know, I came across him here once."

"What? How come you never told me?"

"Marsha? Kiss my ass."

"Sorry. What happened?"

"He gave me the title of a song and held out his beret till I put in some money."

"What was the title?"

"Oh, it was good—'I Keep Learning Things I Never Meant to Know.' You better believe I used it."

This made me too sad to laugh the way Wiley expected. "I hope you gave him a lot of money then. 'Bye, Wiley."

On my way out of the house, I spun the radio dial to a soul station. "Knock yourself out," I told Patina.

The airport had been built about fifteen miles outside of town in what had once been a peach orchard. There used to be only one airline that flew in and out of here, but now there were four. As a result, two new, elaborately elongated wings had sprouted off each side of the original building. Maybe this was a selling point to all the northern businessmen who were expected to come South to have their asses saved. How could they experience redemption in a place where they deplaned on portable stair steps, then stood inside the nearest door until their luggage arrived? If they were going to believe, they needed Jetways and a long walk to baggage claim. Whatever the theory, it was spoiled by how rarely more than one plane was ever on the ground at the same time. Instead of making the airport appear bigger and busier, the new wings just made it seem cavernous and empty.

Being late, I ran what seemed a good half mile to reach the gate where Paul's flight from Charlotte was arriving, sighting not a soul along the way except the security guard who X-rayed my purse. When I got to the gate, the Jetway was just being attached to the plane.

As I threaded my way through people to take up a position where Paul would be sure to see me, someone reached out to tap my shoulder and I turned around to find Jody, his face tight with tension. I should have known why he was here, especially when I saw Calvin standing by his side, but I mindlessly assumed that they, too, had come to meet Paul's plane.

"I'm very happy for you," Calvin said. "But not that happy. We're here for Mr. and Mrs. Lurrey."

"I thought they weren't due until tomorrow morning."

"Change of plans, they decided not to spend the night in New York and flew straight through."

They were flying first class, too. At least, that's the conclusion I reached when the Lurreys stepped out of the Jetway before anyone else, Sol bearing Eileen along with a solicitous hand on her back. They seemed older than my parents now, worn out from more than just jet lag, and more dignified, too. Making an error far more plausible than mine, they mistook me for a member of their greeting party, but not the one who had to be dealt with straight away. That was Jody, and they took him in with such evident relief that Jody almost—but not quite—looked happy to be hugged.

Uncle Sol turned to me first, pecking my cheek and then waiting for me to take my turn on his, just like always except that he didn't say, "Give your old uncle a little sugar." Then came Eileen. "Sister," she said, cupping my chin in her hand and just looking at me, her eyes letting me know what a complicated thing our separation had been for her, too, and if it weren't for the reticence I saw in the set of her mouth, I would have held her in my arms the way I did the last time I saw her. I thought I knew what that expression meant. It meant she anticipated more problems ahead, problems she couldn't postpone addressing any longer.

Before I could speak, Paul loped over and swept me up into an exuberant kiss. He was carrying a beat-up canvas shoulder bag and wearing his Munch T-shirt. Not having much of a memory for the few snapshots he'd seen of my parents, Paul initially mistook the Lurreys for them. He was starting to kiss Eileen when I explained who she was, and then his mouth made a little oval of surprise, something like the mouth of the man on his shirt. He still looked like that as I walked him over to an empty gate so everyone could have a little more privacy.

When the Lurreys passed by on their way to baggage claim, Jody reached out and grabbed Paul by the brass buckle of his webbed belt. "See?" he said to Calvin. "I told you so."

Chapter 18

PAUL WAS right about his presence providing a positive distraction. In fact, among the Roses, the grown-ups were so taken with him that I wondered if they had all along harbored some previously unsuspected desperation on my behalf. The twins' response to Paul was closer to my own. They were most impressed with his ability to speak at great length in the cranky, irritated voice of Donald Duck.

"Say something else," the twins squealed.

"Zip your lips," Paul told them in the duck voice. "You're getting on my nerves."

Joyce wanted to ask the Lurreys to join us for dinner at Piedmont Valley, but I told her they were exhausted, it was better to wait. I told myself it was better for me to wait, too, to give Eileen more time to appreciate Jody's progress before I tried to see her.

Cathy wanted to go somewhere other than the country club so the twins wouldn't have to be so well-dressed and well-behaved, but Daniel was adamant, convinced that Paul would enjoy the place. "You might find it interesting," I told Paul in our room at the Marriott. He was putting on his khaki pants and black linen jacket, the only dress-up clothes he owned. He looked nice, but rattled.

"I'll be all right," he said. "Just don't roll your eyes at me."

There were any number of times that night when I could

have easily done that. Like, for instance, when one of Daniel's golfing buddies told a racist joke in the bar; Paul said nothing but checked his watch, as though noting for future reference the passing of time between his arrival in the South and the telling of this joke. Or when the maitre d' insisted that Paul "borrow" a tie before entering the dining room. Or when Paul made the mistake of ordering a sauced-to-death red snapper that wasn't nearly so good as the chili dog and fried onion rings he had earlier that day at Bybee's. Or when one of Flip's classmates from the Citadel came over to the table and the two of them knocked the enormous stones of their school rings together, a ritual that ardent alumni employ in lieu of a handshake. Or when the twins grew antsy waiting for the adults to finish, and Flip turned to them and spoke in his company commander voice: "Quiet, maggots."

"Don't call them that in public," Cathy said, spooning ice cream into Baby Eugene's mouth.

"He doesn't mean it literally," Joyce explained to Paul over Flip's assurances that he had been speaking from the bottom of his heart. "It's something upperclassmen call freshman cadets."

"They won't let girls go to the Citadel," Missy informed Paul, "because girls administrate."

"That's *menstruate*, Missy," Paul said, then seemed surprised when Cathy stopped her from repeating the word after him.

"Be nice, now," she told her daughter. "People won't like you if you're not a nice girl."

It was still early by West Coast time when we got back to the Marriott, but Paul flung himself onto the bed as if it were a life raft in a wind-struck sea, obviously exhausted by projecting the wonderfulness of himself.

"I wanted to tell Missy that her aunt isn't always so nice,

and that's why I like her," Paul said. "But I didn't think that would go over so well, either." I could already see he would never want to do this again, but that it would have been much worse if we hadn't rented a room. When I realized I had forgotten to bring toothpaste, Paul told me to look in his shoulder bag. Unzipping the top, I discovered an old recital portrait that Paul had somehow smuggled out of Joyce's studio, where she kept it tacked to the wall. I was about fifteen, wearing a spangled red leotard and a big fake smile.

"How," I demanded, "did you get your stubby little paws on this picture?"

"Joyce said you'd be mad at her for giving it to me, but I talked her into it anyway." He sounded pleased with himself.

"I'm tearing it up right now."

"No you're not." He leapt from the bed to protect the photograph from destruction. "Fair's fair—you've got old pictures of me." He was referring to a pair of snapshots I'd gotten from *his* mother, one of a still-blond, three-year-old Paul in a safety-pinned sunsuit, his head nearly wide as his shoulders, and another of him at five sitting in a back-yard apple tree, shirtless and cocky-looking in belted over-alls that he obviously insisted on wearing every day. I had them in wood frames on my bureau.

"Those are different," I said. "Just looking at those pictures melts my heart."

"That's more or less how I feel about this one."

Although our room undoubtedly harbored the ghosts of far more businessmen than trysting lovers, those words changed and charged the atmosphere enough so that I put votive candles into ashtrays by the bed and lit them.

We undressed each other carefully, as though exposing far more than flesh with each shed garment. It felt risky,

riskier than if we had just stripped and flung ourselves at
each other in wild abandon, a dance that, for us, was far
more familiar. I traced Paul's lips with my finger and he
reached out to take my hand, rubbing his face into my palm
with dark, serious eyes locked so hard into mine that I
couldn't turn away, not for a second, even when being
looked at this way became so unbearable I wanted nothing
more than to bury my face in his shoulder. As we eased
back against the pillows, I forced myself to lie absolutely
defenseless in his arms, until I realized with a sudden rush
of sorrow that this was how he had always lain in mine.
Paul kissed at my eyes, catching tears with his tongue.
"Are you okay with this?" he asked, and I nodded emphatically. "This is what I want." "Me, too." And that embold-
ened me enough to lay down the tracks of my desire in a
way he would find impossible to miss. It seemed as if I
couldn't take him in with enough of my senses, that everywhere I touched—the ropy muscles of his neck, the hollow
groove of his hip, the soft, beckoning skin below his navel—
had to be tasted and inhaled as well. When we were
wrapped together too closely for me to wander, our breath
and murmurs became a kind of music that I pulsed and
quickened to, and from how Paul answered, with his own
purposeful hesitations and woozy, syncopated kisses, I
knew that he was hearing it exactly the same way.

Afterward, when the heat left our bodies and we shivered in the mechanically cool air, I reached out for the edge
of the bedspread to pull over us, moving carefully again,
but now only so that we would stay connected.

On the way back from Moonville yesterday, Joyce had
wondered if I should tell Paul about Randolph. "He might
get the wrong idea," she said. Now I decided that anybody
who could love me in that recital portrait could understand
a lot more than Joyce and Randolph. And so when Paul

began talking about what had happened between Jody and me in Athens, I didn't try and change the subject.

"When you're that age," he said, "it's a sort of craziness all by itself. Normal craziness would be hard to tell from some other kind that was just beginning to happen. Maybe there were some signals you missed, maybe not. But Jody didn't get pushed over the edge just because of you."

"How do you know?"

"I don't."

"Nobody else does either."

"What happened to the others who were diagnosed?"

"Well, Stevie Segal I told you about. He killed himself. Debbie Rittenbaum got kicked out of the Hari Krishnas in San Francisco and said they'd brainwashed her."

"She was right."

"But probably for all the wrong reasons."

"What's her story?"

"The last I heard, she was living in a group home out there."

"Anybody else?"

"Billy Shane. His parents divorced and moved away after he got diagnosed, so I don't know what happened to him. I asked Flip, but Flip says Billy Shane probably just inhaled too much model car glue when he was a kid."

"Geez." Paul sat up to light a cigarette. "What is it about this place?"

"Maybe they're not all the same. Maybe there's a mis-diagnosed manic depressive in there somewhere. Or maybe Jody was supposed to be our one out of every hundred that you read about getting schizophrenia, but because of all the people moving here from everywhere else we got too rich a batch. We got too many other places' one-out-of-a-hundred mixed in with ours."

"That's not how they figure statistics, Marsha, town by town."

"Yeah, I don't know what I'm talking about. But sometimes it's easier when you think you know the reason, even if it doesn't really make sense."

"Not sometimes," Paul said, yawning. "Always."

Lying awake after Paul fell asleep, I thought about how his mother, when she gave me those pictures of him, told me of the nightmares he had after his father died, and how difficult it was for her to comfort him. If I were to make this particular incident over into an anecdote for the family reunions story, the wife would have to seize upon the mother-in-law's story as an explanation, and ultimately a cure, for some puzzling marital dilemma—why her husband was afraid of her leaving him, maybe, or why he was an insomniac. For me, though, it only explained that loving someone is dangerous.

Sometimes I would stare at those old pictures of Paul as though projecting all my comforting energy backward into a time before I was born, providing all the exactly right words and touches that would end up soothing him in the here and now. I didn't actually believe this was possible, of course. But I sort of liked the idea that Paul might be similarly inclined in my behalf. And while I had my doubts about a photograph of me pretending to tap dance being an appropriate medium, maybe it was worth letting him keep the goddamn thing after all. Maybe it was a good balance, him enjoying this previous version of me looking unwittingly ridiculous in the same way I enjoyed a previous version of him looking unwittingly adorable.

I couldn't figure out why this should be true, only that it had to do with an urge to put the past at your disposal, so complete and unbroken a chain that you honestly couldn't tell where one part ended and another began, so that the parts were all endless and you were all one.

I ran into Gloria Honeycutt the next morning, pushing a luggage rack loaded with cardboard boxes through the hotel lobby. "Hey, Marsha," she hollered, her voice echoing up the elevator chutes that cut through the building's core, sounding much the way it did blaring out of a megaphone at pep club rallies. "Can you give me a hand?"

Leaving Paul at the newsstand, I ran ahead of her to open the double doors to the Poinsett Ballroom. "You're here awful early!" Gloria said.

"So are you. What are we early for?"

"Decorating. Are you one of my volunteers?"

"No," I said, "we're just staying in the hotel."

"Well, if you change your mind," Gloria said, "I could sure use some help." She pawed through a pile of Wade Hampton annuals and Confederate-colored streamers to find a clipboard. "We're going to check off everybody's name who's coming, cut their pictures out of the yearbook, and paste them onto name tags. Gee," she said looking at her clipboard, "there must be some mistake. We did this by maidens, and yours isn't here."

"I didn't sign up."

She handed me a schedule of events which, apart from tonight's party, included a picnic tomorrow afternoon. "No biggie," Gloria said. "It's fifteen dollars per couple at the door."

"Does that include drinks?" I was remembering a time some years ago when I had been here for Christmas and ran into Gloria at the liquor store, buying a bottle of rum. "It's for a fruit cake," she cried out when she saw me, mindful as ever of her status as the daughter of Bishop Fulmer's musical director.

"The committee took a vote," Gloria said now, absolving herself once more, "so there's a cash bar." Then, gung-ho again, "I'll make sure you're on the list. What's your married name? That goes underneath."

After breakfast, I tried to reach Jody at his apartment, his parents at their house, and Nancy in Atlanta, but no one answered anywhere. When I walked down the street to Calvin's store, which was just opening, Calvin avoided my questions with a long discourse on custom tailoring men's pants according to whether they dressed right or left. I had to buy a belt for Paul—a leather one with a silver-plate buckle—before he'd tell me that the Lurreys had gone to North Carolina. "Why? When are they coming back?"

"I don't know, they didn't say."

"Sounds like trouble."

"Maybe. But have you ever heard of a chicken snake?"

"No. Please tell me this is going to be more to the point than dressing right or left."

"My granddaddy told me about chicken snakes. They'd raid the hen house and swallow eggs whole. Then they'd have to hurl themselves around against the walls so the eggs would break inside and they could digest them."

"Jesus, Calvin. First you tell me to be cool, and now you want me to hurl myself around the hen house?"

"Some things you just got to give time to trickle down."

"*More* time? That's obviously been my big mistake here."

"Sorry. Maybe if you'd bought a suit I could've come up with something better."

Everybody else told me to be patient, too. Maybe the Lurreys were taking Nancy's children to camp. Maybe they had gone to the music festival in Brevard. Sol had a cousin with a Buick dealership up that way—maybe they went there to get Jody a new car (this last idea from Daniel, naturally).

Unconvinced, I went to the museum with Paul to meet Joyce, who wanted to give him a tour. Considering its size and location, the museum had a nice enough contemporary collection. "Although it does seem strange," Paul said, "that they haven't bought a piece made after nineteen seventy-five. They ought to auction off one of their better Jasper Johns things and invest in more current stuff."

"They'll never sell *him*," Joyce said. "He's a native son. Besides, they can't. For all intents and purposes, the donors still own all the paintings here. Not to mention the director."

"That's the kind of thing," Paul said, "that makes me feel as though I might as well be selling shoes."

"Or refrigerators," Joyce added darkly, evidently thinking of Amway.

"And not a single nude," Paul said, "in the entire joint." Which launched Joyce into the story of how I had once made her take down the nude in her bedroom so I wouldn't go to hell down a sliding board of nails. Paul laughed, but I knew the person he had been thinking of in the first place was Jody, the one who really had gone down that sliding board.

When Paul and I returned to the hotel early that evening, I steered us clear of the reunion by avoiding the lobby and taking the elevator in the garage up to our floor. The telephone's message light was blinking when we got inside the room, so I dialed the operator, hoping that one of the Lurreys had called. They hadn't. "A Mr. Marvin Hamlisch," the operator said, "is in room seven-oh-nine, waiting to hear from you." Which meant, I knew, that Wiley was here. I was going to blow him off until he told me that he had a

check for Jody, a kind of royalty payment for "I Keep
Learning Things I Never Meant to Know."

Wiley had brought with him a portable stereo system
that sounded remarkably good for something so small and
tinny-looking. When we got to his room, it was vibrating
with the voice of Mahalia Jackson. I looked through the
case Wiley kept his tapes in, finding far more music that
wasn't country than was. There were, however, several
demo tapes by Nashville songwriters Wiley worked with
and whose names I recognized only from our conversations.

"Pretend we're in the pitching room with you, Wiley," I
said. "Plug us a song."

"What a vile idea," Wiley groaned.

"Come on, let's have it. I want to hear all the clichés."

"Okay," Wiley said, "if it'll make you happy." He leaned
forward confidentially and spoke in a fake-hearty voice.
"This song I want you to hear," he said, "is a hit. It was on
hold for Alabama, it was on hold for Dwight Yoakum, but
they just didn't punch it. It's different, that's the thing that
might've scared them. But if I had to hang a label, I'd say
George Jones meets Lyle Lovett, heartfelt with a hip hook."
Then he played a song called, "I Don't Have to Stick With
You (I'm Stuck Already)." Afterward, there was a long silence.

"I think it's very moving, Wiley," I said.

"Tell the truth, Wiley," Paul said. "Do you really like that
shit?"

"Paul?" Wiley said. "Kiss my ass."

Pretty soon, I had drunk enough Bourbon to stop calling
the Lurreys' house every half hour, and the boys had
enough to think the reunion might be entertaining. "At
least," Paul said in the elevator, "it's centrally located."

"Yeah," Wiley said. "Just like sex."

*   *   *

Happily for him, Wiley didn't look anything like the high school picture on his name tag. The same would have been true at our tenth reunion, too, but neither of us had bothered to attend that one. Since the last time most of these people had seen Wiley, his face had thinned out, giving way to some rather dramatic bone structure. With his strawberry blond mustache and thick mane of wavy hair, he looked more than a little like the image of General Wade Hampton on the reunion sweatshirts being sold at the door for twenty bucks apiece. Wiley was small, about Jody's size, but in his crisp white shirt and black jeans, he made all the old football players, who had dressed for this event as though for golf, seem beefy and dull.

Among the girls who had once ignored Wiley, several were now divorced. One of them, Beverly Sharp, already drunk at eight-thirty, stuck her tongue into Wiley's ear and tried to pocket his room key. "If I were a more immature son-of-a-bitch," Wiley said, joining us at the bar after he escaped Beverly, "I could do some damage here."

"Don't hold back on our account," I said. "Maybe you can get a song out of it. 'She was the homecoming queen who spurned me'—lots of stuff to play with there. Homecoming, coming home, just coming in general, spurning, sperming . . ."

"You don't have much of an ear for lyrics," Wiley told me, "if you think country songs can talk about sperm."

Just then, a small, delicately built woman sidled up between Wiley and me. She was wearing a turquoise shantung sheath that, along with her Lulu-like bob, made her look like a red-haired Suzie Wong. "I once had a boyfriend," she announced in a feathery, girlish voice, "whose come tasted like carnations and honey. Wish I'd kept him. The next one's tasted just like it smelled—bleach. Sort of made me feel like I was taking in laundry."

"Now *here's* somebody," Paul said, "I'd like to talk to."

I recognized her right away. And at the sight of her missing ring finger, I couldn't help thinking that Betty Jo Lowe was so perfectly feminine, it almost seemed like a piece of jewelry she had forgotten to wear.

"Hey, Betty Jo," I said.

"Hey, yourself." She leaned over to give me a kiss, which was nice. Apart from Beverly Sharp, few people at the reunion seemed so expressively fond of the people they were meeting up with again. "I'm here because my mother just had a triple bypass," Betty Jo said. "What's your excuse?"

I had to introduce Betty Jo not only to Paul but to Wiley, who, despite being an outcast like Betty Jo in high school, hadn't been nearly wild enough for her to take notice of him then. Now they had more in common. Betty Jo, as it turned out, married a guitar player she met in a methadone clinic, and together they moved to Nashville, where he became a popular session man. They were divorced now, with joint custody of a daughter named Luna, and Betty Jo owned an antique clothing store that specialized in Hawaiian shirts. Drugs had become so much a part of the past that she described herself as a born-again vegetarian.

I couldn't blame Paul for finding Betty Jo more interesting than anyone else he'd met in the Poinsett Ballroom tonight, a category that by now included Jimbo. He was there with his wife, a woman who finished school a few years behind us. After two children and an equal number of failed businesses, Jimbo was now partners with a former Clemson running back in a home security company—the very company, he told me, that would soon be outfitting my parents' house with an alarm system. If we had been alone, having a beer on neutral territory the way we usually did when I came to visit, Jimbo and I might have joked about this. But without the jokes, Jimbo just made me afraid he was heading for the sort of heartbreak that hustlers around here seemed prone to when the stakes got boring. As much trouble as he probably would have gotten into, politics might have actually been a better bet for him than business. He didn't remind me of himself so much anymore as he did Joyce's Randolph, and how I was tolerant of him in much the same way she had once been tolerant of Jimbo.

While Betty Jo, Wiley, and Paul entertained each other with discreetly whispered speculations about various reunionites ("He sells artificial limbs," "She's an astronaut," "They were married in a Jacuzzi," etc.), I noticed Marie and Mack among the people in the middle of the room who were dancing.

I headed off solo for Marie, wanting to take her by surprise. I hoped that if I could do that, she wouldn't have time to remember how she thought she ought to act with me. When Mack turned her out for a spin, I grabbed her hand and began dancing with her myself, sliding into one of the shag steps we used to make up together. If I had been trying, I would never have remembered where to put my feet. But dancing with Marie, it all came back. Marie danced the boy's part, leading me into a fancy turn, crisscrossing arms over shoulders, and I pulled her into a hug, still moving my feet in time to the music.

It would have been nice if we could have kept on that way for a little longer, just taking each other in, but Marie was embarrassed now. "We better stop," she said, backing off. "They'll all think we're lesbians!"

"Oh, good," I said, but then, I wasn't the one who still felt guilty about having to get married. At least, that's what I imagined Marie wanted to tell me.

Marie and Mack now lived in a house that had a pool, and she asked all of us—Wiley, Paul, Betty Jo, and me—to join them there for a swim. This sounded pretty good for a couple of reasons. For one thing, the hotel cooling system seemed to be flagging, and the ballroom was sticky and close. For another, although everyone clearly felt they had exhausted the reunion's possibilities, it was still fairly early.

I hadn't been to Marie's home in years, and since Mack was in real estate, they moved around a lot. "We'll follow you in my car," I told Marie.

Mack seemed puzzled. "Didn't Marie tell you?" he said.

"Tell me what?"

"We're living in the old Lurrey house."

"I was *going* to tell her," Marie said, avoiding my eyes. "I just didn't have the chance yet."

I had heard from Gypsy Claverie, now a therapist in New York, that visiting the house where you grew up is supposed to be a highly evocative experience. Since my parents still lived in the house where I grew up, I never got enough distance on it to test this theory. But because I had spent so much time in the Lurreys' old house, going there now had a similar sort of effect. It might have been easier to assimilate if the current occupants were strangers. Then I could have nursed my memories along with one part of my mind while using another to tell them when the basement had been turned into a rec room, or what the Roman numerals at the bottom of the swimming pool signified. As it was, the situation felt too loaded. Marie, who tried out her first bikini here, had plenty of associations all her own.

"I think it's wrong what they say about places from the past seeming smaller," I offered. "But the trees are definitely larger."

"I wasn't half so keen on the house as Marie," Mack said as he showed us around. "The lot's kind of stingy, and the house itself was pretty standard once you got past the pool.

289

But the neighborhood's in transition—a couple of black families moved in on the next block—so it was cheap enough that we could afford it."

Mack and Marie weren't the first to live here since the Lurreys, but they had made the most changes. Marie was a demon gardener, like Eileen, so she had kept up the rose bushes, camellias, and azaleas. She had the red brick exterior painted white, though, and alterations indoors were even more extensive: The kitchen was remodeled, the carpets taken up so the pine floors could be refinished, and the living room made contiguous with what had once been a separated dining room and kitchen. Marie was proud that she saved money by being her own contractor, hiring out and supervising all the work.

In addition to LaDonna, now fourteen, Marie had another daughter who was eleven. They were away tonight, staying with Marie's mother. But from the family pictures that lined the bookshelves, I could tell that the youngest, with her snub nose, enormous eyes, and dimpled chin, was a duplicate of Marie at that age. Just like she spit her, as Marie would say.

Marie kept towels and bathing suits in the bathroom off the basement rec room, the least transformed part of the house. Mack's piano now stood in the corner formerly occupied by Uncle Sol's, surrounded by recording equipment. In his spare time, Mack wrote radio jingles for local businesses, which he sang with Marie. A fairly recent newspaper story about the advertising ventures of these former beach music stars had been framed and hung on the wall. "Their record may be a collector's item," the story said, "but their music is still with us, whether we know it or not."

"LaDonna's got a good two inches on you and Betty Jo," Marie told us while she hunted up a bathing suit that Betty Jo could wear.

"It's the hormones they put in chicken now," Betty Jo said. "Makes 'em big and sassy."

"Does Jody know you live here?" I asked Marie.

She shrugged and shivered a little, as if the mention of his name spooked her. "It's kind of like moving in some-place where somebody died," she said. "You'd just as soon not talk about it."

"But nothing bad happened to him here—nothing like what you're thinking, anyway."

"Well, *I* want to know how he's doing," Betty Jo said, so I told her what had been nagging at me, that for all I knew, the Lurreys had taken him off to some nice place to be locked up today.

"There's a saint for people who aren't quite right in the head," Betty Jo said. "Saint Dymphna, that's her name. I heard about her from this Creole lady who runs a magic potion shop in New Orleans. This was back when I thought herb tea might help keep me from going nuts."

"Why did you think you were going nuts?" Marie asked.

"Oh, probably because I was a junkie."

Marie silently handed over a bathing suit to Betty Jo, clearly having second thoughts about the evening.

"I think I'd rather Jody were a junkie," I said. "Or, failing that, that I believed in saints."

Betty Jo gave a deep sigh. "Say a prayer to Saint Dym-phna anyway. It can't hurt."

The night was so humid it was hard to be comfortable without swimming. After a short while in the water, we all seemed to be observing the same unspoken rules. First the women and men separated by gender, clustering on the steps and hanging off the sides of the pool. Then there was a time of mixed couples—Paul with Marie, Betty Jo with Wiley, me with Mack. And then, good will having been es-tablished all the way around, we could finally sit at a patio table lit with citronella candles, dripping dry and drinking beer to stay cool, our skins cast with rippling watery shadows from the pool lights.

Wiley pulled a joint out of his cigarette pack and asked if lighting it would offend anyone. "Fine with me," Mack said. "No neighbors close enough to smell it. Besides, nobody we know ever has any, and Marie's kind of curious to try."

"Don't listen to him," Marie said. "I am not!"

"It's my opinion," Betty Jo said, "that men enjoy grass more than women. Women don't generally have so much standing between them and that state of mind."

Wiley's stuff was strong, and Marie, who had only recently quit smoking cigarettes, took a number of wary but full-lunged hits. At first, everyone just seemed more at ease. Wiley and Betty Jo decided they preferred to converse while floating on their backs in the pool. Mack went into the rec room for a boom box and put on an Aretha Franklin tape. Marie fetched more beer and a bag of pretzels. Paul stared at the Roman numerals at the bottom of the pool. "Just how many pairs of panties are we looking at here?" he asked, but no one, as it turned out, could read Roman numerals well enough to tell for sure.

"That's sad," I said. Because I was stoned, it suddenly seemed absolutely vital that I know what that number was. "We're a bunch of idiots."

"No we're not," Wiley said. "We just live in a digital age."

"I wouldn't have come here," Betty Jo said, "if I'd known there'd be a math test."

"I bet Jody would know," I said. And at that, Marie launched into a diatribe about how wasteful it was to throw away used spice bottles, the kind you buy in the grocery store, and she told us all the different uses for hers that she'd found—refilling the bottles with spices bought in bulk, or dried herbs from her garden, and converting them into travel-sized containers for shampoo, conditioner, body lotion, etc. When Marie finally stopped talking, she looked baffled and afraid. "I'm not making any sense," she said.

"We know what you mean," Paul told her.

"Well, I don't!" Marie shivered and put on a shirt. "And I think I'm going to be sick."

"You're just a little off-balance, sweetie," I told her. "You'll probably feel better if we take a walk."

"I can't run into anybody I know like this!"

"We'll walk around inside, then. Come on."

With my arm around Marie's waist, we walked in a continuous loop through the second floor of what was now her house. She didn't want any lights on, which wasn't an obstacle because despite the renovations, I remembered the layout pretty well. Every time we stepped through what had once been a wall, I felt like we were a pair of cartoon Caspers.

My voice seemed to soothe Marie, so I said whatever came to mind. "I have a friend in Seattle named Felicity," I told her, "who's kind of a witch."

"Do you call her sweetie?"

"Sometimes. Felicity says that whenever she moves into a place where someone else has lived before, she burns candles in the corners of every room. That's a custom she picked up in a part of the world I can't remember anymore. It's supposed to banish any bad spirits that might be hanging around."

"Why'd you say that?" Marie asked, sounding nervous again. "Does it feel to you like bad spirits are hanging around here?"

"I just don't think you need to be worrying about anybody getting sick because Jody did."

I moved my hand up from around Marie's waist to stroke

her hair. It was cut to her shoulders now, the only blonde in it chemically acquired streaks. The style, though, looked pretty much the same as always. "Does your mother still set your hair for you," I asked, "or do you manage that by yourself now?"

"LaDonna does it for me when Mama can't . . . He used to be so cute, Marsha."

"He's still pretty cute, actually."

"Remember how I used to go to temple with y'all?"

"Sure. Afterward you and my father would sing show tunes on the way to Howard Johnson's for a soda."

"Well, I don't know exactly why, but somehow God used to seem closer in that temple."

"Maybe it was the Hebrew. You could kind of make up what people were saying when they prayed in Hebrew because you didn't understand it. Maybe you made up stuff in your head that was better than what everybody was actually saying."

"Maybe it's because everything got kind of confused after we started changing religions. First we switched from Baptist to Presbyterian, and you couldn't testify anymore. Then we were Methodist, and you couldn't believe in predestination anymore. Then I married Mack and got to be Episcopal, like him, and they think Methodists are tacky 'cause their churches are carpeted and they don't have stained glass windows. God just got to be about rules. Marsha?"

"What?"

"This is much better than talking about spice bottles."

"Yeah, I think so, too."

"I don't feel quite so crazy now."

"You probably only felt crazy because your brain got stuck on spice bottles when you really wanted to be thinking about something else."

"Is that how it works?"

"Sometimes."

When we looped again through the family room, Marie turned on a light and dragged me over to the bookcase, which was filled with snapshot albums, a recent edition of the World Book encyclopedia, and companion volumes to several PBS series. Marie found what she was looking for, an autobiography of a French Jewish diplomat who had been in a concentration camp. "Here," she said, earnestly pressing the book on me the way I had once pressed *Exodus* on her when we were kids. "I found this at a garage sale, and when I read it, I thought of you."

I wondered then if Marie had been drawn to live here because, scary as it was on account of Jody, this house had something to do with feeling closer to God. It seemed crazy, all right, crazy enough to be true. We continued on our rounds. When I had to pee, Marie, not wanting to be alone, came with me into the bathroom that once divided Jody's and Nancy's rooms, rooms that now belonged to her daughters.

"Jody and I used to come in here when we were supposed to be sleeping and tell each other stories," I told Marie.

She was sitting on the cabinet beneath *Teen* magazine portraits of Corey Haim and Debbie Gibson that were taped to the mirror, illuminated by a Muppet Babies nightlight. When I went to the sink to wash my hands, Marie swiped at her eyes and I could see that she was crying. "I'm so sorry about Jody," she said. And then, in an instant, I was crying, too. Marie hugged me in a way she had been afraid to at the reunion and I slobbered on her shoulder, drawing her down to the floor to sit with me by the cabinet, which, of course, I was much too big to fit into now. "It's all right, sweetie," Marie said as she patted my back, rocking me gently against her chest for a long time, until the part of her shirt where my head lay was soaked and I was done.

After I got into the car with Paul to leave Marie's, I noticed a lone figure standing in the darkness at the corner, lighting a cigarette. Jody. At first my heart leapt. He hadn't been put away somewhere! Then it sank. Not yet. If he took shortcuts through parking lots and subdivisions, he was only a mile or so from his apartment. But here, where everybody drove, the fact of his walking so far was mildly alarming. "Take your time," Paul said as I left to go to him.

"Hey, do you come here often?" I asked Jody, trying not to infect him with my apprehension.

"Only when I'm in the neighborhood." I couldn't tell if he was joking. He picked up the paper cup at his feet and took a sip. "I've been walking since I got back from dinner. First I walked to Bybee's to get an iced tea, and I saw some people from before, people from high school."

"Yeah, there was a reunion tonight."

"That's what they said. They were real nice to me, Mashie." He sounded surprised. "They wanted to know why I wasn't at the party. I told them I don't much go to parties."

"I'm sure you were invited. You graduated, didn't you?"

"Number twelve, class of seventy-four." He must have been referring to his academic ranking in our class.

"None of us could read the numerals at the bottom of the pool," I told Jody. "Do you remember that one?"

"Ten thousand, one hundred and sixty-nine."

"Marie Gilbert lives here now."

"She probably doesn't remember me."

"Of course she does. Would you like to go in and say hello?"

"No."

"Because you don't want to go inside?"

"Because that's not why I came this way, okay? And if I went inside, she would think it was."

"So," I took a deep breath, "how was North Carolina?"

Silence.

"Jody?"

As he wordlessly lit one cigarette off another, my anxiety rushed out at him. "Jody, what's going on? Are you okay? Are you—"

"No, I'm not hearing any fucking voices!"

"That's good." I racked my brain for a way to get information without making him more upset. "Okay, I'll start. There was this guy who had been given a choice. He could move to Atlanta to live with his sister or he could move to Palm Beach and be near his parents."

"Crappy choice."

"But his family really cares about him, they're just afraid. Maybe he needs to make more of an effort, show them they don't have to worry so much about him."

"Crappy choice," Jody repeated.

"Why?"

"Because there's someplace else he'd rather be."

I didn't like the sound of that, curt and dismissive, as though nothing I might do could help. Or I didn't care enough to try. "Listen, Jody," I said, "I have to tell you something. I felt bad for a really long time about how I was when we were together in Athens. After we . . . made love." It was too dark for me to see Jody's face well enough to gauge his reaction. I felt a trickle of sweat running down between my breasts as I tried to convince myself that the impulse to talk to him about this was clean enough that it would make things better instead of worse, no matter his illness. "You were scared and that scared me, no one's to blame. But I should have been there after you got sick.

That really was my fault, and I'm sorry. I don't want that to happen again, so—"

"Stick to the story, Mashie," he said, but not in a cranky way, more like he'd taken as much of it in as he could and needed me to be back in the here and now with him.

"Right. Okay. There's someplace else he'd rather be. Where do you suppose that is?"

"I *know* where it is." Now I held my breath, wondering if he was going to say Seattle. Instead, what he said was, "Here."

"What? You're kidding! Why?"

"He's been a lot of places and done a lot of things. It wasn't always this way, but now he feels safer here."

"You're sure?" Jody nodded in a definitive way. "I'll see what I can do," I told him, hoping he couldn't hear all the doubt rising up inside my throat. "Come on, let's get you home."

"No," he said, "I want to be alone." Then, after putting a few steps between us, he turned back. "They told me there's a picnic tomorrow."

"Yeah, it's part of the reunion. Do you want to go?"

"It might be fun," he shrugged, walking away again.

I watched the retreating glow of his cigarette for a few seconds. "I'll pick you up," I called after him, and gave a late-morning time. "We'll go together." He said something that I couldn't quite make out, his voice muffled in the ratcheting sound of crickets, but it sounded as if he were agreeing.

Chapter 19

WHILE PAUL and I made fried chicken and potato salad for the picnic, Joyce followed us around the kitchen with a sponge, cleaning up in our wake. "Now you can see why I had to leave home before I started cooking anything other than canned soup," I told Paul.

"I was just trying to save you time afterward," Joyce protested.

"Nope," I said, "that's not it. You don't like messes."

"We *are* two of the messiest cooks around," Paul pointed out.

"But Joyce never liked cooking all that much, right?"

"I used to," she said, "for parties. When you were kids, we gave dinner parties for each other all the time." She laughed like a geisha, covering her mouth with her hand. "I was just remembering one of mine. Everyone got so blasted before dinner—Daniel must have made the martinis extra strong. Anyway, I came in here to light the chafing dish for Swedish meatballs, and I was gone so long that Sol came back to see what was the matter. My matches kept going out in the breeze, I told him, but we were both so bombed that neither one of us thought of closing the windows. Sol decided what we should do was get under the sink because the matches wouldn't go out in there. So we cleared out everything and we crawled partway in with the chafing dish. Eileen was mad as hell when she found us like that, but we were so hysterical she finally realized we weren't up to any funny stuff—at least, not the kind she thought."

"I'll bet we were all here that night," I said. "The four of us, I mean."

"It was late, you were probably in bed."

It didn't seem worth mentioning how easy it had been to spy on my parents' parties since there were windows on all sides of the porch that ran along the first floor of the house. Through these windows it was possible to survey the entire adult party area, including the kitchen. If you kept your head low, you could see a lot without getting caught. Jody had probably crept out of Flip's bedroom, seen his father and my mother underneath the sink, and decided that it looked like enough fun for us to try to emulate them the next time we told stories.

These were the sort of connections—different from a pet turtle, Captain Willy Falaw, or Roman numerals—that seemed furthest out of Jody's reach. And so I felt as if I'd just been given another memory of his to keep with mine.

We were running so late that I hustled us out of the house, making a mental note to call Eileen from Jody's apartment so that she would know what we were doing. And to arrange a meeting with her afterward. Surely a successful social outing would only strengthen Jody's case.

It wasn't terribly hot yet, not by local standards, but Paul's forehead was already dripping sweat. He hated to sweat, and rarely ever did in the Northwest except when he went out to run and expected to. His idea of picnic weather was to have it just hot enough so that taking off your shirt might be pleasant, but not essential to comfort. On the way to Jody's apartment, he turned worrisome. Did

I remember to get directions to the picnic? Did I think it was going to rain? Wasn't I concerned that mayonnaise would turn rancid in the heat and the potato salad would poison us?

"You'd be much happier right now if you were an atomic particle," I told him. "Then you could be in two places at once."

"Haven't I taught you anything?" He turned an air conditioner vent directly onto his face. "Only *sub*atomic particles can be in two places at once."

"You can't deny you'd rather be in your studio."

"Yeah, but I'd almost always rather be in my studio."

"You've got to be wondering by now," I persisted, "why you ever wanted to come here."

"Listen, bub," Paul said reassuringly, "shut up." Pulling out his T-shirt collar, he aimed cool air at his chest. "Maybe one reason it's good I'm here is that I can go back to D.C. with you and help you move."

I wanted to stop the car and have a real conversation, but I didn't want to keep Jody waiting any longer. Besides, the road we were traveling was an ugly commercial strip. I didn't want to be discussing something so important with Paul in a Kmart parking lot. But I didn't really want to talk about anything else, either. "That's quite a leap you've made there, bucko."

"I know." He sounded anxious.

"Now that you've been exposed to some of my more disgusting personality defects, it would almost make more sense at this point if you wanted to stall for time."

"Is that what you want?"

"No. I'm just confused."

"You're not confused. You're scared. And so am I, really. I mainly wanted to see how it sounded, and it sounded a lot better than I thought it would. Only now I feel a little like the way I did the first time I said I loved you, and I had to sit there waiting forever for a response."

"Only because I was too overcome to speak."

"That's not it. You were scared then, too."

"I was driving then, too. Maybe that's the problem. You want my undivided attention at the very moment when, if you got it, you might wind up dead. Or seriously maimed."

"Gee, and I thought I was being romantic."

"You were." We were at a stop light now, so I could lean over and kiss him long enough to miss the change to green, causing the driver behind us to honk.

"Well," Paul said, "does it feel possible?"

"Yes," I said slowly. "Moving definitely feels possible. More possible than anything else I can imagine."

"If it feels possible now, maybe it'll feel inspired later, once we're ready to leave." Paul looked out his window as we passed the L'il Rebel Drive-In, which he took in with obvious distaste. "Leaving," he added, "being the operative word."

"You remind me of Jody. He used to hate it here a lot more than I ever did. And now this is where he wants to be."

"Do you really think he means it?" Paul shook his head, baffled. Not that Paul agreed with my parents, who felt that since Jody was so childlike, so vulnerable, Sol and Eileen might be doing what was best in sending him off to assisted-living land. It was just that Paul had a hard time believing that Jody's urge to stay was less convincing evidence of illness than voices telling him to go.

The majority of Jody's neighbors at Riverbend were either late to rise on Saturday mornings or loath to leave their apartments. The only visible resident was a young man waxing his car in the shade of a lone elm by the entrance gates. Empty Corona bottles were scattered by the pool, remnants of the night before. Behind the complex, where the Saluda River petered out into a narrow, muddy stream, insects undeterred by suspect suds in the water swarmed so thickly you could hear them through the sound of a big rig changing gears on the nearby highway.

Although the curtains in Jody's apartment were closed, the door was ajar. I called Jody's name and waited a moment before pushing the door open wider. "Be right down," a female voice called from upstairs.

Stepping inside, Paul and I watched as a matronly woman who might have been wearing one of Uncle Lud's model coats descended the steps. At the sight of Paul she began to twitter and pat her tightly permed hair. "I'm Miz Jenkins," she said, "the resident manager. Excuse my appearance, but I'm not really supposed to be working today."

Mrs. Jenkins gave me a stern but friendly look, as though I might be technically innocent but was still in trouble and ought to know why. "Mr. Lurrey," she said, "has done a little damage here, I'm afraid."

"Where is Jody?"

"He called himself a cab right after I started my inspection."

"What?"

"He said he was going to your mother's house."

"There must be some mistake," I muttered, so rattled that I didn't even wonder how she knew me.

"Come with me, I'll show you," she said, and we followed Mrs. Jenkins mutely up the stairs to Jody's bedroom. "The condition of this carpet goes well beyond normal wear and tear," she said. Then she pointed up at Jody's iridescent stars. "The painters are going to charge me extra for scraping those doohickeys off the ceiling. So I'll be withholding all but a smidge of the security deposit, Miz Slotkin." Slotkin was Nancy's married name. "If you want to come to the office with me, I'll write you a check."

"I'm not Jody's sister," I told her.

"You're not? I could've sworn you were . . . but then, we only ever talked once—on the phone, yesterday, when she called to break the lease. I told her I understood. Someone like him belongs with his family, if you ask me."

I ran to the phone and called Eileen. "Nancy was just leaving to pick him up," she said. "Oh God, this really is the last straw."

I told her not to panic, that I'd be there as soon as I could. When I hung up the phone, Mrs. Jenkins was telling Paul about a nephew of hers from Valdosta. "He went off to Calgary, Canada, because he said that's where God told him Elvis was going to reincarnate. They arrested him at this hospital where he went to try and test the babies who'd been born there by playing Elvis for them. I mean, can you imagine? Elvis a Canadian? It just about broke my sister's heart. Of course, if everyone thought about Elvis the way I do, he'd still be alive and driving a truck."

At the bottom of Stone Mountain were scruffy lots with prefab houses and wide-bodied trailers, temporary places that seemed staked to the ground by the satellite dishes beside them. Higher up, as the road began to wind, these gave way to sprawling old brick colonials on the pine-covered core of the mountain. On the edge side, rocky and uneven, were all the newer homes, glorified cedar cabins with sloping roofs, skylights, turrets, and catwalks.

As I raced to the Lurreys' house, we didn't pass a single taxicab.

Although sited high on the core side, the Lurreys' place, with its wood and lack of right angles, looked more like houses on the edge. From here you could see downtown to the east and Sol's factory, the cornerstone of a new industrial park, off to the south. To the west were the Blue Ridge Mountains, bumps compared to the Olympics or Cascades, but far bigger than this overgrown hill, which could have chipped off and rolled away after some long ago earthquake.

The gravel drive to the Lurreys' house was packed with vehicles—Sol's, Eileen's, Juanita's, and a station wagon with Georgia plates that was presumably Nancy's. Eileen and Nancy were standing out on the porch, a broad stretch of planking set into a Japanese-style rock garden. "No sign of him yet," Eileen said worriedly. "Sol's waiting by the phone."

"I knew it was a bad idea," Nancy said, "letting him go back to his place."

"What was I supposed to do?" Eileen asked. "Lock him up?" And then, with a look at me, "Whatever you may think, Marsha, our intention is *not* to lock him up."

"All I'm trying to say," Nancy sighed, "all I've *been* trying to say for some time now, is that he doesn't do well with choices."

I found myself staring at Nancy. What struck me wasn't her coolness, or her eldest child's snap and authority. That much had been evident from our telephone conversations. It was more how all that distinguished Nancy now from my earliest memories of Eileen were her close-cropped hairdo and the cut of the clothes she wore.

After I introduced Paul to Nancy, nobody spoke for too long a while. "I'm calling the police," Nancy said, going back inside. Eileen apologized to Paul. "I'm sorry we had to meet under these circumstances." Then Paul, who knew I wanted to be alone with Eileen, said he'd go back to my parents' house and wait to hear from me.

"Jody doesn't want to move," I told Eileen as Paul drove off. "He wants to stay here, that's the problem. That's why he left the last time."

"I can't discuss this with you now," Eileen started out. Then her shoulders began to shake and she covered her face with her hands. "I'm too old for this," she said.

"You don't know what happened," I told her. "And even if he did run off somewhere—"

"Please, Marsha."

I took Eileen's arm and led her over to sit on the edge of the porch. She reached into the pocket of her linen slacks for a Kleenex and dabbed behind her glasses at her eyes, composing herself again. "It's true I don't know exactly what your plans for him are," I pressed on, "but I think you should let him stay."

She snapped her head around to face me. "What do you know about it? Do *you* want to take responsibility for him now?"

I was reminded of Paul's question, asked at a time that felt very distant. Just how responsible do you want to be? Responsible enough, I decided, to realize the solutions that mattered most now weren't to be found on the needle end of a syringe. I was beginning to understand what might appeal to Jody about being here untethered from the Stone Mountain house and the underwear outlet. Maybe when the past didn't have much of a place left in your mind, it could be all the more important that it have some kind of quiet life pulsing through your surroundings, recalling every so often what might otherwise slip away. Then again, maybe not. But it might be entirely possible that my only real responsibility here would turn out to be arguing for such things.

"I'm sorry," I told Eileen, "I wasn't faulting you."

"You've been with Jody for a few days, but I've been struggling with this for eleven years now. I've held him when he couldn't do anything but cry over what was going wrong with his mind. I've watched him when he was so sedated he could barely move. I've gone to places where I didn't know a soul because he'd been put in jail. I can imagine how badly you must feel after not seeing him for so long, but really, it was for the best."

"I'm not so sure."

Eileen took off her glasses to rub at a smudge with the tail of her vest, then put them on again and stared out at the road. "It wasn't as though he was coming down with something you would benefit from by being exposed to it."

She must have been referring to how she and Joyce, whenever one of us got something like chicken pox or measles, would throw us all together, hoping that the healthy ones would get infected and everybody would be done with being sick in roughly the same time span. I could see why the analogy came to mind, but it was hard enough drumming up some dignity without Eileen conjuring pictures of us as pajamaed children dotted with Calamine lotion. "At least," I said, "I would have been a part of it."

"You ought to be grateful that you weren't. It's horrible, having this take over someone you love. I hope you don't think *me* ungrateful for how you've tried to help. In a way it was always what I hoped you might do, but could never let myself expect. For fear of being disappointed. I just couldn't bear the idea of watching your feelings toward him change. Please don't think I have no regrets. I do. But I have to say, what you've been through with Jody is simple compared to how things were in the time that I'm speaking of. We didn't know anything then, that was the worst of it."

"What about the others?" There were, after all, the others. "What about Stevie, and Debbie Rittenbaum, and Billy Shane?"

"It wasn't like now, Marsha, with people feeling so free about airing their troubles to everyone. And what if we had?"

What if they had? Would it have been any harder to get a rabbi than it always was? Would French tire companies build their factories somewhere else? Would we all be less special somehow? I thought I had given up the burden of that sort of specialness a long time ago, but being with Eileen made me realize how very close to the surface it still lay because just then, I couldn't think of anything else to explain why we were here after all these years, having this particular conversation.

Eileen let her question hang in the air before continuing. "Whenever Jody disappeared, before we knew where he was, one of the things we worried about—one of the *many* things we worried about—was that he had discovered where you were."

"Did you think he might hurt me?"

"Or that you might hurt him." She paused for a moment, letting the significance of this register. "Who could know how it would go? Things were fairly quiet these last few years, so Sol and I began to travel more, began to try to have our lives apart from him. But when I heard he went to Seattle, well, we just can't deal with it starting all over again. There aren't many places we would seriously consider for Jody. The one in North Carolina is expensive, but we're happy to pay for the best."

"Who recommended this place?"

"His doctor here. The one he went to before you set him up with someone else. I don't know if that was such a good idea, Marsha. There's enough confusion in his life right now."

"Well, it's a confusing situation, isn't it?" Agitated by the humidity, a piece of hair sprung loose from my barrette and fell across my eyes. Eileen watched as I tried to blow it out of the way with an exasperated puff of air. When that didn't work, Eileen cocked her head at me and reached out to take hold of the spiraling curl, then slowly wrapped it backward around her forefinger like a piece of ribbon. She spoke softly, as though to herself. "Curls whatever way you comb it." Lifting my eyes to hers, I found myself wishing that the barrette might break, and that the hands I reached for now could hover around my head for the rest of the afternoon, coaxing everything into its proper place.

"There's one confusion I'm hoping you might settle," Eileen murmured. "It wasn't just a coincidence, Jody going to Seattle, was it?"

"That's hard to say."

"I think if you know that he went there to see you, I have a right to know, too."

"Maybe," I said. "But maybe there are some things that are okay being just his."

Eileen nodded, not exactly pleased with this explanation, but my confidence in giving it seemed to comfort her in some small way.

Juanita came out with iced teas for us, greeting me as though my arrival had been inevitable. "Well, *there* you are," she said, giving my shoulder a squeeze.

"And there's Jody." Eileen jumped to her feet as a Yellow Cab pulled off the road. Jody paid the driver and emerged with an expression on his face that was difficult to read, showing traces of both excitement and fearfulness. "You had everybody mighty worried, Joy-boy," Juanita said, then went inside to tell the others that Jody had arrived.

"Where were you, son?" Eileen asked evenly.

"I was joining a club," he said.

Please Jody, I silently urged. Talk sense to her.

"They really want me, too."

Uh-oh.

"It took a long time because I was making friends."

Not good, not good at all. Eileen looked at Jody with such concern that I knew she thought he was having a relapse. But there was nothing on the relapse list we made together that said you know you're getting sick again when you find yourself thinking that other people care about you.

"They'll help me get another job," Jody went on. "One I like better. And if you won't let me keep my apartment, they'll find me a new one." Jody reached into the pocket of his jeans for a card and handed it to Eileen. I read over her shoulder: Horizon Clubhouse, 256 North Hampton Avenue.

"How'd you find out about this place?" I asked Jody.

"From Dr. Gower."

Eileen looked puzzled. "His new psychiatrist," I told her.

While Jody ate lunch in the kitchen, Nancy tracked Dr. Gower down at home and grilled him for details. "Well, it *sounds* legitimate," she said dubiously, joining the rest of us in the living room. "A social worker runs the program."

"A social worker?" Uncle Sol said. "Not a medical doctor?"

"Probably can't afford one," Nancy said. "It's nonprofit, gets state funds."

Uncle Sol frowned. "People at those places can be well-meaning, but . . ."

Eileen just sat there, silently judging, and so I addressed my objections to her. "That's not fair. At least give it a chance, at least take a look. Why don't you call Monday morning—make an appointment with this social worker so you can see for yourself?"

"No," Eileen said, getting up to leave the room with such a determined air that I sank back into the sofa, feeling defeated. A few seconds later Eileen reappeared in the doorway with her purse and car keys, beckoning me to join her. "I want to go now."

"Why did you want me to come?" I asked as Eileen drove down the mountain.

"To ask good questions," she said. "That's what you do for a living, isn't it?"

"Sort of," I said, shifting in my seat.

She pressed her lips into a faint smile. "At least I was more or less right about what you would be when you grew up."

Was she measuring me? What did she mean? That I had fallen short of her expectations? Exceeded them? Or ended up in some gray murky middle area? I wanted to give her more credit than that, though. I wanted to give her credit for meaning to say that essence doesn't change, and at least I had been able to grow up with mine more or less intact.

Hampton Avenue was one of the only streets in town where there were houses with plaques on them certifying historic status. I spotted number 256, a large Victorian with a wraparound porch. It was the kind of high-ceilinged, tree-shaded place that could stay comfortable in this heat without air conditioning. As we climbed the steps, there came through open windows the sounds of talk, laughter, and the smack of balls on Ping-Pong tables.

Inside, there was a steady stream of people coming and going. At the front desk, a plump woman with peachy, poreless skin listened as a young man asked her where the

class on drugs was meeting today. She consulted a clipboard and said, "Upstairs, room five." Then, noticing us,
"Hi, can I help y'all?"

As Eileen watched the young man climb the long, curved
staircase, I wondered if she was thinking, like me, how he
was about the same age as Jody when he became ill. Remembering my job, I turned to the woman behind the desk. "Do
you mind my asking what class that was you sent him to?"

"It teaches all about the different medications people
with schizophrenia take."

"Will that help him?"

But she was still wondering how *she* could help *us*. "Are
you interested in becoming a member?"

"No, but we"—I pulled Eileen forward—"have someone
in our family who is."

"If you can wait until my break—" she began.

"I'll be glad to give them a tour, Martha," came a voice
from behind us. "Mark Davis," he said, sticking out his
hand, "I'm director here. I've been in the capitol for budget
meetings, just came by to pick up my mail."

By the time our tour was over, my mouth was dry from
asking questions—about support activities, job training,
and Mark Davis's philosophy on medication. And he had
introduced us to half a dozen of the club's one hundred and
sixty members, including the young man who had come for
the class on drugs. His family sent him out from California
because there wasn't a program there like this. "Before I
came here" he said, "they had me in a place where I spent
all day making leather belts and ashtrays. And going to
group therapy. Yak yak yak yak yak. For *hours*. I hated it.
I mean, I *really* hated it."

Eileen jumped in with an urgent question of her own.
"And do you like it here?"

"Yeah," he told her. And then, with a glance at Mark, who spoke with a heavy coastal drawl, "I'm even getting used to how funny some people talk."

Later, when we were alone with Mark on the porch, he said, "I used to work in a place like the one he described. There are lots, from bare bones to fancy. But the one thing they all have in common is that they're about sustaining people with mental illness. They're not about rehabilitating them."

Eileen stiffened. "What exactly do you mean by rehabilitation?"

"Oh, making it so that they can feel good about who they are. Making it so that they can have all the same things the rest of us want—a nice place to live, relationships with people they matter to, a decent job that puts money in their pockets."

"You haven't even met my son. What makes you think he can handle these things?"

"What," Mark replied, "makes you think he can't?"

At that, Eileen reached into her purse for more Kleenex. "I've lived here all my life," she said, shaking her head. "I don't know why I never heard about this place."

"It's so easy," he said gently, "for a family to get isolated inside this illness." Then, brightening, "Although we *were* in the news a few years ago. Of course, it was bad news. I mean, heaven forbid they should ever run a story about someone with a mental illness who's holding down a job for the first time in twenty years, or gone back to school for their degree."

"Right, where's the hook?" I said, summoning the remembered voices of newspaper editors who often asked me that. "Got to have a hook."

"And the only hook they understand is if someone commits a crime. Then it's front page stuff, 'Mental Patient Commits Crime.' "

"So you were in the news," Eileen prompted.

"That's right. We were negotiating the purchase of our apartment complex when the neighbors took us to court. It was bad enough the mentally ill were hanging out here in the daytime—they didn't want them living around here, too, driving down the property values. We won on appeal, property values stayed the same, and last year, one of the women who led the fight against us came to me for help because her daughter had just been diagnosed. Now her daughter lives in one of our apartments."

"Wow," I said. "That's a great story."

"I know." He spoke without the slightest hint of malice. "I just love telling it."

That night, I left Paul with my family and stayed to have dinner on the mountain with the Lurreys. It wasn't exactly a celebration. No one spoke of Horizon Clubhouse to Jody in anything but "we'll see" terms. But the tension was so abated that I lingered after dinner, drifting into the living room while Sol played his ebony baby grand and slipping onto the bench beside him. Sol looked at me and smiled. "Know what this one is?"

Name That Tune was one of the only games Sol had ever played with us. " 'Mean to Me'?" I guessed.

"That's right. How about this?" He played a few bars of another melody.

"That one I don't know."

"Why sure you do. It's your old uncle's favorite songwriter. Listen a little longer."

"Oh, right—'Ole Buttermilk Sky,' Hoagy Carmichael. I've got an album of Hoagy Carmichael, playing and singing some of his songs. I thought of you when I bought it."

Sol just nodded, as though happy to be remembered this way. "This one," he said, "was our courting song." He didn't have much of a voice, so Sol's singing was a lot like his talking, slow and lazy. " *'Two sleepy people,'* " he crooned as Eileen came in from the kitchen to listen, a dish towel over her shoulder, " *'too much in love to say good night.'* "

I looked between the two of them for a second, wondering how much sooner, if things had been otherwise, I might have realized that they were the set of parents who had always been the most like lovers.

Chapter 20

As Jody began training for a job in the Sparta library's microfilm department, I went to work, too. For several days running, I sat at a table in the history section, the only one equipped with electrical outlets, and hammered out a piece on my laptop that I sent by overnight mail to Carolyn, my editor in New York. A few hours before Paul and I were due to leave town, I called Carolyn from a phone booth in the library lobby, where I was waiting for Jody. "Did you get it?" I asked her.

"Well, I *received* it, Marsha. But I can't honestly say I *got* it. In fact, I'm wondering now if maybe you've *lost* it. What were you thinking?"

"It's about a reunion."

"Yeah, but nobody's married."

"Nope. Not yet."

"And the style's all wrong. It reads like, like, a chapter from a book, maybe."

"Do you really think so?"

"I didn't know you could write like this. Of course, our advertisers—I mean, our readers, aren't particularly interested in delusional people."

"I thought you'd say that."

"Now I've got to write it myself."

"Just picture your copy facing a turkey. That was my problem. I just couldn't see that goddamn turkey."

"You know, I didn't expect you to be so cheerful about paying back your advance."

Looking across the library lobby, I saw that Jody was finished with his shift and coming my way. "Me, neither," I said. "Hey, gotta run. Watch the mail for that check!" I hung up and stepped outside the booth to wave at Jody. "Over here!"

"Shhhh!" he said, finger to his lips.

As we walked to my car, I asked him how it was going. "Okay," he said.

"Better than the underwear outlet?"

"*Anything's* better than the underwear outlet."

Jody got in on the driver's side and sat waiting for me to give him the keys. "I just had the oil changed," I told him. "This little green light on the dash comes on when it's time to do it again. The brakes were relined last spring, the clutch is new, and the tires have got at least another twenty thousand miles left on them."

Jody nodded impatiently, letting me know how it felt to be on Daniel's end of these conversations. "All right," I told him. "It's yours now."

Jody removed a check from his wallet and gave it to me. The amount wasn't what I expected. "I thought we said three thousand."

"Dad checked—it's worth four."

"Geez, this is a *big* help."

Each set of parents had their own reasons for objecting to this transfer of property, but as far as Jody and I were concerned, we were doing each other a favor. He needed transportation, and I needed money. I tucked the new title papers, the ones I had just gotten at the Motor Vehicle Department that switched ownership to me, inside the car manual, where I told Calvin they'd be. Calvin was going to take care of rearranging Jody's insurance policy. There was no reason to expect any problems; although Jody had been arrested in several different states, his driving record was perfect.

Leaving my car with Jody was good practice for everything else that would soon have to be shed in the process of moving from one Washington to the other. Spring cleaning would be a joke compared to the piles of clothes, books, records, magazines, and furniture that I would soon be selling or disposing of, but just the idea of getting rid of stuff, more stuff, somehow made me feel light. And energetic, too. Enough to think that if I wanted to, I could write fluffy dialogue for a cat with the back of my hand. We were going to have to find a bigger place in Seattle, that was a given. Still, I knew that when my pruned-down belongings finally caught up with me, I'd probably wonder at wanting to keep even that much.

As for Jody, soon there would be other ways of picturing him: living in the new two-bedroom apartment that Eileen and Sol, who was selling his business to another northern corporation ripe for redemption, would share when they came to town for visits; working at a library where, for some reason probably having to do with it being located in the South, hardly any of the dispossessed ever congregated; and creating a social life for himself. But for the time being, I could at least conjure an image of Jody here in Sparta, driving this particular car. Which might have been the real reason why I wanted him to have it.

Jody fidgeted, bored with the transaction details. "Can we please go now?"

"Sure," I said, handing him the keys.

I had already said goodbye to my parents, and Joyce was picking up Paul at Flip's, where we'd been staying for the last week, to take him to the airport. I didn't want my own trip to the airport to be with anyone but Jody.

After he had driven out of town and merged onto the interstate, Jody told me about a dream he had the night before. "I was walking down the street wearing a metal minus sign across my chest," he said.

"The sign was made out of *metal?*" I wanted to be sure he hadn't said mental.

"Yeah. And everybody else was wearing a metal sign too, only theirs were pluses. Then something happened in the atmosphere, a kind of hurricane, and it only affected metal."

"A kind of magnetic hurricane?"

"I guess so. In a very short second—a *split* second—all the pluses turned into minuses. Their cross bars were blown away in the storm and everyone was the same. But in another second, all the minuses around me turned into slashes."

Jody seemed to lose interest in the dream as he passed a slow-moving truck. "So all the minuses turned into slashes?" I repeated.

"Yeah. Diagonal slashes. I wanted to see if I'd turned into a diagonal, too. But I woke up before I could look down and check."

Just hearing this dream made me feel better about leaving Jody. Maybe I wanted to think it was a piece of something outside him—something even bigger than what he'd already set in motion, a vision from Saint Dymphna.

"You don't have to come in if you don't want to," I said as Jody pulled up in front of the airport, clearly intending to drop me off at the curb.

"I don't."

He opened the trunk, in which the tube that held his kites still lay, and I removed my bags. Jody was clearly uncomfortable, in a hurry to leave, and I was so leery of adding to his anxiety that I just stood waving as he drove away, not looking back at me once. Still, it didn't feel good, being left behind when I wanted more.

Inside, I went to the counter where Paul was being issued a new ticket, one that would take him back to Seattle by way of D.C. Later, at the airport gate, we sat in silence, as though each of us needed a quiet segue into the novelty of boarding the same plane together for the first time.

We moved to get in line as the departure of our flight was announced. I turned at the sound of my name being hollered. It was Jody, running and out of breath, his arms full of objects—the box of tapes I had left in the car, my Walkman, and his kite tube. "You forgot these," he panted as I reached his side.

I took the tapes and the Walkman. "I'll make you copies of the tapes, okay?"

"Okay," Jody shrugged, "but I'm pretty sick of most of them." He tried to give me the tube with his fish kites in it, but I shook my head. "I won't use them here," he said.

"You have to keep them, they're what your dream was about."

"I didn't dream about kites."

"You dreamed about a miracle. '*I believe in mackerels,*'" I sang. It took Jody a second, probably because I sang so badly, but he got my drift. "'*You tuna fish,*'" he finished. "Not everything is a song, Sister."

I swallowed hard. "Yes, it is. If you really think about it, it is." Jody glanced over at Paul as he stepped out of the boarding line to wait for me. "I wouldn't be able to love him," I told Jody, "if I didn't love you, too."

"You mean before," he said, "don't you?"

"Quit splitting things up and taking sides. Before *and* after."

Jody looked at me as though to say pay attention, I'm about to do something now that isn't easy. I expected words, an actual goodbye, the kind he had been incapable of earlier. Instead, Jody leaned close and kissed me lightly on the lips. As he drew away from that kiss, it was with all the grace and consideration of someone reluctant, now that his gift had been given, to make too much of the effort that lay behind it. I was completely undone, in a way I made no attempt to conceal because of how very much I had needed this, more than I could ever let myself imagine. Jody seemed to know it, too. Otherwise, why would he have stayed with me until my composure returned?

Tucking his kites beneath his arm, Jody walked over to where Paul was standing. Paul reached out to shake hands, and Jody shook his head no, taking Paul aback for a second until Jody put down his kites and reached up to gather Paul in a quick hug. Which, considering Jody's difficulty with touching, had to startle Paul even more.

Just after takeoff, I saw what could pass for a happy ending. Flying low to the ground, the plane's wings shadowed an orchard full of ripe, succulent peaches, and above the trees, also flying, were splashes of magenta, cyan, and yellow dipping and diving in the breeze, colors so definite and distinct that even when mixed, their brilliance is not diminished. But in order to see this, I had to close my eyes.

Acknowledgments

I am especially indebted to Barbara Branscomb, the gifted editor and writer who midwifed this work with such remarkable insight, generosity, and humor.

I would like to thank Nancy Nordhoff and Cottages at Hedgebrook for a nurturing residency as well as the opportunity to meet Valerie J. Brooks and Jean Brody, fellow writers who gave crucial criticism and encouragement along the way. I also thank Libby Burke, Beverly McDevitt, Anise Kirkpatrick, and Silvia Peto for their warm embrace of my intentions, which carried me far. Many a hazy patch seemed to come clear after lunches at the Snappy Dragon, where Jack Remick, Stewart Stern, and Bob Ray shined the light of their storytelling experience on a weekly basis; thanks, guys.

I am grateful to my parents, Bette Lee and Marvin Coburn, for their unquestioning support and faith.

Thanks to Kent Carroll and Martine Bellen for making the process of publication so stimulating and enjoyable.

Finally, I would like to express my appreciation for E. Fuller Torrey's books on schizophrenia and mental illness, invaluable references rich in humanity as well as science.